J.D. 10/5/16

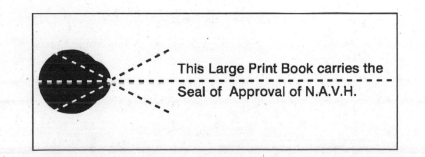

This Large Print Book carries the
Seal of Approval of N.A.V.H.

RETURN TO SENDER

RETURN TO SENDER

FERN MICHAELS

WHEELER PUBLISHING
A part of Gale, Cengage Learning

GALE
CENGAGE Learning

Detroit • New York • San Francisco • New Haven, Conn • Waterville, Maine • London

GALE
CENGAGE Learning™

LIBRARY OF CONGRESS CATALOGING-IN-PUBLICATION DATA

Michaels, Fern.
   Return to sender / by Fern Michaels.
      p. cm. — (Wheeler large print hardcover)
   ISBN-13: 978-1-4104-2198-2
   ISBN-10: 1-4104-2198-8
   1. Single mothers—Fiction. 2. Self-actualization (Psychology)
in women—Fiction. 3. Mothers and sons—Fiction. 4. Revenge—
Fiction. 5. Large type books. I. Title.
   PS3563.I27R58 2010
   813'.54—dc22   2010008386

Published in 2010 by arrangement with Kensington Books, an imprint
of Kensington Publishing Corp.

Printed in the United States of America
1 2 3 4 5 6 7 14 13 12 11 10

RETURN TO SENDER

PROLOGUE

January 13, 1989
Dalton, Georgia

Rosalind Townsend, whom everyone called Lin, held her newborn son tightly in her arms as the orderly wheeled her to the hospital's administration office. A nurse tried to take him from her so she could tend to the business of her release, but she refused.

After eighteen hours of agonizing labor without any medication, she'd delivered a healthy six-pound-eight-ounce baby boy. She wasn't about to let him out of her sight.

She'd named him William Michael Townsend. A good solid name. She would call him Will.

Like his father's, Will's hair was a deep black, so dark it appeared to be blue. Lin wasn't sure about his eyes at that point. She'd read in her baby book that a newborn's eye color wasn't true at birth. Nothing about him resembled her, as she was fair-haired, with unusual silver-colored eyes and milk white skin.

She gazed down at the securely wrapped bundle in her arms and ran her thumb across his delicate cheek. Soft as silk. He yawned, revealing tender pink gums. Lin smiled down at her son. No matter what her circumstances, she made a vow to herself; she would devote her life to caring for this precious little child.

Lin had spent the past seven months preparing for this day. During the day she worked at J & G Carpet Mills as a secretary. Five evenings a week and weekend mornings, she waited tables at Jack's Diner. Other than what it cost for rent, food, and utilities, Lin saved every cent she made. She had to be conservative because it was just her and Will. She'd allowed herself a week off from both jobs so she could bond with her son, adjust to her new life as a mother. While she would love spending more time with her son, being the sole caregiver and provider made that impossible. She'd lucked out when Sally, a coworker at Jack's and a single mother to boot, had asked her if she would sit for her two-year-old daughter Lizzie. In return, Sally would look after the baby on the days that she wasn't working.

Lin had agreed because she had to. There were still the days to cover, but Sally gave her a list of reliable sitters she'd used in the past. Dear Sally. Only five years older than Lin but so much wiser to the ways of the world. They were fast becoming good friends. Sally was the complete opposite of Lin — tall, olive-skinned, with beautiful brown eyes that had a slight upward slant, giving her an oriental look. Lin had called three of the sitters, two high-school girls and one elderly woman. She would meet with them later in the week. Lin was sure that if Sally approved, she would as well.

Sadly, there would be no help from Will's father or her parents. Lin recalled her father's cruel words when he learned she was pregnant. *May you burn in hell, you little harlot! You've disgraced my good name. Get out of my house. I don't ever want to lay eyes on you again or your bastard child!*

Lin had appealed to her mother in the hope she would intervene, but, as usual, her mother had cowered behind her father, accepting his word as law. Lin would never allow a man to intimidate her the way her father did her mother.

Never.

"Miss?"

Lin directed her attention back to the

9

woman behind the administration desk. "Yes?"

"If you'll sign here and initial here." The woman slid a single sheet of paper across the desk.

Lin signed the paper, releasing the hospital from any liability. Since she had no health insurance and refused public assistance, she could afford to stay in the hospital only for twenty-four hours. She'd spend the next two years paying a hundred dollars a month until her debt was paid in full.

The woman behind the desk reached into a drawer and pulled out a thick envelope. "Here, take these. You might find them useful."

Lin took the envelope, peered inside. Coupons for diapers, formula, baby lotion, and anything else one might need. She gave her a wan smile. "Thank you."

"You're welcome."

Throughout her pregnancy, she had visited the local dollar store once a month. She'd purchased generic brands of baby items that were on the list of layette necessities she'd read about in the baby book given to her by her obstetrician. Lin didn't have extra money to spend on a homecoming outfit for the baby, so she'd gone to Goodwill and found a secondhand pale blue sweater set.

She'd carefully hand-washed it in Dreft detergent. Subsequently it had looked good as new. Someday, she swore to herself, her son wouldn't have to wear secondhand clothes.

The orderly wheeled her back to her room, where she dressed in the maternity clothes she'd worn when admitted to the hospital the day before. She ran her hand across her flat stomach. Now she would be able to wear the uniform Jack required, thus saving wear and tear on her few meager outfits. She gazed around the room to make sure she wasn't leaving anything behind. Had it been only twenty-four hours since the taxi had dropped her off at the emergency room? It seemed like a week.

Lin carefully removed the sweater set, which she'd placed in her overnight bag. With ease, she dressed her son, smiling at the results. Will looked like a little prince in his Goodwill blue outfit. Briefly, she thought of his father and their weeklong affair. What would his reaction be when he saw his son for the first time? After months of indecision, she'd finally written him another letter two months ago, the first one since she had been on her own, and mailed it to his parents' address in New York, the only way she knew to contact him. She'd begged

11

Nancy Johnson, a girl Will's father had introduced her to, for his phone number as well, but she'd been adamant about not revealing more of her friend's personal life. She'd told Lin that if Nicholas wanted her to have his phone number, he would have given it to her. The harsh words had stung, but there was more at stake than her raw feelings. She had a child to consider. She'd written a lengthy letter, revealing her pregnancy, telling Nicholas he would be a father shortly after the new year. Weeks had passed without a response. Then, just last week, she'd trudged to the mailbox, only to find the letter she'd sent unopened, marked RETURN TO SENDER.

What's one more rejection? she'd asked herself.

Her father hadn't accepted her, either. Her mother had once told her that he'd always dreamed of having a son. At the time, Lin had been terribly hurt, but as the years passed, she learned to set those feelings aside. She'd been the best daughter she knew how to be in hopes of gaining some kind of approval, and maybe even a bit of love and affection from both parents, but that was not to be. When she told her parents about the decision to keep her baby, they were mortified and humiliated. She'd

12

been tossed out of the only home she'd ever known with nothing more than the clothes on her back.

A soft mewling sound jerked her out of the past. "It's okay, little one. I'm right here."

With the quilt Irma, Jack's wife, had made for him, Lin gently wrapped Will in a snug bundle. It was below freezing outside. Lin had halfheartedly listened to the local weather report as it blared from the television mounted above her bed. An ice storm was predicted. Meteorologists said it could be the worst in north Georgia history. With only two small electric space heaters, her garage apartment would be freezing. How she wished she could take Will to her childhood home. While it wasn't filled with love, at least it would be warm.

But Lin recalled the torturous evenings of her childhood. She would rather die than subject her son to such a strict and oftentimes cruel upbringing. Every evening, as far back as she could remember, she'd had to pray while kneeling on the hardwood floor in the living room as her father read from the Bible.

A die-hard Southern Baptist who considered himself a man of God, her father had constructed a pulpit for himself in the center of the living room, from which he would gaze down at her with disdain, as though she weren't good enough. Then, if that weren't bad enough, he'd make her recite the names of all the books of the Bible in order. If she missed one, he would make her start from the beginning until she named them correctly. Once, when she was about seven or eight, she remembered spending an entire night on her knees, praying. She'd prayed hard, her father watching her the entire time. Little did he know, she'd been praying for his immediate death. Many times she'd wet herself while on her knees in prayer. Her father wouldn't allow her to change her clothes or bathe afterward.

"The devil lives inside you, girly! Taking a shower ain't gonna cleanse your dirty soul!"

She'd winced the first time she'd heard those words. After a while, she became immune to his cruel words. She'd even gotten used to smelling like urine. The kids at school were relentless, calling her Miss Stinky Pants. And she would do what she always did when she was hurting.

She prayed.

Every night that she knelt on that cold, hard floor, she prayed for her father's death. Not once in the seventeen years that she had lived in her father's house had he ever relented on this evening ritual. She had thick, ugly calluses on her knees to prove it.

When she left home, or rather when she was thrown out, she made a promise to herself: she would *never, ever* kneel again.

Freezing definitely held more appeal.

She checked the room one last time. One of the nurses waited to wheel her downstairs, where the hospital's courtesy van would take her and Will home.

In the lobby the automatic doors opened, and a gush of icy air greeted her, smacking her in the face. She held Will close to her with one arm and carried her small overnight bag with the other. The driver, an older black man, opened the door and reached for her bag. "You best hop inside, Miss. This here cold ain't good for the young'un." He nodded at the bundle in her arms.

Shivering, Lin stepped carefully up into the van. Thankful for the warm air blowing from the heater's vents, she sat on the hard vinyl seat and realized she was still very sore from the delivery. Her breasts felt as though they would explode. She couldn't wait to get home to nurse Will. She'd be able to do so only during the week she was home. Then she'd have to resort to formula. She'd calculated the expense, and while it was very costly, she would manage. Unfortunately, she had no choice.

"Thank you," she said to the driver as she placed Will in the car seat beside her. When Lin had discovered she was pregnant, she'd been frightened, fearful of having inherited her parents' harsh and unloving manner. However, when Will was placed in her arms, the love she felt for him was the most natural thing in the world. Her worries had been for naught.

When mother and son were secure in their seats, the driver made his way through the parking lot. Waiting at the traffic light, he perused a stack of papers attached to a clipboard. "Tunnel Hill, ma'am?"

"Yes, just make a left on Lafayette, then take the second right." Lin hated having to take Will home to a one-room garage apartment. Someday they would have a home with a big yard with flowers, a white picket fence, and lots of trees for him to climb. Will would have a swing set, and she'd watch him play. Yes, she would see to it that Will had a good home, and whatever it took, she would make sure he had an education.

Lin remembered her father telling her years before that it was foolish for women to go to college, a waste of money. He'd assured her then that he would not contribute to her education, so after she'd preenrolled at Dalton Junior College during her senior year of high school, she'd saved enough money for the first year.

Having spent three terrifying nights alone in a cheap motel after her father threw her out, she'd made her first adult decision. Instead of using the money for college, she'd paid three months' rent on an apartment. In retrospect, her father's attitude had worked to her favor, since it had forced her to save for her education. If not, there wouldn't even be a place for her to bring Will.

The driver parked in her landlady's driveway. She hurriedly removed Will from the car seat and took her bag from the driver. "Thank you. I appreciate the ride."

"Jus' doin' my job, miss. Now scoot on outta here. That ice storm's gonna hit real soon."

"Yes, I know. Thanks again for the ride."

Lin felt rather than saw the driver watching her as he slowly reversed down the long driveway. She didn't feel creepy at all, because she knew he was good and decent and just wanted to make sure she made it inside safely. A stranger cared more about her well-being than her own flesh and blood. Sad. But she smiled at her thoughts.

She had the greatest gift ever, right there in her very own arms.

Holding Will tightly against her chest, she plodded down the long drive that led to the garage apartment. She felt for the key in her pocket, then stopped when she heard a whining noise. Putting her bag on the ground, she checked Will, but he was sound asleep. She heard the sound again.

"What the heck?" she said out loud.

At the bottom of the steep wooden steps on the side of the garage that led to her apartment, Lin spotted a small dog and walked behind the steps where he hovered. Holding Will tightly, she held out her hand. Its brownish red fur matted with clumps of dirt, the ribs clearly visible, the poor dog looked scruffy and cold. He or she, she wasn't sure of the animal's gender, whined before standing on all fours, limping over to Lin, and licking her outstretched hand.

She laughed. "You sure know the way to a girl's heart."

"Woof, woof."

With the ice storm ready to hit, there was no way Lin could leave the poor dog outside. She fluffed the matted fur between its ears and decided that the dog was going inside with her.

" 'Scruffy,' that's what I'm going to call

you for now. Come on, puppy. Follow me."

The dog obeyed, staying a foot behind Lin as she made her way up the rickety steps while holding Will against her chest.

Unlocking the door, Lin stepped inside and dropped her bag on the floor. Timidly, Scruffy waited to be invited in. "Come on, Scruffy. You're staying here tonight. Something tells me we're going to get along just fine."

Two unwanted strays, Lin thought.

Scruffy scurried inside and sat patiently on the kitchen floor. With Will still clutched to her chest, Lin grabbed a plastic bowl from her single cupboard, filled it with water, and placed it on the cracked olive green linoleum. She took two hot dogs out of her minirefrigerator, broke them into small pieces, and placed them on a saucer next to the bowl of water. "This should tide you over for a bit. I've got to feed the little guy now."

Scruffy looked at her with big round eyes. Lin swore she saw thankfulness in the dog's brown-eyed gaze.

With her son still clutched in her arms, Lin managed to remove her jacket before loosening the blanket surrounding him. Making the necessary adjustments to her clothing, Lin began to nurse her son. Reclining on the floral-patterned sofa, she relaxed for the first time in a long time. Her son was fed and content. She'd inherited an adorable dog, however temporary, and she was warm.

For a while, that would do. Someday their lives would be different.

Lin stared at the sleeping infant in her arms. "I promise you, little guy, you'll have the best life ever." Then, as an afterthought, she added, "No matter what I have to do."

■ ■ ■ ■

PART ONE

■ ■ ■ ■

CHAPTER 1

Friday, August 31, 2007
New York University

Will's deep brown eyes sparkled with excitement, his enthusiasm contagious, as he and Lin left University Hall, a crowded dormitory for freshmen located at Union Square. If all went as planned, Will would reside in New York City for the next four years before moving on to graduate school to study at North Carolina State University's College of Veterinary Medicine, one of the most prestigious veterinary institutions in the country.

"I just hate that you're so far away from home. And in New York City, no less," Lin said for the umpteenth time. "With all the remodeling and holiday parties going on at the restaurant, I doubt I'll be able to make the trip north for Thanksgiving. I don't want you to spend your holiday alone."

"Mom, I said I'd come home if I could.

And I will. I promise," Will said. "Besides, I'm a big boy now. I just might like spending some time alone in this big city full of hot chicks."

Laughing, Lin replied, "I'm sure you would." She watched her son as they rode the elevator downstairs. Over six feet tall, with thick raven black hair, Will was the spitting image of his father, or at least her memory of him.

Lin recalled all those years ago when she'd first met his father. She'd fallen head over heels in love while he'd been visiting a friend in Georgia. Briefly, Lin wondered if Will would follow in her footsteps or his father's. She prayed it wasn't the latter, though she had to admit, she really didn't know how he'd turned out, but she didn't want her son to take after a man who denied his son's existence. Lin knew he was very wealthy, but that didn't mean he was a good man. Good men took care of their children, acknowledged them.

Three weeks after she'd brought Will home from the hospital, she'd sent his father a copy of their son's birth announcement, along with a copy of the birth certificate. She'd shamelessly added a picture of herself just in case he'd forgotten their brief affair. Throughout the years, she had continued to send items marking Will's accomplishments, the milestones reached as he grew up. Photos of the first day of school; first lost tooth; then, as he aged, driver's license; first date — anything she thought a father would have been proud of. Again, all had come back, unopened and marked RETURN TO SENDER. After so many years of this, she should have learned, should have known that Will's father had no desire to acknowledge him. To this very day she'd never told Will, for fear it would affect him in a way that she wouldn't be able to handle. Recalling the hurt, then the anger each time she and her son were rejected, Lin tucked away the memories of the man she'd given herself to so many years ago, the man she'd loved, the man who had so callously discarded all traces of their romance and, in so doing, failed to acknowledge their son's existence. When Will had turned twelve, she'd told him his father had died in an accident. It had seemed enough at the time.

But as Jack, her former employer and substitute father, always said, "The past is prologue, kiddo." And he was right. She'd put that part of her life behind her and moved forward.

The elevator doors swished open. The main floor was empty but for a few couples gathered in the corner, speaking in hushed tones. Most of the parents were either visiting other dorms or preparing for the evening banquet. Will hadn't wanted to attend, but Lin had insisted, telling him several of the university's alumni would be speaking. She'd teased him, saying he might be among them one day. He'd reluctantly agreed, but Lin knew that if he truly hadn't wanted to attend, he would have been more persistent.

She glanced at the exquisite diamond watch on her slender wrist, a gift from Jack and Irma the day she'd made her last payment on the diner she'd purchased from them eight years ago. "I'll meet you in the banquet hall at seven. Are you sure you don't want to come back to the hotel?"

Will cupped her elbow, guiding her toward the exit. "No. Actually, I think I might take a nap. Aaron doesn't arrive until tomorrow. It might be the last chance I have for some time alone. I want to take advantage of it."

Will and his dorm mate, Aaron Levy, had met through the Internet during the summer. Though they hadn't met in person, Will assured her they'd get along just fine. They were studying to become veterinarians, and both shared an avid love of baseball.

"Better set your alarm," Lin suggested. Will slept like the dead.

"Good idea." He gave her a hug, then stepped back, his gaze suddenly full of concern. "You'll be okay on your own for a while?"

Lin patted her son's arm. "Of course I will. This is my first trip to the city. There are dozens of things to do. I doubt I'll have a minute to spare. Though I don't think I'll do any sightseeing today, since I made an appointment to have my hair and nails done at the hotel spa."

Will laughed. "That's a first. You never do that kind of stuff. What gives?"

"It's not every day a mother sends her son off to college." She gently pushed him away. "Now, go on with you, or there'll be no time to relax. I'll see you at seven."

Will waved. "Seven, then."

Lin gave him a thumbs-up sign, her signal to him that all was a go. She pushed the glass door open and stepped outside. The late-afternoon sun shone brightly through the oak trees, casting all sorts of irregular shapes and shadows on the sidewalk. The autumn air was cool and crisp. Lin walked down the sidewalk and breathed deeply, suddenly deliriously happy with the life she'd made for herself. She stopped for a moment, remembering all the struggles, the ups and downs, and how hard she'd worked to get to where she was. Abundant, fulfilled, completely comfortable with her life, she picked up her pace, feeling somewhat foolish and silly for her thoughts. She laughed, the sound seemingly odd since she was walking alone, no one to hear her. That was okay, too. Life was good. She was happy, Will's future appeared bright and exciting. The only dark spot in her life was her father. Her mother had died shortly after Lin had moved into Mrs. Turner's garage apartment. She'd had to read about it in the obituaries. Lin had called her father, asking how her mother had died. He told her she'd fallen down the basement steps. She suspected otherwise but knew it would be useless, possibly even dangerous to her and her unborn child, if she were to pry into the circumstances surrounding her mother's death. She'd tried to establish a relationship with her father on more than one occasion through the years, and each time he'd rebuffed her, telling her she was the devil's spawn. Her father now resided in Atlanta, in a very upscale nursing home, at her expense. Lin was sure his pure meanness had launched him into early-onset Alzheimer's.

Lin thought it was time for her to proceed at her own leisurely pace, kick back, and totally relax for the first time in a very, very long time.

Lin continued to ponder her life as she walked down the sidewalk, toward a line of waiting taxis. After ten years of working at Jack's Diner, when she'd learned that Jack and Irma were considering closing the place, she'd come up with a plan. Though she'd skimped and saved most of her life, for once, she was about to splurge and do something so out of character, Jack thought she'd taken temporary leave of her senses. She'd offered him a fifty-thousand-dollar down payment, a cut of the profits, and a promissory note on the balance if they would sell her the diner. It took all of two minutes for Jack and Irma to accept her offer. Since they had never had children, didn't think they'd have a chance in hell of selling the diner, given the local economy, closing the doors had seemed their only option.

Lin laughed.

She'd worked her tail off day and night and most weekends to attract a new clientele, a younger crowd with money to burn. She'd applied for a liquor license and changed the menu to healthier fare while still remaining true to some of the comfort foods Jack's was known for, such as his famous meat loaf and mashed potatoes. Within a year Jack's was booked every night of the week, and weekends, months in advance. From there, she'd started catering private parties. With so much success, she'd decided it was time to add on to the diner. In addition to two large private banquet rooms that would accommodate five hundred guests when combined, she'd added three moderately sized private rooms for smaller groups. The remodeling was in its final stages when she left for New York the day before. She'd left Sally, her dearest friend and manager, in charge of last-minute details.

Lin quickened her pace as she saw that the line of taxis at the end of the block had dwindled down to three. She waved her hand in the air to alert the cabbie. Yanking the yellow-orange door open, she slid inside, where the smell of stale smoke and fried onions filled her nostrils. She wrinkled her nose in disgust. "The Helmsley Park Lane." She'd always wanted to say that to a New York cabdriver. Though it wasn't the most elite or expensive hotel in the city, it was one that had captured her imagination over the years. Its infamous owner, known far and wide by the well-deserved epithet the Queen of Mean, had been quite visible in the news media when Lin was younger, especially when she'd been tried and convicted for tax evasion, extortion, and mail fraud, and had died less than two weeks ago.

Through blasts of horns, shouts from sidewalk vendors hawking their wares, the occasional bicyclist weaving in and out of the traffic, Lin enjoyed the scenery during the quick cab ride back to the hotel. New York was unlike any city in the world. Of course, she hadn't traveled outside the state of Georgia, so where this sudden knowledge came from, she hadn't a clue, but still she knew there was no other place like New York. It had its own unique *everything*, right down to the smell of the city.

The taxi stopped in front of the Helmsley. Lin handed the driver a twenty, telling him to keep the change. Hurrying, Lin practically floated through the turnstile doors as though she were on air. She felt like Cinderella, and the banquet would be her very own ball, with Will acting as her handsome prince. He would croak if he knew her thoughts. Nonetheless, she was excited about the evening ahead.

She dashed to the elevator doors with only seconds to spare. She'd lost track of time, and her salon appointment was in five minutes. They'd asked her to wear a blouse

31

that buttoned in the front so she wouldn't mess up her new do before the banquet. She punched the button to the forty-sixth floor, from which she had an unbelievable view of the city and Central Park. Lin cringed when she thought of the cost, but remembered this was just a onetime treat, and she was doing it in style.

She slid the keycard into the slot on the door and pushed the door inward. Overcome by the sheer luxuriousness, she simply stared at her surroundings, taking them in. Lavender walls with white wainscoting, cream-colored antique tables at either end of the lavender floral sofa. The bedroom color scheme matched, though the coverlet on her bed was a deep, royal purple. She raced over to the large walk-in closet, grabbed a white button-up blouse, and headed to the bathroom. This, too, was beyond opulent. The marble, a deep Jacuzzi tub, a shower that could hold at least eight people, thick, soft lavender bath towels, bars of lilac soap, and bath beads placed in crystal containers gave Lin such a feeling of luxury, and it was such a novel feeling, she considered staying in the room her entire trip. She laughed, then spoke out loud. "Sally would really think I've lost my marbles." She'd discussed her New York trip with Sally, and they'd made a list of all the must-see places. If she returned empty-handed, Sally would wring her neck. She'd bring her back something special.

They'd practically raised the kids together, and Sally felt like the older sister she'd never had. And she'd bring Elizabeth, Sally's daughter, something smart and sexy. She'd opted to attend Emory University in Atlanta instead of leaving the state, as Will had. Sally had told Lin she was glad. Not only did she not have to pay out-of-state tuition, but Lizzie was able to come home on the weekends. She would graduate next year. Where had the time gone?

She hurried downstairs to the spa for her afternoon of pampering.

Three hours later Lin returned to her room to dress for the banquet. The hairstylist had talked her into a pedicure and a facial. After an afternoon of being catered to, she felt like royalty. Of course, it all came at a price, one so high she didn't dare give it another thought, or she'd have such a case of the guilts that she'd ruin the evening for herself and Will. No, she reminded herself again, this was a once-in-a-lifetime trip. As she had explained to Will, it wasn't every day that he went away to college. Besides, she wanted to look her best at the banquet, knowing there would be many well-to-do parents attending with their children. No way did she want to cause Will any embarrassment just because she was a small-town hick who ran a diner. Her accomplishments might mean something in Dalton, but here in New York City she would just be seen as a country bumpkin trying to keep up with the big-city folk, even though her net worth these days could probably match that of many of New York's movers and shakers.

Discarding her self-doubts, Lin took her dress out of its garment bag. She'd ordered it from a Macy's catalog four months ago. She slid the black, long-sleeved silk over her head, allowing the dress to swathe her slender body. Lin looked at her reflection in the full-length mirror. With all the skipped meals and extra work at the diner, she'd lost weight since purchasing the dress. Still, the curve-hugging dress emphasized her tiny waist. She twirled around in front of the mirror. *Not bad for an old woman,* she thought.

"Shoot, I'm not *that* old." She cast another look in the mirror, slipped her feet into her ruby red slingbacks, which she'd been dying to wear since she'd purchased them two years ago. Lin remembered buying them on a trip to Atlanta as a prize to celebrate her first million. On paper, of course, but still it was monumental to her since she'd clawed her way to the top. It hadn't been all rainbows and lollipops, either.

Clipping on the garnet earrings Sally and Irma had given her for her thirtieth birthday, she returned to the mirror for one last look before heading downstairs.

Five foot three, maybe a hundred pounds soaking wet, Lin scrutinized her image. The stylist had flat-ironed her long blond hair, assuring her that it was the current style, and, no, she was not too old to wear her hair down. Her face had a rosy glow courtesy of Lancôme and a facial. The manicurist had given her a French manicure, telling her that it, too, was "in vogue." After leaving the spa, she'd returned to her room with a few make-up tricks under her belt, plus her hairstylist had sashayed back and forth, showing her the fashionable way to strut her stuff so that she'd be noticed when making an entrance. While that was the last thing on her mind, she'd had a blast with the women, more than she cared to admit. Lin had confessed that she hadn't had time for such things as a girl, but she hadn't explained why.

She glanced at her watch. Six fifteen. It was time for Cinderella to hail her carriage.

"Get off it!" If she continued thinking along those lines, she would have to commit herself.

Lin visualized her mental checklist. Purse, lipstick, wallet, cell phone, and keycard. All of a sudden her hands began to shake, and her stomach twisted in knots. It wasn't like she would be the only parent there. Unsure why she was so jittery, she shrugged her feelings aside, telling herself she simply wanted to make a good impression on Will's professors and classmates. Plus, she wasn't on her own turf, and that in and of itself had the power to turn her insides to mush.

Instead of exiting through the turnstile doors, Lin allowed the doorman to open the door for her. Discreetly, she placed a twenty in his hand and hoped it was enough. Sally had told her you had to tip everyone for everything in the city. Lin calculated she'd be broke in less than a year if she remained in New York.

"Thank you, ma'am," the elderly man said as he escorted her to a waiting taxi.

Okay, that was worth the twenty bucks. She would've hated to chase down a taxi in the red heels.

The inside of the taxi was warm. Lin offered up a silent prayer of thanks that there were no strange odors permeating the closed-in space. She would hate to arrive at the banquet smelling like cigarettes and onions.

More blaring horns, shouts, and tires squealing could be heard. Lin enjoyed watching the throngs of people on the streets as the driver managed to weave through the traffic. Lord, she loved the hubbub, but she didn't think she could tolerate it on a daily basis.

Poor Will. She smiled. *Not* poor Will. After the slow pace of Dalton, he would welcome this. It was one of the many reasons he'd chosen to attend NYU in the first place. He'd wanted a taste of the big city. Lin thought he was about to get his wish and then some.

Twenty minutes later the taxi stopped in front of the building where the banquet was being held. She offered up two twenties, telling the driver to keep the change.

"Do you want me to pick you up later?" the driver asked as he jumped out to open her door. Lin thought the tip must have been a tad too generous.

"Uh, I'm not sure. Do you have a card?" she asked.

He laughed. "No card, lady, but if you want a return ride, you gotta ask for it."

"Of course. Midnight. Be here at midnight." Now she was starting to *sound* like Cinderella.

"Will do."

Her transportation taken care of, Lin stepped out into the cool night air.

CHAPTER 2

Nicholas Pemberton Jr. took the elevator from the twenty-second floor to the main lobby of the Chrysler Building. He sailed across the onyx and amber marble floors toward the exit. He never once looked up at the ceiling, where Edward Trumbull had created a striking mural depicting scenes of the past from Chrysler's assembly line. The skyscraper's history held no appeal for him whatsoever.

Reeling through the turnstile doors, he stood on the sidewalk and sucked in gulps of exhaust fumes and the scent of burnt sausages.

He needed air.

Blaring horns from the hundreds of taxis blasted in the late afternoon; shouts, squealing brakes, and the sound of footsteps on the sidewalk thundered in his ears. Bits of conversations buzzed past him; cell phones rang. Nick even felt the vibration of the subway beneath him. Sounds were heightened. He took another deep breath and leaned against the brick wall for support.

After leaving his physician's office, Nick continued to deny the information he'd just been given.

Clearly, it was not possible. He felt fine.

His mind veered to the appointment he'd had only minutes ago.

Since his last visit over a year ago, Dr. Warner had replaced his former receptionist with a hot-looking blonde, not a day over twenty. She wore a vibrant pink skirt that barely covered the cheeks of her ass and a sheer blouse that allowed him a view of her black bra. Her blond hair was piled on top of her head in a messy top-knot, secured with a pencil. He shook his head at what currently constituted office wear. What the hell was the world coming to? He followed her wiggling ass to a pair of solid cherry double doors, which led into the inner sanctum of the private office, where life-and-death decisions were made on a daily basis.

She tapped on the door, then opened it for Nick.

"Thanks," he said.

She offered him a killer smile before returning to her desk.

He nodded in return.

At six-three, Nick was tall. Those who knew him thought him handsome, with his sleek black hair tinged with just the right amount of gray at the temples. Whiskey-colored eyes matched his deeply tanned skin. At forty-three, Nicholas Pemberton could have easily passed for a man in his late twenties.

When silver-haired Dr. Warner stood, he towered over his patient. Nick guessed the man to be at least six foot six. Clear blue eyes stared at him as if he were a specimen under a microscope. Nick had never felt totally comfortable around the man. Maybe it was time to switch doctors.

The doctor extended a large hand across the expanse of his desktop. "Nice to see you, Nick."

Nick shook his hand. "I'll be the judge of that."

Dr. Warner smiled, but it didn't reach his eyes. "You don't waste time, do you?" He gestured to the chairs across from his desk. "Please, have a seat."

Nicholas Pemberton sat down in what he knew to be an antique French Louis XVI gilt chair, which faced an enormous desk, custom-made to fit the man who sat behind it.

He tried an I-don't-give-a-damn attitude to bolster his confidence. He took a deep breath, hoping it would calm his jitters. "Go on, just spit it out. You didn't take me away from making millions to discuss my cholesterol."

He'd had his yearly physical two weeks ago, after Chelsea, his wife, had reminded him he'd already rescheduled three times. And there he was, on pins and needles, waiting for some life-changing illness to screw things up, or at least that was what he believed. Hell, maybe he'd caught a sexually transmitted disease, and Dr. Warner was just being discreet. He'd been with a woman he'd met in Chicago a few weeks ago. She'd been a helluva romp, but he'd assumed she was clean in the disease department. Yes, that was what it had to be. He'd be a bit more choosy the next time he decided to dip his dick into unknown territory.

Dr. Warner didn't mince words. "Your blood tests came back. I think we need a few more tests to rule out a thing or two."

He knew it! That bitch. He couldn't even remember her name. Once he found out, she'd be sorry she ever laid eyes on him.

Pumped up by his own diagnosis, Nick spoke. "So how bad is it? Can we cure whatever it is with a shot of penicillin?"

Dr. Warner placed his elbows on the desk, strumming his long fingers against each other. "I wish it were that simple."

"Then what is it? Do I need an operation? Dammit, I feel fine. I told Chelsea that when she forced me to get a physical."

"Then thank her when you go home tonight. We did a CBC screen." The doctor opened a manila folder, thumbing through several pale pink papers. "The results are questionable. Your white count is extremely high."

"Exactly what do you mean by 'questionable'? And how high is high?" Nick prompted impatiently. He didn't have time for bullshit. He had a multibillion-dollar shipping company to run. Pemberton Transport hadn't become one of the largest shipping companies in the world by sitting on its ass or by his ass waiting for someone else to make him millions. Nick looked at the custom-made Rolex on his wrist. "I have a meeting in an hour. I'll be lucky to make it at this rate. Just tell me what I need to do, and I'll make the arrangements."

Dr. Warner rolled off the numbers from his blood tests, knowing Nick wouldn't really comprehend the data just then. He closed the folder. "Very well." He removed a business card from a side drawer in his desk. "Schedule an appointment with Reeves as soon as possible." He placed the business card on the edge of the desk.

Nick scrutinized the card. Dr. Warner observed his patient. The veins in Nick's neck pulsated, and he would bet anything that his blood pressure had just shot up. He'd seen this reaction in thousands of patients. He'd felt sympathy for most of them. With Nick, it was all he could do to contain his composure. He didn't like the man; that was the bottom line. Still, the man was his patient, and he was ethically bound to do the best he could for him, no matter the circumstances.

Dr. Warner saw that Nick's hands shook when he extended the card to him. "What is *this?*" Even the man's voice trembled.

Dr. Warner hated to be so blunt, but the bastard had asked for it. "It is what it is."

"So, you're saying I have cancer?" Nick shot back. "An oncologist *and* a hematologist? What the hell!"

The doctor cleared his throat. "I'm not saying that at all. What I'm suggesting is a specialist. Your blood tests aren't normal. I wouldn't want to play guessing games with your health, Nick. I think a second opinion and more extensive tests are needed before an accurate diagnosis can be made." His malpractice insurance premiums were out of this world as it was. The last thing he needed was some hotshot business tycoon taking him to the cleaners. He'd rather play it safe.

Nick paced back and forth in front of the large desk. "So you're saying this is out of your league?"

He really wanted to slap the son of a bitch, but ethics and etiquette prevented him from acting on his impulse. Dr. Warner had always disliked Nick's know-it-all attitude and the man himself. The possibility that Nick had a life-threatening illness wasn't going to change the way he felt about the obnoxious, pompous ass.

"No, not at all." *The smug bastard,* Dr. Warner thought. "I think you need to see a specialist. I could be overreacting. I simply want to play it safe," Dr. Warner explained, though he knew he wasn't overreacting. Something was seriously wrong with Nick's blood tests. Even though he detested the guy, he wanted him to receive the best medical care available. Evan Reeves was tops in his field.

Hatefully, Nick said, "So what are you waiting for? Make me a damned appointment."

Fists clenched beneath his desk, Dr.

Warner replied, "I'm afraid you'll have to do that yourself. Or maybe you can get Chelsea to set something up for you. I wouldn't waste a lot of time on deciding, Nick. This is serious."

Nick stuffed the card in his pocket and stormed out of the office without saying another word. Dr. Warner suddenly felt very sorry for Chelsea.

He supposed he could have had Sheri, his receptionist, make the appointment. That was part of her duties. If it had been any other patient, he would have set it up himself. Simply put, Nicholas Pemberton rubbed him the wrong way. Always had and probably always would.

Squealing tires brought Nick out of his reverie. He took a deep breath, hoping to clear his head. Exhaust fumes from the line of waiting taxis forced him to cough deeply while he perused the line of vehicles, in search of his driver.

Surely Warner is mistaken, he thought.

He couldn't be ill. Hell, he felt better than he had in years. Though he had to admit, he had been feeling more tired than usual the past couple of weeks, but he'd attributed that to long hours at the office with hardly any sleep.

46

He spied his sleek black Town Car.

Tall, with a C-shaped stoop in his back, Herbert was a wiry old man with a tuft of white hair encircling an otherwise bald head. Nick opened the rear door before his chauffeur had a chance to get out and perform the duty he'd performed thousands of times for him and his father. For a brief second, Nick had an unexpected pang of compassion for the old guy; Herbert should have retired a long, long time ago.

"Where to, sir?" Herbert asked in a gravelly voice.

Good question, Nick thought. "Just drive around for a bit. I need to think."

"As you wish, sir."

Nick looked at his watch as they crawled along in the heavy traffic. Despite it being the Friday of Labor Day weekend, he'd scheduled a two o'clock meeting with his office staff. It could be postponed. That night he had to attend a banquet for incoming freshmen at NYU. He wanted to skip that, too, but he knew a few of the attending alumni. It would be in his best interest to attend just to rub elbows with a few of Wall Street's movers and shakers. One never knew.

"Herbert, take me to the office."

The old driver nodded his acquiescence

and rammed his foot on the accelerator, weaving in and out of traffic. Twenty minutes later they stopped in front of the Empire State Building, the home of Pemberton Transport's main offices.

Nick got out of the car, gave a casual wave to Herbert, then bolted toward the building. He didn't want to explain where he'd been for the past hour. Stuffing his hands in his pocket, he felt the small square card Dr. Warner gave him. *Dr. Reeves.* Nick wasn't sure if he was going to call the guy or not. He'd have him checked out first. *If,* and that was a big *if,* he was sick, he would make damned sure he had the best medical care money could buy.

After going through security like everyone else who entered the building, he rode the elevator up to the thirty-second floor. Rosa, his personal secretary, greeted him in the usual manner. A drink — coffee in the morning, tea in the afternoon — and the latest editions of the *Wall Street Journal,* the *Washington Post,* the *Japan Times,* and London's *Financial Times* were customarily on a large coffee table, waiting for his perusal.

"Mr. Pemberton." Rosa followed him to his private office. She placed a pot of tea on a side table next to a comfortable sofa.

She'd spread the newspapers out for him to view.

Nick removed his jacket, loosened his tie, and relaxed into the plushness of the cushions. "Thank you, Rosa."

"Will you be needing anything for this afternoon's meeting?"

Damn! He'd almost forgotten. "Yes. I want it canceled."

"But —"

"No buts, Rosa. Just do as I say. I've had some terrible news that I have to deal with. Tell the staff I'm unavailable until further notice."

"Yes, sir." Rosa was short and chubby, with coffee brown hair and matching eyes. She'd served him well the past fifteen years, though lately she was becoming a bit too nosy for his tastes. He'd make a note to watch her. If she got out of line, she would be replaced in minutes. Pemberton Transport's employees were just that. Employees. As his father always said, "If you're too nice, they'll screw your eyes out. Too stern, and you'll be doing the work of fifty."

Normally, Nick tried to achieve a happy medium. However, it wasn't a good day. He needed silence in order to make plans for the future. If something were to happen to him, the business automatically went to

Chelsea. While she was smart, Nick knew she'd sell out in a heartbeat if given the opportunity. If only he'd had a son to inherit everything, one he could've molded to be just like him. Sadly, as long as he was married to Chelsea, it wasn't going to happen. Besides, they were too set in their ways to bother with a child. *And too old,* he thought.

He took his personal cell phone from the bottom drawer and called Jason Vinery, a very discreet and very expensive private detective he kept on the payroll. Just in case.

Jason picked up on the first ring. "JV Investigations."

"Two things," Nick said.

"And a good afternoon to you, Mr. Pemberton." The last was said with a great deal of sarcasm.

"I don't have the luxury of time. I need you to check out a doctor." Nick looked at the card palmed in his hand. "An Evan Reeves. An oncologist. And I want you to find out the name of a woman I recently . . . met. I was in Chicago. She was staying at the Fairmont. Find out her name. Then I want a background check on her. See if she's had any sexually transmitted diseases."

"And if she has?" Jason prompted.

"It's none of your business," Nick said angrily.

50

"I see."

"I'm sure you *think* you do. Call my private cell when you have news. I don't want Chelsea or Rosa getting wind of this." The bastard was paid well for his discretion. How dare the son of a bitch question him?

Nick described the woman he wanted Jason to check out, told him the dates they were together. Then Nick lied, saying he and the doctor shared a mutual financial interest. He needed to know if the man could produce the financing their venture required.

With that temporarily taken care of, Nick drank his tea, even though it was only lukewarm. He skimmed a few headlines in the papers Rosa had laid out, but found his attention drifting.

"Screw it," he said out loud. He brushed the papers aside in a heap, searching for the cell phone he'd used only minutes ago. After locating it beneath the cushions, he punched in Herbert's number.

"Yes, Mr. Pemberton?"

Reliable as always. Nick could always count on the old guy, he'd give him that.

"I'm ready to go home."

"Yes, sir. I'll be waiting at the usual location," Herbert replied.

Nick grabbed his jacket from the back of the sofa, stuffed the phone in his hip pocket, and locked the door behind him. Rosa had a set of keys to his private office in case of an emergency, but she knew better than to enter without his requesting her presence. If he was gone and something occurred that she considered an emergency, she was instructed to call him immediately.

Nick made his way to the elevator without encountering any of his office staff. He didn't want to explain canceling the meeting to anyone. He had too much to consider.

What if I do have cancer or some other life-altering disease?

He'd survive because he was a survivor. This was just a blip on the screen of life. It wouldn't surprise him at all if Warner was blowing a little smoke up his ass. He didn't like the man, and he knew the feeling was mutual. Maybe he wanted to scare him, make him think twice about canceling any future appointments. But Nick knew Warner had scruples. He'd never resort to such ludicrous behavior just because he didn't like a patient. Most likely, he had something that a few shots and a prescription would take care of. With that thought in mind, he stepped out of the elevator, then quickly made his way to the waiting Town Car.

"Afternoon, sir," Herbert said while opening the door. "Taking the afternoon off. Very good, sir."

Nick nodded, acknowledging the old guy but unwilling to explain his unusual change in schedule. Let him think what he wanted.

His cell phone rang. Caller ID showed it was Jason.

"What?" Nick barked.

"Pleasant as ever, I see," Jason replied.

"This isn't a damned social call. Just tell me what you found out."

Nick heard Jason's hateful chuckle over the wires. This would be the last time he would use his services. He didn't care if he was the best damned private eye in the world. In his opinion, there was always someone better. And he would make damned sure to find an agency that would put JV's to shame.

"*Nada* to any sexually transmitted diseases. By the way, her name is Karen Hollister. Your buddy Evan Reeves is listed as one of the top oncologists in the country. Not yet a multimillionaire, but his finances are very sound. Investments are wise. Nothing fishy about either at this point. Do you want me to continue digging until I find something . . . unscrupulous?"

Nick pondered the question. One never

knew when you might need useful information; however, with the people in question, he didn't need any more details about either of them. "No. That's all. Send your final bill to my office. I won't be using your agency in the future." Nick flashed a sardonic grin. Too bad Jason couldn't see him.

"What?"

"Good-bye." Nick clicked the END button, preventing further conversation. Jason Vinery had just lost his biggest account.

Herbert expertly maneuvered the Lincoln through Manhattan's perpetual traffic, slamming on the brakes when a pedestrian stepped in front of the car.

Nick grabbed the headrest in front of him. "Damned idiots!"

Unruffled as usual, Herbert said, "Yes, sir. There are many of them in the city."

Nick took a deep breath before responding. "Be careful. I don't want to die just yet."

Herbert chuckled. "Sir, you're young. You have a long life ahead of you."

He wasn't so sure after the visit with Dr. Warner. "I can only hope," he replied to the old guy. Suddenly he wished Herbert would stop with the "sir" shit all the time. He was about to speak his mind when they pulled into the underground garage and the spot reserved solely for him, the owner of the luxurious penthouse apartment, which he'd purchased for a song after graduating from college. Being at the top suited him just fine.

"Nicholas, I wish we didn't have to attend this tasteless banquet. I don't understand why you accepted the invitation, and furthermore, why are we riding with the top down? It's cold, but I suppose you don't feel cold. Not Nicholas Pemberton," Chelsea whined. "I've more important things to do than waste my time welcoming a bunch of snotty kids to New York."

Nick had deliberately chosen to drive his silver BMW Z8 with the top down. He did what he could to annoy his wife. In fact, whenever the opportunity arose, he took great pleasure in making her miserable. She annoyed the hell out of him. Nick figured Chelsea was just pissed because her updo was becoming an up-down.

"Get that smirk off your face!" she shouted.

Nick smiled. Yes, she was pissed. "I don't have a smirk on my face. I'm simply smiling."

Chelsea's dark brown eyes glowered at him. "If you call that a smile, I'll kiss your ass. Of course, it's possible you're thinking about one of those sluts that you seem to delight in. Don't think I don't know about them, because I do. I'm not stupid, Nicholas."

He took a deep breath, shifted gears, swerving sharply to avoid a pothole. "I'm not hiding anything from you." That was an outright lie. They both knew it. Chelsea wasn't a saint herself. She'd had as many affairs as he'd had. As long as she was happy, performed when he asked her to, he didn't care how many men she slept with. He was sure the feelings were mutual.

Chelsea liked to play the role of betrayed wife when it suited her. Usually it meant she was about to hit him up for a large sum of money for one of her endless charities.

"Stop kidding yourself. I know what you do. I used to be one of your 'other women,' remember?"

Nick knew where she was going, and wanted to put a halt to it before it started. It was best to agree with her and go on. "Yes. How could I forget? Trash from the Bronx. You've reminded me almost daily for the past nineteen years. I realize I was engaged to Cathryn Carlyle when you set out to seduce me. Of course, when you told me you were pregnant, I had to do the right thing. How fucking stupid of me."

56

A month after their wedding Chelsea had conveniently miscarried. He'd wanted to divorce her, to beg Cathryn to take him back. When his father found out, he told Nick he would disown him if he divorced Chelsea. After all, Pembertons simply did not divorce. They could screw around as much as they wanted, provided they were discreet. Divorce was an absolute no-no. Marriage was till death do you part. His mother had died when he was three. He didn't remember her, and his father hadn't taken the time to encourage his memory, either. He'd been too busy making millions to care for him. Nick had been raised by housekeepers and the occasional nanny.

"You can leave anytime, Nicholas."

"I can, can't I?" he shot back. When his father had died two years ago, Nick couldn't wait to give Chelsea the heave-ho. But the son of a bitch had made certain that Nick would kiss his ass from the grave and beyond. A stipulation in the will stated that if he divorced Chelsea, Pemberton Transport would go public. Under the terms of the will, his shares would become nonvoting shares, allowing the major stockholders in the corporation complete control. Even if he retained his position as CEO, he would be nothing more than a figurehead, at the

57

mercy of the board of directors. However, if he were to produce an heir with Chelsea, the stipulation would be null and void. At forty-one, Chelsea was too old to have children. Pure and simple, he was stuck with her. Hell, she was menopausal. They'd tried throughout the years, but a child hadn't been in their stars. Part of him was glad. He didn't want the lifetime responsibility of raising a child. He was too self-centered and knew it. Chelsea, on the other hand, would have loved a child. Not that she was the motherly type. She wasn't. Having a child would simply be another means of digging as deeply into his pockets as she could. It was all about the money for Chelsea. He liked it, too. Born into wealth, Nicholas Pemberton couldn't imagine a life without all his millions.

The traffic slowed to a halt as Nick turned onto Union Street. The building where the banquet was being held blazed with lights. Limos, Hummers, and Mercedes were lined up to make the turn into the self-serve parking area.

"See? I knew this would be low-class. They're making us park our own vehicle!"

"Shut up, Chelsea. It won't kill you to walk around the corner. As a matter of fact, you might work off some of that extra weight you've been carrying around." He said that just to tick her off. She was as thin as a rail. He got out of the car and walked around to open the passenger door for her. Never knew who might be watching them. Appearances were everything in his world.

Chelsea shot daggers at him. "You're a true prick, Nick. But you already know that, don't you?"

"So you say. Let's just go inside and make nice to all the snotty kids. A lot of society women went to college, you know. You might bump into some of your friends on the catering staff. It's a shame you didn't have the opportunity to get an education."

He knew how her lack of education shamed her. Tossing it in her face now and then did his heart good.

"The shame is that I fell for a liar like you."

Nick placed his hand on her elbow, leading her to the sidewalk. "It is. You've had such a pitiful life. I almost feel sorry for you."

The couple continued to walk toward the bright lights. Music blared; shouts of laughter could be heard through the open doors. Nick cleared his throat, raked a hand through his hair, and led his wife inside.

Couples dressed in their finest had gathered in small groups throughout the foyer. Nick plastered a smile on his face. He glanced around, searching for a familiar face, only to stop when he noticed a woman in a black wrap. She was so striking that it almost took his breath away. And there was something vaguely familiar about her.

Dropping Chelsea's hand, he said, "Go find our table. I'll be there in few a minutes."

Appearances and Chelsea were all but forgotten as he made his way across the foyer to the coat-check counter.

CHAPTER 3

Soon after entering the university building, Lin sheepishly relinquished her wrap to the young woman at the coat-check counter. Everywhere she looked, women glistened in their dazzling evening gowns, their jewel-like hues filling the large room with colors as bright as the shimmering lights on a Christmas tree. Many wore sparkling jewels around their necks, and diamonds dripped from their ears like giant teardrops. The men looked as though they'd jumped right off the pages of the latest edition of *GQ*. Slacks creased to perfection, no one appeared to have a hair out of place. She'd never seen so many beautifully dressed people in one room. It reminded her of a night at the Oscars. She felt drab in comparison.

The main room buzzed with dozens of voices and numerous accents. Nervously, Lin brushed a strand of hair away from her face as she searched the crowd for Will. Seeing him directly across from her, she held her arm high in the air in hopes of gaining his attention. When several seconds passed without him acknowledging her, she dropped her arm to her side, feeling like a silly schoolgirl attending her first dance. She should've asked Sally to come with her, but someone had to stay behind to oversee the remainder of the remodeling.

Lin spied a waiter coming toward her as he carefully managed to balance a tray of champagne flutes overflowing with the pale bubbly liquid. She removed a long-stemmed flute when he paused in front of her. She murmured a soft thank-you. Standing in the center of the room, Lin once again searched the crowd for Will. When she could no longer spot him, she inched her way through the masses of parents and professors, coming to rest against a wall, where she could observe the guests. *A true wallflower.* The thought brought a smile to her lips.

Lin lifted the elegant flute to her lips, preparing to take a sip of champagne, only to stop in midair when she noticed a man directly in her line of vision, staring at her. Uncomfortable under his perusal, she cast her gaze in the opposite direction, hoping Will would magically emerge from the

62

crowd. When he didn't, Lin again caught the eye of the man she'd observed watching her mere seconds ago. She felt extremely uncomfortable when she saw him smiling at her, and with each step he took, he shortened the distance between them. Lin looked from left to right, hoping to see someone else, anyone else. When she glanced at him a second time, he quickly approached one of the many waiters, lifting two flutes of champagne off the tray. Lifting one flute in her direction, he raised a raven black eyebrow as if in question.

Her heart skipped a beat. There was something about the man that unnerved her, something vaguely familiar. Once he was close enough for her actually to delineate his features, her heart pounded so hard in her chest that, for a second, she feared she would die of cardiac arrest right there on the spot. Feeling dizzy, she gulped her entire flute of champagne and quickly placed the flute on a nearby windowsill. Immediately scanning the area for the ladies' room, Lin saw a sign indicating that its location was just to her right.

It wasn't possible, yet her common sense told her it was highly probable!

Lin practically ran across the room, the heels of her red pumps making clicking sounds against the floor like frantic Morse code. *Help me! Help me! Help me!*

She slammed into the ladies' room door like a matador into a raging bull. In her heart she had always known that this moment would come, had feared it like a terminal illness, but the reality was much worse than she'd ever imagined.

Lin was 99 percent positive that the man who'd been staring at her was Nicholas Pemberton! Yes, he was older, but it was almost impossible to forget those sculpted features, the dark eyes, the thick black hair. Especially since Will mirrored his father in almost every way. Looks, build, height. Memories flashed before her eyes like movie stills, each one becoming more precise than the previous one.

It wasn't supposed to be this way. Lin recalled all the letters she'd sent to him, the letters she carried in a messenger bag, letters that were never out of her sight. Why she'd carried them around with her all these years, she didn't know. Maybe she was fearful Will would come across them. Whatever the reason, Nicholas Pemberton had lost his chance to claim Will as his son years ago. Hell would freeze over and crack before she'd let him have a second chance.

Standing in front of the sink, she ran cold

water over her wrists. She'd read somewhere that was supposed to be calming. It wasn't working. Sweat dotted her forehead, and her hands trembled as she removed a tissue from its container.

Why tonight of all nights? She and Will had talked about this day for the past two years. No way would she allow it to be spoiled by the man who'd denied his son for the past nineteen years. And what was even worse, she'd never told Will who his father was. When he'd been old enough to understand, she'd told him about a brief romance she'd had, in which he'd been conceived, saying his father was killed in an accident. Lin remembered how guilty she felt, but at the time it had seemed like the right thing to do. Now she questioned her decision.

Lin inhaled and exhaled as she'd been taught in her yoga class, hoping the deep breathing would calm her fractured nerves. It wasn't helping. If anything, she felt like she was hyperventilating.

She needed to calm down. *Think.*

Entering one of the stalls, she placed her purse on the plastic shelf provided, then sat on the commode, using it as a chair.

If Nicholas were to see Will, Lin doubted he'd see the resemblance. If he had truly recognized her, wouldn't he have called out to her, said something to gain her attention? Of course he would have, she told herself. Most likely he'd mistaken her for another woman. That had to be it.

With that thought in mind, Lin slipped out of the stall, washed her hands, and reapplied her lipstick. She flipped open her cell phone to check the time. Seven twenty. Will probably thought she'd lost track of the time.

Head up, shoulders back, Lin stepped out of the ladies' room, unobserved. What if she ran into Nicholas while Will was present? Would either of them put two and two together?

No! I'm being ridiculous. The odds are in my favor.

Deciding she would allow nothing to ruin this special night, with her head still held high, shoulders squared, Lin marched across the parquet floors as though she owned them. Scanning the throngs of people, her heart settled into a normal *thump, thump, thump* when she recognized Will with a group of young men hanging in a cluster near the coat-check counter.

Fixing a smile on her face, Lin hurried toward her son. "I've been looking all over for you."

Will took her hand and held it. "Me too.

66

Guys, this is my mother. Lin Townsend."

Several approving nods were directed her way, along with "Nice to meet you" and "Welcome to New York." After shaking hands with a few of the young men, who went their separate ways, Lin and Will were finally alone.

"What do you think so far?" Will asked as he escorted her to their assigned table near the stage.

Lin wondered why they were seated so close to the guest speakers, but was afraid to ask. "I think this is . . . terrific! There is so much to see and learn in this city. I want you to take advantage of this opportunity."

Will pulled her chair out for her. She sat down, looking around for the person who had the power to turn her life into a nightmare. When there was no sign of him, she relaxed, but only a little. Lin knew better than to let her guard down.

Will sat next to her. "We've been over this before, Mom. I'll see all the stuff you and Sally suggested. I have the list in my dorm, pinned on the bulletin board. I've got four years. I don't think Ellis Island or the Empire State Building is going anywhere in the near future. There's plenty of time." His eyes sparkled with mischief as he gave her one of his goofy grins.

Lin returned the smile. "Of course there is. I just know how overwhelming the first year of college can be. Not by experience, but Lizzie had a terrible time keeping up her freshman year. Remember?"

Will laughed out loud. "Yeah. I remember Lizzie telling me about all the guys she dated. That's why she couldn't keep up with her classwork."

"Sally kept a tight rein on her. She needed to test the waters."

His grin widened even more. "I completely understand."

"Don't get any ideas about mimicking her behavior. You're a young man. I wouldn't want you to become a father too soon. . . . Just be smart, Will. Don't be foolish like I was."

"Mom, we've had this conversation a hundred times. I promise not to get a girl pregnant. Besides, you're too young to become a grandma just yet."

Throughout the years Lin had reiterated how priceless a family was, but planning ahead was the wisest choice. Will knew of her struggles. He'd been right there with her. She'd done her best to see that he hadn't gone without the latest toys and clothes. And then, when he'd turned sixteen, she'd purchased his first car. While not brand spanking new, like the ones some of his friends owned, it was in good shape cosmetically, and the engine purred like a kitten. All in all, Lin thought she'd been an okay parent. Of course, Sally, Irma, and Jack had been there to offer advice when she needed it. Oftentimes, she'd simply needed a shoulder to lean on, and they'd been there for her then as well. Despite their humble beginnings, Will had turned into a fine young man. Lin was proud to call him her son.

"I'll take that as a compliment. Now, did you get to take that nap you wanted this afternoon?"

"Yes, but it wasn't easy with all the guys screaming and carrying on. Like in scream-ing and acting like a bunch of banshees." Will laughed. "You know how guys act when they're grouped together."

Yes, she did, and, sad to say, it frightened the wits out of her. She recalled the party she'd attended in Atlanta, the men, or rather the *boys,* she'd met. Will was the result.

"It's an exciting day for most of them. Leaving home for the first time." Lin's mind drifted back to her first day on her own. She'd had nothing but the clothes on her back when her father had tossed her out. Fortunately, she'd saved most of the money she'd earned baby-sitting and cleaning houses. Instead of using her hard-earned money for college, she'd used it to provide a roof over her and Will's heads. She remembered those first three nights in a local hotel before finding the garage apartment. She'd been terrified. Once she'd overcome her initial fear, Lin's common sense and work ethic kicked in. She'd worked two jobs, managed to take care of Will and make a decent life for the two of them. They'd stayed in the apartment until Will started kindergarten; then she'd purchased her first house. A two-bedroom fixer-upper was all she'd been able to afford, but, with her never-ending optimism and tons of hard work, she'd made it into a happy home. She'd had her white picket fence, and Will had had his swing set and tree house. Five years after purchasing the diner, she'd saved enough to build her dream home, and they'd lived there ever since. Life had been good to her because she'd worked very hard to make it happen.

"Yeah, I guess you could say that. Most of the guys have family here in the city, or at least those that I've met so far. Are you sure you'll be okay?"

Lin hated the way her son worried about her. She wanted his life to be carefree and unencumbered with the responsibilities she'd had at his age. "I'm fine, Will. I have the diner to occupy my time. If all goes as planned, there won't be much left for anything else." She knew his next statement would be something along the lines of her being alone. Will often encouraged her to date, settle down, get married, but dating had been at the bottom of her list, and there it still rested. There were too many other things she wanted to accomplish.

Will watched her out of the corner of his eye before his grin turned serious. "I won't remind you that you'll be completely alone now that I'm here. It might be a good time to hook up with one of those dating services I see on TV all the time. Who knows? You might meet a millionaire or the love of your life."

Lin took a deep breath, shook her head in disagreement. Like she'd ever go that route. She wasn't desperate yet. "You don't give up, do you? Never mind. Don't answer that."

A high-pitched screech from the microphone next to the podium directed the guests' attention to the front stage.

Saved by a squeal, thought Lin.

The buzz in the banquet hall died down to a soft hum as the guests made their way to their seats. Hundreds of people gathered to listen to speeches by the alumni, whom they hoped their children would someday emulate.

The first speech — if you could even call it that — was short and sweet, given by the dean of students, a rotund man as tall as he was wide. Curly red hair rimmed his head, reminding Lin of Bozo the Clown. The wire-framed glasses perched at the tip of his nose looked as though they were ready to slide off and soar into the air. Lin thought of a ski slope, for some crazy reason.

"First, I'd like to welcome all the incoming students." The dean stopped, waiting for the applause to die down. He gave a few facts about the school and its staff, coming to a speedy ending as he announced dinner was ready to be served. He joked about their needing sustenance in order to endure the guest speakers.

An hour later, after their plates were removed and dessert was served, Lin relaxed and actually enjoyed listening to the humorous stories from many of the former alumni. They all welcomed the new students and spent a few minutes discussing the value of the education they had received at NYU. And then came the closing speaker for the night.

Nicholas Pemberton was taller than she remembered. His Greek-god looks had only gotten better with age. The sculpted cheekbones, square chin, and dark eyes were just like her son's. She clenched her fists to hide their shaking. Stealing a nervous glance at Will told her all was well in that department. He listened intently as Nick told of his days at NYU.

"And to think I was going to give all this up for a pretty blonde," Nick said, his hands held out to both sides, as though he were about to embrace the room.

The guests laughed and spoke among themselves.

Lin's head shot up like a high temperature. Was he referring to her?

"— And she married my best friend," he said in ending.

Lin was so shocked, she hadn't heard all that he'd said. Will looked at her strangely. She took a sip of lukewarm water, smiled at her son. She leaned over to whisper to him. "I need to go. I . . . I ordered the taxi to return now. You won't mind if I leave early?"

Though her behavior was unusual, Will seemed to accept her excuse. "There'll be a line of taxis waiting when this shindig lets out. Sure you don't want to wait?"

Lin took a deep breath. "No, I'm feeling

73

very tired. I think I'll go. You can tell me what I missed tomorrow. Call me when you're up and about. We'll have brunch."

"Okay. I'll walk you out."

"No!" Lin said, loud enough for the speaker to pause and stare down at her. *Oh, my God! This isn't happening.* She had never anticipated something like this. Not in her worst nightmare!

She had to leave. Immediately.

She bent over to give Will a kiss and walked out of the banquet hall. If there were stares following her retreating back, she didn't know, because there was no way in hell she was going to turn around to look.

Stepping outside into the cool night air revived her. Will was right. The taxis were starting to line up next to the curb. She hurried to the one closest to her. The taxi driver she'd asked to wait wouldn't have any trouble finding another fare.

"The Helmsley Park Lane," she announced to the driver as she slid onto the backseat. He was about to put the car in drive when the passenger door opposite her was yanked open.

"This cab's taken," the driver said with a heavy Brooklyn accent. "Sorry, bucko."

"Yes, I just need to speak to the lady for a moment."

Nicholas Pemberton had followed her!

Lin turned her gaze on the one man who had had the power to make her son's life better, the man who had never given a second thought to the son he'd fathered, discarding him like yesterday's garbage. She wouldn't give the bastard the satisfaction of speaking to him.

He leaned in through the open door. "You must think I've lost my mind. I saw you earlier tonight by the coat-check counter. You forgot this." He placed her black wrap on the seat next to her.

Lin's heart rate rapidly increased as he leaned in closer. He smelled clean and rich. She felt his breath on her skin, warm and minty, as he spoke. "I had to get out of that room full of stuffed shirts." When he smiled at her, she almost returned it with one of her own.

Nicholas Pemberton was a charming son of a bitch; she'd best remember that little fact. She turned her head in the opposite direction so she didn't have to look at him. "Thank you. Please, just go," she said to the taxi driver.

Nick stepped away from the car, slamming the door as he did so. Lin was sure she heard him utter something but couldn't make out what it was. It didn't matter. All that mattered to her was escaping those dark, questioning eyes.

"Could you please speed up?" she asked. She'd always heard that taxi drivers in New York drove like bats out of hell. It was just her luck to get one who obeyed the speed limit. She needed to put as much distance between her and Nicholas Pemberton as quickly as humanly possible.

The driver put the pedal to the metal.

"Thanks," Lin said.

"Anytime, but if I get a ticket, you're gonna be sorry."

"I'll take the chance," Lin replied. She closed her eyes, hoping the driver would be quiet. She had to think.

Never in a million years had she imagined herself in such a situation. Those first few weeks alone with Will had been the hardest. She'd often imagined what it would have been like to have a husband there to relieve her when she'd been so tired, it was all she could do to keep her eyes open. That was when she'd started writing the letters again, even though the previous ones had been returned unopened. As each one came back, Lin would make up some wild excuse for why Nick couldn't come for her and their son. After years of doing that, she finally admitted to herself that she was nothing more than a spring fling to Nick, if that. Now here she was, an adult, in a city of millions, and he was the first man she had seen. Knowing it was pure coincidence didn't help, either. There was no way he could have known Will would be attending NYU. Hell, he didn't even know that the kid existed. Finding her in the crowd of hundreds, Lin also put down to coincidence. It had to be, she assured herself once again, since Nicholas Pemberton hadn't the first clue that he had fathered a child. Her worries were unnecessary. The odds of Will and Nick meeting face-to-face were slim. Even if they did, it wouldn't matter. Yes, the resemblance was remarkable, but only to those who knew. And only two people knew what had happened that long-ago night.

The taxi pulled up to the curb in front of the Helmsley. Lin breathed a sigh of relief. She gave the guy a fifty-dollar bill. "Keep the change."

"Thanks, lady."

Lin would've paid a thousand dollars if she'd had to, anything to get the hell away from Nick. Recognizing her, the doorman assisted Lin as she emerged from the taxi. After reaching into her purse, she tucked a ten-dollar bill into the palm of his white-gloved hand. She'd best find an ATM soon.

Her supply of cash was dwindling faster than she'd anticipated.

Back in her room, she took off the black dress, swearing she would never wear it again, because it would evoke too much anger. She stuffed it into a laundry bag for disposal. She'd seen enough garbage cans on the streets of Manhattan. Someone would be in for a nice surprise on discovering the dress.

In the bathroom she filled the Jacuzzi tub with hot water, poured some bath salts beneath the flow, then grabbed a Diet Coke from the minibar. Lin kept her cell phone with her. She looked at the clock. Eleven. Sally would still be up. She piled her hair on top of her head, securing it with a barrette. After immersing herself in the warm, scented water, Lin dialed her best friend's cell number.

Sally picked up on the first ring. "I had a feeling it was you. What's up?"

"You can thank caller ID for that feeling, and you're never going to believe what I'm about to tell you. Are you sitting down?"

"Actually, I was just about to leave the restaurant. I stayed late to make sure the crew cleaned up after themselves. You should've seen the piles of garbage they left yesterday. I wanted to fire the entire lot of them, but this late in the game we'd be lucky to find replacements."

At that moment Lin couldn't have cared less about the diner. "So do whatever you think needs to be done. You're the manager."

"Lin!" Sally cried. "This is your baby, remember?"

"Yes, but that's not why I called." Lin paused, suddenly unsure if she wanted to tell Sally about the evening. *Yes. No. Hell, yes! I have to tell someone.*

"You sound excited. You're not hurt, are you?" Sally asked, her voice rising a notch.

"No, no. I'm fine. Physically at least." Lin rubbed her foot across the pulsing jet of water at the end of the huge tub. "And before you ask, Will is fine, too."

"You know me well. So, tell me what it is you're just dying to tell me. I can hear it in your voice. It's something big, isn't it? Did you meet someone?"

Here goes, Lin thought. "Yes and yes."

"Shit-house mouse! Lin, don't give me that crap! Either spit it out, or I'm hanging up. I hate it when you drag things out. You know that!" the voice on the other end of the line screeched.

Lin wasn't purposely trying to drag out the conversation. She just wasn't sure where to start. The beginning would probably be best. "Tonight, when I first arrived at the banquet for the incoming students, I was searching the crowd for Will when I saw this man looking at me. There was something about him that was familiar. Then he took a flute of champagne from a waiter, lifted it in my direction, as though he wanted to know if it was okay for him to bring it to me."

"Don't tell me you screwed this up, Lin. Please. You know what a short supply of sophisticated men we have in Dalton. And the ones that are remotely half-assed smart are married or gay."

"If you'll stop interrupting me, I'll finish."

"Sorry. Go on."

"The closer this guy came to me, the more familiar he became. I had to do a double take just to make sure I wasn't seeing things. I'm still in shock, Sally, because it was the one and only Mr. Nicholas Pemberton." Lin waited, allowing Sally a minute to soak up the info.

After more than a minute Sally spoke. "Are you sure?" she hissed.

"Of course I'm sure. If I was even the least bit unsure when I first saw him, I was convinced one hundred percent when the dean introduced him as the closing speaker.

80

He hasn't changed at all. He's as handsome as ever, maybe even more so."

"Go on," Sally encouraged.

"When he stood at the podium, making his speech, I swear I thought I would faint. My hands were shaking so bad, it's a miracle my jewelry didn't fly off. I didn't know what to do, so I told Will I had to go. Said I'd ordered a taxi. When he offered to walk me out, I all but shouted 'No,' so the entire crowd heard me. Nick stopped talking. Luckily, I found a taxi, and as we were about to leave, Nicholas raced over to the car. I just knew he was going to say my name. I . . . Then he placed my wrap on the seat, telling me I'd left it at the coat-check counter. He must have seen me check it when I arrived."

"That's it?" Sally stated.

"I think it's more than enough! What if he recognized me?" Lin took a drink of her Diet Coke. "What could I have told Will at that point, today of all days?"

"In the back of your mind you had to know this day would come. Or did you think the perfect life you created for Will wouldn't change? I know, I know he doesn't know about Nick, but the chance has always been there that he'd find out. He's bound to ask questions about his father, that *fictional*

81

father who just happened to die in an accident. Besides, you can't haul those damned letters around forever."

Tears filled Lin's eyes when she realized the mess she'd made. Her intention had been to protect Will. "I'm going to burn those letters tonight, as soon as I get out of the tub. There's a giant ashtray in the sitting area, and several books of matches. I am going to watch as they burn, Sally. I swear. I don't want Will to find them. Ever. If they're gone, then every trace of my relationship with Nick will be wiped off the face of the earth."

"I'm not so sure I'd get rid of those letters. You never know. Someday you might need them."

Lin blotted her eyes with a damp washcloth. "I can't imagine why, unless I want to continue to torture myself. They're so juvenile, Sally. I swear, I can't believe I stooped that low. I practically begged the guy to come and rescue Will and me."

"You did what any young girl in your shoes would've done. You were seventeen! Cut yourself some slack, Lin."

"That's easy for you to say. You haven't read the letters."

"I wouldn't, either, Lin. Those are your private words and thoughts. Quit beating yourself up. You said yourself that Nicholas didn't recognize you. I would forget it ever happened."

Lin sniffed, then dabbed at her eyes with the hem of a bath towel hanging next to the tub. "I guess you're right. If he remembered me, surely he would've said something. I just can't help but think something tragic is going to happen. It's like seeing Nick has opened a can of worms. I don't like the feeling, either. What if something happens to Will while he's in the city? I would never forgive myself, Sally. I'd be better off dead. I wouldn't have a life if it weren't for Will. Hell, that son of a bitch father of mine would've killed me, too, if I hadn't escaped. Well, that's not quite true — he tossed me out. It's just easier for me to think I escaped on my own. I thank God I was pregnant." It had always been Lin's belief that her father had shoved her mother down those steep basement steps. Her mother's death was too timely, too convenient. There were times when she was sorry she hadn't had the death investigated. And all those times she'd convinced herself that Will was more important.

"Stop it! You can't let this get to you. Nick is not going to find out about Will."

"I can only hope."

"What if he does? Would that truly be the end of the world?" Sally asked.

Lin heard the car door slam. Sally was home. They'd talked the entire drive.

"It isn't Nick's feelings I'm concerned with. It's Will's. I've always taught him to tell the truth, no matter what. What kind of mother teaches a child to be honest when her own life is nothing but a lie?"

"Knowing Will, he'd understand. Oh, he might be pissed for a while, but in time I think he'd get over it. You've been good to him, Lin. Hell, you've been just as good to me and Lizzie. I would've left Dalton a long time ago if not for you. You gave me a reason to stay."

"I did?" Lin questioned.

"Hell, yes! You're like a sister to me. You gave me the best job ever. You pay me way more than I'm worth. And don't say it's not true, because we both know it is."

"You're worth every cent, and you know it."

"I am, aren't I?"

They both laughed.

"I don't know what I would've done all these years without you, Jack, and Irma. Ya'll are my real family." Lin's Southern accent was much more pronounced when she was upset.

"It doesn't take blood ties to be a family. I think of that every time I look at Lizzie. I'd kill someone over that girl." Lizzie was Sally's sister's child. Mary Kay had died just weeks after giving birth to Lizzie. Sally had taken her and raised her as her own, knowing that Carl, her brother-in-law, would've treated Lizzie as badly as he'd treated Mary Kay.

"I know what you mean. If anyone were to harm a hair on Will's head, I wouldn't think twice about killing them. As a matter of fact, I don't know of any mother who wouldn't kill to protect her children."

"We're both in agreement on that. You have to be turning into a raisin by now. I'm home. I'm ready to call it a night."

"Sorry to keep blabbing. I'll call you tomorrow. We'll finish this conversation then. Night, Sally."

"Night, kiddo."

CHAPTER 4

Saturday, September 1, 2007
New York City

Lin hugged Will good-bye one last time before heading to her gate to catch her flight home to Dalton. They'd had brunch at Tavern on the Green, and frankly, Lin hadn't been impressed at all. The furnishings were old and shabby, and she knew that brunch at Jack's Diner would put theirs to shame.

When they'd finished their meal, Lin had told Will that Sally needed her to return as soon possible, as there were issues with the contractors that only Lin could resolve. She had agreed to return soon, telling Will they'd see the tourist attractions together. He'd accepted her excuse without question. She'd promised to call as soon as she arrived in Atlanta. Sally would be picking her up at Hartsfield-Jackson International. They'd make the two-hour drive north to

Dalton together, during which they could talk without interruptions.

Lin's experience in New York was her first big excursion on her own. Born in Dalton, at Hamilton Memorial Hospital, Lin had attended Dalton High, where she'd been an honor student. Having a father who spent most of his free time either preaching to her or to the unlucky ones who happened to have the misfortune of knowing him hadn't made her the most popular girl in school. In fact she'd had no real friends. She'd wished for a friend, someone she could talk to, someone to hang out with, but then she would think of her life and how different it was from the lives of the kids she went to school with and was glad she didn't have to make excuses for her family's lifestyle.

She'd gotten over her family shame in elementary school. Years of being called Miss Stinky Pants had hardened her. The few times her mode of dress had been made fun of in high school, she would silently agree with whatever was said and go on as usual. This was normal to her.

As a businesswoman, Lin had earned the respect of her peers. She'd taken the good with the bad and come out ahead. Or such were her thoughts until she'd bumped into Nicholas Pemberton. Despite her unease at flying, she tried to rest on the flight, telling herself it was the only time she'd have to relax over the next few days, but her thoughts wouldn't let her. She kept seeing Nick's face when he'd followed her to the taxi. He was beyond sexy. She'd give him that. Like a fine wine, he'd improved with age. Big-time. She wondered if he'd ever thought about her. Had he been curious how her life had turned out? Hell, no! If he had been, he certainly would have known how to contact her. She'd written enough letters. And in each one she'd listed her phone number and told him the exact time to call. *If* he wanted to, she'd always added. She'd write the times down in her journal. When the time arrived, she would sit by the phone, waiting for a call that never came. She often feared that if she didn't, that would be the one time she would miss his call. Of course, the phone never did ring.

When they landed in Atlanta, Lin breathed a sigh of relief. She was glad to be on the ground. She'd spent the past two hours try-ing to come up with a plan, something to even the score. Lin had spent so many years struggling. If Nicholas Pemberton hadn't been such an ass, things might've been easier for her and Will. She'd truly believed Nick would have at the very least offered financial support when he learned of her pregnancy. Of course, that had never happened, because the jerk had never bothered to read her letters. She was hurt, and she was very, *very* angry.

Anger ate at her as she made her way through the mob of travelers. She had never been one to be vindictive, but thoughts of all she and Will had endured throughout the years enraged her. There had been many times when she fed Will store-brand powdered macaroni and cheese, and she'd had to make the box last for at least two meals. She remembered once, right after she brought him home from the hospital, finances were so tight, she'd scrounged through the couch cushions, searching for change. She'd managed to dig up thirty-five cents. From there she'd walked three miles to the grocery store, where she'd purchased three packages of ramen noodles. That had comprised a week's worth of groceries for her. Then, of course, once she went back to work, she'd had babysitters to pay, formula to buy. No, there hadn't been anything extra those first few years. When she'd managed to start saving, she'd vowed that she and her son would never be hungry again. They might have to wear secondhand clothes and repair the holes in their shoes, but they wouldn't go hungry.

Tears welled in her eyes when she recalled her past. A pity party wasn't her style. She removed a tissue from her pocket and wiped her eyes. What was that saying she and Sally were always quoting? "Don't get mad, get even."

As of that moment, that was exactly what she planned to do. She would figure out the details later. For now, she knew this was something she had to do in order to get on with her life. Being completely honest with herself, she admitted that she had always hoped that Nick would look for her, be her knight in shining armor, discover they had a child together. And once he found out, that he would marry her and they would all live happily ever after.

Right! I'll make my own happily ever after!

Determined more than ever, Lin hustled through the airport, glad she hadn't checked any luggage. She dialed Sally's cell number. "I'm here."

"I'm in the parking lot. Be there in ten."

Lin closed her phone and raced through the airport as fast as she could so Sally wouldn't have to circle the airport a second time. Lin stepped outside just as Sally pulled up in her new Hummer. Lin climbed inside, gave her friend a quick hug, and

90

fastened her seat belt.

"It's good to be home."

"Like you've been gone a long time," Sally teased.

"I know, but you know me. I'm a homebody. Though it was nice to take a trip, it sure as heck didn't turn out the way I'd planned."

"As long as Will is safely tucked away in his new world of academia, that's what matters most. He was the reason you made the trip in the first place," Sally reminded her.

"You're right. I'm just ticked that I had to leave early. Why did I allow that low-life scum sucker to intimidate me? Will you listen to the way I'm talking? I'm sorry. I didn't mean that. No, no, that's a lie. I did mean it. My father would wash my mouth out with soap if he heard me."

"You'll have to answer that yourself. Personally, I would've gone on as though nothing had happened. Really, nothing did happen, when you stop and think about it. You saw him. He saw you. Apparently, he didn't recognize you." Sally paused. "That's what's bothering you, isn't it? You wanted him to recognize you, and he didn't. I know you too well, Lin."

Lin hated to admit it to anyone, but Sally was partially right. It hurt that she'd made no impression whatsoever on her son's father. "I think that's part of it. Hell, I don't know. I know I was shocked to see him. And I know something else. This has to stay between us. Promise me that whatever you do, you won't spill the beans on what I'm about to propose."

"Okay. I promise. Now, out with it." Sally took the exit leading to I-75 North. Once she was on the freeway, she set the Hummer to cruise control. "I'm all ears."

"You know as well as I do that Will and I had some lean times in the beginning." Lin wanted to lay the foundation for what she was about to do, in hopes that Sally would understand and agree to help her with her plans.

"Of course I do. I remember when you came into Jack's, asking for a job. Even though you weren't showing, I knew you were pregnant. I think Irma did, too. All Jack saw was another set of arms and legs to serve up his concoctions." Sally laughed. "You didn't have anyone fooled. We all fell in love with you, and as they say, the rest is history."

Lin hoped her proposal wouldn't tarnish Sally's image of her. "I could've had a much easier go of it had Nicholas been willing to read my letters. I can't explain why he chose

92

to ignore me, and at this point I don't care any longer. What I do care about, though, is this. He's a very wealthy man. I want to find out just how wealthy he is. Maybe mess with his finances a bit. Make him jump through a few hoops. Sort of like I had to."

Sally shot her a wicked grin. "Are you thinking what I think you're thinking?"

Lin laughed. "Tell me what you're thinking first."

"You want to mess with old Nick's bank accounts, maybe steal his identity?"

"Something along those lines. I don't even know where to begin. What I do know is this — I want the bastard to suffer a little bit. Let him wonder where his next meal is coming from. Not that I expect that to happen literally, but people with fortunes expect the world to jump at their beck and call. I want Nick and his wife to have a few restless nights." There, it was out in the open. "So what are your thoughts?"

Sally raised an eyebrow, then smiled. "I like it. Now, all we have to do is come up with a plan where he gets a good financial fucking without us getting caught. I assume you've given thought to what will happen if we're caught?"

"Sorry to say I didn't get that far in my thinking. I wanted to see what your reaction was first before I go full bore."

"No, you wanted to see if I would help you." Sally laughed.

"That, too," Lin said with a wicked smirk of her own.

"What about the diner?" Sally asked.

Lin raised her eyebrows in question. "You don't think I can do both?"

"It's not a question of what I think. It's what you can do. Think you can run a business while trying to destroy someone else's?"

"People do it all the time," Lin said airily. "At least they do in the news accounts I've read."

"Yes, but you're not like those people, Lin. You're honest and decent."

"Thanks. I think. Look at it this way. Let's just say I'm about to jump off the wagon for a while. Give me a couple of months to do what needs to be done, and then I'll put the Miss Goody Two-shoes hat back on."

As they were approaching Cartersville, Sally took the first exit. "I need something to drink and a trip to the restroom."

"Sally, are you angry with me?" Lin asked suddenly.

"No! What makes you think I'm angry?"

"You're stopping in the middle of a very delicate conversation. I thought maybe you were trying to avoid the subject."

"No, I have to pee, Lin. Seriously. I'm thirsty, too." Sally pulled into a rinky-dink mom-and-pop gas station that looked as though it'd seen better days. "Get us something to drink while I hit the ladies' room."

"Sure, I'll be right back."

Lin removed a ten-dollar bill from her purse and went inside the musty little station. An old icebox-style Coke machine hummed as she removed two frosted bottles of Diet Coke. She used the opener on the machine to flip the metal tops off. She hadn't seen a machine like this in years. She placed the drinks on the counter.

"Two bucks," said a woman of indeterminate age.

Lin held her hand out for her change. "Thanks."

"Anytime, missy."

Lin had a huge grin on her face as she went back to the Hummer. *Missy.* For a minute Lin thought the old gal was going to call her Miss Stinky Pants. Sally was waiting for her.

"This place is in a time warp. I swear the toilets were those old black kind with the pull chain attached." Shaking her head, Sally drove up to the on-ramp leading to I-75 North.

"You should've seen the Coke machine. That place is probably full of antiques."

"Lots of these old mom-and-pop stores have them. I don't think they care about updating to the newer, more modern way. Sometimes I think the old ways were the best."

"I don't," Lin said. "I like modern conveniences."

"And you're going to need some high-tech software if you're planning on screwing with Mr. Pemberton's finances."

"How do you know that?" Lin asked.

"I watch TV."

"Remember that computer geek that used to come to the diner, the one who reminded me of Pee-wee Herman?" Lin asked.

"Yeah. What about him?"

"I bet he'd know how to get his hands on the software we need."

Sally glanced at her. "May I ask how you're going to approach him? Better yet, how do you plan to find him? He doesn't come in the diner anymore. Maybe he moved."

Lin took a deep breath. "I honestly haven't thought that far ahead. I need to sit down and make a concrete plan, something do-able."

"If it were me, I'd hire the best PI money

could buy. You've got tons of the stuff now. What are you saving it for? Will's college is paid for. The diner's mortgage is paid off. I think you should put some of that fortune of yours to good use here so you won't be jumping all over the page. Hire the best. Tell him what you want, and more important, make sure to explain money is no object."

"I think you like spending my money. Don't kid yourself, Sally dear. You've raked in a bundle yourself. We're both lucky we made those investments way back when."

"True. Paid for Lizzie's college."

"And that swanky nursing home for my father. We can't forget that."

Sally took the Walnut Avenue exit in Dalton before shooting Lin a dark look. "You know as well as I do that you wouldn't put your father in some decrepit old folks' home. Though he deserves it. One with hardwood floors."

Lin gave her a half smile. "If I did that, I'd be on his level, Sal. It's not me, anyway. If he doesn't get his comeuppance here on earth, he will in the afterlife."

"We can only hope," Sally added.

"I don't have any qualms about putting the screws to Nicholas Pemberton, though. That doesn't say a whole lot about me, now does it?"

Sally made a sharp right turn onto Morningside Drive, where she and Lin both had built their dream homes. As she pulled into Lin's driveway, she said, "Look, if you want to get back at him, you need to put your principles and your conscience aside. Ask for forgiveness when it's over. You keep thinking like this, you'll get screwed all over again."

Lin opened the passenger door, took her bag from the backseat. "Yeah, you're right, as usual. Want to come in for a drink?"

"Can't. I promised Kelly Ann I'd work her shift tonight."

"I'm impressed," Lin said. "Just don't overdo it. I need your help now more than ever."

"Not to worry. There's plenty of me to spare. I'll call you tonight."

"Thanks, Sally. I don't know what I'd do without you."

Sally pulled out of the driveway, waving as she turned onto the street. Lin really didn't know what she'd do without Sally. She was the big sister she never had.

For that alone, she was beyond thankful.

It had taken a full week before Nicholas Pemberton could get an appointment with

Dr. Reeves, and by the time the day of the appointment arrived, he had no patience left. To make matters worse, he'd already been in Evan Reeves's office for two hours without seeing the great man himself.

They'd taken numerous blood samples, asked every medical question known to man, then asked him to wait. He did not like waiting. Especially in a cubicle the size of his clothes closet.

In an hour he had another Friday meeting with his staff. If Dr. Reeves didn't make an appearance by then, he would have to come to Nick. Nick glanced at his Rolex for the tenth time. As he was about to leave, the door opened.

Dr. Reeves was not what Nick had expected. He was in his mid-to late thirties, was deeply tanned, and had longish blond hair. Wide shoulders tapered to a narrow waist. *He must work out,* Nick thought. In fact, he looked more like a beach bum than a doctor. Women would certainly find him attractive.

"Mr. Pemberton" — the doctor held out a hand — "I'm Evan Reeves. Sorry we kept you waiting so long. Dr. Warner asked that we wait for the results of your blood work."

Nick leaned against an examining table. "And?" he inquired impatiently.

"He was right to be concerned." Dr. Reeves took a deep breath. "Let's go to my office. These rooms are too small to breathe in."

Maybe the guy wasn't so bad, after all.

"Yes, they are."

Nick followed him down a narrow hall. At the end, Dr. Reeves opened a door to his left, stood back, and motioned for Nick to come inside.

"Please, have a seat."

Nick sat down in an awkward plastic chair, one of those modern-looking things that was supposed to be comfortable. "So, am I going to die?" Nick didn't want to waste time on idle chatter. He had things to do.

Dr. Reeves sat at his desk. He picked up a sheet of paper and scanned the results. "I'll do everything in my power to keep you from dying, Mr. Pemberton."

Nick's pulse rate increased. He raked a hand through his hair and felt his hand tremble. "This is serious, isn't it?"

"I'm afraid so."

"Give it to me straight up. I don't want the sugarcoated version." Nick jammed both hands in his pockets to hide his tremors. He did not want to appear vulnerable or afraid to the doctor.

Dr. Reeves swiped a dark hand through his messy hair. "Okay. I think you have leukemia. We'll need to do a bone-marrow test to confirm my findings, but at this point, I think I'm on the money. I see this every day."

It took Nick several minutes to absorb the doctor's words. He didn't interrupt him, and for that Nick was grateful. A deep breath didn't help at all. Chelsea swore by them, but he thought her stupid. What did she know?

"Then let's do this test. I want to be one hundred percent sure."

"All right. You'll have to be hospitalized —"

"Are you serious? For a goddamn test? I have a meeting in less than an hour!"

"Mr. Pemberton, this is very serious. It can be life threatening. If my suspicion is correct, you don't have time to worry about meetings. This disease can be devastating in its swiftness. Sometimes we have only a matter of weeks to treat leukemia."

A thousand thoughts surged through Nick's mind. He could die. Soon, according to the doctor. Maybe he should get another opinion. But Reeves was the best in his field; he'd gained that much information from Vinery before firing him. He *was* the second opinion.

"Then let's not waste time. Set the test up now. I'll make a few phone calls to clear my schedule."

"Of course." Dr. Reeves picked up the phone on his desk, swiveled around in his chair, facing the bookshelves behind his desk. He spoke quietly into the phone. Turning around, he got up and walked to the door. "If you'll follow me, I'll have my staff take care of your admission. There's a bit of paperwork involved." The doctor paused before leaving him in the hands of his staff. "Is there someone you'd like to call? Maybe I can make a call for you?"

Nick was touched by the doctor's kindness, and it surprised him. Normally, he was not a sentimental man, yet it wasn't every day he was told he had a serious, possibly fatal illness. "I'll call my office. They can take care of rescheduling."

"Good. Then let's get this paperwork started. I don't know what the world is coming to when it takes longer to fill out the forms than it does to do the actual procedure itself," Dr. Reeves commented with a trace of ridicule for the system of which he was an integral part.

"If you'll have a seat," said a young woman, motioning, "we'll get through this as quickly as possible."

Nick nodded, gave the young woman his insurance card and driver's license before taking a seat opposite her. Nick took his cell phone from his jacket pocket. He dialed Rosa's direct number. She answered immediately.

"Rosa, I want you to cancel all my meetings and appointments for the next . . ." He paused, unsure of how long. He wasn't even sure how long he would live at this point. "Cancel everything for the next two weeks. Something's come up, and I cannot work around it. Have Gerald take some of my appointments. Cancel the trip to China. It can wait. Call Chelsea. Ask her to meet me at Presbyterian Hospital. Tell her to pack an overnight bag and bring it with her. And, Rosa, if I hear of one single word of this conversation floating around the office, I'll fire the entire staff. Is that understood?"

"Yes, Mr. Pemberton. Sir, I . . . uh, hope you'll be fine."

"Trust me, I will. I'll call you first thing in the morning. And remember, not a word to anyone." He flipped his cell phone off, not giving Rosa a chance to say anything else. Nick didn't want her concern or her pity. He would be fine. He would accept nothing less. Pemberton men lived long, illustrious lives. His father had been eighty-nine when he died. Nick expected to beat the old bastard by at least a year. No way was his old man going to greet him at the gates of hell anytime in the near future.

It took over an hour to fill out the paperwork, or rather it took the young woman behind the computer that long to type it into the computer system. Nick would never tolerate such inadequacy.

"You'll need to sign these papers now. It'll save you from doing it when you're uncomfortable right before the marrow extraction." The young lady slid a stack of papers across the desk.

"What is that supposed to mean? Dr. Reeves didn't explain anything about being uncomfortable." He sounded like a whiny child, not the chief executive officer of a multibillion-dollar corporation.

"I'm sorry. I thought he did. I'll be right back," the woman said vaguely.

Ten minutes later Dr. Reeves sat across from Nick in the same seat his secretary, or whatever the hell she was, had just vacated. "I apologize. I was hoping to get back to you before we got this far. The procedure is quite simple actually. First, we'll numb a small area of skin. Then we use a Jamshidi needle. It's a long, hollow needle that's inserted into your hip bone. We'll withdraw samples of blood, bone, and, of course, your bone marrow. From there I'll send them to the pathologist, who will examine them under a microscope. After I get the results, you and I will discuss a treatment plan."

"If this is so simple, why bother admitting me? Can't this be done as an outpatient?" Nick said.

"Sure, it can. However, if the results are positive, and you're already in the hospital, we can begin treatment right away."

"I suppose that makes sense," Nick agreed.

"I'll have more answers as soon as we complete the test."

Nick nodded. "I'll see you at the hospital, then."

Dr. Reeves placed a comforting arm on Nick's shoulder. "You're gonna have a hell of a fight on your hands, but something tells me you won't be defeated."

"Thank you." Nick felt humbled, and it pissed him off. He didn't like the feeling. Damn it to hell, he didn't like *feeling*.

Almost a week later Lin was too keyed up to even think about going to bed. It was too early, anyway. She made a pot of herbal tea to take into her office. She hadn't been able to stop thinking about Nicholas Pemberton, about what she wanted to do to him. Lin wanted him to suffer in the way she'd suffered, but realized time and circumstances had changed since that fateful week of their romance. His suffering would be on a different level. She smiled at the mere thought.

Lin sat at the Victorian mahogany twin-pedestal desk that she'd bought the previous year as a birthday gift to herself. She opened her laptop, clicked onto the Internet. Having given herself time to see if she really wanted to go through with shafting Nick, she decided it was time to start. No time like the present, as Irma would say.

Clicking onto Google, she typed in Nicholas Pemberton's name. There were more than three hundred thousand hits. Starting with the first one, she was directed to the home page of Pemberton Transport. She skimmed through a brief history of the company, where she noted that Nick's father, Nicholas Pemberton Sr., had passed away two years ago. Nick was now CEO. She read through a few more paragraphs, learned there were hundreds of employees. Most important, the company was financially sound. Lin hadn't a clue how to wreck Pemberton Transport's finances directly, but she vowed if she couldn't, then she'd find someone who would.

She Googled top private detectives in the United States. There were gazillions. Lin thought it best to hire one located in New York City, thinking expenses would be less. She scrolled through dozens of names, then stopped when she saw JV Investigations. It was located in the Empire State Building, the same building that housed Pemberton Transport's main offices. JV Investigations' Web site revealed that its clients were primarily large corporations, and the services offered included vetting potential employees and consultants, as well as protecting the secrecy of proprietary corporate information. Wouldn't it be interesting if she could hire a detective agency that operated right under Nick Pemberton's nose, so to speak? She clicked the PRINT button. She would tell Sally about JV Investigations later on since she wanted her opinion.

Her computer zinged, letting her know she'd received an e-mail. Her local humane society. How could she have forgotten? Lin sometimes volunteered as a "foster parent" to care for pets until a decent home could be found. She'd had Scruffy for seventeen years. She'd promised herself she'd adopt a dog and maybe a cat or two as soon as the remodeling on the diner was complete.

They were checking in to see when she would be able to start serving as a foster parent. Typing a quick e-mail to Evelyn, the coordinator for the foster program, she replied that she thought that she would be able to serve in two or three weeks, depending upon how long some important matters took to be settled.

Continuing to research Nick, she opened a page from the *New York Times.* A photograph of a much younger Nick and a beautiful young woman wearing their finest. The article said the couple had announced their engagement. The wedding date was set for early June, just a couple of months after she'd had her spring fling with him. She read further. Apparently, she wasn't the first woman Nick had been engaged to. A New York gossip columnist had questioned the seriousness of his current engagement since he'd recently broken off with Cathryn Carlyle, to whom he'd been engaged for four years.

Lin clicked onto yet another page, one featuring an article about Pemberton Transport's humanitarian acts. That page showed a much older version of Nick and his wife, Chelsea. *What a prissy name,* she thought. He deserved to be married to someone named Chelsea. Lin smiled at her own wickedness. They were being honored for donating five million dollars to an upscale children's home.

Stunned, Lin read the entire article. Then read it a second time to make sure she hadn't misread anything. Fuming, Lin clicked the PRINT button again. Sally had to see this to believe it. Five million dollars. Just like that. According to the article, Pemberton Transport gave large sums of money to the orphanage every year. Nick was quoted in the article as saying, "It makes me feel good to give to kids in need. All children need to feel safe and secure."

What a crock! Maybe that was Nick's way of assuaging his guilt. But then Lin remembered that, as far as Nick was concerned, he had nothing to feel guilty about. He didn't know he had a son. Maybe he didn't even remember their weeklong fling. *No matter,* she thought. Nicholas Pemberton's world was about to be turned topsy-turvy in the worst possible way.

CHAPTER 5

"Nurse," Chelsea shouted into the hand-held intercom beside Nick's bed, "see to it that these sheets are changed immediately. And he will not wear that horrid hospital gown." She tossed the portable intercom aside, managing to tangle it with the tubes and wires connected to her husband. "I'm sorry you have to stay here. This is terrible. Why can't they treat you at home? I think you should tell that . . . doctor that you want to leave. Are you sure he even has a medical degree? Besides, I can't stay here all day. I have a dozen things going right now. I just don't believe what they're saying. You don't look sick at all. Just tired. You spend too much time working."

"And if I didn't, I suppose you'd get off your ass and find a job. Damn, I forgot. You're not qualified to do anything except *spend* my money," Nick said hatefully.

"Why do you always have to remind me

of my lack of education? You didn't seem to mind when we first met. I should divorce you. Wouldn't that give the business world a wonderful opportunity? Pemberton Transport up for grabs. Your poor father, God rest his soul. He didn't care if I drew another breath while he was alive, but in dying, the dear old buzzard saw to it that I'd be taken care of for the rest of my life. I think I'll call the florist and take flowers to the cemetery. I'm going to order the most expensive arrangement money can buy. Your father would want that, Nick. After all, it's his money. Don't forget."

"Get out, Chelsea. Go the fuck home before I have security toss you out on your ass. You're no more concerned about my health than Rosa is. Actually, I believe she *was* concerned when I called her earlier. I'm going to give her a big raise. Hell, I think I'll send her and her family to Hawaii for Christmas this year. Since it's the old man's money, he'd want me to do that. Makes a good impression, don't you think?" Nick raked his gaze over his wife. Black Chanel skirt and jacket that had cost him thousands. Blond hair bleached to look as though she had been born with it. He could only imagine what the upkeep was on that. Didn't she tell him once her hairdresser did

111

Oprah's hair? Only the best for his wife. She'd had her eyes done, a neck lift, a mini face-lift. Her lips were so thick from collagen injections that sometimes her words came out garbled when she spoke. To think she was only forty-one years old. Diamonds glistened from her ears and fingers. Her high-maintenance lifestyle was about to stop. As soon as he was up and about, he would cut off her lines of credit at all those designer shops she was so fond of and her credit cards as well.

"Why are you staring at me like that?" Chelsea quickly removed a solid gold compact from her Chanel bag. She looked at herself and apparently liked what she saw, because she snapped the compact shut, returning it to the designer bag.

"I want you out of here now. As a matter of fact, I don't want you coming back. I'll call Rosa if I need anything. Now leave," Nick snarled.

"You make me sick, you know that? Of course you do." She smirked. "But not enough to divorce me. I hope you die, Nick. I truly do. As a matter of fact, as soon as I leave the flowers on your father's grave, I'm going to Mass. I'm going to light as many of those tacky candles as possible and pray that you leave this hospital in a body bag."

Nick flung the sheets aside and started to leap off the bed, until he remembered the tubes in his body. "Get out!" he screamed loudly and with such force that the nurse came running into the room.

"What's going on? Mr. Pemberton, you can't sit up so quickly. You need to lie still until the anesthetic wears off." The nurse pushed him back on the bed. "Ma'am, is there something you wanted? I was the nurse who took your call. I had a minor emergency with another patient." She smoothed over the sheets and untangled the mess Nick and Chelsea had made of the tubes and wires.

Chelsea looked at her as though she were nothing more than dirt beneath her fingernails. "I thought my husband might like softer sheets and his own pajamas, but he's just convinced me that he doesn't need me for anything."

"Good night, Chelsea," Nick said between clenched teeth.

"*Good-bye,* Nicholas." She swaggered out of the room as though she were royalty.

Nick really hated her at times. All she did was spend his money. There had to be a way around his father's will. The son of a bitch had controlled him his entire life. If only he'd had a son or a daughter, he could have divorced her, as he had intended to do until his father told him about the contents of the will. Just the thought made him smile. While he was thinking about it, he removed the cell phone he'd hidden beneath his pillow and dialed Rosa's private number. Madison Avenue and Fifth Avenue were about to lose one of their best clients. No more Chanel, Gucci, or Christian Dior for Chelsea. She'd be lucky if he allowed her to shop at Wal-Mart.

"Pemberton Transport," Rosa said loud and clear.

"Rosa, I need a favor."

"Of course, Mr. Pemberton. What can I do?"

"I want you to close all of Mrs. Pemberton's lines of credit and credit-card accounts today."

"Yes, sir. Will there be anything else?" she asked.

Yes, but the rest he'd have to do himself as soon as he was out of the hospital. "No, that will be all. If Mrs. Pemberton comes to the office, whatever you do, do not allow her to enter my private office. Is that understood, Rosa?"

"Absolutely, sir," she replied.

"All right then. Good-bye." He punched the END button with a smirk on his face.

He wished he could see the look on Chelsea's face when she realized her accounts were no longer active. Her embarrassment alone would be priceless.

Dr. Reeves entered the room, forcing him to put all thoughts of Chelsea aside.

The doctor spoke in a somber voice. "I've just gotten the results of your test."

"They aren't good, are they?" Nick asked.

"No, Mr. Pemberton, they are not good. It's what I expected. Remember, I see this day in and day out," Dr. Reeves explained.

"Give it to me straight so I can work this into my schedule," Nick said, as though he were working around an unplanned vacation.

"Let me explain a few things about the disease. That will help you understand what you're going through."

"All right," Nick said.

"Leukemia is cancer of blood-forming tissue, like bone marrow. Types of leukemia are grouped by the type of cell affected and by the rate of cell growth. Leukemia is either acute or chronic."

"And which kind do I have?" Nick asked.

"Chronic lymphocytic leukemia. It's most common in adults between the ages of forty and seventy. Reading your test results, I determined that you have a very fast-moving form of the disease. We'll start with chemo-therapy, maybe even some radiation. You can do this on an outpatient basis after your initial treatment. Then we'll have you come in every few days for a treatment and to check your progress."

"What happens if that doesn't work?"

"Then you may have to consider a bone-marrow transplant. Of course, that depends on finding a suitable match. Your children or siblings should provide a match, so that shouldn't be a problem."

Nick's blood pressure soared. "I don't have any children or siblings!"

Dr. Reeves took a deep breath. "First, we don't know that we'll even need to go that far, and secondly, we have other tests we can do that will determine how far your leukemia will progress. Special tests are done on the blood and bone-marrow cells to look at characteristics of the leukemic cells. The tests used include something called a FISH test. This is used to determine the presence of chromosomal abnormalities. There is an immunoglobulin gene mutation status, known as IgVH. It can help us predict a more aggressive course of treatment if not mutated and also a more favorable course if mutated.

"I know this is a lot to swallow right

now. My best advice, do what we suggest. There will be times when you won't feel ill and will want to overdo it. Then there'll be other times that you'll be so wiped out from the chemo, you won't have the strength to move. I guess what I'm trying to say is that you have to trust me and let me do my job."

As hard as it was to relinquish control, Nick knew that if he were to beat the leukemia, and he had all the confidence in the world that he would, he would have to do exactly as the doctor ordered. "I understand. So, when do we get started?"

"First thing tomorrow morning. We'll be doing more blood work throughout the day. It won't be fun, but we've got a great staff. They'll get you anything you need."

Nick nodded and wondered if the staff would be willing to donate material for a bone-marrow transplant if it came down to that. Somehow, he thought not.

Ten days after she had first come across the reference to JV Investigations, Lin heard the phone ringing after midnight and grabbed the cordless phone from the end table. "Hello." She'd fallen asleep on the love seat in her office.

"I told you I'd call. The restaurant was

swamped tonight. Sorry it's so late," Sally said.

"It's okay. I was just dozing on the sofa. I'm still in my office," Lin said, now wide awake. "You want to stop by or wait until tomorrow?"

"I'm too wired for bed. Put on a pot of coffee. I'll stop at Krispy Kreme for dough-nuts," Sally suggested.

"Deal."

Twenty minutes later both women were sitting in Lin's homey kitchen, munching on doughnuts and swigging coffee like they were doing shots.

"I still can't believe the bastard donated five million dollars to an orphanage. Can you imagine the kind of life you and Will would've had if he'd just done the right thing and helped you out?"

"If he'd been a part of it, I suspect we would've been nothing more than a piece of property to him. From the looks of what I've read, he's all about money and making big impressions."

"Phony as a three-dollar bill," Sally added.

Lin got up to make a second pot of cof-fee. "Yeah, but I almost feel sorry for his wife."

"I don't. I'm sure she knew what she was getting into when they married. Most likely she married him for his money."

"From all the articles I've read about her, she can't be all that bad. Says she's on the board of directors for several different charities."

"And you're too naive. Women like her want to be on those boards. It makes them look good."

"Maybe. I just hope there's a trace of decency in her."

Sally laughed loudly. "You're too damn nice, you know that?"

Lin raised her brow. "You think so? Wait and remind me when I'm knee deep in the dark stuff I'm about to shovel in Nick Pemberton's backyard. I'll need some encouragement then."

"I will. We need to plan. We've already talked this thing to death, Lin. Now we need something concrete, a starting point."

"After a lot of thinking, I agree with you about hiring a private detective." Lin had already told Sally earlier in the week about JV Investigations and the kind of corporate work they did. "I'm going to call them first thing in the morning. I may have to make another trip to the city, but I won't know until I speak with the head of the agency." Lin glanced at the clock. "It's three in the morning. Why don't you stay in the guest room tonight?"

"I think I will. There's nothing at the house that needs my immediate attention. I'm sure Clovis is out prowling and whoring around tonight." Clovis was a male cat Sally had adopted when Lizzie went away to college. Since day one she'd never been able to keep him inside at night.

"At least we know someone who's getting laid," Lin teased.

"Get your mind out of the gutter, Lin. Clovis has been fixed — he just likes to scope out his options."

"You're the one who said he was whoring. There's a nightshirt in the bottom drawer, the one with Tinker Bell on it. Same one you wore last time. You know where everything is. We should've built our houses next door to each other, instead of down the street."

"We'd be at each other's houses all the time, then. I like living three blocks away from you," Sally said with a huge grin.

"It does work, doesn't it?" Lin added. "I'm gonna call it a night. I'll see you in the morning." Lin rinsed their mugs and turned off the coffeemaker before heading down the hall to her bedroom. She heard Sally's "night night" and smiled. She couldn't have picked a more compatible friend if she'd

120

tried. They were as close as two women could be. Sisters most of the time, and occasionally they mothered one another when the situation called for it.

In her bedroom Lin removed her jeans and blouse, slipped into a silky red sleep shirt, and crawled beneath the covers, suddenly glad she'd splurged on the thousand-count Egyptian linens. Within minutes she drifted off to sleep.

Sun trickled in through the slats as dust motes flitted through the air like tiny stars dancing in space. Lin cracked one eye open and looked at the clock. Ten o'clock. Damn! She never slept this late. Jumping out of the bed, she raced down the hall to the guest room, where Sally was curled up in a ball in the center of the bed.

"Get up!" Lin called as she yanked the covers off her friend.

"What the heck!" Sally muttered as she inched up against the headboard. "Are you nuts?"

"Yes. I mean no. It's ten in the morning. Someone needs to open the diner."

"Haven't you learned by now that I cover our asses when needed?" Sally asked.

"Yes, I have. You didn't mention anything last night."

"Kelly Ann promised to open since I covered for her last night. There's a full crew until this evening. Since you woke me up, you're going to have to make a pot of coffee before I go home."

"Not a problem, but first I'm going to call JV Investigations." Lin swirled out of the bedroom to her office. She found the paper with the number on it and, before she could change her mind or think of an excuse not to do what she was about to do, dialed the number.

"JV Investigations," a deep male voice boomed over the wire.

Lin's throat closed up. She swallowed before she could utter a single word. This wasn't as easy as she'd thought. "I . . . I would like to hire an investigator." There. She'd said it.

"For what?" the deep male voice demanded.

"What do you mean, for what? I want to . . . I need to get some dirt . . . some information on someone," Lin said.

"We dig dirt. Pardon the pun," the deep voice replied.

Lin smiled. A sense of humor was good. "I've never done this before. I'm not sure of the proper protocol."

"I can tell."

"Really?" Lin asked.

"Sure. After all, I am an investigator."

"Of course. Do you ask the questions, or do I just . . . I don't know. . . ." Lin hesitated. "Do I tell you what I want you to do?"

"That's usually the way it works. But if it'll make it easier, I can ask a few questions."

"Yes. I think that would work. Go for it." Lin took the cordless phone into the kitchen, where she put on a pot of coffee. This could take a while.

"Are you in New York State?" the deep voice questioned.

"Do I need to be?"

"Look, lady, if you keep answering my questions with a question, we'll be here all day, and frankly, I don't have all day. If Mabel Dee hadn't called in sick, you wouldn't be speaking to me now. By the way, I'm Jason Vinery."

"Then you're the one I need to talk to. You see, I am looking to . . . investigate a businessman located in your building. And I live in Georgia."

"I thought I detected a Georgia twang. So who's the unlucky bastard?"

"Nicholas Pemberton." There, she'd said it.

A cackle of laughter came from Jason Vinery. "Are you serious?"

"Yes, of course I am, unless there's a conflict of interest. On your Web site I saw the kind of work you do, and it occurred to me that maybe you had done work for Pemberton Transport. Is that going to be a problem? Should I go somewhere else?"

"Look, if I didn't need the money, this'd be pro bono. The spying business slows down when the economy is bad."

"Does that mean you'll take the job?" Lin asked.

"Absolutely."

She let out a breath she hadn't been aware of holding. "Thank you."

"So, Georgia lady, what do you want to know?"

Lin wondered for a moment if she should give him a phony name, but then realized if he was half as good an investigator as it said on his Web site, he'd find her out in a heartbeat. "I'm Lin Townsend."

"Okay, Lin Townsend, now that we've got that critical information out of the way, what would you like in the way of *dirt?*"

Lin took a deep breath. Something told her she could tell this man exactly what she wanted, and he'd comply. From what he had said, it sounded like he was not at all fond of Nicholas. She wondered what that was all about. "Before I tell you, is there some kind of confidentiality agreement you have? Something to assure me that you won't go running to the cops when I tell you what kind of 'dirt' I'm after?"

"You'll have to trust me, Lin. I don't know you. You don't know me. In this business, that's not always a bad thing. To answer your question, you have my word that our conversation stays between the two of us. Now, if my lines are bugged, which I doubt because Mabel Dee does a sweep daily, or if you're recording this, then I can't guarantee squat."

"I'm not recording anything, nor is my phone bugged, at least not as far as I know," Lin said.

"Then you trust me?" Jason queried.

Lin didn't have a choice. Besides, she'd felt that kick in her gut that she swore by. It had gotten her through some major decisions in her life. There was no reason to stop relying on it. "Yes, I believe I do."

"Then let's hear it."

Okay, here goes. "I want to tie up his . . . credit, his bank accounts, his stock accounts . . . make it impossible for him to access his money. Make him sweat. I want to make him squirm. Be clear about this. I do not — repeat, *do not* — want to steal any of it. Just tie his hands so he can't get to any of it. I want the bastard to pay for his s—" She'd almost made a fatal mistake. Whatever she told Jason, she could not reveal that she had a son by Nick. That could ruin everything.

"So you want me to steal his identity? You do realize that he's a very prominent businessman? Not just in Manhattan, but around the world."

"I don't want his identity. I just want him to suffer. Wonder where his next meal is coming from. I want him to know what it's like to have to put cardboard in his shoes to keep his feet warm, those kinds of things."

"Hmm. This is serious stuff you're talking about."

"If you don't want to take the job, I understand," Lin said, even though she didn't.

"Slow down. I didn't say I didn't want the job. I just want you to know if we're caught, we'll both be in a heap of trouble. Stealing one's identity is too easy to trace. If I were looking to ruin a man of Nicholas Pemberton's stature, I'd go for something else besides his pockets or the state of his shoes. I would suggest this. . . ."

For the next thirty minutes, Jason Vinery

mapped out his plan for Nick's fall from grace. Lin loved the detective's plan and couldn't wait to get started, but it was going to take some maneuvering on her part. She prayed she'd be able to convince Sally to take part in what was to come.

She'd start immediately. Hurrying before Sally could question her, she whipped up a batter for the blueberry pancakes Sally loved. Thank goodness she had all the ingredients. She found a pound of bacon in the freezer. She pried the slices apart with a fork and tossed them into her favorite iron skillet. She made a fresh pot of coffee since she'd drained the last one while she was on the phone with Jason.

Sally still wore her Tinker Bell nightshirt when she meandered into the kitchen. The look on her face almost made Lin burst out laughing.

Lin turned around to the stove so she could flip the bacon. "Why don't you go take a hot shower? By the time you're finished, breakfast will be ready. I'm making your favorite blueberry pancakes." Lin stalled by stirring the batter. When Sally didn't say anything, she turned around. "What?" Lin asked in an innocent voice.

"You *never* make breakfast, Lin. What gives?"

"Can't a girl do something nice for her best friend?" Lin stated. "Go on, get in the shower."

Sally eyed her suspiciously but did as she was told. Ten minutes later she was back in the kitchen in the same nightshirt, but her hair was dripping wet.

"You can use my hair dryer," said Lin.

"I don't want to dry my hair. I want coffee. And those pancakes." Sally sat down on one of the oak bar stools placed around the island in the center of the kitchen.

"Coming right up." Lin placed a bright red mug filled with steaming coffee in front of Sally and a plate piled high with pancakes. The microwave beeped. "I heated the syrup, too. That Vermont stuff you like so much." She took the mini-pitcher of syrup from the microwave and poured it over Sally's pancakes.

"I'm going to drink this coffee, eat these pancakes. Then I am going to get up, go to my car, where I will proceed to drive the three blocks to my house." Sally took a bite of her pancakes. A sip of coffee.

"What are you trying to say? You don't like my gesture of friendship?" It was all Lin could do to keep a straight face.

"I've known you too long. I know when you've got something up your sleeve." Sally forked another bite of her pancakes.

Taking a deep breath, Lin burst out laughing as she held her hands up in defeat. "You're right. You know me too well. Actually, I've come up with a plan. Well, I didn't personally come up with the plan. It was Jason Vinery's idea. He's the JV of JV Investigations. I spoke to him while you were sleeping."

With a slight smile on her face, Sally asked, "So what is this big plan that has you hopping around the kitchen like Martha Stewart on crack?"

"Promise to hear me out rather than rushing to judgment?" Lin requested.

"Just spit it out. You know I don't make rash decisions."

While Sally took the last bite of her pancakes, Lin retrieved the coffeepot from its burner and refilled their cups. Lin explained Vinery's plan and what would be required of her. She described Sally's role and waited for her to respond.

Amazed, Sally asked, "You're serious about this, aren't you?"

"Very," Lin said flatly.

"*If,* and it's a big *if,* I decide to take part in this insane idea, what about the diner? Someone has to be here to run the place."

"Actually, I've already thought that out.

You know how Irma says Jack's being underfoot all the time is driving her to drink? I thought it would be perfect if we asked him to act as temporary manager for a few weeks. The remodeling is basically finished. All the dishes and flatware are in the stockroom. Everything that I've ordered has been delivered on time. That shocked the crap out of me, too. I know there are some cracks here and there, but we can fill them in as we go. So, am I crazy or what?"

"One hundred percent certifiable." Sally closed her eyes for a minute, then opened them, looking Lin squarely in the face. "If we screw this up, we're all going to be in a very large heap of . . . of you know what. Maybe even jail," she said ominously.

"Yes, those were Jason's exact words. That's why I want to make sure you're up for the challenge."

"There is Lizzie to think of. But then again, she's an adult. If I went to prison for a year or two, she'd be okay. I'm sure she'd never speak to me again, but I've said that so many times, I've lost count. So, I guess you can count me in. You'll have to make arrangements for Clovis," she added with a smile.

"Done. Irma loves cats. She'll take good care of him."

"You're sure? Of everything?" Sally inquired.

"As sure as the sun will rise tomorrow."

"Then what are we waiting for? Let's get this show on the road, Lin."

CHAPTER 6

Monday, October 1, 2007
New York City

It was Nick's first day back at the office since he'd been diagnosed with leukemia. He'd lost fifteen pounds since beginning the treatment. His hair was thinning by the minute. For the moment, his energy level had rebounded some, and before he had to undergo another round of treatments, he had Herbert drive him to the office, explaining that he had to check on the staff. Not that he owed Herbert any explanation. He never gave explanations. Another one of his new quirks. He wasn't sure if he liked the change or not.

Herbert must have alerted Rosa that he was coming, because as usual she had several newspapers spread out on the large coffee table and a pot of coffee waiting. The thought of drinking coffee made Nick gag. Even his taste buds were rebelling.

132

"Good morning, sir," Rosa called from outside his office door. "Is there anything else I can get you?"

Nick thought she sounded like one of the phony nurses at the hospital. "Yes. I'd like a pot of chamomile tea with honey and lemon. This coffee is disgusting."

"But, sir, you always drink cof—"

"I don't drink coffee anymore. Now get the goddamned tea, like I asked." Jesus Christ, what was wrong with him? One minute he was being considerate of old Herbert, and the next minute he was chewing out Rosa. He winced as he realized he was starting to sound more and more like his father every day. The bastard.

"Yes, sir. Right away, sir." Rosa bolted out of the doorway as though she'd seen a ghost. The way her boss looked just then, maybe she had. None of the staff had been told the nature of his illness, only that he was sick and was expected to make a full recovery.

Nick bit down on his lower lip as he tried not to think about the looks on the faces of his staff as he walked down the long hall to his office. They'd been shocked to see him. That was a given. More than likely they were shocked at how terrible he looked. As one, they'd looked away or just given him an airy wave. What was that old saying? If you don't acknowledge something, you can pretend you didn't see or hear it.

Not bothering with the newspapers laid out on the table, Nick immediately went to his desk, where he booted up his laptop. Ever since he'd cut off Chelsea's lines of credit, he'd received several notices from his bank, a bank he'd borrowed millions from in the past — a bank that was now putting a temporary freeze on his line of credit and his personal accounts. What was up with that? *When the cat's away, the mouse will play, or something like that.* Where the hell did that thought come from? Surely his wife wasn't smart enough to . . . What? He had to admit, he didn't know.

Not wanting to alert Chelsea that he knew what she was up to, he'd been acting as though nothing were awry. He didn't want to call the bank from home or send them an e-mail, fearing she would find out he was onto her. No, he was going to play it nice and slow. Too bad he had the damn treatments to contend with. He was the first to admit he wasn't firing on all cylinders.

He pulled up his accounts from the Bank of Manhattan, punching in a series of security codes. Nothing came up. He tried a second time. Still nothing.

"Rosa!" he screamed at the top of his lungs. "Get in here right *now!*"

The dumpy little woman came flying around the corner with a tray in her hands. "Sir, I'm working as fast as I can. Here is your tea. We didn't have any lemon, and I had to send out for some."

"Has Chelsea been in my office? I swear, if you lie to me, I'll fire you on the spot." Nick stood up, even though he felt wobbly and unsteady. He wasn't about to allow his authority to be undermined by a damned illness. No way.

"Sir, you told me she wasn't allowed in your office. I have respected that order. Mrs. Pemberton was here, but I followed your orders. In fact, sir, I kept the key to your office in my purse. She did *not* enter your office. Sir."

Nicholas looked into the frightened woman's eyes and decided she was telling the truth. Rosa was almost a saint, but he knew how persuasive Chelsea could be when money was at stake. "You're positive?"

"Absolutely, sir," she said. Hesitantly, she placed the pot of tea on the coffee table, where the newspapers were scattered about.

"Has anyone else been inside my office?" Nick demanded. "Anyone at all?"

"Again, sir, I did just as you instructed. I

didn't even let the cleaning crew in to clean. I'm sorry about the dust."

Nick nodded. "It's all right, Rosa. I'm sorry I snapped at you."

"Yes, sir."

Nick closed his eyes. He needed to get a grip on things. He'd just made his secretary cry and practically accused her of conspiring with his wife to do him in. Yes, sir, he was definitely in line for the Boss of the Year Award.

Suddenly weak, he sat down. He'd done just what Dr. Reeves had told him not to do. He'd felt fine that morning, but at the moment he wasn't even sure if he had the energy to summon Herbert. Nick allowed himself a moment to relax. Taking a deep breath to calm himself, he carefully typed his pass codes into the computer. Again, he was denied access to his accounts. He chewed on his lower lip as he contemplated his next move. He gave his head a slight shake and dialed the number of Andrew Miller, his personal investment banker and the chief financial adviser for Pemberton Transport.

The investment banker picked up on the first ring. "Miller," the voice said curtly.

"I'm being denied access to my personal accounts. What's going on, Andrew?"

"Nicholas! Good to hear from you. You must be feeling better. I heard you were a bit under the weather. Yes, I'm aware of the problem, and I sent you a couple of letters advising you of the fact. Possibly your mail piled up, or you just didn't get to it. It appears that someone other than you has managed to change your security codes. We put a freeze on all your accounts until our fraud team can trace that person to the originating source."

"How long is that going to take?" Nick asked in a shaky voice. God, even his voice sounded like the rest of him, broken down and brittle.

"I can't give you a specific answer. Sometimes it takes only a day. Other times it could take weeks, possibly as long as a month. It all depends on how smart the person changing the codes is."

"That's it? I can't get into my own accounts, and you can't even tell me how long it's going to take? No, no, I don't do business that way. Either find the culprit, or your ass is grass by the end of the day. I'll move every single account I have once I gain access. Are we clear on this, Andrew?"

"Nick, this isn't something I have a lot of control over. Do you need cash? I'd be happy to front you a few thousand,"

Andrew offered.

Nick clenched his teeth. Dr. Reeves's words rang in his ears. He tried to calm down. "I don't need cash, Miller. I want results. I'll call you first thing in the morning." His hand was shaking so badly, he had trouble fitting the phone back into its cradle.

Nick sank back into his leather chair. All of his earlier strength was gone. It had to be Chelsea. She'd thrown the hissy fit of a five-year-old when she found out her line of credit had been cut off. It had given him great pleasure watching her as she'd literally flung herself on the floor, then crawled to him as though he were a king. She'd begged and pleaded, but he hadn't relented. She'd hardly spoken a word to him since.

Nick didn't think Chelsea was smart enough to go after him financially, but apparently he'd underestimated her. Yes, she was cunning, sneaky, and manipulative, but when it came to anything remotely technical, the woman was dumber than a doornail. Or pretended to be. Maybe she knew some hackers who had been only too glad to offer up their services for . . . whatever Chelsea was prepared to pay.

She'd screwed with the wrong person. Or she was screwing the person who was screwing him. Now *that* made sense. Chelsea was a very attractive woman, he'd give her that. It was one of the reasons he'd been conned into thinking that he slept with her in the first place. It was also the biggest regret of his life. His engagement to Cathryn had been severed immediately because of that little indiscretion. Of course, Chelsea had told his father she was expecting Nick's child. Controlling as ever, his father hadn't wasted a second when it came time to plan their wedding.

They'd had their photographs taken, their engagement announced in the *New York Times.* Somehow his father had managed to get them in *Town & Country* just two weeks before the June issue hit the stands. He recalled his wedding day in vivid detail. He remembered throwing up before heading to St. Patrick's Cathedral. That they'd actually married in a church had seemed a mockery to Nick at the time. How his father had managed to secure the famous cathedral in the city on such short notice, he hadn't a clue. Later he learned that Pemberton Transport had financed a major remodeling project for the church. Money talked then, and it had best speak up now, he thought as he tried to log on to his accounts once more before summoning Herbert to drive him home.

Access denied.

Chelsea would rue the day she messed with him. When he got through with her, she'd be lucky to be alive.

On the first Wednesday in October, Lin and Sally were discussing the apartment in SoHo that Jason Vinery had found for them.

"I can't believe I'm paying five thousand dollars a month for this dump. It hardly seems worth it," said Lin. The small apartment was about the size of Lin's living room back in Dalton.

"Jason was lucky to find this, remember?"

"So he says. It just seems so . . . wasteful spending that amount of money for such a hole-in-the-wall. Think of what I could do with all that money. I could have all the chairs in the diner reupholstered in leather. Rich, warm buttery leather."

"This was your idea, Lin. Live with it," Sally said.

"I'm sorry. When Jason said we'd need to rent an apartment for a couple of months, I certainly envisioned something larger. At least two bedrooms."

"Stop whining. At least he found us a set of single beds. I haven't slept in a single bed since I was a kid. It'll be fun. It won't be forever, Lin. You've got to stay focused. This is one of the sacrifices we agreed to."

Lin wandered around the three small rooms. A living room the size of her walk-in closet, a bathroom with a tub half the size of hers at home, and a bedroom barely able to hold the two beds. It was a joke. They couldn't walk in the bedroom at the same time without bumping into one another. The kitchen was nothing more than a sink with a minifridge. There was no stove — only a microwave, which sat on a counter not more than three feet long.

"I'm glad we aren't planning on cooking," Lin remarked as she wandered across the room to the kitchen. "Much," she added with a trace of her old humor.

Part one of their plan was already in motion. Jason's "source" had said Nicholas was furious when he learned he couldn't access his personal bank accounts. Even though she knew it was only temporary, it brought a smile to Lin's face.

Let the games begin.

They'd been in New York for two days when Jason told them it was time for a little bit of fun, and he could use their help. It was risky, but when he explained his idea to them, both Lin and Sally were excited.

"Do you think this will backfire?" Lin asked Sally, as they both plopped down on the cream-colored sofa, the only decent piece of furniture in the apartment. They'd just finished unpacking, if you could even call it unpacking. They'd left their luggage open on top of the beds. At night they would simply slide it beneath their beds. Their toothbrushes and toiletries were stacked precariously on top of the toilet tank.

"Not if we're careful and do exactly as Jason says. He said the first thing we have to do is get the clothes. He said there's a thrift shop on Mulberry Street. You want to walk or hail a cab?" Sally asked.

"Let's walk. I need the fresh air after being cooped up like a chicken."

Sally stood up and stretched. "Then let's go. We don't have that much time. Remember, it gets dark here early. We'll have to rush to get back to the apartment for our makeovers."

"I can hardly wait," Lin agreed.

Together they walked down the streets of SoHo, marveling at all the shops, the restaurants, and the variety of people. It was like a kaleidoscope of life. Both women tried their best not to look like tourists. It was all about blending in, according to Vinery.

"I'm so glad we're here together. Too bad we can't call Will and have him meet us for dinner while we're here," Sally said.

"Jason doesn't know I have a son, and I want to keep it that way. At least for now. I don't want to give him any reason to investigate me personally, but I'm thinking the guy is going to do it, anyway. If I was him, that would be the first thing I'd do. As far as Will knows, we're both in Dalton, busting our buns, getting ready for the holiday parties. I just wish I didn't feel so guilty about lying to my own son."

Sally reached for Lin's hand. "It's for Will that you're doing this, and don't you forget it even for one minute."

"No, not really, Sally. If I'm honest with myself, it's for me. I want to see that bastard suffer the way Will and I had to suffer. His son ate macaroni and cheese for weeks at a time when he was younger. I didn't even have enough money to feed him properly. He was three before he knew what a damned ear of fresh corn was. It's a miracle he didn't have rickets or some such disease from a vitamin deficiency. I want Nicholas to live in fear, like I had to those first few years. Fear of anything, whether it be his last meal, or fear that he'll lose his last dollar."

I remember when Will was around four years old. I took him to McDonald's for breakfast. It was his first time there. Can you believe that? I remember feeling as though something was missing. I felt out of sorts. At first I thought it was because we were actually going to a restaurant for a meal. I remembered thinking that I'd always felt fear as a child, but then when I saw how tough it was to raise a child alone, the fear I'd felt as a kid almost seemed like a joke compared to what I felt each time I walked into Winn-Dixie or Kroger. I feared I wouldn't be able to provide enough. It was always there, nagging like a damned toothache. Never enough. Never enough. Then it hit me that morning at McDonald's. I realized the daily fear was gone. I actually felt normal for the first time in my life. In a McDonald's. Can you believe that?" Lin shook her head in wonderment.

Sally knuckled the tears in her eyes. "Look how far you've come, Lin. Your hard times are nothing more than a distant memory. You should be proud of all you've accomplished."

"I suppose. I just did what anyone else would've done had they been in my shoes. Nothing spectacular."

"You're a survivor, Lin. Will is lucky to have you for a mother."

Lin grinned. "He is, isn't he?"

Sally gave her a gentle shove. "You witch!"

They both laughed until their sides ached.

Lin's mascara ran down her face, but she didn't care. She was on a mission to right a terrible wrong. "Look at that." She pointed to a street sign. "We're on Bleecker Street. Let's go to that bakery, the one from *Sex and the City.* The Magnolia Bakery. Their cupcakes are supposed to be some of the best in the city."

"That's the smartest thing you've said all day. Let's run," Sally suggested.

Together they ran down the street to the famed bakery. Once inside, there were so many cupcakes to choose from, they ordered one of each.

"I bet you've gained back all that weight you lost," Sally said after they'd eaten six cupcakes apiece.

"And then some. I know when I go home, I'm going to dream about those cupcakes. They're to die for!" Lin exclaimed.

They walked another block before spying the thrift shop tucked in an alleyway.

"Just where Jason said it would be," Lin commented.

The place was called Frugality. Lin guessed this was supposed to be a hip name for what she thought of as a used-clothing store, something she thought she'd never have to visit again, but desperate times called for desperate measures. Not that she couldn't afford to shop on Madison Avenue. She could. It was simply a matter of common sense.

They entered the store. Lin was surprised to find it so organized and neat. A young girl with coal black hair, and so many piercings she reminded Lin of a pincushion, greeted them.

"Can I help you find anything?" she asked.

They told her what they were searching for, and she directed them to a half-price table at the back of the store.

"Look at these," Sally called as she held up a pair of black slacks.

Lin walked to the back of the store.

"Oh my gosh," Sally whispered. "They're Chanel. Size six. Five bucks. I'll take it."

"You go, girl," Lin said. "Let me see what else we can find."

The two of them rummaged through the piles of clothing, finding everything they needed for tonight's adventure. Now all they had to do was wait for Jason's call.

Chelsea Pemberton had never been more mortified in her life. The minute she'd found out her husband had canceled her lines of credit and credit cards, she'd sneaked his American Express from his wallet while he showered. The way he looked told her he wasn't long for this world. He couldn't die soon enough as far as she was concerned.

Reluctantly, she'd had to share Herbert today since Nick was due for his Wednesday chemotherapy treatment midmorning. She'd told him she was having lunch in the Village with friends. What did he know? She could've told him she was dining with the Pope in Peru, and he wouldn't have acknowledged her. She prayed for his sudden death. Maybe an air bubble would form in his IV line. She'd heard that was deadly. Whatever the means, she wanted the son of a bitch dead. With him out of the picture, she'd have complete control of his fortune. Pemberton Transport would be up for grabs. At the right price, of course. She smiled. Nick would kill her if he knew what she was thinking, and if he didn't, her dead father-in-law would reach up from beyond the grave and try to pull her right down into the depths of hell with him. She smiled at the thought.

"Herbert, I need to make a stop at Van Cleef & Arpels."

She knew he'd tell Nicholas if asked. The old sod was loyal to the Pembertons. Chelsea couldn't understand why, since they treated most of the hired help like eighteenth-century slaves, though she had to admit, she enjoyed abusing their services as much as Nick did.

"I'll need you to wait."

"Of course you do," Herbert replied in what Chelsea felt was a condescending tone. She'd make sure to mention this to Nick, for whatever it was worth.

Herbert expertly maneuvered the Lincoln Town Car through the midtown traffic. Lin looked at her Tiffany watch, a gift from Nick when he'd been trying to impress Joel Stein, an investment banker he'd taken to dinner when he'd been trying to lure him away from J.P. Morgan. It hadn't worked. Apparently good old sharp-as-a-tack Joel had seen right through his phony malarkey. Though Chelsea had to admit, she'd been pleasantly surprised when Nick whipped out the famous blue box while at dinner.

Unbeknownst to her husband, she was about to purchase an exquisite Caresse d'Eole ring she'd seen in Van Cleef & Arpels. His American Express bill would be a tad on the high side by the end of the month.

"Ma'am," Herbert said as he pulled in front of the famous jewelers.

Chelsea hurried into the shop. Herbert had been instructed to return to the hospital in three hours. She didn't have time to browse.

A small man wearing a custom-tailored suit greeted her at the door. "Mrs. Pemberton, how wonderful to see you."

Chelsea loved the recognition. "Yes, I must have the Caresse d'Eole ring I saw last month."

The man smiled at her. "Of course, madam. Follow me."

She followed the man to the back of the store, where he removed the ring from its case. "This is one of our most beautiful pieces. Here." He reached for her hand. "Allow me."

Chelsea gazed at the ring of white gold and diamonds. She deserved this. "I'll take it."

"Are you sure of the sizing?"

"It's perfect, almost as though it were made for me. Now, if you'll hurry along. My driver is waiting." She thrived on ordering around what she thought of as the "little people." She smiled. In this instance the phrase "little people" was quite literal. How pleased she was!

The man made fast work of wrapping the ring in beautiful cream-colored wrapping paper. "Would madam care to charge this to her Van Cleef & Arpels account?"

Madam would *love* to, she thought. However, Mr. Pemberton, the bastard who'd closed her account, had decided otherwise. "I'll be using American Express." She removed the card from her bag and gave it to the clerk. She tucked the bag under her arm. She couldn't wait to wear the ring in front of Nick. She'd show him it wasn't so easy to prevent her from getting what she wanted.

When the clerk returned to the front of the store, his face was red. When he spoke, it was in a hushed voice. "Madam, there seems to be a problem. Mr. Pemberton's card has been denied."

"What do you mean?" she shouted. "There must be some mistake. You've done something wrong. Try again." Chelsea felt the heat rise from the tips of her toes to the top of her head.

The clerk ran to the back of the store, only to return minutes later. "I am very sorry, madam. The card was denied. Perhaps Mr. Pemberton . . ." His words trailed off.

Chelsea knew what he wanted to say. *Perhaps Mr. Pemberton has canceled the account.* "Never mind. Give me back my card. I will *never* visit this store again!" She tossed the package on the counter and ran out the door, humiliated beyond belief.

Herbert was waiting. The moment he saw her, he got out of the car to open her door for her.

"Get out of my way!" she shouted. She could open the goddamned door herself. Did he think she was stupid? Of course she was stupid — she had been stupid for years. More times than she could remember, she'd stood rooted to the ground while she waited for the old man to extricate his arthritic body out of the car to come around and open the door for her when she could have so easily done it herself and spared Herbert his pain.

He complied.

In the backseat, Chelsea fumed. Nicholas had just humiliated her for the last time.

"Where would you like to go now, Mrs. Pemberton?" Herbert asked.

The lunch date had been nothing more than a lie, but she'd never admit it. "I'm too upset to go anywhere. You can take me back to the penthouse."

A spark of an idea started to form on the drive home. If it worked, Nicholas Pemberton was as good as dead.

Lin and Sally waited outside the SoHo

apartment for Jason Vinery. Each wore the secondhand black slacks and shirts they'd purchased at Frugality, and each wore gloves.

Jason said he would provide them with ski masks. They'd disguised themselves with hats and heavy make-up. They barely recognized each other.

"I can't believe we're doing this," Lin said as she scanned the street, looking for Jason's black Lincoln Navigator. "We look like a couple of Forty-second Street hookers."

Mimicking Zsa Zsa Gabor, Sally said, "I think we look divine, *dahhhling.* Especially these itch-from-hell gloves."

"If we get caught, you know we'll be sent away for a while," Lin stated matter-of-factly.

"What? Are you trying to back out?"

"No, I just want you to be sure you're in for the long haul. Jason says this will go off without a hitch. I trust him. He hates Nicholas Pemberton as much as I do. He's not putting his butt on the line just for us, you know?" Lin said.

"I know. I wonder why."

"I don't really care what his reason is for wanting to ruin Nick as long as he does what I'm paying him to do."

"Here he comes," Sally said. "I don't think

we'll have to worry about him not keeping his end of the bargain."

The shiny black SUV pulled up to the curb. Lin opened the passenger door to the back, where both women climbed aboard. Lin hated SUVs. She'd take her sporty red Porsche any day of the week.

Jason Vinery was the total opposite of what Lin expected when she first met him. On the phone he sounded sexy and self-assured. He *was* very self-assured, but the sexy part had just been her imagination. He stood barely five feet tall. He wore his long brown hair in a ponytail and had two gold hoops in his ears. Lin couldn't find a part of his exposed arms that weren't covered in tattoos. She and Sally had both wondered if the tattoos went below the belt. She smiled at the thought.

"Are you ladies ready to have some fun?" Jason inquired as they sped away from the curb.

"I'm not sure what we're about to do could be classified as fun," Sally observed.

"You'll have the time of your life. It's truly harmless. I promise. I've done this a time or two and never once has anyone complained or been hurt. I've never been caught, either, but you two already know that. Now, I want to go over our plans one more time."

Jason repeated his instructions, reminding them of their roles.

Entrance to the penthouse apartment located on Madison Avenue could be attained only by invitation. However, as one of the top PIs in the city, Jason knew that anything could be had for a price. When he consulted Lin, she had been shocked at the amount but had readily agreed to it.

Jason drove to the underground parking garage, where he spoke to the attendant, then left his keys. Once they were out of earshot, Lin spoke up.

"How do you know that attendant won't inform someone that an unauthorized vehicle is parking in Nick Pemberton's reserved spot?"

"The guy loves money, and he knows how to cover his ass. Trust me. This isn't the first time I've had to use his services. Don't worry. Let me do the hard part, and you two ladies simply do what we planned. You ready to rock and roll?" Jason asked.

The women looked at one another.

"I guess it's now or never," Lin said.

Sally nodded her agreement.

The trio entered a service elevator located at the back of the underground garage. "This is the elevator the delivery people use. It wouldn't look right if a pizza was delivered in the main lobby," Jason said, punching the button that would take them to the penthouse apartment. "Okay, girls, put your masks on. Once we step off the elevator, the security cameras scan the area every fifteen seconds. Remember, look down and walk fast, just the way we timed it. Are we ready?" Jason asked once more before the doors swished open. He wore a white chef's top, with his hair tucked beneath a white hat. If the situation hadn't been so serious, Lin would have burst out laughing.

Lin and Sally nodded solemnly.

Together, the trio walked quickly out of the line of the security cameras.

"You two stay behind me at all times," said Jason.

Both nodded their agreement a second time.

"We're ready," Lin whispered.

Jason stood as tall as possible, then rang the doorbell to the penthouse. He leaned against the door, hoping to hear footsteps. Nothing. He punched the bell a second time.

All three heard a loud unpleasant voice shouting as they leaned against the door. "Who is it? The doorman didn't send anyone up here."

Jason looked at the pair behind him. "It's

now or never."

Both women stepped back and to the side of Jason, per their instructions. Before anyone could utter a word, the heavy wooden door flew open.

A tall blond woman wearing a pink silk robe stared at Jason. "Who are you?"

"Mr. Pemberton asked me to . . ." Jason didn't have to finish the sentence, because he'd jabbed Chelsea in the neck with a hypodermic needle loaded with liquid Valium. In seconds she collapsed like a pile of bricks.

Lin grabbed Chelsea's arms, and Sally took hold of each leg. Jason ran ahead of them to open the elevator. The doors parted like the Red Sea.

Once inside the elevator, Lin let go of Nick's wife. She looked at Jason, her eyes round as dinner plates. "You think she's all right? Lord, I would hate to hurt her."

"Trust me, she'll be waking up soon enough. I bet you anything you'll wish she'd stayed out a little longer. Something tells me this is one feisty bitch," Jason replied.

Sally laughed. "I've got the duct tape and blindfold. I won't hesitate to use it either."

They stood stock-still as the elevator delivered them to the garage level.

"Girls, you wait here while I get the car.

When you see the lights flash on and off, grab her and run like you've never run before. We've got ten seconds. Ready?"

"Let's just get this over with," Lin whispered, still shocked at what they were doing.

Swiftly, the doors opened, Jason ran out, and then Sally hit the CLOSE button.

Together, Sally and Lin counted. "One, two, three . . . eight, nine, ten."

Sally hit the OPEN button, grabbed Chelsea's legs. Lin had both arms secured. With their prisoner swinging like a hammock between them, they ran as soon as they spied Jason's flashing headlights. His timing was impeccable.

They tossed Chelsea in the backseat, and both women climbed in after her.

Careening out of the parking lot, Jason almost hit a pedestrian. "Asshole," he shouted. "Damn New Yorkers never pay attention."

Lin looked at Sally and smiled. Sally was the first to speak. She whispered so both could hear her. "So you're not always the cool cucumber you claim to be."

"Hey, I didn't plan on running over someone," Vinery shot back.

"Sorry. I'm just trying to lighten things up," Sally said.

"They're lively enough. Thank you very much," Lin said in a low voice. "Think she can hear us?"

"No. Stop worrying. As soon as we dump her off, she'll probably wake up screaming. Let's prepare for the worst. I bet her mouth runs like a nasty case of the shits," said Jason.

"That's disgusting," Sally said with a smile.

"Yeah, it is," Lin added.

"Sorry, girls."

The rest of the short drive was silent, all three absorbed in their own thoughts. Each wondering if that night would be their last night of freedom.

CHAPTER 7

Nick heard Chelsea's loud shouting from the front of the penthouse but didn't bother trying to find out what her problem was. He was too sick to get out of bed. He'd vomited nonstop the entire afternoon. Only in the past hour had the waves of nausea subsided. Nick wasn't sure how much more of the chemotherapy treatments he could stand. Dr. Reeves had explained to him that his treatment would be very aggressive, almost deadly in its side effects.

He'd heard a few of the other patients complaining, saying that sometimes they'd prefer death to the horror of the treatments. At the time he'd laughed at them. At the moment, however, he agreed with them completely. He'd lost twelve more pounds according to the doctor. Nick couldn't remember the last meal he'd kept down; hell, he couldn't remember his last real meal. He'd been reduced to green and yellow Jell-O and weak chicken broth. He craved a shot of good whiskey, but alcohol wasn't allowed during the treatments.

In his weakened state, he felt like less of a man, and he hated the feeling. Depending on others to do the very basic tasks he'd never given much thought to was demeaning. A male nurse helped him shower. Helped him dress. Savile Row was no longer his mode of dress. Ralph Lauren pajamas and cotton socks comprised his daily wardrobe. Nick thought that he was experiencing what it must be like to get old. Though nothing about his body worked right, his mind was as clear and crisp as a waterfall. That was what had him so pissed.

Shiploads of merchandise waited for his decision — Gerald couldn't seem to do anything right. Nick planned to relieve him of his duties as soon as he returned to the office. Rosa called him daily with reports. Pemberton Transport was by no means in trouble, but a few more months of backlogged shipments, and it would show. Nick needed what little energy he had to fight this belittling disease.

His cell phone rang. Since it was in the bed next to him, he answered. "Hello."

"Is this Nicholas Pemberton?"

"Who wants to know?" he shot back. Nick

160

smiled, thinking he sounded more like himself than he had in days.

"It doesn't matter who wants to know. If you're as smart as you think you are, you'll listen, because I'm only going to say this once."

"Who is this?" Nick demanded.

"You're not very smart, are you?"

Nick took a deep breath. "What do you want?"

"Listen very carefully. I have your wife. She is alive and well. She'll be returned to you that way if you follow these instructions exactly."

Nick burst out laughing. "Is this some kind of a joke? Because if it's not, then keep the bitch. Do whatever you want with her." Nick punched the END button, grateful for the laugh.

The phone rang again. Nick answered.

"This isn't a joke. If you look around your penthouse, you'll find Mrs. Pemberton is nowhere to be found. She is wearing a beautiful pink silk gown."

"Hold on." Weak, Nick managed to hobble to the hallway. "Chelsea, where are you?" He waited for an answer. Nothing. He'd try another tactic, one sure to send her running to his room. "Chelsea dear, I promise to open all your charge accounts first thing in the morning." Still nothing. He spoke into the cell phone. "You're serious?"

"Yes. Now, I want you to listen and listen good. I've repeated myself one too many times already. This is what you have to do if you want to see your wife alive."

Nick listened to the ridiculous instructions. He was tempted to hang up but figured he needed Chelsea around just in case the nurse didn't show up. If not for that, he would have told the caller, who obviously thought he gave a hoot about his wife, to buzz off. Chuckling at the ridiculousness of it all, he congratulated himself on the performance he had put on over the years to give whoever this was the impression that he gave a damn about Chelsea rather than wishing with his entire being that she would just die. But since, for the moment, she was still useful to him, he took great care to remember all the details.

Lin pushed the beat-up wheelchair slowly, as though it took every ounce of energy she possessed. Lucky for them, Chelsea was still out cold. Just in case she started to rouse, Jason had given her a second shot, but with less Valium. It was in her pocket, in a ziplock bag. Sally walked alongside her down Madison Avenue. They both looked like homeless hookers. They were receiving stares from everyone, though none of the well-dressed New Yorkers would look her or Sally directly in the eye. Lin could have cared less. She was disguised with a hat and more piled-on make-up. She knew there was no chance of running into Will or Nick. They knew for a fact that Nick was home, safely tucked in bed.

Jason had carefully outlined their route. From Madison Avenue they would walk to Herald Square, where they would take either the N, Q, or R train to Times Square. From there they would catch the number 1 train straight to Harlem. Once there, they were to deliver Chelsea to the steps at the offices of former president Bill Clinton. Reporters from the *New York Post* and the *Times* would be waiting.

"What are you thinking?" Sally asked.

"You really want to know?"

"I asked you, so I guess I do," Sally insisted.

"I'm thinking it's not going to be so easy pushing her through the subway." Lin laughed. "Seriously, I'm nervous. If this works, I'm going to laugh my ass off. If it doesn't, I was thinking what I would say to Will to explain all . . . this."

"Stop worrying. We're not going to get

caught, and if Will does find out, you'll deal with it, just like you've dealt with problems in the past. Don't borrow trouble, Lin."

"I suppose you're right." Lin shoved the chair over a metal grate on the sidewalk, thankful Chelsea was thin.

People scattered around Herald Square like ants at a picnic. Lin and Sally maneuvered the wheelchair down the steep flight of steps leading underground to the N, Q, and R trains. Once on the platform, they waited along with dozens of others for their train. They barely had time to wheel Chelsea onto the train before the electronic doors closed. Ten minutes later they arrived at Times Square.

"Let's hurry. The number one train doesn't come as often as the others, according to Jason," said Lin as she pushed Chelsea, who, thank God, appeared to be ill and just sleeping.

Sally ran ahead to locate the track for the train to Harlem.

Through the throngs of people ahead of her, Lin caught a glimpse of Sally waving her hands in the air. She'd located the train. Lin elbowed and shoved her way through the passengers emerging from the incoming trains. She was out of breath when she caught up with Sally.

"This way," Sally shouted.

Lin pushed Chelsea onto the train, thankful they were on the last leg of the journey. When the doors finally closed, Lin, who was out of breath and sweating like a mule, spoke up. "I think we've both lost our minds."

"Just wait until tomorrow, when this hits the papers!"

"Yes, but we don't know if that'll happen. Jason didn't make any promises, only that he would 'leak' the story to those reporters. What they choose to do with the information is up to them and their respective newspapers." Lin wasn't sure if she wanted to see tonight's stunt plastered on the front page of a newspaper.

Mentally chastising herself, she knew she had to focus on the ultimate goal: ruin Nicholas Pemberton's reputation, no matter what it took. This stunt was only the beginning. Lin prayed for forgiveness. Daily. At the rate she was going, she'd soon be asking by the hour.

The subway cars traveled so fast that Lin had a death grip on one of the metal poles that paralleled the seats. With her other hand she clung to one handle of the wheelchair, while Sally gripped the other. It was all she could do to maintain her balance.

The train came to an abrupt stop, announcing their arrival in Harlem. Hustling Chelsea in the wheelchair was easier this time around. It was late, and there weren't that many people hanging around, waiting to travel to and from Harlem.

"Let's get a taxi. Jason said there would be several waiting."

True to his word, there was a line of taxis waiting as they emerged from the subway.

Sally found a van that was equipped to hold the wheelchair. Lin had worried about this, wondering how they were going to manage the chair and Chelsea. Things were running as smooth as silk.

"Where to, ladies?" the taxi driver inquired. "I ain't so sure yous should be out in this part of town at this time of night. While it ain't as bad as it used to be, it ain't too safe."

"We want to go to President Clinton's office," Lin said quickly.

The whites of the driver's eyes glowed like shiny pearls as he gazed at them through his rearview mirror. "You for real? I can tell ya this. It ain't open."

"We're meeting someone," Sally offered.

"Well, then let's not keep your folks waitin'." The driver shifted the van into drive and sped away from the curb as

166

though he were in a NASCAR race.

When they managed to get both the wheelchair and Chelsea out of the van, Sally paid the driver, giving him a hefty tip, with the promise of more to come if he would agree to wait for them three blocks from Clinton's office. The driver agreed. Crazy women, someone had to look out for them. And it was easy money. His wife was going to be so happy.

Winded as she pushed the wheelchair uphill, Lin stopped to catch her breath. "Five minutes, and that's it. I refuse to stay here any longer than that. Just so you know."

"What makes you think I want to hang around here any longer than we have to? Come on, let's get her to the steps like we promised. From there the reporters can take over," Sally said. "If they even show," she added.

Once they'd adjusted the locks on the wheelchair, they waited exactly five minutes. As soon as they saw two men with camera equipment walking toward them, they hurried down the steps and ran the three blocks to where the handicapped taxi waited. They jumped inside the van, telling the driver to take them back to Madison Avenue.

"You girls sure are a long way from home. I can tell by them accents. But don't worry.

I didn't see a thing that ya did. No, sirree, I did not see a thing."

Lin creased her brow. She whispered in Sally's ear, "Do you think he'll report what he saw?"

"I doubt it, but it doesn't matter. We're not going to look like we do now. Remember?"

"True."

For the next twenty minutes, both women were silent. When the van reached their destination, Sally crammed another wad of money in the man's hand before hurrying to catch up with Lin, who'd taken off the second they came to a stop.

"I can't wait to see how this turns out," Sally said as they walked down Madison Avenue, searching for a taxi. Neither was in a rush now that they were out of Harlem and away from Chelsea and the reporters.

"Me either. This is a true life-changing moment. I don't feel good about this, Sally. I feel soiled and dirty. It reminds me of when kids at school used to call me Miss Stinky Pants. I don't like it one bit."

"Hey, it's okay. Don't wimp out now. Remember those mac-and-cheese days. Remember Will."

"I know, but it's not poor Chelsea's fault."

"Forget 'poor Chelsea.' I doubt the

woman knows the word. Let's take the subway, see what kind of weirdos are riding it this late at night."

Lin rolled her eyes. "And you think we look normal?"

They eyed one another and burst into fits of laughter.

Nick threw a jacket over his pajama top and slipped a pair of khaki slacks over the pj bottoms. By the time he located a comfortable pair of shoes, he was exhausted. He crept to the kitchen, where he took his private elevator down to the garage. Herbert had offered to come up and help him down, but Nick wouldn't hear of it. Yes, he was sick, but there was no way in hell he was about to let the public know the extent of his illness. Not yet. He would not relinquish control. He had a way to go, but he was extremely confident he'd win the battle in the war to save his life.

Herbert was waiting for him when the elevator doors swished open. "Good evening, sir."

Nick nodded. He didn't want to chitchat. He would follow the ridiculous instructions the anonymous caller had given. If Chelsea had actually been kidnapped, he would find out soon enough.

The odd thing about the entire situation was that the caller hadn't asked for ransom! Nick's instructions were to be at the location he was given at a certain time if he wanted his wife safely at home, where she belonged. Hell, there wasn't even a hint of a threat. If this was something Chelsea had orchestrated to gain his attention, she was about to see a side of him that he knew she wouldn't like.

Once inside the car, Nick sank into the plush leather seats, thinking of a million different ways he'd like to kill Chelsea. Even after Nick had discovered that any unborn child Chelsea had carried until her miscarriage, if there had ever been a child, could not have been his, his father had threatened to disinherit him should he divorce. His father had not cared that Chelsea had tricked Nick into thinking that Nick and Chelsea had slept together the night they had met at the frat party. It had not mattered to his father that Chelsea had come to the frat party with knockout drops all prepared and had caught the big fish, Nicholas Pemberton, heir to Pemberton Transport. Pembertons did not divorce. So with the threat of disinheritance hanging over his head, Nick had stayed his hand. Hoping against hope that his father had not managed to tie his hands via his will, Nick had intended to divorce Chelsea soon after his father's death. But the will had put an end to those plans.

And now here he was, running around with his goddamned chauffeur in the middle of the night. She would pay for this, one way or another.

Herbert waited until they were out of the garage before speaking. "May I ask where you would like to go, sir?"

Nick was glad it was dark. Glad he wouldn't be able to see the look on the old man's face when he told him where he wanted to go.

"Harlem. I need to go to Clinton's office."

Herbert glanced in his rearview mirror. His look said it all. "Of course," he replied.

Nick felt obligated to the old man, hated that he'd dragged him out in the middle of the night. He owed him an explanation, even if it was a lie. "It's a prank. Something set up by NYU, an initiation of sorts. Since I spoke at their inaugural banquet last month, they invited me to . . . help. I'd forgotten until the call came in. I'd prefer this remain within the confines of this vehicle."

"Absolutely, sir. My lips are sealed."

Nick admitted to himself it was a rather

crafty lie. When Herbert saw who was waiting at the end of this long drive, he'd have questions, but Nick was in charge. He didn't need to explain himself any more than necessary.

The rest of the drive was silent, and for this boon Nick was grateful. It took too much of his waning strength to carry on a conversation. If he didn't see a change in his health soon, he would have to tell his household staff and swear them to secrecy. They had to suspect he had something other than a bad case of flu. Chelsea had told all of them he had the flu. Of course, he could have that deadly bird flu, but Nick figured they wouldn't fall for that, either, because he would've already died.

"Sir, we've arrived," Herbert stated half an hour later.

Nick sat up straight and pushed the electric power button down, revealing the commotion on the darkened street. The night air was chilly and raw, settling into his already aching bones. He made a pretense of waiting. Then, when he could stall no longer, he eased out of the Lincoln. "Stay here. I'll be right back."

"Yes, sir," came Herbert's usual response.

Expecting gangs, streets crammed with prostitutes and low-life scumbags, Nick was taken aback when he saw groups of people walking together, some in deep conversation, others laughing loudly, nothing even remotely menacing. Of course, this wasn't his favorite area, but it certainly wasn't what he'd envisioned. It had been years since he'd ventured into that neighborhood. In spite of its lack of crazies, psychos, and general nuts, he knew he wouldn't return there anytime soon. If Chelsea pulled a similar stunt, she'd be on her own.

It was slow going as he walked the short block to the former president's office. He should have had Herbert drive him, but he preferred to keep whatever Chelsea's surprise was between the two of them. At least for the moment.

He shuddered when a gust of cool air greeted him. He should have worn a sweater under his jacket, but under normal conditions Nick wouldn't even have bothered. Since getting sick, he found that he was cold most of the time.

Up ahead he saw two men. They seemed to be fascinated with something or someone. He picked up his pace as much as he was able to. Who knew? They could be attacking Chelsea, which wouldn't be such a bad thing, he thought as he trudged the last few feet to the front of Clinton's office.

173

At the top of the stairs leading to the former president's office, Nick saw a woman in a wheelchair. She moaned softly, and her head appeared to be slumped at an unnatural angle. He forced himself up the stairs and, as he did so, he saw the two men racing down the street. He heard an engine crank, then tires squeal as a vehicle lurched out of the darkness. In the distance the car's taillights glowed like two evil bloodred eyes.

When Nick reached the top of the stairs, he was short of breath. Pausing for a few seconds to gain control of his failing body, he almost jumped out of his skin when he heard the moaning again.

"Where . . . am I?"

The woman in the chair was speaking and had his full attention. "Chelsea? Are you okay? What the hell happened to you?"

She tried to look up at him, but her neck lolled to one side. "Nick," she whispered.

"I'm right here. Look, I don't know how you got here or why you're here, but we've got to get back to the penthouse." Nick took stock of the wheelchair, unlocked the wheels, then walked behind to grasp the handles. Thank God there was a handicap ramp off to the right of the stairs. Using what was left of his waning strength, Nick pushed the wheelchair, stopped to catch his breath, then resumed pushing her back to the Lincoln.

"Where am I?" Chelsea asked in a hoarse whisper.

"Not now. Let's get you into the car. We can talk there," Nick said between labored breaths.

She must have understood what he said, because she didn't utter another word while he summoned Herbert to help him ease her out of the chair.

"Sir, this looks like more than a college prank. Should I locate a police officer?" asked Herbert.

"Hell no! The last thing I need is some nosy-ass cop asking questions. This *is* a college prank that went too far. I'll take care of it. Now, help me get her into the backseat."

Between the two of them they managed to get Chelsea inside the car. Nick left the wheelchair on the sidewalk, knowing it wouldn't remain there for long. Once Chelsea was inside the car, Nick got in beside her.

"Herbert, take us home. And whatever you do, please don't mention this ridiculous . . . adventure to any of the household staff."

"Of course, sir," Herbert replied.

Chelsea whimpered.

Nick took her hand. "Shhh. Don't say anything. Just relax."

A million different scenarios were running through his head. None of them gave him the slightest indication of what was wrong. He hadn't looked at the caller ID when the so-called kidnapper phoned. He would as soon as they got home, but anyone in his right mind would know not to call on a traceable line. Nick tried to think of all the people he'd pissed off, but there were too many to enumerate. Chelsea didn't have that many true friends, but he wasn't sure that she had an enemy that would go to such lengths. And for what? To get him out of the house? That made no sense at all. If the incident was something Chelsea and one of her boyfriends had concocted, he'd make sure she suffered.

Still, Nick couldn't see Chelsea putting herself in such a risky situation. He was sure she was either drunk or had been drugged. Maybe she'd taken some of his sleeping pills. Whatever she'd taken, he couldn't see her purposely going to Harlem in the middle of the night to wait for him to come to her rescue. Chelsea had to have been forced because she would never go to that part of the city willingly. It was simply beneath her.

The traffic wasn't heavy that time of night,

and Nick was glad. The venture had cost him all his strength. Fifteen minutes later Herbert drove into the parking garage.

"Herbert, if you'll help me get Chelsea to the elevator, I think I can handle her from there."

"Yes, sir. Sir, I can help you . . . inside."

"That won't be necessary, Herbert." Nick knew the old guy wanted to help, but he simply wanted to get inside and forget the world for the next few hours. "I appreciate the offer, though."

Herbert nodded.

Chelsea was as limp as a wet noodle as they each took an arm.

"Move your feet, Chelsea. I can't do this alone," Nick grumbled. Damn her for putting him in such a humiliating position.

Chelsea put one foot in front of the other. When they reached the elevator, Nick grabbed his wife around the waist when Herbert released his hold on her.

"I'll take it from here. Remember, not a word to anyone," said Nick.

Herbert gave his usual nod and stepped back as the elevator doors closed.

Nick held Chelsea upright as they rode up to the penthouse. What he'd really have liked to do was leave her in a heap right there in the elevator. When whatever she was on wore off, he figured she'd find her way home. But after all the bullshit he'd been through that night, he figured he might as well see that she was safe and sound.

The door swished open. Nick practically dragged Chelsea to the living room. He plopped her on the leather sofa, found one of her jackets, and tossed it over her. Sure that nothing could be done about the situation until morning, Nick slowly walked back to his bedroom. Crawling into bed, he closed his eyes, and for a moment he felt a rush of fear so sudden, his heart raced and his mouth felt dry.

What if *he didn't* wake up in the morning?

CHAPTER 8

Jason Vinery used his foot to tap on the door. "Come on, my hands are full." He was trying to perform a balancing act with three cups of coffee and the newspapers. The *Times* and the *Post,* a copy for him and copies for the girls. "Open the door!" he shouted.

Lin was dreaming about a sexy, dark-haired man when she heard Jason at the door. "Is it morning already? Damn, I just went to sleep." She listened for Sally, sound asleep in the upper bunk. "I know you're awake, so get up." Lin grabbed her robe from the foot of the bed. "If you don't wake up, I'm going to drink all the coffee and make you wait."

Sally shoved the covers aside. "You're a real pain in the ass, you know that?"

Lin laughed. "Yeah, so? What are you gonna do about it?"

"It's too early for this. Answer the door

before someone calls the police."

Lin counted her steps as she walked to the front door. Ten. *Big room,* she thought.

She unlocked the dead bolt, released the security chain, and saw Jason. "What are you doing here this early? I've had only two hours' sleep, if that." She opened the door, standing aside to allow Jason room to enter the cracker box.

"I thought you might want to read how last night's adventure played out. I even brought coffee. If you'd rather I leave . . ."

Lin shook her head. "No, I'm just tired. . . . I didn't sleep much. Come on in."

Jason sat the container of coffees on the small counter that constituted the kitchen. He reached in his pockets, removing sugar, cream, and stir sticks. "I wasn't sure how you took your coffee," he said, indicating the pile of sugars and cream.

Lin took one of the large cups of Starbucks coffee and motioned for Jason to follow her to the sofa. "Let me see the papers."

Jason snagged a coffee for himself before bringing the papers over to her. "Tell me this isn't good."

Lin was almost afraid to read them, afraid that somehow they'd been found out. She took a sip of hot coffee before reaching for

180

the paper.

"It made the front page," Jason added.

The *Post's* headline: PEMBERTON WIFE VICTIM OF DOMESTIC ABUSE!

Chelsea Pemberton was found drugged and beaten on the steps of former president Clinton's office.

It is unknown at this time how or why she was at that location. Sources believe she was taken to the location by her husband, Nicholas Pemberton, CEO of Pemberton Transport.

Charges have not been filed at the time of this writing.

The rest of the article was simply details about Pemberton Transport and the family.

The headline of the *New York Times* blared: PEMBERTON PACKS A PUNCH!

More of the same. Lin's hands trembled when she placed the paper down beside her. "This is more than I hoped for! I . . . I don't know what to say."

"Chalk one up for the good guys, Lin. It's time Pemberton received some of the crap he's been dishing out to others for the past twenty years. The man doesn't have a lot of close friends. After these articles, I doubt that what few he has will want to be seen with him. Reputation is everything in his world."

"So what happens next? Will they arrest him?" Lin asked.

"That's up to Chelsea, if she convinces herself this really happened. If the DA's office decides to pursue charges, he will be formally charged, will have to make a plea to the judge. I doubt it'll go that far, since there is a proof factor involved here, but it'll take him a while to erase this mess. He deserves it, Lin. He's stepped on and kicked so many people since taking over as CEO that you're just one of many who want to see him get what he deserves. The line is very long, trust me."

Briefly, Lin wondered if Jason had any idea exactly why she wanted to ruin Nick's reputation. If he did, he'd kept it to himself. And the why didn't really matter to Jason. Of that she was sure. She was certain he had plenty of reasons himself. Nick was a former client, something Jason had let slip when they first met, so Jason probably knew who'd been screwed by whom and for how long.

Sally chose that moment to grace them with her presence. "So did it make the papers?" She reached for the *Post* and skimmed the feature story. "Whoa! This is good stuff, Jason. Do I smell coffee?"

"There's Starbucks in the kitchen. You

might have to nuke it if you want it hot," Lin added.

Lin took another sip of coffee. "So what's next on the list? I don't see how we can top messing with his bank accounts and this." She indicated the pile of newspapers on the sofa.

"This is just the tip of the iceberg. You want something lasting, something that will plague him for the rest of his life." Jason furrowed his brow. "I think that's what you're looking for. Am I right?"

Lin took a deep breath, suddenly unsure of just how much she wanted to mess with the Pembertons. Already she'd felt somewhat vindicated, but she knew it wouldn't last. When she looked back on those times when Will was a toddler, all her struggles, she knew the two *pranks,* if you could even call them that, were nothing in comparison to what her son's father deserved.

"Yes, like I said before, I want him to feel fear, pure heart-pounding fear. Whatever it takes to do that, short of murder, I'm in."

Nick carefully opened his eyes, searching for the pearly gates of heaven. When he didn't see them, he thought he'd been condemned to the fires of hell, until he saw Nora, his housekeeper, picking up the clothes he'd dropped on his way to bed last night. He'd managed to survive another day.

He looked to his right. The digital clock read 10:30. "Where is Mrs. Pemberton?" Nick asked, easing himself out of the bed.

"I believe she's in the shower. She mentioned she wasn't feeling well when I came in this morning."

Nick's thoughts raced back to the events of the night before. Someone had to pay for what she'd put him through, not to mention the embarrassment she'd caused him. He was sick, maybe dying, for God's sake. Didn't anyone care? Suddenly he felt like crying when he thought of how Herbert and his cronies were probably having a good laugh at his expense right then.

"Would you like some tea and toast?" Nora inquired.

No, what he'd like was his old life back. Before the leukemia. "No, I'm not hungry this morning," Nick replied. "Thank you for asking," he added as an afterthought.

"Very well." Nora made fast work of straightening the room. At the door she turned to him. "If you need anything, I'll be in the kitchen."

Nick waved her away. "Tell Mrs. Pemberton I want to see her."

"Yes, sir," Nora said.

Before he lost what little privacy he had, Nick called Andrew Miller. He answered immediately.

"Have you found the son of a bitch responsible for screwing with my accounts?"

"Good morning, Nick. To answer your question, no. We're still working on tracing him. As I explained, it could take a few days, even a few weeks. If you're in need of a large amount of cash, there shouldn't be a problem. I can have the loan department set up a line of credit if you need it."

He truly didn't have much fight left in him, and the day was young. It wasn't as though that was the only bank he did business with. Today was Andrew's lucky day. "No, I don't need another line of credit. As soon as you learn who is responsible for this, I want you to call me."

"Sure. I want to find this jerk as much as you do, Nick. This doesn't look good for the bank."

"Fine. Make sure you stay on top of it." Nick slammed the phone down. He was tired. Business dealings were his life. Until his disease was under control, Nick knew he'd have to back off being the hard-ass that he'd always been. Not that he was going to ease off any of the bastards who were employed by Pemberton Transport. PT, as he thought of it, hadn't become a multibillion-dollar shipping company by his letting someone else run the show. He knew he had a rough time ahead of him. Nick wished he had more trust in his employees. Maybe if he'd been easier to work with . . . but no, he wasn't going to get chummy with his hired help at this point in his career.

A tap at the door. "Nick?" Chelsea stepped inside his room.

They'd had separate bedrooms for years. Nick liked it that way, and he knew Chelsea did, too. The one rule he'd insisted upon when they decided to have separate rooms was that under no circumstances would either of them bring another bed partner home.

Nick sat back down on the bed, drained already. He hadn't even brushed his teeth.

Chelsea looked like the wrath of God.

He motioned for her to sit down. "Do you want to tell me about last night?"

She shook her head from left to right. Her face was ashen; purple shadows underscored her eyes. She looked terrible. "That's just it. I can't seem to remember anything. I woke up this morning on the sofa. The last thing I remember was answering the door."

Nick watched his wife. She actually appeared confused. "You really don't remember?" he asked.

"Why would I lie? What is it I'm supposed to remember?" Chelsea questioned.

His cell phone rang. "What?" he barked into the receiver. "Who is this?" Nick listened for several seconds, then tossed the phone on the bed. "Have you seen the papers this morning?"

"No. I'm telling you I woke up, took a shower, and here I am. Nora doesn't even have the coffee ready. I think we need to consider hiring another housekeeper. She can't seem to stay on top of her duties." Chelsea looked at her husband. "Are you all right? You don't look well, Nick."

"Nora!" he called out at the top of his lungs.

A breathless Nora entered the room. "Yes?"

"Bring me the newspapers now," Nick said.

"Yes, Mr. Pemberton, right away."

"And coffee, Nora. That is something you can handle, isn't it? If not, I will —"

"Shut up, Chelsea," Nick ordered.

"I want a damn cup of coffee! Is that too much to expect?" Chelsea huffed.

Nora returned with the newspapers.

"Nora, make a pot of coffee for Chelsea and leave it on the hall table."

Nora hurried out of the room

"What's all the mystery, Nick? Who were you talking to on the phone?" Chelsea asked.

Nick opened the *Times,* scanned the headlines. Rage unlike any he'd ever known flooded through him. He took a deep breath, then counted to ten. He read the front page of the *Post,* then tossed the paper at Chelsea. "I want you to read very carefully. Then I want to know how the fuck you allowed this to happen."

Chelsea reached for the paper with shaky hands. As she read the headlines, Nick observed her. Her face turned even more pale than it was already. Slowly, she laid the papers at the foot of the bed. Her mouth looked like an O. It appeared as though she was as shocked as he was.

"Is this really me? The gown . . . I . . . It's what I had on this morning when I woke up."

"Yes, it's really you! You don't recognize yourself?"

Chelsea picked up the paper for a second look. "It is me. I swear to you, Nick, I have no memory of this. Someone is playing games with you. With us."

"And you have no idea how this could've happened? Who would go to such great lengths to do this to me? Some of your Bronx clan maybe?"

She shook her head as though in a daze. "Give me a break! Maybe someone you've had bad business dealings with? I truly don't know. I'm as shocked as you are. I swear on my life, Nick, I had nothing to do with this. You've got to believe me! I wouldn't ever, ever go to that terrible part of town. I'd be afraid of getting mugged or, even worse, killed!"

As much as he hated to, he believed her. She wouldn't place herself in harm's way even to get back at him. Finally, he grudgingly said, "It's funny, but I believe you, Chelsea."

Chelsea cast her dark brown eyes at him, reminding him of the first time he saw her at that party all those years ago. She was still a beautiful woman, even though greed and power had taken over her life. She'd become hard and cold. Bitter. *Like me,* he thought.

"Really? You're not saying this to try and trick me?"

"No. The question is, who did this and why? I think it might be a good idea if you called Dr. Warner. He should have a look at you. Check for any venereal diseases or hepatitis or, God forbid, AIDS."

"Nick, I didn't have sex with anyone!"

"How do you know? You said yourself you have no memory of last night."

Chelsea looked down at the Persian rug on the solid cherry floor. The carpet had cost tens of thousands, more than many families earned in a year. She traced the pattern with her bare foot. "A woman knows, Nick. Trust me."

"How?"

"Do you really want me to go into details? Let me say this. There are areas that are tender after a woman has sex. I don't need to draw you a picture, do I?"

He held up a hand. "No, no, I get the picture." He grinned. He'd embarrassed his wife, the woman who had the mouth of a sailor.

"What?"

"Nothing, Chelsea. In nineteen years of marriage I don't think I've ever seen you embarrassed."

"Well, maybe if you paid more attention to me, you might learn something," Chelsea challenged.

"I'm not going to argue with you. We both know this marriage wasn't made in heaven. So don't fool yourself. Right now I need to find out who did this to you, to me. Pemberton Transport could lose several contracts. I can't allow that to happen." Nick raked a hand through his hair. A clump of it fell out. Chelsea saw, and tears sprang to her eyes.

"Nick, I'm sorry what I said that day in the hospital. I don't want you to die. I just get so . . . I don't know. I just get angry at the world when things don't go my way. Is there anything I can do to help you get through this?" She held her hands behind her back, crossing her fingers.

"Actually there is. Keep our name out of the papers. I don't need another scandal. This is bad enough. You could get the word out that I've got something . . . hell, I don't know . . . mono, something debilitating but not life threatening. I worry that if word of my illness gets out, it could cause an uproar among the company's customers and competitors. See what you can do to keep the lid on this. Dr. Reeves says I'm doing as well as he expected. My blood levels are abnormal, but I do have a goddamned blood disease, so I expect that's par for the course."

Nick and Chelsea hadn't talked so civilly to each other in years. Maybe there was hope for them, after all. But that little voice whispered in his ear, *Can you trust her?* He chose to believe not. She'd screwed him too many times in the past, starting with day one.

Nick's cell phone rang again. He dreaded the next few days. "Yes?" he stated.

"Would you like to comment on the article in the *Post*?" a female voice asked.

"How did you get this number? This is a private cellular line!" Nick shouted.

"Mr. Pemberton, do you have any comments?" the female voice asked again.

"No!" Nick clicked the POWER button off. "That was a reporter. I don't know how she got my number. This is going to be a nightmare. I can feel it already."

"I could call a press conference or something. Tell them the story is a lie. It is, Nick. I wouldn't live with a man who knocked me around. I think you know that. I must have been drugged and taken from the house. I can ask Dr. Warner to run a toxicology screen. I'm going to file a police report, too. I'm sure I was taken unwillingly from the penthouse last night. The last thing I remember was hearing the doorbell ring. I . . . I was upset because Nora didn't answer. . . . After that I draw a complete blank. Now, the question is, who did this and what was their motive?"

"I'm calling Trevor." Trevor McDermott had been the family attorney since Nick was in high school. "This is libel or slander."

Nick kept the attorney's number on his speed dial.

When Trevor answered, Nick didn't bother with the usual amenities and started to explain what he and Chelsea thought had really happened. Trevor had read both articles.

"I can file a lawsuit for libel against both papers. It'll take time. And since you're a public figure, there is no chance of winning in court. Moreover, I'm afraid it won't do much to alleviate the rumors. I mean, she was there. The pictures are the proof. I know the publishers of both papers. I might be able to get them to print a retraction, something along those lines. But those pictures . . . Kidnapping, now, that's going to bring in the FBI. You want to go that route or maybe just make a statement, take the heat, and wait for it all to blow over?"

"Chelsea mentioned something about a press conference. What's your take on that?" asked Nick.

"Let's not do anything just yet. Let me make some calls. I'll let you know what, if anything, you'll need to do. For now, my best advice is to lie low. Don't answer your phone unless you recognize the number. Tell your staff if any of them decide to talk to the media, their jobs are history."

"Thanks, Trevor. I won't do anything until I hear from you."

"Good." Trevor promised to call as soon as he had something concrete.

Nick rehashed his conversation with the attorney for Chelsea's benefit.

"Does this mean I shouldn't make an appointment with Dr. Warner?" Chelsea asked.

"Yes. As I said, don't do or say anything to anyone until Trevor gets a handle on all of this. The man's been a damned good attorney for us and the company. He's one of the few people I actually trust. As hard as it may be, Chelsea, you're going to have to stay inside, curb your desire to shop, gossip, and whatever else you do with your time. Is that clear?"

Chelsea walked to the door, then turned around. "I want to say, 'Crystal clear,' but I'm not sure I can keep such a big promise."

Chelsea walked to the kitchen to take a coffee tray with her out to the terrace. Settling herself in the chaise with a cup of steaming coffee, she tried to remember, all those years ago when she'd seen Nick at that stupid party, just what it was that had attracted her to him. Not his good looks. Not his charm. Just his family fortune. She had never been in love with him. She had been in love with his fortune and had tricked him into thinking that it was he who had made her pregnant. Once his father had forced him to marry her, and stay married to her, he had given her a life of luxury. And now she could see that life of luxury starting to crumble around her. She felt a wave of fear unlike anything she'd ever experienced. If something happened to destroy his fortune, what would become of her? God, she'd be just like all those women who thought all they could do was sell real estate. Her thoughts carried her back to that fraternity party nineteen years earlier.

Before she even had a chance to wipe the froth of beer from her upper lip, Nicholas Pemberton strode across the hardwood floor in her direction. Chelsea glanced at her younger friend, Caroline. "He's coming over here!" she whispered. Her face turned a deep, dark shade of crimson.

"So?" Caroline stated, then took another drink of her beer. "Now's your chance to meet him."

Chelsea had to restrain herself from giving Caroline the finger, but it wasn't the right time. Nervous, she licked her lips, tasting the slick cherry lip gloss. As she observed Nicholas Pemberton moving toward them, he stopped to speak to a gorgeous, tall blonde with legs as long as forever. He whispered something in her ear. They laughed. Sure she'd lost her chance to meet the man of her dreams, the man she felt sure she could trick into marriage, Chelsea felt her heart plummet. She just knew they were talking about her. It was obvious she didn't belong there. She was about to tell Caroline it was time to go when Nicholas walked away from the leggy blonde, his eyes totally focused on Chelsea.

He was at least six-two, with oarsman's shoulders, hair a deep shade of black, and whiskey-tinted eyes she could drown in. She almost fainted when he smiled at her. Her face flushed with happiness, and her heart rate quadrupled. She resisted the childish urge to pinch herself.

He walked up to her and held out his hand. "I'm Nicholas Pemberton, and you are?"

"Chelsea Wilson." Her hand remained locked in his warm palm. Shivers shot up and down her spine.

"Well, Chelsea Wilson, what brings you to New York City?"

Thinking she would be tongue-tied, Chelsea surprised herself when she spoke. "I'm staying in Manhattan with a friend." Perfectly normal. She could do this. Nothing to it. She was an adult, not a bumbling teenager. A wealthy man was her only chance to escape the humdrum life she'd been born into. A wealthy man was her ticket out of the mess she'd made of her life with that useless asshole who'd knocked her up. She'd best watch her p's and q's with this one.

Caroline perked up. "She's staying with me."

"And you must be her friend," Nicholas said, extending his hand.

Caroline clasped his strong hand. "Caroline Whitaker. I'm a student at NYU. First year."

He laughed. "I remember those days well. It's not bad, really. If you can stand all the seniors trying to give you girls and guys a hard time, you'll be just fine." He turned his gaze to Chelsea. "So, why haven't I seen you before now? Surely you've attended some of the more . . . uh . . . noted parties?" Nicholas asked Chelsea with a sexy smile.

Demurely, Chelsea lowered her gaze. "This will be my first."

The three laughed.

"Caroline, is that you?" A female barely topping five feet, with long black hair and wire-rimmed glasses, came bounding up to her friend. "Remember me? I was in your English Lit class. I dropped out before the end of the semester."

"Of course I remember you, Holly Jolly! How in the hell did you wind up here?" Caroline asked.

"Long story."

"And she'll be more than happy to tell you while I introduce Chelsea to some of the gang. Right?" Nicholas asked the small girl, but his eyes were on Chelsea.

The small girl glanced at Caroline for confirmation. "Sure," she said, eyes asking a question.

"Come along, Holly," said Caroline. "I think Nicholas wants to get to know Chelsea, who is staying with me for a while. I think we should disappear."

Chelsea waved hi to the black-haired girl, all the while wondering just what Nicholas Pemberton had in mind. Thinking of the knockout drops she had brought with her, she took a small sip of beer while he poured a mug for himself. She did not want to lose her focus when so much depended upon what happened with Nicholas that night.

"Let's find a place to talk." He took her hand and led her into the main room. The party was in full swing. Chelsea observed the guests. Some were dressed to the nines; others wore jeans and T-shirts. Some of the girls wore long dresses, their hair reaching the back of their knees. Hippies. Chelsea smiled. She'd smoked her share of pot with a few in her day.

Nicholas found an empty corner, where he cleared a place for her to sit. She sat down on a brown leather chair while he cleared a space on the floor by their feet so they could set their mugs down.

"Not much room around here tonight," Nicholas said.

"I thought you were going to introduce me to your friends."

Nicholas laughed, revealing perfectly white teeth. "You believed that, huh?"

Chelsea wanted to come across as naive, so she lied. "Of course I believed you."

Nicholas sat on the floor next to both mugs of beer. "When I saw you, I knew I had to meet you, pure and simple." He smiled again. "Scout's honor."

If her heart rate climbed any higher, Chelsea knew her heart would explode right out of her chest. She searched the depths of her soul for a response, but nothing surfaced. She reached for her beer. He caught her hand. Waves of anticipation swept through her. For a second she was so nervous that she thought she might throw up, but the urge passed. Mortified at the thought of puking in front of Nicholas, she begged her unresponsive brain to come up with something to say. "How long have you lived here?"

He leaned against the wall, his caramel eyes gazing into hers. "Most of my life."

Ashamed at her own stupidity, she laughed

in spite of herself. "That was a dumb question." She sounded normal, but she sure as hell didn't feel normal. Chelsea had spent enough time around guys to know her reaction to Nicholas Pemberton was anything but normal. She could see a future with this man. Maybe even marriage, if she could make him think that he had seduced her and made her pregnant, but it had to be that night. She was running out of options fast. Who cared that she'd only known him for less than an hour?

Certainly jumping the gun, *she thought to herself.* Caroline will just love this. And I am not about to screw this up. No way. He can be my ticket to the good life.

"No, it wasn't. I could've just moved here, for all you knew."

The Carpenters' "We've Only Just Begun" played in the background. She forced her cheeks to flame. Gawd! Corny, but she'd act the part. Innocent and charming, hanging on his every word, as though privileged just to be in his presence.

"Want to dance?" Nicholas asked.

Chelsea saw several couples dancing in the middle of the room. Arms wrapped around one another, heads on shoulders while footsteps moved to the rhythm of the music. Someone lowered the lights.

Nicholas took her by the hand and led her

to the middle of the room, where the dancers were grouped closely in a circle.

She let Nicholas guide her to the makeshift dance floor. The song changed, and she would swear someone was reading her mind tonight. Olivia Newton John's "I Honestly Love You" droned in the background.

When she finally allowed herself to relax and enjoy the music, she leaned against Nicholas's chest, the top of her head fitting neatly beneath his chin. Effortlessly, he led her around the room. Chelsea closed her eyes, breathed in his scent. Beer and a musky soap. She wanted to burn the moment in her memory, because she didn't think there would ever be another. This was just a party, she kept telling herself. He was just another guy. But, if she played her cards right, it could be the beginning of something big. Very big. And very rewarding.

They danced two dances; then the beat kicked up. Grand Funk's "The Loco-Motion" blared from the speakers. Dozens of people grabbed their mates and began doing what the song instructed, making a chain and swinging their hips, then jumping up and back. It was a fun song, and Chelsea would've liked to dance, but Nicholas led her back to the corner.

"That's a little too fast for me. What about

you?" Nicholas asked once they were seated.

"It's not that fast!" She laughed.

He grabbed her hand. "Then let's do it!" He pulled her back to the center of the room, where they joined the train of people swinging, jumping, and getting into the song. Someone went to the turntable and set the record to play again. There were at least fifty people squeezed in the center of the room for the second go-round.

After jumping, swinging, and laughing, Chelsea, out of breath, was glad when the fast-moving song ended. "That's a lot of work." She fanned her face with her hands.

"It is, but fun. I can't remember when I last danced."

Chelsea took his words as a good sign. Maybe he didn't have a girlfriend. Maybe the rumors she'd heard about his engagement to Cathryn Carlyle were simply that. Rumors.

"Then you need to go out more," Chelsea offered.

They returned to their seats. "I should, but I'm preparing to work at my father's company full-time. There just aren't enough hours in the day. It doesn't leave me much time for a social life."

Chelsea wondered if this was his way of telling her he wasn't engaged.

She watched his eyes, dark and smoldering, as he stared at her. "It's too loud in here. Do you want to go somewhere quiet where we can talk?"

She looked at her watch. Going on midnight. Chelsea scanned the room in search of Caroline. She spied her across the room, in the corner, with the small girl and a guy she'd met earlier. She waved. Caroline saw her, motioned for her to come over.

"I'll just be a minute," Chelsea explained to Nicholas.

"I'll be right here waiting," he replied.

His words caressed her like a soft, warm rain. She smiled over her shoulder as she made her way to Caroline's side of the room.

Before Chelsea could say a word, Caroline yanked her by the arm, dragging her to a small powder room beneath the staircase. "Do you realize every woman and girl and some of the damned guys here tonight hate you? I can't believe Nicholas Pemberton would . . . Never mind. Just give me the details."

Chelsea set her purse on the sink, removed her cherry lip gloss. She pursed her lips as she peered into the mirror above the sink. "There isn't anything to tell, really. We've danced, and that's about it. He did ask me if I wanted to go somewhere quiet where we could talk. That's why I'm here. You won't mind if I don't come back to your place tonight, will you? If things go as I plan, I might not make it back till the wee hours of the morning."

"You're a real society chick now, aren't you?" Caroline applied some gloss to her own lips. "I suppose it doesn't matter where you actually sleep. As long as I'm the first one to get the details."

"Thanks, Caro. You're a good friend." Chelsea turned around while Caroline repaired her make-up, and then they left the room together. She almost collided with Nicholas as they made their way to the front door.

"You're not trying to sneak out on me, are you?" he asked, his eyes glowing.

Damn! "No, I was telling Caroline not to expect me." Chelsea smiled at him.

Chelsea had one arm in the sleeve of her coat when Nicholas piped up. "I can drive her back to your place. Tomorrow."

Chelsea gave Caroline a keep-your-mouth-shut-or-I'll-kill-you look. "Are you sure?"

Nicholas took Chelsea's hand. "Of course I'm sure. I wouldn't have offered otherwise. Now, why don't you say good-bye to your friend and let's go someplace where we can get to know one another better?" Then: "I'll take good care of her. Promise," Nicholas said to Caroline, a big grin on his face.

"I'm sure you will," Caroline retorted. "Then

I'm going to call it a night. I'll see you later, Chels." She hugged her and whispered, "Details," in her ear.

Chelsea cringed, fearful Nicholas could hear her. He waited while she got her purse and said a last good-bye to Caroline and her two friends.

Ten minutes later they were riding through the streets of Manhattan in his cherry red Corvette. Nicholas turned the heater on, but Chelsea couldn't stop shivering. *Nerves*, she told herself. Wasn't there such a thing as good nerves?

Nicholas shifted into low gear as he came to a stop. "There's this little all-night diner right around the corner. I've been coming here forever. They have the best hamburgers in the world. Are you hungry?"

Having bypassed all the food at the party, Chelsea realized she was starving. "Actually, a hamburger sounds good." She hated red meat, but she sure as hell wasn't going to let that stop her from agreeing to anything he said.

"Then you're about to experience burger heaven." He pulled into an empty spot next to the curb. She reached to open her door, but Nicholas stopped her. "I'll do that."

A real gentleman. Chelsea wasn't sure she'd ever dated one. He came around to her side and opened the door. A blast of night air caused her to shiver even more.

"Come on, let's get you inside before you turn into a Popsicle," he said.

Chelsea let him guide her inside.

"Nick, my man! What brings you out this late?" a bald man with horn-rimmed glasses called out from the kitchen.

"Harry, I came for one of your famous burgers. Brought a friend. Told her they were the best. We'll have two, with the works."

Nicholas led her to a turquoise-colored booth. Shakers for salt and pepper and a napkin holder were the only ornaments on the tabletop. Chelsea removed her coat and slid onto the soft vinyl seat. Thinking Nicholas would sit across from her, she was more than surprised when he slid in beside her.

"I just want to keep you warm. That's all." He gazed into her eyes.

Her stomach flip-flopped, and she looked away. "Who said anything about being cold?" She couldn't think of anything else to say.

"Tell me something about yourself," Nicholas said.

Chelsea opened up to him. She told him about her childhood, that her parents were older when they'd had her, but that's where the truth ended and the lies began. No way was she going to tell him she was from the

Bronx. Who knew where her father was? And her mother, well, when she wasn't screwing some strange guy, she was drinking. No, Chelsea painted a pretty, happy picture for Nicholas. She knew a family's lineage was very important to him.

Their food arrived.

"I hope you're hungry," Nicholas said. The burgers were at least an inch thick and three times that high.

"Wow, this looks fantastic!" she exclaimed. She cut hers in half. She almost lost it when she took the first bite and saw the blood dripping onto her plate. Her system didn't tolerate red meat. Juice dripped on her hands, then onto her plate. "They're messy, too."

"A burger has to be messy to be good in my book."

They finished their burgers, and Nicholas left a generous amount of money on the table, promising to return. Once they were outside, he helped her with her coat. Then, just as she thought he would turn away, he took her in his arms. His lips were warm when they touched hers. Their kiss was light, affectionate, but she took over from there.

When they went back to his place, he was raring to go. After holding him off for a bit by suggesting that they have something more to drink, she slipped him the already prepared knockout drops and started to get him aroused. By the time they got to the bedroom, he was just about out on his feet. She undressed the two of them and slid into bed beside the unconscious Nicholas, waiting for the morning and the inevitable aftermath — marriage. By the time she had the convenient miscarriage, she was already the wife of Nicholas Pemberton, heir to Pemberton Transport and one of the richest men in the business.

Chelsea refilled her cup of coffee. And look at her now. She truly was laughing all the way to the bank. Scratch *laughing*. She had the terrible feeling she was going to be crying, and the bank was suddenly going to be empty.

CHAPTER 9

Lin spent part of the afternoon on the phone with Jack. He'd run into problems that only she could resolve; most involved money.

"Kelly Ann scheduled six New Year's Eve parties. Can you believe that? At this rate I'll have to hire at least two more crews," Lin said after hanging up the phone.

"That's what it's all about, Lin. Making money. You've said it yourself," Sally reminded her.

"I know. I do like having the restaurant, though. It's the only thing I know how to do, besides being Will's mom. I have to be a success, or I might end up marrying some skunk like Nicholas Pemberton just to pay the bills," Lin joked.

"I can't see you stooping to Chelsea's level. Of course, she could've been in love with him. At least in the beginning," Sally said.

Jason had provided them with background information on Chelsea. She came from some nowhere in the Bronx and had become the biggest social climber in the city.

Lin rolled her eyes. "Good old Nick was making the rounds back then. It wasn't easy telling him no. He was slick, and I fell for everything he said. Could be what happened to the current Mrs. Pemberton. When I think about these letters I haul around, I want to burn them. But like you reminded me that day I was ready to burn them, I might need them someday."

Sally gathered up the morning papers and tucked them under the sofa. "So what's next on the list?"

"Jason says to lie low for a few days. He wants to see where this leads. I think he wants to make sure our butts are covered before we attempt anything else. Nick and Chelsea will be on their guard at this point, and for sure the police have been alerted, so what he said makes sense."

"You're right. It does make sense. Then why don't the two of us take in the sights? We've practically been shut-ins since we arrived."

"You know I would love to, but I just can't take the slightest risk of bumping into Will. I know the odds are in my favor that I won't, but I've got too much at stake to take another risk, Sally. Sorry."

Sally smiled. "You know we don't have to stay in New York. Let's go home to Dalton and come back when Jason says the coast is clear."

Lin felt as though she'd been given the Hope Diamond. "I can't believe I didn't think of that! There isn't a thing in the world to keep us here. We can work a couple of days, give Jack and Kelly Ann some time off, or at least help out." Lin gave Sally a high five.

"What are we waiting for? Let's pack. We'll call Jason from the airport."

They made quick work of removing the suitcases stored beneath the bunk bed. They tossed in their toiletry items, then made sure to disconnect all things electric.

"I'll run the garbage out if you'll get us a cab. I'll meet you out front," Sally said.

"Deal." Lin said, feeling as lighthearted as she did the day she'd attended Will's banquet. *Before seeing Nicholas,* she thought.

Scanning the small apartment one last time, Lin took their luggage, placed it on the hall floor, then locked the door. Not that they'd left anything worth stealing behind, but this was New York City. Inserting her key into the final dead bolt, Lin heard the reassuring click, then ran outside to hail a taxi.

Ten minutes later they were on their way to JFK.

"I hope we can get a flight out tonight," Lin said.

"Shoot, Lin, this is New York! Of course they'll have a flight. We might have to pay out the kazoo, but who cares? We've both got boatloads of money. Why not enjoy it?" Sally teased.

"There you go again, spending my money, but it's okay. Like you said, why not enjoy it? I can't see hanging out in that cracker box any longer than necessary. You want to call Jason now or wait till we're home?" Lin asked.

"Call him when we get to the airport. Just to make sure we're actually leaving," Sally said.

"This coming from 'Shoot, Lin, this is New York. Of course they'll have a flight.' " Lin shook her head.

The taxi driver must've heard them, because he spoke in a thick, unidentifiable accent. "Where you go?"

Lin and Sally looked at each other. "Atlanta."

He nodded. "They have flight to all major city."

212

"Thanks," Lin said, then leaned over and whispered to Sally, "I think."

Traffic was bumper to bumper as they made their way out of Manhattan to JFK, located smack-dab in the heart of Queens. An hour later the taxi driver dropped them off at the airport. Lin paid for the ride and hustled over to a skycap at the American Airlines counter.

"I need two tickets on your next flight to Atlanta. One way." Lin cast a questioning glance at Sally. "I don't know when we'll return."

"Fine with me," said Sally.

The young man clicked at the computer's keyboard. "Flight four-five-eight-one leaves at eleven tonight."

"Perfect. I'll take two tickets." Lin removed her American Express and her driver's license from her wallet. Sally followed suit.

"Told you we'd get a flight," Sally smarted off.

"Yeah, yeah, whatever. Here, give the man your ID, or we'll miss the flight." Lin took Sally's license from her and gave them to the skycap.

"I bet he thinks you're older than you really are," Lin said matter-of-factly. Both women cackled.

"You're slowly digging your grave, Lin," Sally shot back.

"So you say."

They took their boarding passes and IDs from the young man.

"Have a great trip," he said.

"Thanks," Lin replied for both of them. "We will."

Thirty minutes later they'd managed to get through security. "I can't believe you still wear white granny panties," Sally said with an air of haughtiness.

"I can't believe they dug through my luggage like they were mining for gold. Since nine-eleven, I swear there is no privacy anymore. And it's none of your business what kind of underwear I wear." Lin looked from side to side, making sure no one saw her as she gave her dear friend the single-digit salute.

Laughing, Sally continued her razzing. "Take a word of advice. If you plan on getting laid in the near future, make a trip to Victoria's Secret first."

"And you're such a sexpot."

"At least I keep my undies up to date. A girl can never be too prepared."

Lin kept up the light teasing banter. "I didn't know you cared."

"Someone has to."

As they waited for their flight number to be called, Lin suddenly couldn't wait to get home. To her own bed, her own bathroom, her own life. She needed to spend quality time at the diner. Their "mission" hadn't turned out to be as simple as she'd originally expected.

"I'm ready to call it a day," Sally said as they walked slowly down the ramp to the plane.

"Don't zonk out on me now. You know flying isn't my favorite mode of transportation. You have to hold my hand, at least during the takeoff," Lin teased, but she was quite serious. She did not like the idea of being inside what she thought of as a metal bullet soaring through the air at an astounding rate of speed.

"Quit whining," Sally said as she stepped on the plane.

"You're some friend," Lin complained.

Both laughed and found their way to their seats. Lin relaxed while they were still on the ground. She couldn't get home soon enough.

Atlanta, here we come.

Two days after Chelsea's abduction, like sand flowing through an hourglass, Nick's once-orderly life was slowly slipping through his fingers, completely beyond his control. It was just a little over a month since the deadly cancer cells had invaded his body, demanding that he surrender to their commands. He would not give up the fight, no matter what he had to do.

"Herbert, I'm not sure how long I'll be today. I'll call you when I'm ready to return to the penthouse." Out of necessity, he'd had to tell Herbert the truth about his illness. Nick had sworn him to secrecy.

"Of course."

Herbert pulled up to the side of the curb, where one of Dr. Reeves's nurses waited outside the office with a wheelchair to take Nick up to the seventeenth floor for his chemotherapy. When he finished, he had another series of tests to go through. Dr. Reeves said the results that day would be critical in determining how well he was responding to the treatments.

"Good afternoon, Mr. Pemberton," the nurse said cheerfully.

Somewhat distracted, he replied, "I wish."

All the nurses knew him by then, knew he wasn't an easy patient to care for. He was demanding and often cruel. Nick didn't care what they thought of him. They were mere instruments to be used in order to bring a killer disease under control. As long as he thought of them that way, he could hold himself together. Nick couldn't look at them as sympathetic health-care providers who wanted to do whatever was in their power to make his journey through hell easier. No, if he thought of them as something real, something touchable, he would become vulnerable and weak in their eyes. Always powerful, Nick couldn't allow a disease, something he couldn't even see, couldn't even touch, to control him. Yes, the drugs that fought the disease made him wish he were dead, but once the effects wore off, he immediately started the renewal process. Then it would begin all over again.

That day was a milestone of sorts.

The nurse pushed him down the hall to the chemo suite. Hospital recliners circled a large room, where IV poles, basins, and ice chips were the order of the day. He'd gotten used to the drab atmosphere, the sickly smell of decay, the pain and suffering of all who entered. It angered him. Tremendously. He did not want to be there among the hopeless and the diseased. He told himself he didn't belong there. He was too young to die. Then he glanced around the suite at the other patients, some much younger than his forty-three years, and Nick knew without a doubt that they didn't want to die, either.

It was an unspoken thought among them all, young and old.

An oncology nurse assisted him to the recliner. After several adjustments to the IV, she cleaned an area on his hand with an alcohol pad. "Mr. Pemberton, if you'd allow us to insert the chemo port, we wouldn't have to jab and poke you. Your hands and arms look terrible."

Nick didn't need to be reminded that he looked like a heroin addict. "I'll suffer through it," he said flatly. Nick refused to have a foreign object implanted in his chest, even though Dr. Reeves highly recommended the procedure.

"It's your choice," the nurse said.

She inserted the needle in the vein just below his third knuckle on his left hand, then hooked the IV line to the small hose protruding from his hand. Within minutes the lifesaving drugs would course through his system, targeting and, hopefully, destroying the leukemia cells.

The treatment usually took about three to four hours from start to finish.

Rosa sent daily updates to his iPhone. He would listen on his headset while getting his treatment. It made the time pass quickly and took his mind off what was real, what was happening to him while he sat in this uncomfortable excuse for a recliner. He would make notes for her, and when his body finished rejecting the poisons that were his cure, he would call her with his answers. Gerald was still useless. Nick suspected his staff knew he was seriously ill, but so far no one had had the courage or the nerve to discuss his future as CEO of Pemberton Transport.

When Nick finished his chemo, another nurse took him down one floor, where he would have more blood work, and they would extract more bone marrow.

After the anesthesiologist numbed his hip area, he gave him something to relax. Dr. Reeves came in the room. He looked at his chart, made a notation, then stood where Nick could see him. "How are you feeling?"

Nick grimaced. "I've been better."

"That's what all my patients say. If it keeps up, I'm liable to get a complex."

"I wouldn't want to be responsible for that." *Enough,* Nick thought to himself. *Do what the hell you came to do and get it over with.*

"Okay, I'm going to withdraw some fluid. This should be over within a few minutes. Just relax." Dr. Reeves stepped to the other side of the bed, where a surgical nurse had the Jamshidi needle ready for him. He slowly inserted the needle, moved it up and down, then side to side before removing it. "All done."

Nick released the breath he'd been holding. "Can't say this is one of my favorite things to do, but that wasn't as bad as the first time."

After they cleaned and covered the injected area, Nick rolled over to his back. He pushed the button on the side of his bed allowing him to sit up straight.

"First time is always the worst," Dr. Reeves said.

There didn't seem to be any response to that statement, so Nick kept quiet.

The nurse drew more blood, wrote something on a white label, then took the fluid from the Jamshidi needle.

"I'm going to wait for them," Dr. Reeves said.

"Tell the lab stat the results. I'll take this down myself," the nurse said.

"Thanks." Dr. Reeves looked at Nick, as though trying to gauge his mood. He was like mercury. One minute he was up, and the next he was down. "It shouldn't take more than an hour, possibly less."

"Are you saying I have to stay here and wait?" Nick asked.

"Yes, at least until the anesthetic wears

off. Is this a problem?"

"Of course it's a problem. My entire life is nothing but one giant goddamned problem!"

Dr. Reeves waited, allowing him to vent, but Nick went silent, his thoughts all over the map.

"Then let's hope it gets better," the doctor encouraged.

It has to, Nick thought, *because there's no fucking way it could get any worse.*

When Lin woke on Friday, it took her a minute to realize she was still home in Dalton, in her own bedroom. She smiled. Energized, she bounced out of bed to the kitchen, where she readied a pot of coffee. Seconds after she clicked the ON switch, the enticing aroma of the heady brew filled the kitchen. Waiting for the coffee, she looked around her home at the openness, all the glorious space. In Manhattan a place that size would cost millions.

Filling her mug with coffee, she took it into the bathroom with her, took a quick shower, dressed in jeans and a bright red sweater, put her hair in a sleek ponytail, and returned to the kitchen for more coffee before heading to her office, where she had a pile of mail she had picked up the day

221

before from the post office but had not gotten around to dealing with. She would sort through it before going to the diner.

Lin attacked the pile with a vengeance, mostly final bills from the remodeling. She wrote out a dozen checks, scribbled out a thank-you note to Jean Le Boeuf, a food critic from the *Atlanta Journal-Constitution,* and, lastly, wrote a hefty check covering another year for her father's stay at the nursing home in Atlanta. With the hard mail, as she liked to call it, finished, she clicked on her computer to read her e-mail, checked the stock market, saw that it had taken a nosedive. Scrolling through her e-mail, she hoped there would be something from Will.

There were 226 e-mails, most of them spam. Nothing from Will, which disappointed her, but he'd only been away a little more than a month at this point. His weekly phone calls would have to suffice.

An e-mail from Jason Vinery caught her attention. She clicked on the link he'd sent, to the *Post.* Apparently, they'd issued something of a retraction, which had appeared in yesterday's paper. Simply stated, it said the reporter who wrote the article had "misquoted his source." Lin smiled. That was an understatement. In a personal e-mail he said as soon as his next "escapade" was safe to execute, he would call her. She clicked through a few other e-mails.

With nothing more at home needing her immediate attention, Lin grabbed a handful of grapes to eat on the drive to the diner and her purse. Thirty minutes later she was in the kitchen with Jack, going over the evening's special.

"Jack, we just can't have meat loaf every night of the week."

In a gruff voice he said, "It worked for thirty years. I don't see why it won't work for another thirty."

Dear Jack, Lin thought. His meat loaf was to die for, but not every night of the week. Not wanting to hurt his feelings, she continued, "People are much more health conscious these days. We do the meat loaf on Wednesday. Customers look forward to that, but they also like a change, a surprise of sorts."

Jack shook his balding head and threw his hands up in the air. "This younger generation amazes me! You want me to run the show, and when I try, you tell me all you want is fish and lettuce, nothing hearty that'll stick to your bones, like my meat loaf and mashed potatoes. What do I know?"

Lin smiled, remembering her days as a waitress. Jack had pretended to be tough and mean, but he'd been such a softy. He'd always made her think of the animated Mr. Clean, with his bald head and stocky build. All these years later he was still trying to act like a hard-nosed grill cook, like the guy from the seventies sitcom *Alice*.

"How about we compromise? Let's do the meat loaf as a lunch special tomorrow."

"Hey, you're the boss. You do what you want. I'm just an old man." Jack wiped his hands with a towel, then tucked it in the waist of his apron.

At seventy-five, Jack was anything but old. He could pass for a man of sixty, at most. He had stayed in shape after retiring by joining a gym and was the number one player on a senior tennis team. Irma had never looked or acted her age, either. Lin loved this about them, loved that they hadn't withered away and died when they'd retired. The couple remained a bundle of energy.

"You're not old, and you know it," Lin teased. "I'm going to write the specials on the computer and print them out." Impulsively, she gave the old guy a hug. He returned it with a hefty squeeze of his own.

Smiling, Jack propelled her out of his way. "Go on now. Do that menu thing you're so fond of."

Lin entered her private office, a small room off the back of the prep kitchen. The daily specials were printed out in a different font and color depending on the item. Salads, dark green, meats were different shades of brown and red. Cutesy, but it was just one of the little extras she enjoyed doing. Lin would insert them into leather menu holders, and the hostess would then place them on each table as the customers were seated.

Kelly Ann had done an excellent job when she'd booked the parties for New Year's. Each guest's menu was itemized right down to the color of candles they preferred. This wasn't something that Jack's would normally do, but Lin thought Kelly Ann smart for thinking of it and made a mental note to mention this to her. Lin made a list for the restaurant-supply specialty store: extra flatware, colored tablecloths, napkins. The food was next. After spending an hour organizing the food list in order of what could be purchased ahead of time and what would have to wait until the last minute, Lin stood up, stretching the kinks from her neck and back.

Taking the menus with the lunch and dinner specials to the hostess's stand, Lin grinned when she saw Sally. "I knew you'd materialize sooner or later. After all, lazy-bones, you slept the entire day yesterday. Or, at least, you didn't show up here."

"Yeah, wild horses couldn't keep me away. Actually, I would've been here earlier, but I stopped by Irma's to check on Clovis. Irma swears he hasn't journeyed out at night." Sally laughed at the image. "I'm not sure I believe her. I think she's just telling me that so I won't worry about the old satyr."

Lin stacked the menus beneath the hostess's stand. "I'm sure he's in good hands. You worry too much."

"Me? Worry?" Sally rolled her eyes upward. "I don't think so."

"Nonsense. Here, help me wipe these down." Lin handed her a tray of saltshakers and pepper mills, along with a clean, damp cloth. Making sure no one was around to overhear her, Lin took a step, closing the distance between them. "Jason sent me an e-mail. The *Post* printed a retraction yesterday. Something along the lines of their source being misquoted."

"I'm surprised they did that," Sally said. "Seems too easy."

"I thought so, too. Remember, Nick's a powerful man. I'm sure he has contacts all over the world. When I think of that, it scares the bejesus out of me. With his money and power, it would be easy for him to find me out. I'm not even sure I want to continue to . . . try to topple his tower." Lin paused, waiting to see how her words affected Sally. "I don't know if it's even worth the time and effort." She'd already invested thousands into bringing about his downfall, and she hadn't even put a scratch on his empire, much less the man himself.

Sally took her arm, turning her so that they faced one another. "You don't have to do this. This is a choice you made, and you can undo it. If you're not comfortable continuing, you need to stop. No one knows about it, except for Jason. He's certainly not going to reveal anything. Really, if you stop and think about it, you didn't even *do* anything. Yes, he's locked out of his personal bank accounts for a few days or weeks. Yes, his reputation might need a bit of polishing after that report in the paper. It will probably take a life-or-death experience to have an effect on him, so unless you're willing to threaten him physically, I agree with you. It'll take a lot more than Jason and our 'pranks' to hurt him."

Lin felt as though the weight of the world had been lifted from her shoulders. She could relax, look herself in the mirror without doubts and second thoughts. She knew what she had to do. So what if Nicholas Pemberton had skipped out on his duties as a parent? In all fairness to Will, he really hadn't suffered because of this. She had. Though, if she admitted it, she'd become stronger, more capable, and probably the astute businesswoman she was today because of the situation. What she was about to do, she must do on her own. She had to let go and do things her own way.

She took a deep breath, smiled, and forced a feeling of lightheartedness. "I'm going to call Jason and tell him to forget it. It's just not worth the time and the stress."

"And don't forget the money," Sally added.

"How could I? You can't stop reminding me!" Lin stacked the salts and peppers on the tray. "As I said, I could've spent that money on something useful. Like these chairs." She nodded at the chairs placed throughout the main dining room. "Now Kelly Ann won't have to work like a slave during the holidays. With the three of us here to help with the planning, the New Year's parties and the Christmas parties will go off without a hitch. Help me put these on the tables. We're opening in twenty minutes."

They placed the saltshakers and pepper

mills on the tables, made sure the silverware sparkled, the napkins were folded just right, and the water glasses glistened like platinum.

"I think we're ready to unlock the doors. I'm glad we had this time to . . . reflect," said Lin.

Sally laughed and hugged her. "Yeah, if you want to call what we've been doing 'reflecting,' then I think it's the smartest 'reflecting' we've done all week."

Lin paused, then announced, "I'm calling this off right now. Remember that old adage, 'What goes around, comes around'? I'm sure it'll catch up with Nick someday."

She was positive that it would.

CHAPTER 10

Nick couldn't wait to tell Chelsea his news. She wouldn't like it, but tough.

"Herbert, I'll be needing your services tonight. I plan to take Mrs. Pemberton out to dinner. To celebrate." She wasn't going to get rid of him that easily.

"That's wonderful, sir. You haven't been out in quite a while."

Nick thought the old geezer would ask what it was he was going to celebrate, but he didn't, so Nick explained. "Dr. Reeves told me I could taper back on the chemotherapy today. My red blood cells are almost back to normal. Platelets are normal. Hell, even my liver and spleen are good as new. No swelling, nothing." Nick knew he'd whip the leukemia's ass, just to prove he wasn't a loser.

A smile crinkled Herbert's already

230

wrinkled face even more. "Congratulations, sir. That's the best news I've heard all day."

"Indeed it is."

Nick was still weak, the aftereffects of the treatment just as severe as before, but knowing he wouldn't have to undergo another treatment for a month seemed to obliterate the nausea and the weakness he usually experienced afterward. He even felt hungry for the first time in weeks. Knowing that was most likely psychological, and he'd be as sick as ever, didn't matter. It was simply a case of mind over matter. If he could keep going until he arrived home, he could rest before taking Chelsea out to dinner. He couldn't wait to see the look on her face when he told her he was going to live, after all, if anything, just to spite her. The thought brought him immense pleasure.

Herbert pulled into the garage. Still very weak, Nick refused the man's help getting to the elevator. He was a Pemberton, and Pembertons did not lose. At anything. Ever. It simply never occurred to him that there was a first time for everything.

Standing erect, he waited for the elevator doors to open. Inside the elevator, he slumped a bit, but as soon as the doors opened, he stood straight and tall. He was going to use his brain to help him conquer the disease. More mind over matter.

Entering through the kitchen, Nick nodded at Nora.

"How are you today, Mr. Pemberton?" she asked with genuine concern in her voice.

"I'm on the road to recovery, Nora, and thank you for asking."

The short, squat woman raised her black eyebrows and smiled. "Wonderful news, sir. Just wonderful. Shall I make a pot of tea for when you're settled in?"

"That would be wonderful. And maybe something sweet to go along with it."

"Of course." Nora smiled, thinking she had just the perfect dessert for him. She'd baked oatmeal raisin cookies just that morning.

Nick went to his suite of rooms. He was about to lie down when the first round of nausea hit him. Racing to the bathroom, he spent the next hour heaving. When he had regained his strength, he managed to crawl into the shower and let hot pelts of water beat against his thin, sallow skin. He managed to scrub the vomit off his face and wash his hair. Shaving took too much energy.

He slipped a pair of boxers on before climbing beneath the covers. He saw the pot of tea and cookies sitting on a tray. He drew in a deep breath. Just then the thought of putting anything in his mouth made him gag. So much for mind over matter.

After he relaxed for a while, his stomach calmed down enough for him to take small sips of tea. The cookies weren't looking all that bad, either. He took one off the plate and bit into it. *Heaven,* he thought as he took another bite. Never having had much of a sweet tooth, he'd found since getting sick, he constantly had cravings for sweet desserts, cakes and pies. All the things he never ate. It was as though being ill had humanized him in a way he had never thought possible. Eating something that wasn't beneficial to his health in the past had been something men much weaker than him would choose to do. His body had been strong, fit. He'd spent many hours in the gym making sure he remained in top form. And here he was now, like some schoolboy, getting excited about what was for dessert. It was the illness, he guessed. Probably the chemo made his body crave things it shouldn't. Whatever the reason, no matter how he tried to rationalize it, if it was sweet, and he could keep it down, he would eat it.

Exhausted, but feeling much better, Nick decided to take Chelsea out, after all. He'd sip tea if he couldn't eat. Besides, he needed to be out in the public eye. Places where he was usually seen. They'd go to the club.

He wasn't dead yet.

Lin spent the morning and afternoon at the diner, then went home to change for the dinner crowd. While it wasn't required, since Jack's was casual dining, Lin believed that as the owner, she needed to stand out from the staff. In the evenings, when she saw she wasn't being intrusive, Lin went to each table when her patrons were finished with their meal, spoke with them, and thanked them for their business. She liked the personal touch, and so did her customers. The last few hours were trying, but she managed to get through the evening without thinking about all the terrible lies she'd told.

And she was about to add a trail of lies to follow those. She remembered how her father used to tell her if you told one lie, then you had to tell another to cover that one up, and, before you knew it, you'd told so many lies, you couldn't keep them straight. If this was his legacy to her, she was about to put it into action.

She'd worry about forgiveness later. Just like Scarlett, her idol.

It was after one when she returned home. Sally was too tired to stop in for their usual doughnuts and coffee. Lin was glad because she had plans to make. With Sally around, it would be impossible.

Lin put on a pot of coffee after changing into sweats and a T-shirt. She scrunched her hair on top of her head, using a plastic clip to secure it. She took her laptop to the kitchen and plugged it in. While she waited for the computer to boot up, she poured herself a cup of coffee. Telling herself she was being silly, she could not do what she was about to do in her home office. It seemed wrong, like a traitor had invaded her space. Why she thought the kitchen table a better place, she didn't know. It felt more communal, less personal.

Clicking on her e-mail, she sent Jason Vinery a lengthy message. If his answer was as she expected, she would start formulating her plans immediately. If not, then she'd go to plan B. Whatever plan B was.

When she heard the familiar *ding* letting her know she had received an e-mail, Lin's heart raced, and her palms were suddenly damp. The e-mail was from Jason. She read it, then read through it a second time. Yes! He'd agreed to her plans.

Feeling relieved, yet hyperexcited about her mission, Lin shut the computer down. Too wound up to sleep, she went outside.

The night air was cool against her skin. She was glad for the warmth of her sweatshirt. She walked the length of the porch, glad that she'd spent the extra money. An extension of her home.

When she'd first imagined this house, she'd told the architects her dream and it had materialized. Her favorite area was the porch, which wrapped around the entire perimeter of the house. Lin spent as much time there as she did inside, weather permitting. She'd made the place homey and comfortable, with outdoor furniture with plump cushions, lots of colorful throw pillows. There were side tables with plants placed next to rocking chairs, and benches. Books and reading lamps sat next to her favorite chair for those wet days, when she loved nothing more than to hear the sound of rain pelting against the metal roof while reading one of her cherished mystery novels, an addiction she no longer tried to hide.

Lin had created her dream home. It hadn't been easy, but it was hers, lock, stock, and barrel. No mortgage, no liens. She'd spent many sleepless nights wondering how she could afford such a costly investment, but she had saved and invested wisely throughout the years, and was able to swing the cost easily. Now that her dreams had come to fruition, she was about to jeopardize everything she'd worked for just to get even.

Relaxing in the old maple rocker she'd restored last summer, she tucked her feet beneath her. The old chair creaked as she teetered back and forth, its sound comforting, reassuring. Frogs, crickets, and the occasional nightingale enlivened the darkness. Their nighttime harmony complemented her mood, secretive and cunning. Lin sipped her cold coffee as she plotted. There were kinks in her plans, but between her and Jason, they'd work through them.

Hating to lie to her best friend, she justified doing so by telling herself it was for Sally's benefit. She'd seen the look on her face on Friday, when Lin told her any future screwing around with Nick was over. The relief was Lin's deciding factor. She cared about Sally too much to ask her to step up to the plate once again. Sally was right when she said it would take a life-or-death experience to even the score. Somehow, Lin was going to make that happen.

Lin had her work cut out for her. Knowing she'd need a clear head, she sat a while longer, rocking to the night sounds, before she finally got up and went inside to prepare for bed. Tomorrow would be here soon enough. Actually, tomorrow was already there. The sun just hadn't risen.

"I truly don't think you're up for this," Chelsea said as she climbed into the seat next to her husband. "You look awful, Nick, and I'm being kind when I say that."

"It's so nice to know that I can always count on you to cheer me up, I'll give you that," Nick snapped.

"You know what I mean. You're as pale as a ghost, and you've lost so much weight, you look like a Holocaust victim. Someone has to tell you the truth," Chelsea declared. "You really should stay home. Until you . . . uh . . . until you recover."

"I told you I was celebrating. After all I've been through, I deserve this night out. It's a reward to myself. If you'd like Herbert to take you home, that can be arranged."

"I didn't say I wanted to go home. You're always trying to put words in my mouth. Of course I want to go with you to . . . to celebrate. I just think you look like . . . death warmed over." Chelsea smiled, knowing she was raining on Nick's parade. The bastard deserved it.

"I don't know if I should slap you or forgive you your ignorance," Nick commented dryly. Maybe bringing her along wasn't such a good idea.

"I don't think you want a repeat of the *Times* or the *Post*. Or maybe you do? Though I'm sure you wouldn't get a retraction the second time around." Chelsea observed her husband's facial expression. "I guess the *Times* or the *Post* didn't have much of a choice, since the very paper their crap is printed on was aboard one of your cargo ships. Lady Luck certainly watches over you, Nick. I have to give you that."

"Shut up, Chelsea, or I'll have Herbert take you home. This is supposed to be a celebration. For me. I know you're not happy with the news, but I am. The least you can do is pretend you're pleased."

"I didn't say I wasn't happy for you, Nick. You look sick. For the past six weeks you've been trying to convince everyone you're not sick. If they see you now, they'll know you've been lying to them. It's that simple. Make what you want out of it." She turned sullen and glared out the window.

Chelsea had a point, but no way in hell would he agree with her. "They can think what they want to think. They always do. When I live to be in my eighties like my father, I'll have the last laugh."

"Of course, you're a Pemberton. How could I forget?"

Nick pushed the button opening the privacy window that separated the front and back of the Lincoln. "Herbert, please turn around. Mrs. Pemberton would like to go home."

"I did not say that, Nicholas," Chelsea retorted.

Herbert stopped for a traffic light. "Sir?"

Nick watched his wife. "Well? It's your decision. I'm sick of listening to your stupidity."

"Herbert, take us to the club," Chelsea demanded.

The old man directed his gaze to Nick for confirmation. He nodded and closed the window.

Half an hour later the couple were ensconced at their private table at Manhattan's ritzy Supper Club. Nick paid an enormous amount of money for the exclusivity. Privileged people with money only had to name their price. Nick's father had confessed this to him once, when he was only seven years old. At least his father had been right about that. He could buy anything.

Nick smiled at the thought. Even his stupid wife. All he'd had to do to regain her loyalty, not that he needed it, was to reinstate her lines of credit and credit cards. It wouldn't look good if one of Manhattan's wealthiest women didn't have the proper funding. A few weeks' torture had been enough for both of them.

The waiter took their orders, then quickly disappeared. The staff was as discreet as the nonexistent prices on the menu. Chelsea ordered rare prime rib. Her aversion to red meat during the early days of her pregnancy had ceased soon after the night she had snared Nick. Two drinks later, the waiter returned with their food. Nick's stomach clenched when he saw the red blood dripping from the prime rib on Chelsea's plate. He had ordered a bowl of lobster bisque but hadn't been able to bring himself to try it. The smell of seafood suddenly sickened him.

He stared at Chelsea as she forked a bite of the nearly raw meat. He wasn't sure he could contain himself. Quickly excusing himself, he headed to the men's room, where he emptied what remained in his stomach. *Son of a bitch! I should've stayed home. Deep breaths and mind over matter,* he told himself.

As he made his way back to the table, he spied Albert Fine, senior vice president of Chase Manhattan Bank. Nick squared his shoulders and plastered a smile on his face.

"Albert, I haven't seen you around Wall Street lately. What gives?" Nick cajoled the moneyed man.

Albert Fine was tall and thin. His skin matched the color of Nick's, though Nick knew his unnatural pallor wasn't from an illness. The man spent so much of his time making billions, he probably hadn't seen sunlight in years. Thinning gray hair barely covered the brown and purple spots that dotted his head.

"Nick, old boy. Where have you been? Word's out that you'd died and gone straight to hell." Albert smiled as he said this, but Nick saw the question in his gaze as he scrutinized him.

"Then you can put that rumor to rest. I've had . . . *E.coli.* I got hold of some tainted meat a couple of months back. It's taken its toll on me."

"I'll say. You sure that's all?" Albert questioned. "Where on earth did you come across tainted meat? I'll make sure to avoid it." He saw right through Nick's lie.

"Actually, Nora prepared it at home. Nasty stuff."

"It's good to see you're out and about. Give me a call. I know a fellow who could use your services." Albert extended his hand once again.

"I'll do that. Good to see you."

Nick hoped seeing Albert would quash the rumors that he was dying. Dying simply was not good for business.

He returned to the table, where Chelsea was continuing to eat as though she were starving.

Fork and knife in each hand, she stopped in midair. "Why are you looking at me like that?"

He sighed. "Let's go home. I've had enough."

"I haven't finished eating, and I was looking forward to the strawberry pie! This was your idea, remember?"

"Yes, I do remember. I'm leaving now, so either you come with me, or you'll be calling a taxi." Nick called Herbert on his cell phone, telling him they'd be waiting outside in five minutes.

Not wanting to lower herself and ride in a New York taxi, Chelsea took one last bite before racing to the elevator. The doors were closing when she stuck her foot between them. "Wait!" she shrieked.

Nick was grateful no one else was in the elevator with them. When they were alone, Chelsea had the class of a backstreet hooker.

They took the elevator down to the private foyer without speaking. Nick hadn't seen any of the crew that usually frequented the Supper Club. It'd been a pointless evening, except for running into Albert, and Nick had a feeling the banker would delight in spreading even more rumors about him. His earlier optimism felt forced. Hell, what did he know? The goddamned doctor could've lied to him. He might not live to see another day. Fear crawled up his spine like a serpent. Nick did not want to die. He had too much to live for.

Herbert was waiting at the curb when they stepped outside. The October air was sharp, cutting through his thin jacket like a switch-blade. He shivered. "I'm sorry, Chelsea. This evening was a mistake. I don't feel . . . never mind." He'd almost shown her his weakness, his fear of dying. Clearing his mind of negative thoughts, he smiled at his wife. "I appreciate the effort you made this evening. I know I haven't been the easiest person to live with since I was diagnosed with this damned disease. I just want you to know that I . . ." He choked up. "I appreciate your sticking around." God, he *was* sick.

Herbert opened the door, and Chelsea climbed inside. She watched Nick as he made his way around the car. She was shocked at his display of emotion. Maybe there was more to the disease than she'd been told. Though she'd never heard of cancer causing a major personality change, at least in a positive way, maybe there was something Nick wasn't telling her. God, she could only hope he was even sicker than he thought. She wanted him to die. Soon. She had plans. Big plans. But she could and would play the nice wife as long as it suited her to do so and not one minute longer.

"Of course I'll stick around," Chelsea lied with a straight face. "I know we're not the most compatible couple, but, Nick, I would never turn my back on you." She almost believed her own words. She was such an expert at playing games. And to think she'd learned it all at Nick's knee.

"Thanks. I think."

He smiled at her as though she were a favorite pet. Chelsea waited for him to fluff her between the ears. *It* didn't happen.

The short drive home was silent. It was easier to think about killing Nick when he was an ass. His kindness, however, had melted a bit of the ice around her hard heart.

No, Chelsea decided, she much preferred his arrogance.

On Thursday morning Lin crossed her fingers and placed them behind her back, the way she had as a child when she was afraid of getting caught doing something she had no business doing, which wasn't often — given her father's severe disciplinary methods.

Her heart ached with what she had to do, but it had to be done. When it was over, she'd tell Sally the truth. Until then, she'd live with her guilt.

She dialed her best friend's number.

"I've had only one cup of coffee, so this better be good," Sally said when she picked up the phone. Never a hello.

"Caller ID again?" Lin teased.

"You found me out. So what's up?"

Here goes. The mother of all lies. "I . . . The doctors from the nursing home just called." Sweat dotted her upper lip. If Sally saw her, she'd know she was lying. "Apparently, my father has suffered a major heart attack. I need to go to Atlanta." Lin paused, waiting for Sally to call her a liar. When she didn't, Lin breathed a sigh of relief. So far, so good.

"Okay. So when do we leave?" Sally asked.

Dear Sally. Lin hoped her actions didn't completely damage her friendship. She would never intentionally hurt Sally's feelings. "I need to go by myself. This . . . I need to reconcile with him before he dies.

It's . . . just something I feel I need to do."

"If you're sure, then go. I'll take care of the diner."

Lin closed her eyes. "Thank you. I knew I could count on you. I don't know how long I'll be. Maybe a few days. I'm not sure yet. I'll call you when I can. I remember the last time I visited. Something about cell phones being a no-no." Add that to her ever-lengthening list of lies.

"Just do what you need to do. What about Will?"

"I'm going to call him as soon as I hang up. It's not like he ever knew my father. I probably shouldn't even trouble him with this. So let's not tell him anything yet. I'll just tell him I'm making the trip to visit." More lies.

"You know best. So when do you leave?" Sally asked.

"Soon. Today."

"Call me when you get there so I'll know you made it safely, okay?"

"Thanks, Sally. I will."

Lin hung up the phone. She'd risen before dawn to prepare for her trip. She'd packed, put a hold on her mail via e-mail.

With nothing left to do, she walked through the house one last time, made sure the windows and doors were locked. She didn't activate the alarm, knowing Sally would be in and out. There wasn't a lot of crime in Dalton, anyway.

With her bags already in the car, Lin grabbed the morning paper from the front lawn, sticking it inside her messenger bag. She never traveled without her letters to Nick; it was sort of sick, but it was something she had to do. With nothing left to keep her, she pulled her bright red Porsche out of the drive to head south on I-75.

God willing, her plan would be a success, and she could return to Dalton to resume her life as though nothing had happened. To ease her guilt somewhat, Lin decided that a quick stop at the nursing home was in order. She hadn't seen her father in a very long time. Maybe a visit would reinforce what she was about to do to Nick. If not for her father's mean and evil ways, her life might have turned out differently. Her mother might still be alive, too. She couldn't forget that.

Taking the I-285 exit to Northland Drive, she steered the Porsche into the right lane and made a sharp left turn to the private road leading to the Main House, the upscale facility where her father resided. Lin dreaded going in. Because her visits were so infrequent, the staff always made her feel like a lowlife, an uncaring daughter. If they only knew. At times Lin wondered if her father truly had Alzheimer's. His ability to recall certain events seemed very selective to her.

As a child, she used to pray for his death while kneeling on those cold, hard floors. However, she'd come to think of death as the easy way out for him. She wanted him to suffer on earth as she had. As her mother had. After her mother's death, Lin had heard talk that her father had collected a large sum of money from an insurance policy, though she'd never seen any evidence of it. Of course, she wasn't living at home by then, either. If he had received a large amount of money, he must have hidden it well. Each year she paid an enormous fee for his care. Sometimes Lin wanted to take Sally's advice and let him live his remaining years in squalor, but her conscience didn't allow it. A conscience could be a terrible thing. She just might toss hers into the wind. Soon.

Lin found a parking spot close to the entrance. She wanted to get in and out as quickly and painlessly as possible, though she had her doubts that the latter would be possible.

Upon entering the reception area, one

would think she had entered a grand hotel. Original artwork from Monet to Georgia O'Keeffe adorned the walls. Comfortable chairs and sofas were placed in a semicircle, facing a large window overlooking a perfectly manicured lawn and gardens.

At the reception desk, Lin pushed the CALL button as instructed. Before she could blink an eye, a woman dressed in a dove gray sweater and matching skirt appeared. Lin didn't recognize her. Bony to the point of emaciation, thin brown hair coiled on top of her head, she couldn't disguise her signs of hair loss.

"Yes?" the woman asked in a pleasant voice.

"I'm here to see Clarence Townsend."

The woman nodded. "Of course. I'll need to see your identification. I just started last week, though I'm sure I'll remember your next visit." She smiled.

Probably won't be one, Lin thought. It was her hope this would be her last. She removed her driver's license from her wallet and handed it to the woman.

"Lin Townsend. You must be Mr. Townsend's daughter. I'll walk you to his room."

"Thanks." She walked behind the woman to her father's room, noting that it was a different one from the last time she had been there. Lin followed her down a long hallway, where the resident rooms were located.

"Here we are, room five-eighty-four," the woman said cheerfully. "Your father had his breakfast a while ago. I'm sure he's ready for company. I'll leave you to your visit." She quietly left Lin standing at the door.

Did she knock or just walk in? Confronted with the same dilemma on each of her infrequent visits, Lin always tapped on the door before entering. Not today. She twisted the knob and shoved the door inward with such force, it slammed against the wall.

"What do you want?" her father shouted at her from his La-Z-Boy. "I didn't invite you here. Go away."

Remaining in the doorway, Lin stared at her father. Today must be one of his good days, since he appeared to recognize her. At seventy, her father remained as heavily muscled as he was in his younger days. He wore his thick white hair slicked back from his forehead. His ice blue eyes glared at her. He got out of his chair and came toward her. Lin remained in the doorway.

"I asked you what you want. You deaf, girly?"

Lin wanted to slap him the way he'd slapped her so many times. Instead, she

251

smiled, because she knew it incensed him more than her anger ever could. He might think he could still intimidate her, but Lin knew those days were long gone. She took a step forward, coming as close to him as she could without touching him.

"My hearing is quite good, thanks. Though it's a miracle I never had any permanent damage since you felt it your God-given duty to slap me whenever it suited you." Lin's pulse quickened. She'd wanted to say that to the old bastard for years. It felt really good saying it.

Her father took a wobbly step toward her, his meaty hands doubled into fists. He waved them around. "And I'll do it again! You . . . you slut! Get out of here before the Lord turns you into a pillar of salt! Go now!"

Lin stood her ground. Her father was certainly his old self. For once she didn't care who heard her, didn't care how disrespectful she was. He didn't deserve her respect.

Instead of turning around and leaving as she'd normally do — anything to avoid a confrontation — Lin stared at her father. Defiantly, chin up, daring him to hit her. "That's what real men do, isn't it? They beat their daughters because that's what makes them strong and powerful. Oh, and godlike. How could I forget that? You know what, *Dad?* You make me sick!"

He stumbled, then grabbed the La-Z-Boy for support. "May you rot in hell! You are not the flesh of my flesh, girly! You come in here all high and mighty. Who do you think you are? Does 'honor thy father' mean anything to you?" he bellowed, sending spittle flying from his dark red lips. "Go now! Get thee behind me!" He gestured wildly, his hands flying around, as though battling a swarm of killer bees.

Remaining stock-still, Lin stared at him. "You're really warped, you know that? I pray that you rot in hell. As a matter of fact, I know you're going to hell." She cast a wicked smile at him. "I'm finished with you." Lin recalled all the beatings, the days and nights of forced prayer, the insults. Yes, she was finished. "Before I leave, I'm going to make a detour to the administration office. I'm going to do something I should have done a long, long time ago." Lin eyed her father, searching for some small sign that he regretted what he'd done to her. She saw nothing. "You have about a year left here. If I were you, I'd start praying to that cruel God of yours, because you're going to need someone other than me to foot the bill for this" — Lin glanced around at her father's luxurious quarters — "swanky establishment. On that note, let me say good-bye. I wish I could say it's been nice, but you know as well as I do that it hasn't."

He lurched toward her, hands tightly fisted. She stepped out of the room, refusing to acknowledge his anger. She was finished. Enough was enough. As she hurried toward the administration office, Lin smiled, thinking Sally would be very proud of her at that moment.

Three and a half hours later Lin was at a small private airport just south of Atlanta, where she boarded a private jet bound for New York. Jason had suggested traveling this way in case someone tried to track down her movements. It cost a small fortune. Lin grinned, thinking her dear friend would definitely approve of her lavish spending.

When the Gulfstream landed, Lin peered out the window and spied Jason waiting on the tarmac of the private airstrip. She grabbed her luggage from the overhead bin. When the plane came to a complete stop and the door opened, Lin practically ran down the short flight of steps.

Jason was all smiles as he greeted her. "I'm glad you took my suggestion." He nodded toward the Gulfstream.

"I didn't want to take any chances," Lin said.

"Smart woman. Come on."

Lin rolled her eyes upward. She didn't believe him for a minute.

Once they were inside Jason's SUV, he spoke about their upcoming plans. "We're going to my office. I've got some information I'd like to share with you."

Lin was nervous about visiting the Empire State Building. She told Jason.

"No need to worry. The big man hasn't been in his office lately. Something is going on with him. I'm working on finding out what it is."

"You don't think he suspects anything, do you?" Lin asked, suddenly afraid of what she'd set out to do. Getting caught would ruin everything.

Jason shook his head, his gold hoops bouncing against his neck. "What's to suspect? Trust me, he hasn't a clue. Besides, he's too full of himself and Pemberton Transport." Nick Pemberton was an extremely intelligent businessman who had some of the best contacts in the business. Jason knew that firsthand but didn't want to scare Lin off. He wanted her to succeed. Someone needed to bring the bastard down a notch.

"I hope you're right," Lin said.

"You have to trust me."

"I wouldn't be here if I didn't." Lin would, but she wasn't going to elaborate. Not yet. When the time was right, she'd know. Until then, she'd keep some things under her hat.

"Good."

After an hour of traffic, horns, and people screaming out their car windows, they arrived safely. Lin let out a relieved sigh.

Jason gave his keys to a young Spanish guy in the parking garage. "Thanks, Julio. Later."

Lin chewed her lip, a sure sign of nerves. She remembered how she used to do it as a kid when she knew her father was going to punish her for some so-called crime against the Lord. She hadn't resorted to such childish behavior in years.

From out of nowhere Lin had a flashback of the events leading up to the day she finally realized she was pregnant with Will.

Lin rolled over in bed. It was already eight fifteen! She never slept this late. She ducked beneath the covers, wishing she could stay in bed, where she could savor the memory of Atlanta. Since the party two months ago she hadn't been herself, couldn't forget the sin she'd committed, couldn't deny how much she'd enjoyed committing it with the handsome man she'd given herself to. Her father would kill her if he found out that the week she'd spent in Atlanta under the guise of a mathematical competition was spent partying with a group of Jolene's college friends who attended Emory University. God! Her soul would burn in the fires of hell.

She'd done nothing but sleep and wait by the phone for weeks. She'd spent endless hours remembering her weeklong affair with Nicholas. It'd been the best week of her life, or it had until recently.

But all she wanted to do was lie in bed. Her energy level was a big zero. When her father woke her each morning for breakfast, the mere thought of food gagged her. Lin knew she was wasting time — she should be studying, or at least helping her mother with the household chores — but it was all she could do to get dressed. She hadn't even bothered washing her hair in over a week. The greasy strands lay across her cheek. It was disgusting; she was so ashamed of herself. Knowing she needed to get back on her normal routine, she forced herself to get out of bed and into the shower. Ten minutes later she felt revived. Clean hair. Shaved legs, teeth brushed and flossed. She felt human for the first time in days. She chose a pair of khaki slacks and a navy Hang Ten T-shirt. She went downstairs in search of food, thinking of Nicholas.

She vowed to herself that she was not going to pine away waiting for him to call. He'd said he would. He didn't. Should be the end of the story, but Lin knew as well as she knew what a logarithm was that she'd fallen head over heels, knee deep, "no turning back" in love with Nicholas Pemberton. Obviously, her feelings weren't reciprocated, or he would've called. It was time to get on with her life. No, she would forget that glorious week and move on. She had to because it was becoming more obvious with each passing hour that he had moved on with his.

"It's about time you got up. Go help your mother in the kitchen," her father said. "I was about to come and wake you."

Lin forced herself to act as cheerful as her normal self, whatever that was. "I'm sorry. I was reading the scripture until the wee hours."

"Oh?" Her father seemed pleased.

"Yes, I studied the book of Genesis."

"And you found that . . . What? Appropriate? There are other books of the Bible I would prefer you to study. What have you been doing in that room of yours? And you'd better tell me the truth."

She hated to lie to her father, especially

when it came to religion, but he gave her no choice. "I am telling you the truth! I was reading about Sodom and Gomorrah." In her mind she was Lot's wife, and her father was about to cast her out into a sea of demons.

"I don't believe a word you say! Go have your breakfast. Then help your mother clean up. When you're finished, I want you in the front room. We're going to study the book of Genesis today. In fact, since you enjoy reading that book so much, I'm going to have you memorize it. Now, go on. Get out of my sight!"

Evidence of her mother's baking lingered in the kitchen. Measuring cups and mixing bowls dried in the dish drainer. Her mother never left a thing out of place. Lin was still getting used to the new Harvard gold appliances and the fact that they had a dishwasher, which her mother had yet to use. She said she was afraid the electric bill would be outrageous. She said it was wasteful to have such things.

Wasteful not to use them, Lin thought, but she wouldn't say that to her mother.

She took a muffin from the basket warming on the stove and slathered it with butter and jelly. She poured herself a glass of orange juice. After two small bites of the muffin, she tossed it into the sink before racing to the bathroom.

Falling to her knees, she emptied what little

contents were in her stomach into the toilet, retching until she finally collapsed on the tile floor, where she lay, gasping for air. She couldn't remember being so sick. Using the wall for support, she eased herself upright. Splashing cold water on her face, she spied her reflection in the mirror. Purple moons below her eyes highlighted the unusual silver of her eyes. She looked like a cancer victim. Cupping her hands under the water, she splashed her face again, then rinsed her mouth. She used her mother's hairbrush to smooth her hair. Using her finger, she rubbed a dab of Pepsodent across her teeth.

Barely mobile, she returned to the living room for her Bible lesson. Her father stood at his homemade pulpit. She dreaded what she had to do.

"What's the matter with you? Have you been drinking? I heard you throwing up. Liquor is the devil's drink, young lady! What is it going to take to teach you how to act like a God-fearing young lady?"

Lin cringed, knowing what was coming next.

"You know what it takes, don't you, girl?"

Lin nodded.

"Answer me!" her father shouted from his pulpit.

Lin got down on her knees and began to pray. Prayed that he'd drop dead from a massive heart attack.

"I didn't hear you!" her father shouted in his holier-than-thou voice.

"Prayer, father. It takes prayer." Unable to control herself, Lin vomited on the floor.

"You drunkard! I'll show you! You'll never allow evil to pass through your lips again!"

Her father took a leather strap that he kept hidden beneath his pulpit. His weapon against the devil himself, he called it.

Lin ducked her shoulders, preparing for what was to come. The first lash stung, brought tears to her eyes; the second forced her to grit her teeth together; with the third, she almost chewed her lip off. After that, it was simply a matter of her father tiring out. Ten minutes later she woke up, lying in a puddle of urine and vomit.

"See what you've done!" Her father grabbed her by the hair on the back of her head and slammed her face into the putrid mess. "You will clean this up. Then I want you back on your knees! You understand, girl?"

Lin nodded. Yes, she understood. As though a bright light flashed before her, Lin knew her sickness wasn't from drinking or the muffin she'd just consumed.

She was pregnant, destined for the fires of hell.

"Are you all right?" Jason asked.

Lin had to shake her head from side to side to rid herself of the memory. "I'm fine. Just got caught up in a memory from the past."

Somehow Lin had merged memories of her father and Nick. Each man was treacherous in his own way. Her father was a Bible-thumping hypocrite; Nick, a destroyer of dreams. Both men deserved more than she could call down upon them. She'd just evened the score where her father was concerned. Nicholas Pemberton was next.

Jason regarded her as they made their way to the bank of elevators. "You're sure?"

"I'm okay." And she was. "Actually, I'm going to be just fine," she added.

Revenge was going to be very, *very* sweet.

■ ■ ■ ■

Part Two

■ ■ ■ ■

CHAPTER 11

Jason Vinery's office was completely the opposite of the man himself. Posh and sophisticated, it oozed good taste. JV Investigations took up approximately an eighth of the twenty-fifth floor of the Empire State Building. Jason's decorator had created the illusion of a much bigger area, with lots of open spaces and mirrors, nothing cluttered. Cream-colored chairs had been arranged throughout the reception area to create a cozy, comfortable atmosphere. Lin recognized the Moorcroft vintage pottery set on a shelf behind a sleek desk. Lush green plants had been placed in corners and on tabletops. The effect was refreshing.

"You like?" Jason asked.

Smiling, Lin nodded. "It's not what I expected."

Jason led her to a private room at the end of the short hallway. "That's what they all say," he replied in a teasing tone.

Lin glanced around the room. Small, but open and airy. "I like it." A small walnut desk faced two Queen Anne chairs, which had been placed on each side of the room's only window. *Sparse,* she thought. *Nothing to distract anyone from the job at hand.*

Jason was full of surprises, she'd give him that.

"Have a seat." He gestured to the chairs.

Lin did as instructed. Nerves made her fidgety. If Nick only knew what was about to befall him. Shuddering just to think about it, she composed herself while waiting for Jason to explain their next move.

He sat down in the chair next to her. From a side table he took a folder, opened it, flipped through until he located what he'd been searching for. "What I'm about to share with you isn't public knowledge. Old man Pemberton wielded some major power in his day. He was able to keep this information out of the press. I'm not even sure if Nicholas knows the complete story. He could, but as I said, I don't know. If he does, it won't affect what you're planning." Jason continued to flip through the file, stopping to remove a black-and-white photograph. He held it out to her. "This is Naomi Pemberton before she became ill."

Lin looked at the picture. Will's grandmother. She was beautiful. Dark, wavy hair cascaded down her shoulders. Perfectly arched brows topped almond-shaped eyes. Her mouth was full, almost too full. Naomi Pemberton reminded Lin of Angelina Jolie, the actress well known for her voluptuous lips. Lin thought Naomi's eyes appeared vacant, devoid of any emotion. Empty, like two dark holes. Lin gave the photo back to Jason. "She was very striking. A shame she died so young."

"According to the information I have, Nick would've been around three or four when she died."

"It must have been hard for him growing up without a mother. I can't imagine my . . . It's very tragic, I would think." She'd almost slipped but caught herself. As far as she knew, Jason was still unaware of Will's existence. She wanted to keep it that way for as long as possible.

"He was raised by several housekeepers and a few nannies. None of them stayed very long. I made a few phone calls. Three of these housekeepers and one of the nannies are still alive. They're all in the New York area. According to the women I spoke with, Nick Sr. was a son of a bitch to work for. Each had a similar story. Long hours, barely minimum wage. Apparently, the old man forced them to have sex with him on a regular basis. He told them it was part of their duties; hence the turnover in staff."

Lin's first thought was, *Like father, like son.* But in all fairness to Nick, he hadn't forced himself on her. She'd been more than willing to give herself to him. *Stupid, stupid, stupid,* she thought, but then there was Will. The only regret she had was that the man who'd fathered him had never bothered to even acknowledge his existence. Lin found it hard to comprehend that he'd never once read her letters, never had the least bit of curiosity as to why she continued to write to him all those years. But then again, all she knew was that they had come back to her marked, RETURN TO SENDER.

Lin wasn't sure where the PI was going. "What does this have to do with Nick now?"

Jason held up a tattooed arm. "I'm getting there. Remember, this is all about reputation."

She nodded. "Go on."

"None of the women that I spoke with ever reported Nick Sr.'s behavior to the authorities. One of the women" — he shuffled through the papers — "a Maria Torres, worked for the Pemberton family while Naomi was still alive. Apparently, the employees weren't the only ones who were victims of his abuse. Maria said she'd observed Mr. Pemberton hitting Naomi on more than one occasion."

Lin's stomach churned at the thought. What if Will were to duplicate his grandfather's abusive behavior? My God, the Pembertons were no better than her own father!

"When Nick Jr. was two or three — Maria wasn't sure of his age at the time — Naomi was pregnant with their second child." Jason paused, allowing her to absorb the information. "Mr. Pemberton didn't want another child. He had his heir. Another child would complicate his life, or so Maria said."

Curious, Lin interrupted. "What happened to the child?"

"This is where it gets nasty. Naomi delivered a daughter, but she was stillborn."

Lin drew in a deep breath. "That's heartbreaking." She could only imagine the loss Naomi had felt.

"Medically, there was no explanation for why Naomi delivered a stillborn little girl. She went to the doctor. She wasn't a drinker. Didn't smoke. All the things you're supposed to do to deliver a healthy, normal child, she did. However, she never reported the beatings she received from her husband.

I would guess she was too frightened or too ashamed. Probably both. Maria said when she returned from the hospital, Naomi was never the same. She coddled Nick Jr. more than ever, wouldn't let him out of her sight. Maria said when Mr. Pemberton was home, she would take her son and lock herself and Nick in her room.

"This behavior went on for months. Nick Sr. decided enough was enough and put his foot down. He removed Nicholas from his mother's room. Maria said within days of the child's being taken away, Nick Sr. had his wife committed to an upscale institution in Vermont."

"How terrible for Nick. My God, his father was a monster!" Lin exclaimed. What kind of father did that to his own child? Sadly, she knew from firsthand experience. An evil son of a bitch without feelings, one like her father. She was convinced more than ever that she'd made the right decision by refusing any further financial responsibility for her father and his care.

"It gets worse. Little more than a month later, a male nurse found Naomi dead in her bed. According to the medical examiner's report, she died of a drug overdose."

"I don't see how that's possible if she was in a hospital. Where did she get the drugs?"

"There were others asking the same question. The official report states Naomi was given Thorazine twice a day. It's assumed she stockpiled the drugs. Then, when she felt she had enough to do the job, she did so, causing her own death."

Lin shook her head. "That doesn't sound like something a woman who goes to such great lengths to protect her son would do. Suicide doesn't fit the person this Maria claims to have known."

"I agree. Maria hinted that it was possible Naomi didn't take her own life."

"Why? Does she have proof?" The story was becoming more and more bizarre. Lin didn't understand how the past events related to her current situation.

"If she does, she isn't telling me. At this point in the conversation, she clammed up, said she'd already said more than she should have."

Frustrated, Lin twisted her hands. "Then what was the point in telling you anything? I don't get it."

"The point is, there's a history of domestic violence in the Pemberton family. If this information is available to the public, it will reinforce the claims printed in the *Post* and the *Times*. Remember, it's all about the reputation."

"The powerful and mighty Nicholas Pemberton could get another retraction."

"Maybe. But we don't know that for sure. And even if he did, the damage is done. Not only is Nick Sr. an abuser, but he's passed the admirable trait on to his son. Fortunately, Nick Jr. never had a son. In all likelihood, he would have continued the Pemberton cycle of abuse."

Lin gasped. In her wildest dreams she could never imagine Will as an abuser. "I see." She didn't, but there was nothing she could say without revealing her secret. Questions lingered, but she was afraid to ask them, fearing Jason would suspect she knew more than she was telling.

"I'll send the medical examiner's report to my source at the paper. I've located some Pemberton family photographs to accompany the report. If my plan goes as expected, Nick's reputation will go right down the tubes. I don't want to do anything else just yet. I want to wait and see what kind of reaction we get."

"Who will give you that information? It's not like you have a plant, or whatever they call them, in the Pemberton office, or do you?"

Jason winked at her. "Don't be so sure of that."

"What's that supposed to mean? You can't just . . . say something like that and not back it up, explain it, whatever you want to call it!" Lin challenged.

"I can, and I did. Listen, the less you know about the inner workings of this investigation, the better off you are. As I said, you'll have to trust me, Lin. I've been doing this for a while. I know what I'm doing."

"I'm sure you do, but remember I'm the one who hired you. If you're doing something . . . *underhanded,* I think I should know. You know, just in case." The words were barely out of Lin's mouth when she realized what she'd said. "I meant . . . Oh, who knows what I meant? I'm digging a big hole for myself here, and it doesn't look like you're going to help me dig my way out." She shook her head, a sardonic grin lifting the corners of her mouth.

"Private investigation is oftentimes a sneaky and, yes, underhanded business but legal. I'm not breaking the law, Lin. You'll have to take my word on that. Besides, I've never asked exactly *why* you want to ruin Nicholas" — Jason extended his arms, palms facing forward — "and I don't need or want to know now. It's your business. I guess what I'm trying to say is, let me do my job. If and when the need arises and you need to worry, I'll let you know in plenty of time," he said.

Lin felt like a schoolgirl who'd been chastised by the principal. "I got it. I apologize. In my own defense I guess the only excuse I have is that I'm new to the game."

"Hey, no big deal. Stuff happens. You don't understand, you ask me, and I'll explain, or at least as much as I consider necessary. I do have my sources to protect." Jason flashed a smile so big and bright, Lin couldn't help but laugh.

"Fair enough. What about Naomi's death? If it wasn't accidental, shouldn't there have been an investigation? I can't imagine sweeping something like that under the rug. If you know something about that, then it's your duty to inform the authorities so justice can be served. Killing someone is never an option and should not go unpunished." Lin felt such outrage, she was sputtering.

"I'm checking into that, too. I'm working on locating Naomi's former doctor. Maybe he'll be able to fill in some of the blanks. Naomi had two private nurses attending her while she was at the hospital. I'm trying to locate them also. If we're lucky, they'll talk, unless someone else got to them first. If they won't talk, I'll give this information to the police, and they can take it from there. There is no statute of limitations on murder."

It sounded so cut and dried to her. Was it possible that Will's grandfather had had his wife murdered? Could his beatings have caused their child to be stillborn? Lin needed answers. She couldn't ask Jason to find them unless she was willing to share her true story. And if she did, she would put Will at risk for the public to speculate that he, too, could become an abuser. Even worse, her life's lie would be uncovered. She had to keep her goal in mind. She was there to ruin Nick Pemberton's life big-time, then return to Dalton and resume a quiet, normal life, knowing she'd gotten the revenge she longed for.

Lin stood up, brushing imaginary lint from her jeans. "So now we wait?"

Jason stood up next to her. Placing his arm at the small of her back, he led her out to the small hallway and back to the reception area. Mabel Dee sat at the desk.

"Mabel, this is Lin. She's a new client. Lin, this is Mabel Dee, secretary extraordinaire."

Lin held her hand out to the impeccably

dressed woman, surprised Jason employed a woman her age. With steel gray hair in a youthful pageboy, a round face with a beautiful peaches-and-cream complexion, a sharp black suit with a frilly turquoise blouse, the woman had to be in her seventies, at least.

"Pleased to meet you, Lin. If there is anything you need that cartoon man can't help you with, let me know." Mabel Dee winked at her employer.

Raising her brow, Lin looked at Jason. "Cartoon man?"

"It's Mabel's pet name. Ignore it."

"Of course," Lin replied, smiling at Mabel.

Jason turned to Lin. "For the next couple of days it's a waiting game. Do some shopping. Take in the sights while you can. As soon as I know anything, either Mabel or I will call you. Let's get a taxi to take Ms. Townsend home. Call me if you need anything, okay?"

"I will. Thank you, Jason. I . . . just thanks." Lin couldn't put into words what she really wanted to say, but maybe someday she would be able to. This man was the perfect instrument to use to exact her revenge. Lin figured Jason's feelings about Nick were a bonus. All she could do was wait. She wasn't ready to hit the streets on her own. Maybe another day.

The Monday following the disastrous dinner at Nick's club, Chelsea decided that she needed to speak with Nick's doctor. She was his wife; she needed to know exactly how sick Nick really was. Something told her that her husband wasn't telling her the complete truth. She found Evan Reeves's number on Nick's prescription bottle. She wasn't worried about Nick catching her on the phone, because last night, while he was taking a shower, she'd taken his bottle of Ambien and crushed three ten-milligram capsules in a cup of hot tea. She'd liberally poured on the honey and lemon to mask the taste, but Nick had been in such high spirits after a fairly good day that he hadn't questioned her bringing him the hot drink.

She dialed the number from the prescription bottle. "I need to speak with Dr. Reeves. Yes? Well, no, I'm not a patient. My husband is. Nicholas Pemberton. Yes. Yes, I'll hold." Chelsea peered down the hall just to make sure there was no sign of Nick. With Nick, one could never be too sure, drugged or not. The man was like Arnold Schwarzenegger's character in *The Terminator.* With every attempt on his life, he came back better and stronger than ever.

"Dr. Reeves, hello. Yes, this is she. No, no, Nick is fine. I just had a few questions. You see Nick doesn't tell me anything about his illness. I know he has leukemia, but that's about it. I want to help him, but I can't if I'm not armed with information. I guess what I really want to know is exactly how sick my husband is." Chelsea crossed her fingers, praying the good doctor was about to offer her his sympathies.

"Actually, Nick is doing quite well. When we tested his blood and did another bone-marrow examination last week, his blood tests were fairly normal, so I gave him a four-week reprieve from the chemo. I think he needs to gain some weight, get his strength back. While he certainly isn't out of the woods, he's making remarkable progress."

Chelsea felt like crying. That was not what she wanted to hear. "So, then, he's not dying?" She faked a crying noise.

"I didn't say that, Mrs. Pemberton. The chemotherapy is doing what it's supposed to do. Nick's body can stand the four-week break. In no way is he out of the woods. His type of leukemia moves quickly and can be deadly. Let's just look at this as a respite for your husband. Chemo is very hard on the body."

He could die? Chelsea wanted to jump up and down like a child, but refrained. "Are there symptoms I should look for? Something to indicate he's getting sicker?" She knew she sounded like an idiot, but just then she didn't care, as it was to her advantage to play stupid. She was sure she could get more information out of the good Dr. Reeves by acting naive. And Nick thought it took a college degree to make one smart. *If only.*

"He'll tire out easily. He might even be short of breath. Trust me, Mrs. Pemberton, your husband is very well informed about his illness. If he should take a turn for the worse, he'll know."

"Thank you, Dr. Reeves. I feel much, *much* better knowing Nick is aware of the seriousness of his disease. He sometimes makes light of things." She paused. "Yes, I'll call if I have any more questions. Thank you, Doctor." She hung up the phone. Chelsea knew her smile was as wide as the moon. Good old Nick might not win this battle, after all. She couldn't wait to see him fall from grace, couldn't wait to get control of his fortune.

She was already visualizing his funeral. She'd wear Chanel, of course. And one of those black lace things to hide her face. If possible, she would have the services at St. Patrick's Cathedral. The irony, she loved it! Most likely it would be a full-court press. Foreign dignitaries had attended his father's funeral; no doubt they would feel obligated to attend Nick's as well. The vice president might even show up again. It could be the social event of the season. If she played her cards right, she just might attract a future husband, if she wanted one, while putting dear old Nick six feet under.

Chelsea had plans. She wasn't about to let Nick ruin them by living.

Determined not to sit still and idly watch his life go by without a fight, Nick planned on staying one jump ahead of his disease. He'd spent plenty of time reading the books Dr. Reeves had suggested; he'd even joined an online support group. Chelsea would have a blast making fun of him if she found out. Nick didn't plan on her doing so. The subject of bone-marrow transplants had been weighing heavily on his mind. What would he do if it came to that? Since he had no siblings or children, the likelihood of finding a suitable match in a short time didn't look good. He'd read about the National Marrow Donor Program registry. After he read what the odds were of finding a suitable match, an idea planted itself in the back of his mind. If it came down to the point that he needed a transplant, he was going to do whatever he could to plan for such an event. He was about to put the Pemberton family's money to good use.

Nick Pemberton was going to start a bone-marrow drive. And the winning match would be rewarded with a very large sum of money. A business venture, if you will. It would be the biggest recruiting drive in Manhattan. Hell, he'd get NYU involved. They owed him for that freshman banquet. It would be perfect. The more he thought about it, the more excited he became. Knowing there would have to be an incentive for a bunch of healthy college students to offer to donate their marrow, Nick was going to lure donors in with the promise of the good old green stuff. Cold hard cash. He'd figure out the amount, maybe enough to cover the cost of an iPod or one of those new iPhones. That, of course, wouldn't be the main attraction. If a match was found, Nick would offer the donor ten million dollars. Yes, that was a nice figure. Who wouldn't give up a few blood cells and marrow for the chance at ten million bucks?

"When you're good, you're good." Nick spoke out loud. He had almost four more weeks before his next treatment. Enough time to find some lucky bastard who might very well just save his life.

Feeling extremely tired, Nick remained in bed. He would start the recruiting process by phone. He dialed Trevor McDermott's private number, one that was only to be used for emergencies. Nick figured saving his life certainly constituted an emergency.

"Yes." Trevor picked up on the first ring.

"Trevor, it's Nick."

"Yes. What can I do for you this fine morning, Nick?"

"What I'm about to ask has to remain confidential."

"I'm your attorney, Nicholas. Our conversations are always confidential."

Nick lowered his voice. "Yes, of course. However, if the public were to get wind of this, Pemberton Transport could be in big trouble. My name has to be kept concealed at all costs."

"What is it you want me to do?" Trevor asked.

For the next half hour Nick explained to his attorney what he wanted. Hell, no sense beating around the bush, what he *needed*. He had to tell him of his illness because Trevor knew him well enough to know he wasn't the most charitable person in the world, excluding the orphanage. He contributed to them because it looked good, and it was a hell of a tax write-off. Other than that, his generosity was zip.

"All right. I've never attempted something of this nature, but as the saying goes, there is a first time for everything. Nicholas, you have to do exactly what your doctor says. I'm very familiar with your disease," Trevor said.

"You are? Why didn't you say something?"

"I'm saying it now. My daughter-in-law's brother had the disease a few years ago."

"And how is he doing now?" Nick asked.

Trevor hesitated a moment before speaking. "He died."

Nick was shocked and, for a minute, was at a loss for words. "That's terrible. How . . . Did he have proper medical care?"

"Yes, he had the best medical care. He did everything by the book, just like his doctor told him. This disease is treacherous, Nicholas. You feel fine one minute, and in the next you could . . . Well, I'm sure you're quite aware of the severity of your illness."

Nick took a deep breath. Suddenly his future didn't look so damned bright. "I'm doing all that I can to fight it. That's why I want to do the donor drive. If I need the stuff, I want to have it as soon as possible.

I'm not screwing around with this, Trevor. You know me."

"Good then. I'll get started right away. I'll e-mail you the details as soon as I have them."

"Thanks, Trevor. This just might save my life."

Nick hung the phone up. For the first time since he'd been diagnosed, he seriously considered that there was a chance that he could die. And to think his father thought money could buy anything and everything, as it had for most of his life. Was this the proverbial straw that would break the camel's back? Was he being punished? No, he'd been decent, hardworking. Hell, he had married a scheming, social-climbing gold digger just because he had been fooled into thinking that Chelsea had been carrying his child. Deciding that thinking about his wife and what a fool he had been was getting him bent out of shape, Nick tossed the covers aside, got out of bed, and stepped into the shower.

He would conquer the goddamned disease, or he would damn well die trying. He wasn't a quitter. Twenty minutes later he was dressed in his favorite Savile Row suit. Though it hung on his bony frame, he didn't care. If he acted normal, as if nothing had changed, then it would take his mind off the nightmare disease he wanted no part of.

Nick called Herbert. "I'm going to the office. I'll need you to meet me downstairs in fifteen minutes." It would take him that long to walk to the elevator in the kitchen.

"Yes, sir," came Herbert's usual reply.

An hour later Nick sat at his desk. Rosa was acting like he had the plague. Gerald filled him in on a few matters that only the CEO could handle. He signed several new contracts, read his private mail, and was pleasantly surprised when he saw there was a letter from . . . the woman he'd met in Chicago. Karen Hollister. Maybe when his life returned to normal, he'd arrange for another rendezvous. If he remembered correctly, she was one helluva piece of ass. He smiled. Already things were looking up. He'd never once thought about sex since getting sick. This had to be a good sign. He recalled their passionate day in bed and felt himself harden.

"Hell, yes!" he shouted into the empty room. At least that part of his anatomy hadn't betrayed him.

A tap on the door brought him down to earth.

"Yes?" he snapped irritably. He'd told

Rosa he was not to be interrupted.

"Andrew Miller is here to see you, Mr. Pemberton. Are you ready to see him, or would you like me to schedule another appointment?"

Damn! He'd almost forgotten about Andrew and his accounts. There had been more important issues to deal with of late. Like his possible impending death.

"Sure, send him in," Nick said agreeably.

Andrew Miller was young, late thirties. It was hard to tell. Handsome in a clean-cut way. Boy-next-door type. Brown hair combed to the side. Not a blemish or mark on his face. He looked every bit the consummate professional, just the way his father did.

"Nick, good to see you're back at the helm." Andrew sat down without waiting for an invitation.

"Yes, and it's good to be back. A lot to catch up on. That damned *E.coli* about wiped me out." Nick dared a look at the man seated across from him. If Andrew suspected something other than *E.coli*, it didn't show on his face. Nick suspected it wouldn't have shown on his old man's face, either.

"Makes you want to forgo red meat."

"It does. So what brings you out among

the working class?" Nick asked.

Andrew removed an envelope from his inside jacket pocket. "Here. These are the new access codes for your accounts. While we've yet to find the culprit who did this, the fraud unit is still investigating. They released these codes just this morning. When I called your secretary, she said you were in the office. Thought I'd drop them off to you myself. Once you gain access, of course, you're free to change the codes. I would if I were you. As a matter of fact, I'd change them every few days. It's a pain in the ass, but technology is making it easier and easier for thieves these days."

"I appreciate the personal attention." Nick peered inside the envelope. "I'll change these right away." Nick stood up and held out his hand to Andrew. "Thanks for stopping by."

Andrew shook his outstretched hand. "Anytime, Nick. I'll see you around."

Nick walked with him to the door. "Count on it." One more affirmation of his life: positive thinking.

The minute the door closed behind Andrew, Nick booted up his computer, logged on to his accounts, and changed all the passwords. He was sure Chelsea had something to do with the temporary inconvenience, but he had no proof. He checked the balances and saw they were as they should be. Why would Chelsea do something like that? Wouldn't she have taken a large chunk of money, or at least written a check? One never knew with his wife. Since nothing was lost, he wouldn't mention it to her unless she brought it up. But from that moment on, he'd keep his eye on things.

Checking his e-mail, he saw that Trevor was on the ball already. He'd contacted an ad agency to advertise the upcoming donor recruiting. No mention of money. Nick thought he'd made it perfectly clear that there was a reward of sorts just for donating. If there was nothing to gain, he'd be lucky to assemble even a handful of donors.

He sent a reply to Trevor explaining that. Money was everything to most people. He knew that. Hell, Nick thought, laughing, he'd been raised on the principle that anything or anyone could be bought for a price as long as the price was right. He still believed it, so with his life on the line, he was going to find out if it was true or false.

With Gerald in control, albeit somewhat reluctantly, Nick made arrangements for Herbert to meet him downstairs in twenty minutes.

"I'm leaving for the day. Expect me in the

morning unless I call you. Make sure you have tea. No more coffee. I can't stand the stuff anymore." It was his last order of the day to Rosa.

"Of course, sir. It will be good to have you back," Rosa said.

Nick doubted she really meant it, but it was expected of her, and Rosa always did what was expected. There was something about her that was niggling at him, but he couldn't quite put his finger on it. Maybe it was time for a raise. Yeah, yeah, that was probably it.

"Tomorrow." Nick casually strolled to the bank of elevators in front of the reception area. Wiped out, he didn't want anyone to observe his unusually slow gait. Just a slow stroll to the elevator, down twenty floors, and then he could relax in the car or pass out, whichever came first.

For some reason he couldn't explain, he was more tired than he had expected. That was not a good sign. If he didn't feel more energetic in a few days, he'd call Reeves.

The doors to the main lobby swished open.

"Nicholas, how are you? The rumor mill says you're dying and hell is beckoning," Jason Vinery said to his former client.

Nick stopped dead in his tracks. Lost in

his thoughts, he hadn't paid attention to who was in the lobby.

"You're good at spreading venom around. As you can see, I am alive and well. Spread that around and see what comes of it," Nick snarled as he escaped through the revolving doors.

"Looking at you, I'd say just barely," Jason observed to Nick's retreating back.

Something was seriously wrong with Nicholas Pemberton, and Jason planned to find out. He speed-dialed Mabel Dee. "I want you to put a tail on Nick Pemberton. Call Dave Williams. He's the best. And, Mabel, not a word to Lin." Jason clicked off.

Whistling, Jason walked through the same revolving doors and stepped out onto the street. A gleeful smile on his face, he took a minute to watch as Nick's limo pulled away from the curb.

There was definitely something seriously wrong with the smug bastard.

Could be payback time.

CHAPTER 12

Monday, October 22, 2007
New York City

It took Jason's contacts at both the *Times* and the *Post* more than a week to publish the story of the Pemberton abuse. It made the front pages of both papers, and both included the photograph he'd provided, plus a few others they'd dug up themselves.

Even though it was barely six in the morning, Jason dialed Lin's cell phone. She'd been on pins and needles all last week, waiting, fearful that she would be found out.

"Hello?"

"Get a copy of the *Post* and the *Times,* read them, and then call me back."

"It made the paper," Lin stated flatly, the breath leaving her body in one wild swoop.

"Oh, yeah, and above the fold. Anything concerning the Pembertons is news."

"Oh, my God! I never thought . . . Let me get the papers, and I'll call you back." Lin hung up the phone, slid into the same pair of jeans she'd worn the previous day, an NYU sweatshirt, her Uggs, and she was out the door.

The corner Starbucks had become her hangout for the more than a week she'd been waiting. She hurried to get copies of the papers and a latte.

After paying for her coffee and papers, Lin hurried back to her apartment. She didn't want to risk a public reaction. No, this was something she had to do in the comfort of her own home, apartment, whatever. She simply had to be alone.

Sitting on the sofa, she read the twisted headline in the *Times* first.

LIKE SON, LIKE FATHER!!!

Apparently, the apple doesn't fall far from the tree in the Pemberton family. Sources close to the family say abuse was an everyday occurrence in Nicholas Sr.'s household.

A former employee, who wishes to remain anonymous, told our source that the violence was so bad, the now-deceased Naomi Pemberton would hide in her room for weeks at a time. The employee said she not only feared for her life, but for that of her young son, Nick Jr., as well . . .

Similar to the first story, the article continued with information on Pemberton Transport, which was *then* followed by a sketchy family tree.

The *Post's* story was more of the same.

Lin tossed the papers aside, took another sip of coffee. She dialed Jason's cell phone.

"What do you think?" Jason asked, not bothering with a greeting, because he'd seen Lin's name on his caller ID.

"Part of me feels sorry for Nick Sr. since he isn't alive to defend himself. Another part of me is incredibly sad for Naomi." Then there was the part of her that burned with wild, hot, mind-blowing anger that she'd allowed herself to get involved with Nick. Then it always came back to Will. But she couldn't voice those thoughts to Jason.

"That's it? No 'Job well done'?" Jason inquired in what was supposed to be a teasing tone, but Lin heard a trace of annoyance in his words.

"I can't thank you enough, Jason. I'm overwhelmed, that's all." Was this it? Was this what she'd lied, connived, and spent a small fortune for? Smearing the Pemberton family name? Lin felt let down, as though there should be something more satisfying or *final.*

"We're not through, Lin," Jason said.

She wasn't so sure of that. What was the point in slandering Nick if he didn't know who was doing it and why? She felt nothing close to personal satisfaction. If anything, she felt like a fool.

"Lin?"

"Yes. Sorry. I was thinking."

"Let's see how this plays out. I've had a tail on Nick for the past week. I didn't say anything, because I didn't want to get your hopes up, but something is going on with him, and it's big."

"What do you mean?"

"This will be in the *Times* on Wednesday, so you'll know about it, anyway. Pemberton Transport is sponsoring a bone-marrow drive."

"And why does that matter?" Irritation rang in Lin's voice.

"Two things. First, I ran into Nick the Monday after you came to the office. Secondly, and I'm pretty damn sure of this — actually I'm waiting for this to be confirmed as we speak — but when I saw old Nick, he looked like hell. His suits are tailored. They usually fit him like a glove. When I saw him, I would bet my last dollar he's lost forty or fifty pounds. His clothes hung on him like wet sheets."

"Sorry, Jason. I still don't see what this has to do with me." Lin didn't want to play guessing games.

"Bone-marrow drive. Nick looks like shit. Come on, Lin, don't make me draw you a picture."

She gasped. "He's ill?"

"That's my guess. It gets better. This is what we'll read in the *Times* on Wednesday. Got this from my contact, too. Apparently, old Nick is reaching out to his former alumni connections, because he's recruiting bone-marrow donors. Everything is set up to take place on NYU's campus. He's even offering a five-hundred-dollar payoff for those who donate. I think there's more to the story, but that's all I could get. What I'm trying to say, Lin, is it could be that it's out of our hands, and the good Lord above has stepped in. Sounds to me like the man could be dying. If looks are any indication, I'd say old Nick isn't long for this world."

Lin's hands began to shake, and her mouth was suddenly so dry, she couldn't swallow. She almost choked on her own breath. A thousand different thoughts flashed through her mind, but none would come into focus.

Nick dying?

But wouldn't that be the answer to her prayers? The end of all ends. Death, the sweetest revenge of all. She should be feeling victorious, satisfied, but all she felt was absolute, total, all-consuming fear.

Fear unlike any she'd ever known. Her father's beatings with the strap hadn't struck such fear in her. The early days, when she'd struggled just to keep food in Will's mouth, didn't even begin to compare.

"Lin, are you all right?" Jason asked.

Trying to clear her head and focus on the conversation, she spoke in barely a whisper. "I'm not sure."

"Want me to come over?"

God, no!

"No, I just felt dizzy there for a moment. I wasn't expecting to hear something like that. Death is . . . death is . . . so final."

"Oh, well then, if you're sure. I'm expecting a call from Dave, my tail. As soon as I receive a full report, I'll call you back." Jason paused. "You're sure you're okay? I can send Mabel Dee over. She loves SoHo."

"No, really I'm fine. I appreciate your efforts, Jason." Lin hit the END button on the phone.

She needed to think. Unscramble the images assaulting her brain. One thought at a time.

Will. Nick. NYU. Donors. Blood. DNA.

What if Will were to participate in the donor drive? My God, it would be just like him to do that! He'd always been a charitable kid. Lin's mind flashed back to all the blood drives the local blood bank had held when Nick was in high school. Since Nick had a rare form of blood, *AB negative,* he'd always donated when they asked him, explaining to her that he might save someone's life one day.

Never in a million, hell, never in a zillion, years did Lin think something like this would happen. Never. What were the odds? *Oh God, oh God, oh God!*

She paced the small apartment, raking her hands through her hair. What to do? Call Sally. She'd have to come clean, tell the truth, but if Sally were the friend she knew her to be, she'd understand and offer her support.

She glanced at the time. It was still early. Most likely Sally would still be asleep. It didn't matter. This was life or death. Sort of. She grabbed her cell phone from the sofa and dialed Sally's home number.

Sally picked up on the second ring. "This better be good. Oh, sorry, Lin. Me and my big mouth. Is it your father?"

Where did she begin? The beginning, of course. "No, he's fine. Or he was when I saw him last. This is more important."

"Okay, explain. I'm getting up. Walking to the kitchen to flick the coffeemaker on."

Lin knew Sally didn't function well without her morning caffeine jolt.

"I feel like such a fool. If you don't speak to me ever again after what I'm about to tell you, I'll understand. I just want you to know that, Sally."

"That isn't gonna happen, and you know it. Spill it, Lin."

"My father didn't have a heart attack —"

"— Too bad."

"Sally!"

"That's it?" Sally questioned.

"No, there's more, if you'll stop interrupting me. I went to Atlanta. Basically I told him to kiss off. You'll be happy to know I'm no longer footing the bill for his care."

"What!" Sally shouted.

Lin held the phone away from her ear. "You heard me. That wasn't my intention, but he was such a bastard. Called me a slut and started preaching about the fires of hell. I'd had enough, and I told him so. I went to the administration office, told them I would no longer be responsible for his care as of September. They looked at me as though I were the most evil daughter that ever lived, but I didn't give a damn. He's belittled me for the last time."

"Hallelujah! It's about time you got on

your hind legs and roared. Good for you, Lin."

"I knew you'd be glad to hear that. What I didn't tell you . . . Well, I'm in New York. Remember that day at the diner when we were talking about letting bygones be bygones? I couldn't let it go, Sally. I just couldn't, but I didn't want you involved any more than you were already. It was something I had to do. Alone." Lin waited for the sound of the dial tone.

"And you think I'd stop what? Being your friend? Quit the diner? Lin Townsend, you know me better than that!"

Lin sighed. "I should, huh?"

"Damn straight. Now, tell me what's going on in the Big Apple. Have you seen Will?"

"No, Will thinks I'm in Atlanta, at my father's bedside. I hated to lie, but I didn't know what else to tell him."

"Okay, I can understand that, but what about Sir Nicholas? Have you exacted your revenge or what?"

"That's just it. I have in a way, but it looks as though someone higher up might finish the job for me." Lin told her what Jason suspected.

"Dying? Well, if that isn't sweet revenge, I don't know what is," Sally said coldly.

"I don't want the man to die, Sally! I'm not that coldhearted!"

"He was," Sally reminded her. "A seventeen-year-old who could have been pregnant with his child and he couldn't care enough even to open the letters you sent him. I'd say that's pretty coldhearted."

One of the things Lin admired most about Sally was her ability to cut through the bullshit and go straight for the heart of the matter.

"Put that way, it's cold. I don't care if he dies. Not that I want him to . . . What if Will decides to donate marrow? That's what I'm worried about."

Lin heard clinking noises. Sally pouring coffee.

"You can't allow him to, that's all. Surprise him. Tell him . . . something and keep him away from the school until the drive is over. End of problem."

Could it really be that easy?

"It's the middle of the semester. I can't just pull him away from his classes."

"I didn't say that. Just make sure when he's not in class that he's with you, anywhere but on campus. Tell him you miss him, which we both know is true, so that's not a lie. He's eighteen. Tell him you're taking him out on the town. Nothing like an invitation to party in the Big Apple."

Maybe that could work, Lin thought.

"Why don't you fly up? Between the two of us, we're bound to come up with a plan to keep Will away from campus."

"Maybe. I don't know. Jack is freaking out because I refuse to serve meat loaf every day. Apparently that compromise you reached with him about meat loaf as a lunch special isn't enough to satisfy him. And Kelly Ann thinks she pregnant. She's spent more time in the ladies' room than she has working."

Lin needed to go home, but she couldn't. Not yet. Not when the lie she thought she'd kept hidden from Will was about to be uncovered, or at the very least, there was a chance that it could be. Sally needed to stay in Dalton.

"I'll be fine. Sounds like you have your hands full. I hope Kelly Ann's boyfriend steps up to the plate if she is pregnant. He's such a weirdo."

"My thoughts, too, but kids will be kids. Even though she's twenty-one, Lizzie still acts like a teenager sometimes."

Feeling defeated, Lin took a deep breath, trying to take some interest in their conversation. "I'd always heard girls were more difficult than boys. But listen, I shouldn't

have dumped all this on you. I'm just feeling so mixed up about the whole stupid
mess. Maybe I should've insisted Will go to
college elsewhere. I don't know. There are
so many what-ifs right now."

"Listen, you can 'what-if' yourself to
death, and it will get you nowhere. Stuff
happens. You deal with it. Bottom line,
would it be so terrible if Will were to learn
his father was alive?"

"Yes and no. He'd never trust me again,
and I wouldn't blame him. And what if he
does find out and Nick dies? Where would
that leave him? Me? Us? I can't risk it.
There's too much at stake."

"Let's look at the worst-case scenario.
Number one, Will finds out his father is
alive, and you've lied about it all these years.
You carry that damn messenger bag full of
those letters with you everywhere you go.
Show them to Will. Let him know you made
the effort to include his father in his life.
Number two, this may hurt Will, but at least
he'll know your intentions were good. Rejection from an unknown father is much worse
than rejection from a father you've known
all your life. At least that's my take on it.
Will is eighteen. Nick is his father. Whatever
happens between the two of them, if *anything* were to happen, you will have done

what is right. Will is an understanding young man, Lin. Remember it was you that raised him, not your father, not Nick. He's a good penny."

"I know. I just don't want my son to think less of me. He's all I have, Sally." Tears pooled in Lin's eyes. She used the hem of her sweatshirt to stem the flow.

"Ultimately, the decision is up to you, Lin. I can't make it for you. Whatever happens, we'll deal with it."

How like Sally to put what Lin thought of as a gut-wrenching nightmare into perspective. It really *was* simple. Cut and dried, if you will. But gambling on her son's emotional well-being wasn't something she was willing to do at that point.

"You're a real friend, Sally. I can't imagine what I would've done without you all these years."

"Yeah, whatever. Stop with the sappy stuff. Whatever you decide, I'm here."

As always, Lin thanked her dearest friend before they said goodbye. She was on a mission.

"Man, you're crazy! It says they're paying five hundred bucks. In cash," Will said to his dorm mate, Aaron Levy. "There's a hundred things I could do with five hundred dollars right now." Though Will had plenty of extra money, it came from his mother. This was going to be the first Christmas after he had been away from home. It'd be cool to buy her something really nice with money he'd earned on his own.

"Not me. I hate needles," Aaron explained to his crazy friend.

"And you want to be a vet? Look, man, I don't know what planet you came from, but the last I heard, veterinarians use needles. They give shots. They draw blood. That kinda thing."

"I meant to say that I *personally* hate needles stuck into me." Aaron laughed. "I don't care how much money they're offering."

"Says here the matching donor will receive a ten-million-dollar bonus. Holy crap! Just think of the practice you could start with that kinda money. I'm not afraid of needles. I'm going first thing tomorrow."

"Whatever, dude. All I can say is good luck." Aaron tossed a blue and purple pillow at Will.

"Thanks." Will said. "I'm going to the library. Check you later."

Will's dorm mate was cool in every way except socially. He was shy, didn't have the first desire to meet some of the hottest girls he'd ever laid eyes on. Will couldn't wait to tell Jack about the house of horniness he was living in. The old man was like the grandfather he'd never known. He'd get a kick out of hearing about it for sure. His mom, on the other hand, would blush and shake her head. She was always preaching to him about getting a girl pregnant. Didn't she know he carried a condom wherever he went? Well, he had since starting college. If the opportunity arose — *No pun intended,* he thought to himself and laughed — he was going to be prepared.

The request for bone-marrow donations in the Sunday edition of the *Times* was the perfect opportunity to earn some cash. Wanting to surprise his mother, he decided not to mention anything about it to her. She'd get all antsy and squeamish. He remembered when he was in high school and always donated blood. His mom never understood why he went through what she called "such an ordeal" when you didn't have to. It was just something he liked doing. Maybe he'd saved a life or two. He didn't know.

Since Scruffy had died, Will had known his calling. He'd loved her so much, it was like losing his best friend when she'd died. His mother had told him the story about finding her cowering beneath the steps of her apartment, cold and hungry. If he were able to extend the lives of animals, make their lives healthier and happier, it would give him immense pleasure. At fifteen he'd decided to become a veterinarian and he'd studied hard when he hadn't really wanted to, but his hard work had paid off. He'd been accepted into one of the most prestigious undergraduate vet programs in the country. Will couldn't wait to get his degree. Then he would really be on his way to fulfilling his life's dream.

And ten million dollars would make it so much nicer, if he turned out to be the donor they were looking for.

Lin read the newspaper article for the third time. *Ten million dollars! Five million to an orphanage, and now this.* Her hands shook, she was so mad. The son of a bitch threw fortunes around like pocket change. Her desire for revenge renewed, she called Jason's cell phone.

"I take it you read the paper," he said.

"Ten million dollars. Can you imagine?" Lin asked in amazement. "He'll have so many donors, they'll be crawling out of the cracks like ants at a picnic. But I suppose that's what he's trying to achieve."

"I knew he was sick when I saw him. I checked out leukemia on the Web, and if he has the fast-moving kind, chronic lymphocytic leukemia, odds are he won't live long enough for all the donors to be tested. He could have something else, but I doubt it. Dave tracked him to a Dr. Evan Reeves. He's an oncologist and a hematologist. Smart doctor, from what I hear."

Lin had read about him in the article. He and his office staff would be stationed at the university for one week in order to take blood and buccal swabs from potential donors. This would narrow the typing process to only those that met certain medical criteria, a human leukocyte antigen typing which Lin understood involved a part of a gene that identified similar immune systems. From there it would determine who would undergo the bone-marrow extraction. It was quite a task, and Lin knew that if Will learned of this, he'd be first in line. She had to do whatever she could to prevent that from happening.

"I suppose I should sit tight and see what happens," she said, knowing she had her work cut out for her if she was to prevent Will from doing something that could cause so much pain.

"That's what I would do. I've called Dave

off. There's no reason to have the guy followed. He'll be in the public eye now that he's confessed to being ill. I imagine he's hoping sympathy will replace the outrage from the article in Monday's paper. The man has perfect timing."

"He does. I'm going to stay in the city for a couple of days. Then I need to go home. I have a business to run. Call me if there is anything I need to know."

"I can do that, Lin. I wish . . . Someday I want you to tell me why you're so hell-bent on destroying the man."

She took a deep breath, letting it out slowly. "Maybe. I'll talk with you soon." Lin closed her cell phone. The day might come when she would have to tell Jason, but not just yet. She had to do whatever was in her power to prevent her son from opening a Pandora's box so full of lies, it would take years for her to recover.

After she'd read the article in the paper, the beginnings of an idea had started to take root in her mind. After her talk with Jason, she knew it might backfire, but it was worth a shot.

It was Sunday. Monday morning she would visit Dr. Reeves. He had to see her. It truly was an emergency. With nothing to do, Lin decided to scope out her neighborhood beyond the local Starbucks.

She ran a washcloth over her face, brushed her teeth, and pulled her blond hair up in a ponytail. Grabbing a jacket and her purse, she stood in the hallway and locked the door. Feeling relatively safe in a city this size seemed strange to her, but she did. She'd said hello to her neighbors, a young couple with a set of twins. They were both executives on Wall Street. Lin wondered why they weren't living in a penthouse. Then, remembering the amount of rent she was paying for a one-bedroom apartment, she understood. It would cost a small fortune to house a family of four in this city.

Why is everything always about money? she thought as she pushed her way outside. She thought of the ten million dollars Nick had offered to pay a matching donor. It was within her power to save his life, sort of. Maybe. In all honesty, if it came to that, it would be Will who held Nick's life in his hands.

Feeling empowered by her rationalization, Lin joined a group of others in a line that wrapped around the Magnolia Bakery on Bleecker Street. She needed to gain a few pounds, anyway. She'd eat two of the cupcakes. Maybe three, one for Sally. Hell, she'd get a dozen and take them back to the apartment with her.

Thirty minutes later Lin felt as though she'd burst if she ate another cupcake. She'd picked up a couple of mystery novels at a secondhand bookstore across the street from the bakery. She planned to spend her Sunday afternoon reading.

CHAPTER 13

Monday, October 29, 2007
New York City

Lin swallowed, feeling a lump in her throat the size of a golf ball. Now that she was there, she wasn't sure if she had the nerve to go through with what had seemed like such a good idea just yesterday. *Maybe I should just leave,* she thought. But before she could escape the confines of the small examination room, the door opened. It took a few seconds before Lin could speak. "Hello."

"Hi. I'm Dr. Reeves. It says you're here on a personal matter." He glanced at the clipboard holding the papers she'd just spent twenty minutes on. "Have a seat." He motioned to a metal chair. He hopped on top of the table. He smiled. "You're wearing a dress."

"I know." What an idiot she sounded like. "I mean, of course I do."

Blond hair that was too long, a deep tan, and from what she could tell by the way he filled out his polo shirt, he had the body that went along with the total package. And he was a doctor. Some woman was lucky. Just looking at him made her blush, forget why she'd come in the first place.

"And it's very pretty, too." Lin must've looked shocked, because Dr. Reeves laughed very loudly. "I'm sorry. Most of my patients are sick. You look very healthy to me. And pretty."

Did he say she was pretty? Or was it the dress he thought pretty? Was he actually flirting with her? She looked for a wedding ring. Nada!

"Uh, thanks. I guess. I am healthy as far as I know, though it's been a while since I had my cholesterol checked." Lin could've given herself the V8 smack to the forehead.

"We can check it for you," Dr. Reeves said.

She hadn't expected such a young hunk. Heaven help her, Sally would die if she saw him. That thought caused her to smile. If he didn't stop the unprofessional banter, she didn't know what she was going to do. Feeling like a girl with her first crush, Lin cleared her throat. She had a son to consider. Who cared what the damned doctor looked like?

I do, I do, a little voice whispered in her ear.

"No, that won't be necessary. I'm sure it's fine. As I said on the papers I filled out, this is a personal matter. I saw the article in the *Times.*"

"Yes. Some people have money to burn. If it saves their lives, then who's to say it's a tad on the side of ridiculous? I suppose you want to donate your marrow. It was pretty clear in the paper. We've got a medical team set up on campus. They can do everything that I could do here in the office."

"No, no, it's not that. I don't want to donate my bone marrow." Lin stood up. "This wasn't a good idea. I'm sorry I wasted your time."

"Wait!"

Lin stopped on the way to the door because the handsome doctor blocked her path.

"Please, tell me why you're here. It must be important to you. Otherwise, you wouldn't have come."

Shaking her head, Lin wasn't sure how she should reply. "I'm not sure myself. Obviously, I didn't think this through."

"Okay. I can't force you, but just so you know, whatever you say to me is protected. Patient confidentiality."

"I thought so, but I wasn't sure, since I'm not actually a patient. Does this mean that whatever we discuss, no matter what, it can't be used . . . for one of your patients?" Knowing her words made no sense to the doctor, she was about to correct them when Dr. Reeves spoke.

"I suppose that qualifies as personal. I can't give you a yes or no answer, Ms. Townsend. If it involves something that's unethical, then I can't withhold that information, whatever it may be."

Lin nodded, unsure of what his response meant. "I shouldn't have wasted your time. I'm sorry."

"Wait," the doctor called as she pushed past him to the door. He hesitated; then a quirky smile revealed bright white teeth. "I mean . . . are you hungry?"

Lin looked at the handsome doctor. He was smiling at her. She gave a small smile in return. Maybe he assumed her blood sugar was low or something. "I had a cupcake for breakfast. And a latte. From Starbucks. So to answer your question, no, I'm not really all that hungry."

"Look, it's been a while. I've spent most of my adult life in school. I'm sure there's a much better way to do this."

"Do what?" Lin asked, extremely curious

about Dr. Reeves's strange behavior.

"I'm asking you out on a lunch date."

Lin's eyes doubled in size. "What!"

"I guess that's a no. Like I said, it's been a while since I've asked a beautiful woman on a date. I apologize."

"You're serious, aren't you?" Lin asked, astonished at his words.

"I've never been more serious in my life."

Lin gazed into his eyes. They were a deep blue. Like the Caribbean.

A wry glint appeared in his eyes as he returned her stare. "You have the most unusual eyes I've ever seen. They're . . . silver."

She nodded.

"Does that mean yes to lunch or yes to the eyes?"

Feeling as though she were having an out-of-body experience, Lin nodded a second time before saying, "Yes."

A vague sensation passed between them. Electrical. White hot. It took her a minute to gather her thoughts. Sexual attraction, that was what it was. Dr. Reeves peered at her. Her entire being seemed to be filled with waiting, wanting.

This is ridiculous!

The attraction between them was disturbing in its intensity. Lin licked her lips, wondering what it would feel like to kiss the doctor. What would it feel like to run her hand along the firmness of his chest, the muscles that rippled in his arms? She shook her head. She felt like Dorothy in Oz. Only Dr. Reeves did not resemble the great and powerful Oz in the least. Or the Cowardly Lion, the Tin Man, or the Scarecrow. God, he was manliness magnified times a zillion.

"To both," she finally managed to answer.

"Your eyes are silver, and you'll have lunch with me?" This was framed as a question rather than a statement.

"Yes."

"Wait here. I'll be right back."

She nodded.

What the hell had just happened? Lin could never recall in her entire life being so . . . attracted to, so mesmerized by a man. *My God, he's Nick's doctor!* And she'd just agreed to have lunch with him!

Taking a deep breath, Lin decided to go with it for once. She didn't think anything would come of their sharing a meal. But it would take her mind off her next move — getting Will away from campus as soon as his afternoon classes were over that day.

"Let's go."

"Shouldn't we introduce ourselves or something?" Lin asked as they left Dr.

Reeves's suite of offices.

"I'm Evan Reeves, and I feel like a total jerk. Where are my manners? My mother would kill me. Of course I should introduce myself. I already know that you're Lin Townsend, age thirty-six, in reasonably good health, though your cholesterol might need to be checked. And I know that you wanted to share something personal with me. That's what brought you here in the first place. I also know that whatever it is between us wasn't the kind of *personal* you were referring to when you called my office this morning to schedule an emergency appointment."

"You know more about me than I do you. But then again, I know you're single. At least I hope you are, because I do not go out with married men, even if it is just lunch." Lin looked over and up at Evan. He was smiling.

"So far, so good," he said.

"Uh, you have a mother and a father, I assume. And you went to school so long, you never developed proper dating etiquette. How am I doing?" Lin asked.

"Very well. Now" — he pushed the door open, sending a gush of cool air up to greet them — "where would you like to go? I have an hour and a half, more if I'm willing to

317

make my patients wait, which I'm not, so wherever we go, it'll have to be quick."

He stepped off the curb, his right arm in the air. A taxi came to a full stop just as Evan stepped back on the sidewalk. They got into the taxi.

"You're the one that invited me to lunch. Shouldn't you have thought about this before asking?"

"You're absolutely right, I should have, but I didn't, because I was afraid if I took my eyes off you for one second, you'd disappear."

"I guess I can live with that."

"So, any suggestions? I usually eat lunch at my desk."

Lin knew he thought she lived in the city permanently and knew of the best places to go. She knew only Starbucks, the Magnolia Bakcry, and the mom-and-pop pizza kitchen where she had ordered takeout every evening during the past week. Lin didn't want Evan to know that she wasn't a true New Yorker, even though he had to know by her accent that she wasn't from the New York area.

"I'm not really familiar with this part of the city. Why don't we ask him?" She motioned to their driver.

"Sure. Excuse me." Evan leaned across

the edge of the front seat. "Can you suggest a place where we can get a quick lunch? Someplace nice."

The driver spoke with a heavy New York accent. "Sure do. I'll drop you two off at Grand Central Station. They have everything imaginable, though it ain't fancy. You'll see they have variety."

"Sounds good to me. Are you okay with that, Lin?"

She would've settled for a Sabrett hot dog from the many street vendors but didn't tell him that. "It'll be perfect for both of us since I can take the subway from there. I have another appointment across town." At least that was the truth.

Thirty minutes later they were seated in the food court at Grand Central. She'd chosen a fresh fruit salad, and Evan had opted for fresh shrimp tossed in a lemon butter sauce and salad with mixed tender baby greens and fresh snap peas.

"This is delicious. I wonder where they're getting their off-season fruit? I can't even get this from . . . at my local market." She'd made another slip. She'd almost said she couldn't get fruit this fresh from her supplier in Dalton, but he didn't have the first clue about her chosen profession.

"Hey, it's New York. If it can be had, this

is the place you'll find it."

"Yes, of course. I don't know what I was thinking." She forked a plump strawberry.

"So tell me about yourself. Isn't that what I'm supposed to ask on a first date?" Evan inquired between bites.

Taking a deep breath, Lin knew that was where things could get tricky. Wanting to lie as little as possible, if at all, she couldn't think of a thing to say. "I . . ." Realizing whatever she said would generate even more questions, and not to mention she was so very, *very* tired of lies, she chose the truth, damning its consequences. "I don't live in the city. In fact I have only a three-month lease on my apartment in SoHo. I . . . own a restaurant. In Georgia." She took a large slice of orange and practically crammed it into her mouth.

"Hmm, I don't think you put that on your patient info form," Evan said, a grin showing a dimple in his left cheek. How could she have missed that?

"No, I didn't see the point at the time."

"And why tell me now?" he questioned.

Remembering she wanted to be as honest as possible, Lin said, "I'm tired of lying."

Evan furrowed his brow, took a deep breath. "Is it a problem for you? I know a couple of doctors that can treat that type of thing. It's much more common than you would think."

Laughter exploded from her mouth like an iron ball from a cannon blast. "It seems I haven't explained myself very clearly. First, I can distinguish the truth from a lie. Secondly, I have some personal issues in my life right now, so it just seemed easier to lie than admit the truth. It's something I've had to wrestle with since I was a young girl. Events have sort of catapulted me into a position that may force me to confront someone with a secret I've kept from him his entire life." Lin felt as though a cement block had been lifted from her heavy heart. Waiting for a reaction from Evan, she was stunned when he reached for her hand.

The lighthearted note in Evan's voice was gone when he asked, "Is that what brought you to my office?"

Vowing to continue her crusade of truth, she nodded. "Yes. But it's so complicated, so . . . There are so many other factors to deal with. I've done some things of late that I'm not very proud of."

"I don't understand how I, as an oncologist and hematologist, can be of help to you."

Lin's eyes pooled with tears. *Shit-house mouse!* "I'm sorry." She dabbed her eyes with a paper napkin. "It concerns one of your patients." There. It was out in the open.

"I see."

Lin knew she would have to tell him the full truth. Why, after all these years, she suddenly felt comfortable discussing her most personal secrets with a man she'd known for little more than an hour was beyond her. Lin felt as though she'd known him forever, as though whatever she said, he wouldn't judge her. It was that gut thing again. She would go with it.

"The marrow drive for Nicholas Pemberton, it's connected to that."

"That's public knowledge. It was in the *Times* yesterday. Tell me what's so terrible that you've felt you had to lie about it." He wiped his mouth, tossed his napkin on the tray, then took both of her hands in his.

"I don't even know where to start," Lin said.

"The beginning is usually your best bet."

"Yes, it is. However, it looks like it's time for you to get back to your office, and I do have that appointment I have to make."

"So, I guess this is good-bye. For today, I mean. You're not going to slip away from me, Lin. I mean that. I know it's been less than two hours since we met, but there is something quite unusual between us, wouldn't you agree? I don't want to lose you when I've just found you. God, that's a cliché, huh?"

It was, and she loved it, but she wasn't ready to tell him that. "I think if I don't catch the crosstown train, I'm going to be late." She reached inside her purse, found one of her business cards for Jack's Diner, scribbled her cell-phone number on the back. "So you'll always be able to find me. I'll wait for your call, Evan. I promise. Thank you for the lunch. This has been one of the best days I've had in a long time."

"How about dinner tonight? I should be through around six. Then I have to make my rounds at the hospital. What do you say?"

Here goes nothing. "Could I bring my son along? I'd like for the two of you to meet."

Evan stared at her as though seeing her for the first time. "You're full of surprises, Lin Townsend, I'll give you that. By all means bring your son along. I would like to meet him."

Lin expelled the deep breath she'd taken. *Thank you, Evan Reeves,* she thought as she reached for his hand. *Thank you so very much.*

"We had almost one hundred donors today.

There were so many, the medical teams ran out of swabs and syringes and had to shut down at lunchtime. I'm betting the number will increase with each day," Nick said.

"You sure put your money where your mouth is. I still can't believe you're offering a fortune to the matching donor. Isn't that unethical or something? Trying to bribe people. You and I both know the board isn't going to approve such an expenditure."

"I didn't ask them to. This is coming out of my own pocket. And no, to answer your question, it's not the least bit unethical. Marrow drives are quite common."

"Are you telling me you're using our money for this? I can't believe you would do this to me!" Chelsea paced the living room, stopping in front of the floor-to-ceiling window that looked out over the city. "Have you thought this through? What if you can't find a match, and someone tries to sue you? This is the most absurd thing I've ever heard of. Have you ever thought what will happen if you don't win your battle, Nick?" Chelsea looked at her husband. His face was even more pale than what was becoming the norm.

He slowly made his way across the polished marble floor to where she stood at the window. "It's *my* money, Chelsea. You want me to die, don't you?"

Chelsea looked at him, then cast her eyes back to the view of the city lights. "Of course not. Stop being an idiot."

"Let me make something perfectly clear to you. I don't care if it takes the entire Pemberton fortune, nor do I care if I have to sell out, go public with the company, whatever it takes. None of that matters if I'm not here to reap the rewards of three generations of hard work. If I die before you, not one cent of my money will be left to you. Only through a divorce will you get any of my money, and trust me, I've had my father's will gone over with a fine-tooth comb. You don't want to fuck with me now."

Chelsea walked away from the window, back to the large sofa in front of the fireplace. A fire burned there, spilling a rich, smoky scent throughout the living area. Chelsea hated the smell; it reminded her of the weenie roasts she'd attended as a kid, where many times the hot dog would comprise her only meal for days at a time. She knew what was in Nick's will. Upon his death, unless there was an heir, and she knew that wasn't going to happen in her lifetime, Pemberton Transport was hers. Yes, there were parts of it that she didn't completely understand, but for a price she'd find someone who could. Someone who wasn't on the Pemberton family payroll.

Softening her voice, she said, "I'm just trying to be realistic, Nick."

"Then support what I'm trying to do. You should be at the campus with me. Hell, it wouldn't hurt if you and some of your social-climbing friends volunteered to do something. Provide the damned doctors with one of those fancy catered lunches you're so fond of. Use your connections to influence all those charitable organizations you give my money to. It might even make the *Times*. Think how good that would make you look to all your friends. Why, it wouldn't surprise me if it didn't get you on that Trump guest list you seem to covet."

"As much as I hate to admit it, you're right. I should be doing *something* to help with the drive. I'll make some phone calls later. Why don't you lie down for a bit? I'll bring you a pot of that tea you seem to have developed such a taste for. I think Nora made cranberry scones."

Nick watched his wife. He wanted to think she had something up her sleeve, an ulterior motive, but he honestly couldn't see a trace of deception on her perfectly sculpted face. "That's sounds good, Chels. I think I will lie down for the night. It's been a long day. I still don't have my strength back."

"I know you don't. I'm sure it will take a while to regain your strength. Go on and get ready for bed. I'll be there as soon as I make the tea."

"You surprise me, Chels. You really do," Nick said as he watched his wife go to the kitchen.

She called out to him. "And why is that?"

He walked into the kitchen, where she was filling the kettle with water. "You can be so nice when you want to. Really. Thanks."

Chelsea's heart rate tripled at his words. "Why, thank you, Nick. I'm not a bitch all the time." She smiled at him so he would know she was teasing. "Now go on. Get in bed, and, Nick" — she paused for effect — "don't put on those stodgy old pajamas tonight."

He laughed and shook his head. "I'm not sure I'm 'up' for that just yet."

"Don't worry. I'll take care of everything. All you have to do is lie there and enjoy. Now, go before I change my mind."

Nick scuttled out of the room, grinning from ear to car. At times like this, he almost *liked* his wife. "Don't take too long," he called out to her.

In the kitchen Chelsea waited for the

kettle to come to a boil. She took out the silver tea service that had belonged to Nick's grandmother. Nora did keep it polished, one of the few things she did right. She had never liked the woman, felt she overstepped her boundaries, but all of that was about to change. And soon.

The teakettle whistled. Scooping the loose tea from its special packaging, Chelsea filled the tea ball, put it inside the silver pot, then poured the boiling water on top. Since Nick's illness had begun, she'd made a point to learn how to make tea. Better than Nora's, he'd said. That was good, because when he wanted his tea, she was more than willing to make her special brew for him. She told herself she wouldn't have to do this much longer. Besides, she liked the stuff herself, minus the "extras," of course. After squeezing half a lemon in the fragrant brew, she poured a heaping amount of honey, then a quarter cup of sugar. Next came the fun part. With a mortar and pestle she'd purchased at one of those cheap shops in Chinatown, Chelsea took six ten-milligram Ambien from her pocket, crushed them to a fine powder. For good measure she added three Ativan into the mixture. If this didn't knock Nick on his ass, she didn't know what would. She poured herself a cup of tea before adding the mixture to the silver teapot.

She arranged the scones on a small silver platter, added dessert plates and forks. She washed the mortar and pestle thoroughly, returning it to the cupboard above the commercial-sized freezer. She knew Nora never looked in that cupboard, because inside was a fine layer of dust. For once, the woman's slacking ways had paid off.

Hurrying to Nick's room, she was surprised to find him sprawled totally nude on his bed. He grinned when he saw her. "I bet you thought I'd be asleep, so you wouldn't have to keep your promise."

Chelsea placed the tray on the night table next to the bed. "Not on your life, Nick. I'm looking forward to it, actually." To prove to him she was intent on a night of pleasure, she removed her black Prada slacks and cashmere sweater. She wore a creamy beige bra that left nothing to the imagination, nor did its matching thong.

"You still look good, Chelsea. Damn!"

He watched as she reached behind her and unhooked her bra. Her breasts were perfect round mounds on her chest. They were fake, but the surgeon's work still had the power to get a rise out of Nick. Next, she hooked her thumbs in the waist of her thong, inching it slowly down her long tan legs until it reached her feet. She kicked it away, then stood tall. She smiled when she saw his erection.

"So what'll it be?" she asked, coming toward the bed. Seeing that he was as fully aroused as he'd been in the past, Chelsea had a brief thought that the part she admired about him most hadn't been affected by his illness.

"Why are you smiling?" Nick asked.

"It's been a while." She placed her index finger over his lips. "Shhh, just let me love you, Nick."

In Chelsea's mind this was the last time she and Nick would make love. She wanted to remember it, so she put her heart and soul into the act.

Starting with his lips, she kissed and teased until he moaned. Tracing her tongue along his neck and down to his chest, she dotted light kisses until she reached the dark brown triangle between his legs. She took him in her mouth.

He put his hands behind her head, pushing her down farther.

"Not yet," she murmured. Before he came, she climbed on top of him and centered herself over his erection, then slowly swiveled her hips back and forth to take in all of him. Placing her arms on his chest, she looked into her husband's eyes. "Are you ready?"

"Hmm, beyond."

With lightning speed, she slid up and down his shaft until his body tensed. She leaned into him, thrusting herself up and down until showers of white lights danced behind her closed eyes. She spiraled out of control, calling her husband's name when she reached her peak. He placed a hand on either side of her thighs and slammed into her until he erupted.

Both were panting. Chelsea lay on top of him, feeling his thumping heart. She waited for a few minutes, then slid next to him.

"We're still perfect together, Nick. Even after all these years."

Both had had numerous lovers, but when they were together sexually, it had always worked. It was outside the bedroom where their troubles lay.

Wearing Nick's shirt as a robe, Chelsea walked to the opposite side of the bed, where she poured his tea. "Here, this should be ready to drink by now."

Removing her cup, which she'd poured earlier, she took it back to bed with her. She patted the spot next to her. "Come closer, Nick. I want to be close to you tonight."

"I don't know what brought this change, but I'm not about to complain. Here, hold this." She took his cup of tea while he inched his way to her side of his massive bed. When he was comfortable, she handed him his tea.

Chelsea sipped her tea while casting a glance at Nick. He was drinking his tea, but slowly. "Finish that up so we can go a second round," she teased playfully.

Nick finished his tea in record time.

Chelsea hurried to the other side of the bed, where she took Nick's empty cup and refilled it. "You'll need this." She winked like there was some big joke between them. Nick did as instructed and drained his second cup of the dangerous concoction.

By the time Chelsea made it to the opposite side of the bed, Nick's eyes were droopy. She made a show of touching him, kissing him. After five minutes he was completely gone.

Hurrying before Herbert or, God forbid, Nora showed up unexpectedly, Chelsea scooped up the tray and teacups and raced to the kitchen. Taking the bleach from beneath the sink, she liberally doused Nick's cup and the teapot before filling each with scalding-hot water. Using her hand in order

332

not to leave a trace of the sleeping pills and antidepressant on the sponge, she swirled the hot water around several times, dumped it into the garbage disposal, then added more Clorox to the drain. She'd watched enough episodes of *CSI* to know that anything was traceable. Next, she scoured the cup and teapot with Dawn dish detergent. After swishing the water around for five minutes, Chelsea dumped the soapsuds down the disposal, then poured more bleach down the drain. After thoroughly drying every dish she'd used, she put each and every piece back exactly as she'd found it. Nora might be half-assed when it came to cleaning, but Chelsea had learned from experience that the woman knew where every knife, fork, and spoon was located.

Satisfied she'd left nothing behind, she raced back down the long hall to Nick's bedroom. He was just the way she'd left him. She placed her hand on his neck, feeling for his pulse and finding it steady. It was just as she had expected. Hoping that would change in the next few hours, she was prepared to wait. She needed Nick out of the picture before morning. That way she could put a halt to the marrow drive he'd orchestrated.

She went to her room, tossed Nick's shirt

aside for the dry cleaner, then slipped into her robe before heading back to Nick's room. It was going to be a very long night.

CHAPTER 14

"I can't believe you're here," Will said. "Good thing I didn't have a hot date tonight. So, what's the big surprise you couldn't tell me over the phone? I mean, besides your being here."

Lin laughed at her son. He was such a good sport. She knew it wasn't normal for a guy's mom just to pop up unexpectedly. Lin was glad she hadn't rained on his parade. He'd been studying when she called.

"Be patient." She gave him a quick hug once they were inside the elevator. She didn't want to embarrass him in front of the other guys in the dorm by being one of those doting moms who made their sons cringe.

She'd asked Evan to wait in the lobby. When the doors swished open, they stepped out into the lobby. Lin's heart flip-flopped when she saw Evan smiling at her. She hadn't told him any details about Will. The look of surprise on his face made her smile. Did he think she had a *young* son? Like maybe seven or eight years old. She took his surprise as a compliment that she didn't look old enough to have a college-age son. Her smile grew wider at the thought.

Taking Will by the hand, as she had when he was a child, she led him to where Evan stood by the main doors.

"Will, this is Evan Reeves. Evan, this is my son."

Both men looked perplexed, then laughed.

"I *know* you!" Will said, excitement ringing in his voice as he extended his hand in greeting.

"You're too young," Evan said, looking at Lin, then back at Will.

"I was seventeen when I had Will." So, she was right. She had homed in on Evan's thoughts and was right. She continued to smile and enjoy the flattering comment.

"Nice to meet you, Will. I have to say this is a big surprise. I had no idea," said Evan.

"Yeah, Mom has always been real good at keeping secrets." Will grinned.

Lin tensed, recalling her conversation with Evan that afternoon. Where was this going to go, and where was it going to end up? She shivered at the direction her thoughts were taking her.

"You're the doctor that's leading the marrow drive! I knew I'd seen your face somewhere." Will shook his head. "I won't even ask how you came to be here with my mother. I think you have some explaining to do, Mom." He laughed. "Hey, I went to donate after my second class today. By the time I got there, they'd run out of supplies or something. Think you can get me a pass to the head of the line tomorrow? It has to be early because I have some morning exams."

"Will!" Lin shouted a bit too loudly. "Where are your manners?"

"Oh, come on, Mom. I want to donate. There's ten million bucks at stake."

Lin's hands started to tremble, and her stomach turned to water. Fear leaped up her spine like an icy hand. This was the very thing she wanted to prevent. If she had to do something drastic, it was time. If Will followed through, it would ruin everything. She had yet to confess her lies to Evan, as she had promised she would, but under the circumstances, she wasn't sure that she could.

Evan laughed at Will's excitement. "Yes, Mr. Pemberton certainly knows how to recruit for a cause, I'll give him that."

The trio stepped outside into the cool

night air. For some reason, Lin had thought late October in New York would be icy cold, with possible snow flurries. The air was brisk but not uncomfortable.

"You're his doctor? Do you think the old dude will make it?" Will asked, still as exuberant as ever. He definitely was not picking up on his mother's agitation.

Vehemently, Lin said, "Enough, Will!"

"It's okay, Lin. I don't mind talking about it. However, the 'old dude,' as you put it, is only a few years older than your mom. He should live a long and healthy life, but with this type of disease, one just can't predict the outcome. That's about all I can say without breaching my patient's confidentiality," Evan said.

"Oh, sorry, Dr. Reeves. I didn't think of that. So, Dr. Reeves, how did you meet my mom? This is beyond coincidence. Mom never meets cool guys."

"Will, I swear if you don't take that foot of yours out of your mouth, I'm going to pull it out myself. Then I'm going to find a corner somewhere and make you stand there until you fall asleep."

Will laughed again. It was clear to both Evan and his mother that the young man was enjoying his mother's embarrassment.

"I'm serious, Will," Lin said, her tone

sharpening.

"All right, Mom. You're the boss. So, where are we having dinner tonight?"

"Evan? Any ideas?" Lin asked as they walked over to where a line of taxis waited, smelly fumes blowing forcefully from their exhaust pipes. People shouted profanities, and music with vulgar lyrics boomed from a nearby dorm. The campus was extremely noisy that night. Her first visit had been totally opposite of what she was seeing and hearing. She chalked it all up to young men and women on the loose and out from under their parents' protective wings.

Right then nostalgia stroked Lin like the soft hand of a lover. She longed for the sweet smell of the night-blooming jasmine that bordered her front porch, for her coffee-and-doughnut nights with Sally, and she even missed arguing with Jack over his meat loaf. She should not have come back to New York. She was digging deeper and deeper into a past she had thought, until she saw Nick Pemberton, she'd put behind her. Resurrecting old ghosts wasn't going to accomplish a damned thing.

"Mom, are you okay?" Will asked. "Let's get inside the cab."

Lin shook her head to clear her thoughts. "Sorry, I was . . . trying to think of something exciting to do for dinner."

"It's getting late, all the better restaurants are probably full, but I think I just might have an idea," Evan said.

Evan whispered something to the taxi driver. He turned to Lin and said, "It's a surprise."

"Mom hates surprises. Don't you, Mom?" Will said.

Lin hadn't a clue what was up with her son. Usually he was beyond polite. She guessed it was college and hanging around with a new breed of kids. She made a mental note to speak to him later in the evening about his lack of respect.

"Oh, Will, I don't hate this kind of surprise." She'd never told Will exactly why she hated surprises, since it brought back too many bad memories.

Will turned defensive, not sure exactly what was going on with his mother and the tall, good-looking doctor, who kept watching him. "Well, I remember your always saying you hated to be surprised, saying it was rude, and the person doing the surprising should take into account the recipient's feelings."

Lin tried to force some lightness into her voice. "I did say that, didn't I? As of this very minute I'm turning over a new leaf. I love surprises."

Evan remained quiet during the mother-and-son exchange, but his eyes were full of unasked questions.

Lin favored Evan with a slight upturn of her mouth. "I'm sure whatever you've planned will be perfect." Feeling as though she needed to keep the conversation light and continuous until they arrived at their destination, Lin decided to talk about Will's course of study. "Will is studying to become a veterinarian. When our dog Scruffy died, Will decided he wanted to devote his life to animals. Right, Will?" She raised her eyebrows at her son, hoping he would follow through and talk nonstop about his favorite subject. She needed to get out of the danger zone.

"I love animals. They're like no other, ya know? They never get mad at you, they love you no matter how crappy you look, and they're just the epitome of true friendship. When Scruffy died, I thought I should've been able to save her. I know now that she was old and ready to go, but it just stayed with me. What made you decide to go into medicine, Dr. Reeves?"

This is more like it, Lin thought as she listened intently to their conversation.

Evan took a deep breath. "Like you, I lost

341

someone I loved when I was a kid. I always felt like more could've been done to save her. I've spent most of my life in school, trying to learn as much as I can so that I can save others like her."

"Who was she?" Will asked.

"My little sister. She was four when she was diagnosed with leukemia. I remember the day my mother told me. I was in the sixth grade. I had just gotten home from school, and I was all mad because my best friend, Larry, made the basketball team, and I hadn't. I wasn't the most athletic kid back then. Mom was sitting at the kitchen table, crying. I thought maybe my dad had died or my grandparents. Looking back, I realize that was the most logical conclusion anyone would've come to. When she told me Emily might die, it completely changed my perspective on life."

"Oh, Evan, that's terrible. I'm so sorry," Lin said. She wanted to touch his face, erase the sorrow she saw in his deep blue eyes.

"Yes, I was too. She lived for four years after her initial diagnosis. Our lives centered around her illness so much, I became quite comfortable in the hospital lounges. I liked talking to the doctors. When Emmy had to be hospitalized, I hated it for her, but for me it was like going home. I fit in. Before long, I knew I wanted to study Emmy's kind of cancer. And here I am."

"That's dedication, for sure. I want to hurry through these first four years. I can't wait to start studying the real stuff," Will said.

"I was the same way, but make sure you study hard, especially your sciences. You'll find the extra knowledge invaluable," said Evan.

"Thanks, Dr. Reeves. I appreciate the advice."

"You're welcome. And you can call me Evan."

"Deal," Will said.

So intent was she on the conversation taking place around her, Lin was surprised when the taxi came to a stop.

Evan placed a fifty-dollar bill in the driver's outstretched hand. "That should cover it."

They all got out.

Evan cleared his throat before speaking. "I thought it would be nice if we went inside Thirty Rockefeller Plaza. There are several quick places to eat. Then we can ride to the top if you want. And when we're finished, if you're game, we can ice-skate."

"Oh, Evan, this is fantastic! I've always wanted to ice-skate here. I've never skated at all. I'll probably break my leg," Lin gushed.

"Will?" Evan looked at him.

"It rocks." Will shot Evan a megawatt smile, then gave him a high five.

"Then let's get started," said Evan.

They found a small restaurant inside, where they ate turkey paninis and drank hot chocolate. Since it was getting late, and none of them wanted to miss the opportunity to ice-skate, they skipped going to the top of the building.

Thirty minutes later the three of them cautiously made their way around the rink. Being in the middle, a death grip on both Will and Evan, Lin couldn't remember a time in her life when she'd felt so carefree and silly. She forgot about all her troubles as they circled the rink. Her lips were getting numb from the cold, and her hands tingled, but she didn't want the night to end. None of them were wearing the proper outerwear, but it hadn't been that cold when they'd started out. By now the three of them were freezing.

Thirty minutes later Will took off on his own, as though he'd been skating all his life. Lin was still a bit wobbly but comfortable enough to let go of her viselike hold on Evan's hand. He reached for her hand the second she took it away.

"I like holding your hand," he said.

Lin nodded and squeezed his hand. She decided she liked the feeling. As they circled round and round, Lin couldn't believe the moment was hers, couldn't believe how she'd arrived at that point. At that moment all she cared about was her son and the man who made her feel so safe and . . . protected. She'd always been her own protector, and when Will came along, of course, she'd protected him at every turn. It was a nice feeling, but she was a realist out of necessity. She knew it wasn't going to last. It couldn't. That was the bottom line. She might have a fling with Dr. Reeves before heading back to Dalton, but with their different backgrounds and lifestyles, not to mention the thousands of miles that separated them, she was almost certain nothing could come of such a relationship.

Pushing her thoughts aside, Lin focused on the moment. She wanted to remember every single detail of the night.

She did her best to commit to memory the hundreds of Christmas lights that were being strung throughout Rockefeller Center. Preparations for the giant Christmas tree, which Al Roker or some other television personality would light on Thanksgiving, were being made by workmen, and she was actually seeing it with her very own eyes. At night, no less. In Dalton they rolled up the streets at dusk, and the town shut down. She couldn't wait to tell Sally and Jack about the huge Swarovski crystal snowflake that hung precariously in the center of Manhattan.

She savored the sights and smells and stored them in her memory. Lin looked up at Evan just in time to catch him frowning.

"I need to stop for a minute. My pager just went off. Will you be okay on your own?"

"Of course."

Lin skated slowly, with both arms out from her sides for balance. She would never be able to spin in circles and do all those fancy moves some of the kids could, but that was okay with her. She was content to go slowly and carefully. Feeling she had her balance, she almost fell when Will grabbed her arm.

"Hey, kiddo, enough of that," she warned.

Will's eyes glistened with excitement. "Sorry. I was just trying to help. Man, I should've tried this sooner. It's a blast. Next time let's try Wollman Rink in Central Park. It's bigger. Where'd Evan go?"

"He had a call on his pager he had to take.

Something you'll have to do, too, no matter that your patients will be the four-legged kind."

"Yeah, but I won't mind."

"I know. It's something you've wanted, and you're going after your dream. I'm proud of you, Will. I should tell you that more often, shouldn't I?"

"Thanks, Mom. You do it just often enough so that I don't get cocky. You know, you're pretty successful yourself. I know you don't think so, but you are. You have a tough business, and you just keep at it even when it's hard. I've seen you. I've seen you down, and I've seen you up. You taught me just to roll with both and do your best, and if that isn't good enough, you just try harder, and in the end it will all be okay."

She did say that. Her motto. "Thanks. It hasn't been all that bad. I love what I do. Creating new recipes, mingling with the customers. I think it's in my blood. I always enjoyed looking at my mother's cookbooks whenever I could." They skated in unison, their sharp blades making swishing sounds across the ice.

"Sally said you had a rough way to go as a kid."

Lin hadn't discussed much of her past with Will, didn't want him to know how she'd suffered at the hands of her father, how he'd tossed her out like dirty water when she told him she was keeping her baby. No child should have to endure the harsh life she'd suffered. Even though she knew that she couldn't protect Will from the evil ways of the world forever, she'd done her best to see that his own childhood was everything hers wasn't.

The memory of those years was what had started her vendetta in the first place. Revenge, payback for all the indignities, the heartache, and the misery she'd suffered because Nicholas Pemberton wouldn't step up to the plate. But it seemed stupid to her, because here she was with her son, happy doing things normal families did. It reminded her of that time in McDonald's all those years ago. She and Will were safe, and they were both content. What more could she possibly want?

Evan came soaring up to them. "I hate to do it, but duty calls. A patient of mine was brought to the emergency room. I hate to end the night this way."

"I'm getting tired myself." Lin glanced at her watch. "It's after midnight! I had no idea it was so late. Go on, Evan. Will and I can take the train."

"Absolutely not. You're both coming with

me. You can wait in my office while I check on my patient. Then I'll see both of you home."

"That's too much trouble. Don't you have to be up early?" Lin questioned.

"I'm used to it. I won't take no for an answer. Please, let me do this," Evan replied.

Lin looked at Will. He shrugged and nodded. "Actually, I wouldn't mind seeing your office. It's fine by me if it's okay with my mom."

"Okay, if it's not too much trouble," said Lin, giving in gracefully.

"Let's return these skates. We'll do this again when I'm not on call," said Evan.

Lin thought doctors were always on call, 24-7. "Then let's hurry. I don't want to keep your patient waiting."

They sat down, removed their skates, and returned them to the counter, where they retrieved their shoes. Fifteen minutes later they were speeding to New York Presbyterian.

As the taxi sped through the streets, Lin had an epiphany of sorts. When she'd made that frantic phone call to Evan's office that morning, she had never imagined she and Will would ever be ice-skating with him. *Everything,* she told herself, *happens for a reason.*

Life throwing her another curveball. She smiled, hoping she could handle this particular one.

Making sure the stage was set for the performance of her life, Chelsea waited till almost midnight before dialing 911. Nick's breathing was shallow. She practically screamed his name and got no response. She did it a few more times, hoping she could be heard one floor below.

When the paramedics arrived, she went into her act. "I got up to go to the bathroom. When I checked on my husband, it didn't feel right. His breathing didn't sound . . . I just knew something was wrong." She stopped to wipe the tears from her eyes. "He has leukemia. I . . . Oh please, just get him to the hospital."

"Try to calm down, ma'am," the paramedic said. "Who is his doctor? I'll have the hospital call him."

Chelsea raked her hands through her hair, shaking her head from side to side. Damn, if she were in a movie, she'd be nominated for an Oscar. "I . . . Dr. Reeves. Evan Reeves. Yes, yes, that's his name. He . . . he has other doctors, but Reeves is the one he is seeing now."

"He's at Presbyterian, right?"

She nodded as she continued to sob. "Please just help him. I don't want him to die! Oh God, he's all I have! Please hurry!" she screamed at the top of her lungs.

She was actually enjoying her own performance. Too bad she hadn't thought to record it so she could relive the moment over and over again.

Once they had Nick loaded on the gurney, Chelsea dialed Herbert. He finally picked up on the sixth ring. One more person to get rid of. She'd hire someone young, someone whose services would consist of more than driving her. The thought made her smile. A young, eager stud would fit the bill nicely.

"What took you so long, Herbert? Don't you know you're on call all night?"

Herbert cleared his throat, "I'm sorry, ma'am. It is rather late. What can I do for you at this hour?"

"Mr. Pemberton has been taken to the hospital by ambulance. I need you to be waiting downstairs in five minutes. Hurry up!"

A sudden dilemma presented itself. She didn't want to look too put together, but no way could she show up looking like trailer trash. She squeezed into her Seven jeans, a navy sweater, and black stiletto boots. She arranged her hair in a messy topknot, grabbed her purse, and headed downstairs.

Herbert was waiting in their assigned parking space.

"Let's get a move on. At this rate Mr. Pemberton will die by the time I get there." Secretly she prayed for precisely that to occur.

"Yes, ma'am."

God, he is so stodgy! I can't wait to oust him from his cushy position.

Herbert broke all speed limits, making it to the hospital in record time. He pulled up to the emergency-room entrance, tires squealing.

"Shall I wait here?" he asked.

"Yes, and don't move unless security forces you to park somewhere else! It could be an hour. It could be longer."

Once inside the ER, Chelsea drummed up real tears, and her hands actually shook as she accepted a tissue from a nurse. "Is he going to live? Can I see him? Please, please don't let anything happen to him. I'll die if something happens to him. I swear I will." Chelsea cried louder and harder once she saw she had an audience. A man and a woman with a teenager stared at her.

The man came forward, putting his arm around her. "Mrs. Pemberton, please calm down. Tell me what happened. I'm Dr. Reeves, Mr. Pemberton's oncologist."

Chelsea blinked rapidly when she realized the man was Nick's doctor. She'd never seen him, only spoken to him on the phone. And God, what a piece of eye candy. She cried even harder so he'd wrap his muscular arms around her tighter. She sobbed a few more seconds just to make it look good. "I . . . I had to go to the bathroom, and I always check on him." She actually hiccuped. *Damn, I'm good.* "His breathing was shallow. He didn't look right. Then, when I tried to wake him and didn't get a response, I called nine-one-one. Please tell me you can help him!"

Evan wrapped his arms around her. He observed Lin and Will. Both looked shocked, but Lin seemed frightened. He mouthed the words, "Go to my office." He'd see her later, after he took care of Mrs. Pemberton and her husband.

As soon as she saw Evan bolt through the double doors, Lin grabbed Will's arm and practically dragged him outside. "We can't stay here. We have to leave. Right now!"

Walking fast, Lin pulled her son along, ignoring the questions he was shooting at her. When she finally spied a taxi, she jumped in front of it. "NYU campus," she said, climbing inside, then slamming the door.

"Okay, Mom. That's enough. You're acting way too weird for me. What's wrong? Did that woman in the emergency room scare you? You looked like you had just seen a ghost."

Oh God! Oh God! Oh God! Evan's patient is Nick! The hysterical woman in the ER is his wife! Will's stepmother — sort of!

"Mom!" Will raised his voice. "Tell me what's wrong. You're scaring me."

Lin's face fell into the palms of her hands. Could she ever look her son in the eye again?

What to do? Clearing her throat, Lin swiped at her eyes with the cuff of her shirt. "I'm sorry, Will. That . . . that scene just brought back a bad memory." That was putting it mildly, she thought. "I didn't mean to scare you. Are you okay?"

"I'm fine, Mom, but what do you think Evan's going to think when he finds his office empty? We told him we'd wait. Leaving like that was rude, especially since you drummed into my head all my life that there is no excuse for rudeness. And it's not like you, either."

Lin shook her head. "You're right. I'll call

354

Evan as soon as I get back to my apartment."

"Apartment? Mom, come on, you just got here! You don't have an apartment. Are you sure you're not sick or something? You don't have like a brain tumor or leukemia or anything like that, do you? Is that how you met Evan? Are you his patient?" Fear rang in the young man's voice, and his grip on his mother's arm was fierce.

"No, no. Will, I am physically fine. I meant hotel. I was thinking of your dorm as an apartment. I'll be fine. Just give me a minute." She could not answer his questions, couldn't look into his questioning eyes. Her lies were following her like a stalker, peeping around corners when least expected. Before she knew it, they'd be out in the open for all the world to see. Lin knew it was up to her either to continue the lies or not. At that moment she could barely think, let alone make such a life-changing decision.

"Whatever you say, if you're sure you're all right."

"I'll be fine, Will. It was just a bad moment."

They rode in silence for the rest of the trip. When the driver stopped in front of Will's dorm, Will said, "Look, Mom, you're making me nervous. I can come back to your hotel. Wait for me to get a change of clothes."

"No!" she shouted. "I mean, no, you don't have to do that. Besides, there's just one bed. I'm fine, Will. Just a little shook up, that's all. Trust me. Why don't I meet you here as soon as your classes are out? Maybe we can go to that other ice-skating rink you mentioned. What do you say?" Lin had never been forced to fake cheerfulness for her son's benefit, but it was all she could do just to look at him.

"If you're sure. Look, I can sleep on the floor. Hell, I mean, heck, around here we do it all the time."

"You gonna yak all night or what?" the taxi driver tossed back at her. "The meter's running, lady."

"It's fine. Will, go inside. If it makes you feel better, call my cell phone before you go to your first class. Please?"

"Okay, but I want you to call me as soon as you get to your hotel. Are you staying at the Helmsley?"

God, more lies. "Uh, no. The Sheraton. In Manhattan." Lin would bet there was more than one, but just then all she wanted to do was escape to that dreary little apartment so she could think.

"Then call me when you get there. Promise?" He gave her a thumbs-up and kissed her on the cheek before getting out of the car.

"Night, Will."

"Wait until he's inside," Lin said to the driver.

"It's your dime," the driver replied.

Once Will was inside, Lin gave the driver her address in SoHo.

"You told the kid the Sheraton."

Lin wanted to scream! "I lied, okay! I damn well lied, okay! It's none of your business, anyway, now is it?"

"Calm down, lady, just calm down. You're right. It's none of my business, but you shouldn't lie to your own kid."

Lin took several deep breaths before she actually felt calm. She should apologize to the driver, but it really *was* none of his business.

Thirty minutes later she was safely inside her apartment. She wanted to call Sally, but it was after two in the morning. This wasn't Sally's problem. It was hers. And she had to solve it. Before she forgot, she dialed Will's cell. He picked up on the first ring.

"I was about to call you. What took so long?"

"The driver went the long way. I think I

was his biggest fare of the evening. I'm wiped out, son, so call me in the morning."
Lies, lies, lies.

"Later, Mom."

With that out of the way, Lin walked across the room to what she thought of as an excuse for a kitchen. She'd purchased a coffee-maker at Duane Reade so she'd have coffee when Starbucks wasn't open. She filled the back of the machine with water, scooped three spoons of coffee into the filter, then clicked the ON button.

While waiting for the coffee, Lin took a quick shower and slipped into a pair of sweats and a T-shirt. After pouring herself a large mug of coffee, she collapsed on the sofa.

It was time to think. Really think. She'd made a real mess of her life. Actually, she'd had help. First her father, then Nick. The only two men she'd had any kind of relationship with. She didn't know what had happened to her father to turn him into such a mean, Bible-thumping, evil man. She'd asked her mother about it once, but all she would say was, the past was the past, and that was where it should stay. There'd been no grandparents, no aunts or uncles, no cousins to visit. Just the three of them living in hell.

Lin's eyes glistened as she thought of her mother. What a pitiful life she'd had. She had been a year older than Lin's current age when she'd fallen down the stairs and died. Or been shoved down the basement steps and murdered. She would never know how her mother had really died. What she did know was that her mother had been terrified of her father. Though Lin had never seen him strike her, she knew there were other ways of abusing someone.

She remembered the week she'd spent in Atlanta. At the time it had been the most exciting week of her life.

"Please, don't make me go," Lin Townsend begged. "Jolene, I'll feel foolish. All those rich people. It's just not my thing. But you go ahead. I'll be content to stay here and read that new book I had to sneak inside my luggage." Lin smiled at her new friend, Jolene Norris. Lin was staying with Jolene, who was now a college student in Atlanta. This was the first time Lin had been allowed to sleep over with a friend. In fact, it was the first time she'd ever been invited.

"The one about sex? What's that author's name?" Jolene asked as she discarded another dress on top of her bed.

Reclining on the floor next to the bed, grinning from ear to ear, Lin said, "Erica Jong.

The book is called *Fear of Flying*. My father would kill me if he knew I had a copy."

"For crying out loud, Lin, you're seventeen years old! You can read whatever you want. You don't need their permission. Besides, that book is as old as Methuselah."

"I know that. It's just a matter of respect. Me being an only child and all."

Jolene and Lin attended high school together in Dalton, both were on the math team, and both had won the state tournament. So when the opportunity to go to Atlanta for the math competition had come up, even though Lin knew her father didn't want her to travel to Atlanta, she'd lied, telling him it was required. Though she needed to be there only for three days, her new friend had convinced her to lie so she could extend her stay to a week. Lin had. Her father had actually believed her, but then again, she'd never given him a reason not to.

"I don't know what that has to do with anything. I'm an only child, and look at me."

"That's what I'm talking about. God forbid I should act like you! I mean, you know my father. He's so strict." Her father would kill her good and dead if she ever acted like Jolene.

"It doesn't really matter, anyway. Lin, you have got to go to this party with me. It's the crème de la crème of parties. Do you know what I had to do just to get an invitation?" Jolene held up a slim white hand. "Forget I said that. If you knew, you'd be bouncing off the walls like half the girls in my French Lit class. I have got to make an appearance. I promised the girls details, Lin." Jolene's dark brown eyes crinkled mirthfully. "Please . . ."

"You know I didn't bring any fancy clothes. I can't wear this." Lin peered down at her creamy white painter's pants, which were all the rage in the South, and her black Converse high-tops.

Jolene looked at Lin, her perky nose wrinkling in disgust. "You're absolutely right. You cannot wear that. But since we're the same size, I'm sure I can find something you'll like."

Lin glanced at the pile of dresses heaped on top of the white canopied bed in Jolene's dormitory room. "I'm sure you can."

"You look through this pile, see what you like, and leave the rest to me," Jolene said.

Groaning loudly, Lin pushed herself up, then plopped on the pile of clothes. "It'll take days to go through all this. What day is this party, anyway?" She lifted a pale pink chiffon dress out of the pile, swinging it around to view the back. A large bow at the bottom of the zipper made her laugh out loud.

Jolene yanked the dress from her. "Not that. I wore that to my eighth-grade graduation."

"You're spoiled, Jolene. Since this means so much to you, I've decided to go. But you'll have to do my hair and make-up. You know I'm not worth a flip when it comes to dressing up. Look at the clothes I wear to school. Look at the clothes I brought with me to Atlanta. I'm hopeless."

Jolene gave her a quick hug. "You can't help it. Things will change when you get out from under your father's thumb." She rummaged through the pile. After several look-sees, she found a yellow sleeveless dress with a matching belt. "This is perfect! It'll show off your tiny waist and complement your coloring. Not to mention those silver eyes. You know most of us girls would kill for your eyes." She held the dress up for her inspection.

"Really? I never knew." Lin held the dress up and looked in the mirror. "This will do. Now what about shoes?" she asked, suddenly in party mode.

"I have the perfect pair. Now, let's get on the stick. I want to make a statement when we walk through those doors. I can't believe we're going to a party that college men are attending! Gawd, this is so much better than Dalton High," Jolene said to Lin.

Three days later they were in the backseat of some guy's Camaro on their way to the party.

"This is so . . . exciting! I can't believe I'm here. Thanks for inviting me," Lin said.

"Isn't this better than reading that dirty novel you brought?" Jolene teased.

After they arrived, Jolene held a small packet out to her. "Here, take this and put it in your purse." Jolene handed Lin a compact of Maybelline face powder.

"I feel like Cinderella at the ball," Lin said as they walked through the maze of apartments.

Jolene dug around in her purse. She removed a small foil packet and gave it to Lin. "Just in case."

Lin blinked in surprise, then turned crimson. "What? Where did you get this?"

Jolene took her by the elbow, steering her up the sidewalk. "From my father's medicine cabinet. I have six. Just in case."

Lin stopped in the middle of the sidewalk. "I don't think I'll be needing this." She held out the condom packet. When Jolene refused to take it, Lin crammed it in her purse, praying that she would remember to toss it aside before they got to the party.

It wasn't like she was going to give up her virginity to the first guy she met.

"Never say never, Lin. These guys are good-looking, at least the ones I've met are. They have good names, and their families have lots of money. It wouldn't be such a bad thing if you were to have a fling, you know?" Smiling jauntily, Jolene eyed her friend.

Lin rolled her eyes. "Yes, it would. First of all, that's the furthest thing from my mind. Secondly, I'm saving myself for the man I marry."

Jolene took Lin by the hand and hurried her along. It was already nine. She didn't want to be that late. "Come on. We'll talk about this later. I want to make a grand entrance, all eyes on me. Us." She shot Lin a sheepish look. "You know what I mean," she finished flatly.

Lin nodded, shivering as she raced along the sidewalk. "Do you know anyone at this party?" she asked.

Jolene laughed. "Yeah, a couple guys. How do you think I managed to finagle an invitation? I told you this party is the crème de la crème. They're very particular about who they invite, or that's what Mark told me."

"That's it?"

Lin heard the music blaring, peals of laughter, and car doors slamming. To her it looked more like a party for the governor or something. Limos lined the cul-de-sac as they dropped guests at the entrance to the giant complex.

"Jolene, this doesn't look like just any party to me."

"It's college boys, remember? These people are rich, rich, rich. Even richer than my parents — and they're swimming in the green stuff. Don't worry. They put their pants on the same way as you and me."

If Jolene thought her words reassuring, she needed to think again. "Rich" intimidated Lin.

Three hours later Lin was sure she'd met the man she was going to marry. They had sex in someone's bed. She spent the next four days with the man of her dreams, Nicholas Pemberton.

Lin took another sip of her cold coffee. While she didn't regret having Will, she regretted giving herself to the man who had fathered him.

Her life had turned into a ticking time bomb, and any second her lies would explode, revealing her for what she was. There had to be a way to unravel them without hurting Will.

CHAPTER 15

Evan hurried to his office. He'd spent two hours examining Nicholas Pemberton. Until the lab results came back, he would be as stumped as the ER doctor. He'd questioned Mrs. Pemberton repeatedly, but she'd been too upset to offer any valuable information. He suspected she knew more than she was telling, but at that point there wasn't anything to support his suspicions. He'd always relied on his gut feelings when he couldn't come up with a logical solution to something that eluded him.

Excited at the prospect of seeing Lin again, he entered his office, only to find it completely dark, with no sign of either Lin or Will. He switched on the lights.

"Lin, Will," he called, knowing there wouldn't be an answer. Expecting them to wait two hours had been ridiculous.

Maybe they were in the cafeteria. He turned off the lights and locked the door before he galloped downstairs.

He searched the room. Except for a few tired-looking residents, it was empty. No Lin or Will. He'd known they wouldn't be there, but he'd hoped maybe he was wrong.

Evidently they had gotten tired of waiting. He couldn't blame them.

Evan returned to the ER for one last look to make sure they were really gone. He knew he was being ridiculous, but he wanted to make sure they were truly gone before he went home.

The nurse manning the desk saw him and smiled. "If you're looking for the woman and the boy, they raced out of here like the place was on fire the second you went through those doors." She nodded in the direction of the double doors to the triage area.

Perplexed, Evan questioned her. "Did she say anything? Leave a message?"

"No. But I can tell you this, the way she dragged that kid out of here, there was something going on. Maybe hospitals make her sick or something." The nurse laughed at her own joke.

"You're probably right. Do me a favor. If she or her son shows up, call me." He knew she had a list of all the numbers where he could be reached.

"Sure thing."

Evan thanked her, then stepped out into the brisk night air. The temperature had dropped by at least fifteen degrees. Shivering in spite of his leather jacket, Evan thought perhaps he should move to a warmer climate. The few times a year he was able to escape to California, where he surfed and loaded up on sunshine, were no longer enough. He'd think about it later. Right then he needed to sleep for a few hours before starting all over again.

As usual, there was a cab waiting. He slid into the backseat, giving the driver his address.

"Hey, I've taken you home before. You're that doc that was in the paper, aren't you?"

Would he ever reclaim his anonymity?

Evan shrugged. "That would be me." He didn't want to engage in conversation; all he wanted was to sleep. And dream about Lin Townsend.

"Ten million bucks. I'd donate myself if I could," the driver said. "I read the requirements in the paper. I'm too damned old."

"That's the way it is," Evan commiserated.

When they pulled in front of his building, Evan gave the driver a generous tip and hurried to his apartment on the sixth floor. He dug his keys from his back pocket and unlocked the door. A part of him had hoped he'd find Lin waiting for him in his apartment, but she had no idea where he lived. He was acting like a stupid teenager — another indication he needed to sleep.

Spying his mail on the hall table, he scanned through it, saw nothing that required his immediate attention, and headed for a hot shower.

Like the dutiful wife she wanted to appear to be, Chelsea stayed at Nick's bedside in the ICU for the limited time he could have visitors. When appropriate, she'd cry loudly, sniffling as though she herself were about to die.

Chelsea surmised she'd missed her calling. She felt she was far better at acting the role of a distressed wife than she'd ever been as a "real" wife. It was the money she loved. And the sex, even if it had been infrequent. She enjoyed her position in society as Nick's wife. Chelsea figured she would enjoy being Nick's widow so much more. Life imitating art, or was it the other way around?

She watched him. Tubes were attached to every orifice in his body; a heart monitor bleeped, reminding her the son of a bitch was still alive. She'd been sure the overdose of sleeping pills would've killed him already. The doctors had yet to make a diagnosis, though she knew they were waiting on the lab results. Of course, she knew the pills would show up in a toxicology report. She'd prepared for it.

Lost in thought, Chelsea jumped when she heard the door open. The ER doctor. She couldn't recall his name.

"Mrs. Pemberton, can I speak with you?"

Sick to death of crying, she summoned up another bout of tears for the doctor's benefit. "Of course." She wiped her eyes with a tissue.

"If you could step outside." He motioned to the door.

Chelsea grabbed her bag and another handful of tissues from the box on the stand next to the bed in which, she hoped, her husband would soon die. If only the good doctor could read her mind, she'd be on her way to prison. Laughing inwardly, she couldn't wait to get this done and over with. She had big plans for Nick's money, soon to be *her money.*

All was quiet here in the ICU except for the monitors and the swishing sounds coming from the machines that kept some of the patients breathing.

Standing outside of Nick's room, she

waited for the doctor to tell her what she already knew.

"We've got the results from the lab. I'm afraid it looks as though your husband overdosed on a sleeping pill and an antidepressant. Ambien and Ativan." He let the statement hang in the air.

Chelsea mustered up the required look of shock, then disbelief, then the tears. After a minute or so, she blotted her eyes for the umpteenth time. "This . . . this doesn't surprise me." She sniffed pitifully.

"What makes you say that?"

"It's . . . I'm not sure if I should say anything. Nick likes to keep family problems in the family, where they belong." Chelsea paused, waiting for the expected coaching from the doctor.

He didn't disappoint her.

"Mrs. Pemberton, now isn't the time to withhold information that could possibly save your husband's life. You must tell me if there are issues in your family. I'm a doctor. Anything you tell me remains confidential."

Just as she'd expected, so predictable.

"Well, I suppose if it helps poor Nick. His mother committed suicide when Nick was little more than a toddler. She took an overdose of pills, just like Nick. He says he doesn't remember her, but he must. He's chosen to end his life in the same manner!" With more sobbing and tissue wiping, Chelsea continued her act while waiting for the good doctor to reply.

"Tragic as it may seem, suicide seems to run amok in some families. Certainly I'm not saying this is hereditary, but often people who are suffering mentally or physically, as is the case with your husband, will follow a pattern. Did Mr. Pemberton indicate he was upset this evening?"

If only she could tell him about the seduction.

"He was very quiet. It was early when he went to bed, but since becoming ill that was normal for him. I kissed him good night and went about my business. I spent some time reading, watched television for a while, and then I went to bed. I woke up to go to the bathroom around eleven thirty or so. Something didn't feel right. You know what I mean? It was as if something strange had permeated our house. When I finished in the bathroom, I peeked in on Nick. He appeared to be sleeping. I went over to his bed and adjusted his blankets. He just looked odd to me. I felt for his pulse, but it seemed weak. I know I'm not a nurse or anything, but something told me to shout at Nick. I did several times and got no response. That's when I dialed nine-one-one." Chelsea liked this story even better than the one she'd told to that sexy-looking Dr. Reeves. Maybe when this was all over, he would offer her some sympathy.

"I'll have to report this to the police," the doctor said.

"What? Why would you do that? I told you this was to be kept in the family! Nick would never want this made public. Why, his name would be sullied more than it has been already with those nasty accusations in the paper! No, no, you absolutely cannot do that. You said this would remain confidential, and I expect you to keep your word," Chelsea shouted, not caring that she was drawing the attention of the staff at the nurses' station.

"I understand how you feel, Mrs. Pemberton. However, as a doctor, I am required by law to report an attempted suicide. This won't be reported in the news media, if that's what you're worried about. Mr. Pemberton's condition seems to be improving. It is my hope that he will come out of this with little or no lasting physical side effects."

There was no way in hell Chelsea was going to allow a stupid doctor to ruin her life by saving Nick's! She didn't have an alternate plan yet, but by God, she would come up with one. If she had to get drugs from a pusher to finish off her husband, she would. First, she had to prevent the doctor from contacting the police. The Pemberton name had received enough bad press to last a lifetime. The last thing she needed was some nosy-ass cop prying into their private affairs. Showing her temper would get her nowhere with this doctor. She'd kiss his butt just a little until she came up with another plan.

"I'm sorry. I'm just . . . shocked. I never thought Nick would resort to something like this. I knew he was unhappy because of his illness, but . . ." She wiped her eyes again. "Could you wait and report this after I talk to Dr. Reeves?" She held her breath, waiting for his answer.

"I don't think that should be a problem. Dr. Reeves will be in his office in a few hours. Why don't you go down to the cafeteria and get something to eat? You'll need to keep your strength up for the next few days. When Mr. Pemberton realizes his attempt was unsuccessful, he'll need your support. I would suspect he'll want you by his side as he confronts whatever caused him to attempt taking his life. If you're sick, you won't be doing either one of yourselves a favor."

Chelsea thought the long-winded doctor would never shut up. She didn't care about eating — hell, she'd consumed three cranberry scones while waiting for Nick to kick the bucket. But she needed to think, to plan her next move. "Yes, I think I will. Some tea would be nice." She almost choked on her own words.

"Good. I'll have the nurse page you if there's any change."

"Thank you. Now, where is the cafeteria?"

The "good doctor" gave her directions. Once inside the elevator, she said every dirty word she knew and repeated some. Nick could not live! He'd remember her seduction, remember the tea. The man might be sick, but he was far from stupid. She had to do everything in her power to prevent that from happening. There were more pills at the penthouse. Maybe she could get them and crush them up and cram them down the son of a bitch's throat. And if that didn't do him in, then she'd shoot him — in self-defense, of course.

She began to formulate a new plan. Each time she thought about Nick fighting for his life, she almost laughed out loud. The man had never had to go without, didn't know what it was like to wonder where his next meal was coming from. When she'd met him at the party all those years ago, Lady Luck had been shining down on her. Granted, Nick wasn't even close to the most perfect husband, but she wasn't a perfect wife, either, and had no problem admitting it to herself. Add the fact that she had already been pregnant with another man's child, and she couldn't have picked a better man for the job of becoming her husband and the "father" of her child.

Chelsea poured lukewarm water into a Styrofoam cup, then dunked a Lipton tea bag inside. She paid the tired-looking cashier before she headed back to the ICU waiting room, where she'd have to stay until she was allowed back in Nick's room.

Her mind clicked. When she'd been rummaging through her bag, searching for change to pay for her tea, she'd found the bottle of Xanax her doctor had prescribed for her a month ago, when she'd claimed she was having anxiety attacks. She'd filled the prescription, tossed the bottle into her bag, and forgot about it, because she'd refused to take a drug that might push her out of control. That she still carried them around was a miracle. Maybe, just maybe, those little pills would be the answer to all her problems. They couldn't watch her all the time.

Relieved that she'd come up with a backup plan, she entered the elevator, pushing the button that would return her upstairs, where she could continue playing the role of anxious wife.

When the elevator doors opened, Chelsea thought she'd pushed the wrong button. The three nurses at the desk were standing in front of the desk. Chelsea thought they looked threatening, and her heart started to pound.

"We were just about to come and get you, Mrs. Pemberton," the older of the three nurses said.

Chelsea's heart pounded harder as she prayed that Nick had succumbed to the drug overdose. Summoning a look of fear, she tried to make her tongue work, but it refused to do her bidding. Suddenly all three of them started to smile.

Nurses didn't smile when there was bad news.

"Is he . . . awake? Is he okay? Did something happen? Is he going to be okay?" Chelsea sobbed.

"As soon as they finished pumping his stomach, he woke up," the charge nurse said cheerfully. She made it sound like everyone should get their stomachs pumped from time to time.

Chelsea tried to remember how many bullets were left in the thirty-eight revolver that she'd bought from a junkie years ago. One would be enough.

"That's wonderful," Chelsea cried. "I prayed so hard. God must have heard my prayers."

"Your husband has been asking for you, too. We were just about to page the cafeteria."

Chelsea smiled at the women. Right now the last thing she wanted to do was rush to her husband's bedside. It wouldn't be pretty, she thought, because Nick would have no qualms whatsoever when it came to turning her over to the police. Unless, of course, he didn't realize what had happened.

"Uh . . . I need to use the ladies' room first. Tea . . . tea . . . makes me . . . Please . . . tell Nick I'm on my way," Chelsea sputtered.

When Chelsea saw the nurses could no longer see her, she ran back to the elevator and headed for the main floor. She took her cell phone from her bag and dialed Herbert. For once the old guy picked up on the first ring.

"I need to go home." She closed the phone and stepped outside just as Herbert pulled up to the ambulance lane. Chelsea smiled. She'd bet her last nickel the old man thought his employer had just died.

Soon, Chelsea thought. *Very soon.*

Nick barely opened his eyes. He heard a continuous bleeping sound, followed by excited, yet hushed tones. He was in a strange room. As though he were looking through gauze, the images were fuzzy, undefined. He tried to speak but couldn't seem to remember how.

The voices around him continued. Someone raised his eyelids wide and shined a thin beam of light into his eyes. He felt his eyes burning, felt the liquid pooling down his cheeks.

"Can you hear me, Mr. Pemberton?" a male voice asked.

Gathering every ounce of strength he could, Nick nodded. Once. Twice.

"Relax. You're going to be fine," the voice informed him.

Nick closed his eyes because it took too much effort to keep them open. His head felt fuzzy, and he couldn't focus on anything.

It could have been a minute or ten, he wasn't sure, but when he opened his eyes again, he saw Evan and another man standing at the foot of his bed. Sunlight brightened the room. He must've slept for a while, because it had been dark before.

"Nick, can you hear me?" Evan asked.

Nick nodded.

"He's coming around. Let's allow him to sleep it off a while longer. I think that's the safest treatment plan at this stage," Evan said.

Sleep it off? Have I been drinking? Nick tried to remember but came up empty again.

The voices in the room were louder, or he was more aware, he wasn't sure which, but he heard someone say, "Chelsea." The monotonous *bleep, bleep, bleep* noise suddenly went *bleepbleepbleepbleepbleep.*

"His heart rate is increasing," Evan said.

Nick heard quickened footsteps, then sharp voices issuing commands. Something squeezed his left arm for several seconds before the pressure released.

A blood pressure cuff!

He opened his eyes, blinking rapidly as he tried to clear the fog from his vision. He swallowed. His mouth felt dry as the Mojave Desert. Moving his thickened tongue from side to side took quite a bit of effort. He was thirsty. "Wa-ter," he managed to say in a scratchy voice.

"He's asking for water," the nurse said to Evan.

"Go ahead. It's fine. Just not too much," said Evan.

Nick felt like he'd died and gone to heaven when a flexible straw was placed between his lips. It took a few seconds, but he managed to drink enough to relieve the dryness. He licked his lips. They were cracked and raw.

"Here, let me." A woman rubbed a balm across his lips. "That should help."

Nick tried to smile, but it hurt his cracked lips too much. He offered up a grimace instead. "Thanks."

"You're welcome."

He must have drifted off again, because the next time he opened his eyes, the room was dark. A small light above his bed cast shadows on either side of him. He swallowed, wanting more water. He rubbed his lips together. Someone must have been caring for them, because they were almost back to normal.

Opening his eyes completely, Nick managed to shift himself into a semisitting position. He saw the call button clipped onto the pillow. He pushed it.

Images of a thousand aspirins and jugs of water made him push the button a second time. His head pounded, as though an orchestra were playing a Mahler symphony. He wasn't sure exactly what Mahler symphonies sounded like, but remembered hearing something about how loud they were.

"Wow, you're sitting up. I'm impressed," a nurse said.

He managed a croaky "Why?"

She took a plastic aqua pitcher and filled a paper cup with water. She put the straw in his mouth. He drank it all and asked for more.

"Why am I so thirsty?" He could only whisper, but Nick knew it was the first full sentence he'd said since he'd been admitted to the hospital. He ran a hand up and down both arms, searching for the chemo line, but found nothing.

"You've been asleep for a while. I'm going to get the doctor. I'll be right back."

Evan returned with the nurse. "You're awake. Good. How are you feeling?" He felt Nick's pulse, wrote something on a chart, then handed it to the nurse.

"Like I've been trampled by a herd of angry cattle."

"Well, that's not good, but it's what I expected. You still feeling groggy?"

"Some, but not as bad as before."

"Do you know why you were brought to the hospital?" Evan asked, careful not to put words in his mouth.

"No. It's the leukemia, isn't it?"

"Actually, your blood count is still at a good level. Your white count is elevated a bit, but that's to be expected under the circumstances."

Evan knew that one of Ambien's side effects was temporary loss of memory. With the dose Nick had taken, he was lucky to be alive. Evan hoped that Nick would remember the events of the night before he was rendered unconscious and transported to the ER.

"What circumstances? Don't keep me in the dark, Dr. Reeves. I might be sick, but I haven't taken leave of my senses yet."

That sounded more like the domineering man that Evan knew. He didn't sound like a man who wanted to die, a man who'd just attempted to kill himself with a massive overdose of sleeping pills. Something wasn't right.

"Of course you haven't. I didn't mean to imply otherwise. I want you to concentrate, think back to two nights ago, try to remember what you were doing."

Nick frowned in concentration. "*Two* nights ago? What night is it now? Wednesday? So two nights ago was Monday. I was at home."

"Anything else about that night you remember?"

Nick rubbed his hand across his stubble. "I didn't need a shave?" He laughed.

"A sense of humor is good. Seriously, think back to that night. Did you go anywhere? Do anything unusual?"

Nick had a flash of Chelsea's naked body on top of his. "I had sex with my wife." He grinned. "I remember now. Actually, she seduced me. I was surprised since Chels and I aren't the most compatible couple in the world."

"Okay, sex is good." Evan thought of Lin. He'd tried to call her several times over the past two days, and each time he'd gotten her voice mail. He planned on driving to her apartment tonight, as soon as he left the hospital.

"It was especially good that night. Damn, I shouldn't be discussing this with you."

"Yes, you should, Nick. I'm trying to figure out a few things. Just humor me a few more minutes. I don't need details, just your recollection of Monday night."

"Okay. Chelsea brought me some tea. We drank it after we made love. She , . . she was adamant that I drink a second cup."

Nick paused. "Goddamn her! She put something in my tea, didn't she? She's behind this, isn't she? That bitch. I swear I will kill her when I get my hands on her!"

"Nick, try to calm down. And stop making threats. Someone is liable to hear you. The last thing you need is a visit from the police."

"Did you check . . . do whatever they do to check for drugs? Did you do that?" Nick asked. "She poisoned me, didn't she? Wait! If she did that, how the hell did I get here?"

"A toxicology screen. Yes, we did. We found extremely high levels of Ambien and Ativan in your system. Enough to . . . Your wife called the paramedics, and we got you just in time."

"Kill someone? Is that what you were about to say?"

"Yes," Evan answered. Nick was his patient. His loyalty was to him, not his wife.

"Where is she? Has she been here?"

Evan hated to be the bearer of more bad news, but his patient had to hear it from somebody. "She was here the night you were admitted. She stayed for several hours. When you woke up, she was in the cafeteria. I had just told a couple of nurses to have her paged when she came up. I thought she'd be thrilled with the news. When she came upstairs, one of the nurses told her it looked like you were out of the woods, because you were awake. She said she needed to use the restroom. No one has seen her since."

"That conniving bitch! She laced the tea with drugs. That's why she wanted me to drink the second cup. I've known for a while she wanted me to die. She's been after my money since the day we met. She never made any secret of it, either. I guess the leukemia isn't working fast enough for her. It's . . . it's not easy knowing . . . knowing someone hates you enough that she wants you dead. And then try to . . . Never mind, Doctor. That's my problem, not yours. I'll take care of it when I get out of here."

Nick had just voiced Evan's own thoughts. *A man doesn't offer up ten million dollars if he's about to off himself. No, something is definitely wrong with that picture,* Evan had concluded.

"The ER doctor called the police after the tox screen came back."

"Then where are they? Shouldn't they be here questioning me? I guess they got tired of waiting for me to wake up," Nick said wearily.

Evan hated what he was about to say, but again it was better coming from him than someone else. "Mrs. Pemberton told the staff you took the pills yourself. When someone attempts to take their life, since it's against the law, we have to call the police. A report was filed, but that's all I know at this point."

"That's the most ridiculous thing I've ever heard! No matter how bad it is or was, I'd never try to kill myself. That's just something I would never do. My own mother . . ." Nick closed his eyes, unable to finish whatever he was going to say. Evan saw a lone tear escape his eye.

"I agree, but it's the law, and we have to abide by it, or we could lose our licenses to practice medicine. We don't take risks, Nick." Evan had eased into calling him by his first name. He seemed comfortable with it. Since Nick had been more than a bit formidable during his first office visit, Evan hadn't cared for him as a man all that much, but now he felt like the guy was having more than a bad run of luck. His health was withering away, and his wife wanted him dead. That was enough to piss off a saint.

"I took the Ambien you prescribed only a couple of times. With all the chemo, the last thing I wanted was more drugs floating through my bloodstream. Come to think of it, around the time you told me I could wait a month before my next treatment, I remember thinking I felt unusually tired. I bet she was lacing my tea with the stuff back then, and I was too stupid to know it."

Evan had no doubt that there was some truth in what Nick said. While it wasn't up to him to prove a crime had been committed, it *was* up to him to be honest. If asked his medical opinion of Nick's state of mind, he would have to conclude that his patient was perfectly sane. No one who'd gone to such great lengths to orchestrate such a large, not to mention expensive, bone-marrow drive was, in his professional opinion, the least bit suicidal.

"I can't offer you legal advice, but I can do whatever is in my power to keep you alive," Evan said.

"That's good enough for me. Now, would you suggest I phone the authorities, or should you make the call?" Nick asked briskly.

"As your doctor, I don't want to see you upset. I'll call them and explain your health situation. After that, it's up to them to decide if Mrs. Pemberton's a threat."

"The woman is beyond greedy! She wants my money and will stop at nothing to get her hands on it. Normally, when she wants large chunks of money, we negotiate. I've never really denied her anything. I just didn't think . . . murder is . . . That's so unbelievable, I just can't wrap my mind around it." Evan watched as Nick swiped at his eyes again.

"Let me make a few phone calls, see what I can find out. I'll order something for you to eat. Any special request?"

"I don't care as long as it's not Jell-O or chicken broth."

"I think your system's ready for something a little heartier. Just rest. I'll be back to check on you before I leave for the night."

If Nick's admission turned into an attempted-murder investigation, there was no way Evan would be able to get out of the hospital at a decent hour. He'd have to leave finding Lin to another night.

CHAPTER 16

When Jason had stopped by Lin's apartment on Tuesday, she'd already decided to go back to Dalton. She'd forget about getting revenge on Nick. She also knew it was in her best interest to forget about the man whose mission it was to keep him alive.

Jason Vinery's visit had changed everything.

"You'll get to see the trees changing their colors. Well, maybe not. They've probably changed already. So you'll see a bunch of naked trees," Jason had said as a means of persuasion.

Now here she was, in Jason Vinery's SUV, on her way to Vermont.

"I don't mind telling you this entire story seems as hokey to me as the one about the tooth fairy. I can't believe I let you talk me into this," Lin said, but it was said happily.

"If it were hokey, I wouldn't be here, trust me. I believed the man. He's dying, Lin.

Why would he confess to something so bizarre?"

"You just answered your own question. The man is dying. He's got nothing to lose."

"Okay, I'll give you that. But what's the point? He has no family left. All his millions go to the institution when he dies. He has no reason to do this, other than to get it off his chest. If we make it in time, he's agreed to let me videotape his confession. Said he had proof. That's convincing enough to me."

Lin guessed Jason knew what he was talking about. In her desire to exact her revenge, she had joined forces with Jason, but she was afraid she would never be free of Nick again.

"If you get a valid confession, what do you plan to do with it? Give it to your 'source' at the paper?"

"I haven't gotten that far in my thinking. Maybe I'll just give it to you. You could use it more than me, anyway."

It would be one more secret to keep from Will. Speaking of Will, he hadn't called her today. She took her cell phone out of her purse. Damn, she hadn't bothered to turn it on since she'd turned it off after talking to Will Monday night. The poor kid was probably beside himself with worry.

She had five calls from Will, three from Evan, and two from Sally. *Damn!* She listened to her messages.

"Hey, Mom. Just checking in. It's Tuesday. Missed the donor thing again. Guess I'll try again tomorrow."

Four more messages from Will, the last one sounding more than a little worried. She dialed his cell phone number.

"Mom! Damn, where have you been? I've been worried to death about you. I've been calling and calling."

"That's my line. Honestly, I haven't turned my phone on since we talked Monday night. Not a very responsible parent, huh?" Lin tried to make light of the matter but knew it was a major faux pas where her son was concerned.

"Then why do you have the stupid thing if you're not gonna use it! I was worried, especially after the way you acted the other night at the hospital. Speaking of which, have you heard from Evan? And where are you?"

She'd been anticipating that last question. Not wanting to tell another lie, she opted for the truth. "I'm on my way to Vermont."

"Mom! Have you lost your mind? Forget I said that. Sorry. But what's going on with you? You've been acting weird ever since I started college. You're not suffering with that empty-nest-syndrome thing, are you?"

If only that were it. Lin could deal with that, because that was normal, something many parents experienced.

"No, I'm not, though I miss having you around, Will." She took a deep breath. Once the words were out, she couldn't take them back. "I have to talk to you when I get back from Vermont. Nothing life-threatening or anything, but it will . . . explain my behavior." There, it was out! After more than eighteen years of lying to her son, she was going to tell him the truth about her past, *his* past.

"Ohhh-kay." He dragged the word out the way kids do when they think whatever a parent said was crazy.

Despite the seriousness of the situation, Lin laughed. Will was her son, and nothing she said could take that away. "I'll be back tomorrow, but I want you to promise me something."

"Sure. What is it?"

"Whatever you do, don't do that bone-marrow drive. Will, I'm very serious. This is important. You'll understand why when we talk. Promise me?" she said, crossing her fingers.

"Okay, okay! Geez, what? Do we have

some defective gene or something?"

"No, but promise me."

"I said I would."

"Humor me, Will, and say the words." Lin knew she was about to push her son over the edge, but it couldn't be helped.

She heard his frustrated sigh over the phone. "I promise not to go to the bone-marrow drive until my mommy gives me her permission."

"Will, don't make jokes right now. I have my reasons, and you're going to have to trust me. I'll call you tomorrow, okay?"

"Sure, Mom, whatever you say. Just remember to keep your phone turned on. Sally was getting worried, too."

"I will. Promise." Lin clicked off the phone before Will could ask more questions.

Jason was looking at her as though he, too, thought she was losing her mind.

"Something tells me you're not going to be as easily put off as my son."

Jason kept shaking his head, like one of those bobbleheads on someone's dashboard. "I had no idea you had a son, Lin. What the hell! I don't understand why you felt you had to keep that from me."

"How long before we're in Vermont?" Lin asked.

"Three hours, four if we stop for gas. Why?"

"Because it's going to take me that long to tell you my story."

"Bring it on. I'm all ears."

Two hours and one box of tissues later, Lin finished her story. Jason spoke for the first time. She'd made him promise not to interrupt her.

"And you're falling for the damn doc!"

Lin's mouth dropped open like a cartoon character's. "That's all you've got to say?"

"I knew there was a reason for you to be so hell-bent on revenge. I'm just surprised you waited all these years. What made you decide to drag Pemberton through the dirt now? You didn't tell that part of the story."

"When I saw him at Will's freshman banquet, he looked so . . . rich, so pampered. I'd sent him all those letters and not once had he bothered to read them. I felt like I'd been tossed aside like a day-old paper. And Will, too. God, what kind of man could deny his very own flesh and blood?"

Jason held up his hand as the female voice of the GPS told them they would be arriving at their destination in fifteen minutes. "I love that thing." He paused. "Lin, did it ever occur to you that Nick never received your letters? Maybe he never had the chance to acknowledge Will because he didn't know he existed."

"Oh, please, Jason. You men, you all stick together, don't you?"

"Hey, remember I don't like the guy myself. But if his old man killed his wife, the mother of his son, sending back a bunch of his son's love letters would be mild in comparison, don't ya think?"

Lord, she'd never thought of it that way. Of course, she hadn't known the Pemberton's family history then. Could it be possible? No! She wouldn't go there, because if she did . . . She could *not* go there.

"There's no doubt in my mind the man's a true son of a bitch, but do you really think in a family as powerful and well off as the Pembertons, Nicholas Sr. would run home to catch the daily mail?" Jason said.

"When you put it that way, no, it doesn't make sense," Lin said.

"Look, we're here." Jason said, pointing to a sign that read TARA WOODS.

"Sounds like a country club," Lin said.

"Yeah, but we're about to find out that it's anything but. Dr. Steffani keeps rooms there, or so I was told. I can't imagine being in some nuthouse, let alone living in one."

"You know what they say, a psychiatrist is

as wacky as his patients," Lin said.

"We're about to find out firsthand." Jason removed a small black duffel from the backseat. "Camcorder," he indicated, slinging it over his shoulder.

Tara Woods looked like its namesake. A beautiful old mansion sat smack-dab in the middle of nowhere, surrounded by hundreds of sweet-smelling pine trees. Lin took a deep breath as they walked up the long path to the visitors' area.

"This fresh air is a treat after the city."

"Yeah, it is, but after spending most of my life in the city, you miss it when you're away."

"Jason, we've been gone only half a day."

"I know that. I'm talking about weeks. It's like it's a drug, something you crave. But we're not here to discuss the pros and cons of living in New York City, are we?"

"No, we aren't."

Jason stopped at the entrance, waiting for her to catch up. She'd lagged behind, but knowing the doctor was dying forced her to hurry.

"Once I begin questioning him, you just stay put. Don't say one word, okay? They might throw us out," Jason said.

"I wouldn't do that, Jason. Since we're talking about my son's biological grandfather, I do have a stake in this. I won't say one word, I promise." Lin smiled her first real smile of the day.

Once inside, they were led down several dim hallways, where doors were kept shut and most of the patients were sedated.

"This way," the administrator said. A woman in her early forties, she was attractive in a professional way. Perfectly styled brown hair. Formfitting navy suit. Shoes that were quiet as she led them to Dr. Steffani's rooms. "If you need anything, there's an intercom by the bed. Just press the button, and someone will come." She turned and left before either of them could reply.

Dark-skinned, with a shrunken-type head, Dr. Steffani looked like a shriveled-up potato. Somewhere under all the layers of overlapping skin were a nose, a mouth, and two eyes. Maybe. Lin saw large areas where his skin was missing, sores that oozed pus. She gagged and turned away. As long as he could speak, Lin shouldn't care what he looked like.

A hospital bed was set up in the large room, which, Lin guessed, had served as a ward at one time. A kitchen area faced one wall. A dining table and living-room furniture were on the opposite wall. How sad to be dying with only that to look at.

"Dr. Steffani, I'm Jason Vinery. We spoke on the phone."

Lin stayed behind Jason; she didn't want the old man giving her the evil eye. The place gave her the creeps. When she thought about Nick's poor mother being forced to stay there after she'd lost her baby girl, she wanted to cry.

"Yes, please sit down," said Dr. Steffani. Though he looked like a creature, whatever was killing him didn't affect his voice. He spoke with the confidence of a doctor. "I know you've come a long way. I don't have a lot of time left. Skin cancer, of all things. My actions all those years ago have tormented me. Sometimes I think God is punishing me with this wicked disease, because every time I see myself, I think of it as a reminder. I had Louise take down all the mirrors."

Jason set up his camcorder on a tripod, the lens directed on the doctor's monstrous face.

"There is no way to tell this other than the way it happened. If you have any questions, I would very much appreciate if you would ask them when I finish. This isn't something I've been looking forward to."

"Whatever you're comfortable doing, Doctor. I'm ready when you are." Jason clicked the record button on the camcorder, and its soft buzz filled the cavernous room.

"Look, Steffani, I've given you hundreds and thousands of dollars for that . . . that nuthouse you run. The least you can do is listen to me!" Nicholas Pemberton Sr. wasn't used to having anyone questioning his wishes.

"I'm happy to listen, Nicholas. Stop screaming and calm down. You sound like one of my patients. Now, tell me, what seems to be the problem?"

"It's Naomi. I think she's losing her mind."

In a calm, pleasant voice Dr. Steffani asked, "And what has Mrs. Pemberton done to make you think so?"

"She hides in her room all day. She won't let Nick Jr. out of her sight. I'm afraid if something isn't done, she might hurt my son."

"Nicholas, just because a mother seems to be a bit . . . overprotective of her son doesn't mean she's out to cause him harm. Has she hurt him?"

"No! Er, not that I've seen, anyway. She's become nothing more than a thorn in my side since she lost that damned baby!"

"What did you just say?" Dr. Steffani asked.

"You heard exactly what I said. She was pregnant. She carried the kid around for nine months, and it was dead."

"Stillborn is what we say."

"Dead is dead, Dr. Steffani. She's not right in the head. Imagine what my business associates would think if they knew my wife never left her room. She hasn't been out of the house once since the kid died."

"I'm curious, Nicholas. Did Naomi see an obstetrician throughout her term?"

"What do you think I am? One of those backwoods idiots you seem to be so fond of? Of course she saw a doctor!"

"And was there any indication of trouble? The child was active throughout the pregnancy?"

"How the hell would I know? She was disgusting to look at. She was so fat! I wasn't about to touch that . . . thing causing her stomach to protrude."

"And you felt this way when she was pregnant with Nick Jr., too?"

"What does the way I felt about my wife looking like the Blob have to do with her mental status? She's not normal. For all the money I've passed your way, I would think you'd jump at the chance to care for her."

"Nicholas, calm down. You're going to suffer a stroke. Relax. Take a deep breath."

"Cut the psychobabble!"

"If you want me to help your wife, there are certain things I need to know. If you'd rather consult another doctor, I can recommend someone."

"What is it you want to know?"

"That went on for weeks before he actually brought her to the center, as I called it back then. We talked daily on the phone. He would threaten my career. I would try to calm him down. Finally, it got to the point where I refused his calls. That was before he brought her to the center. I thought he would strike me when he brought Naomi in that sad day. She was so thin. Her eyes were sunken and hollow. I'm sure she barely weighed a hundred pounds. What struck me the most, though, were the bruises all over her body. There were dozens, some yellowed, some purple, and the others, well, they were fresh. When I asked Nicholas if he beat his wife, he raised his hand to me."

"I'll make sure you never practice medicine again if word of this gets out, do you understand? She's crazy! Hitting her is the only way I get a response out of her! She makes me do this, Dr. Steffani. Do you understand, she makes me do this to her!"

"Leave her. I'll see what I can do. Maybe some time away from the city, here in the country with the pure air, maybe she will come around in time."

"I don't trust you, Dr. Steffani! When I leave

here today, the next time I return, it will be to arrange for Naomi's body to be shipped, do you understand, *shipped* back to the city? Do you get my drift?"

"I shook with rage! I'd spent my entire life working to build Tara Woods into a fine institution. Now that I had achieved my goal, I would not allow a man's anger over his wife to ruin my future! Never, no matter what I had to do. Sometimes in medicine, there are casualties. Three months later Nicholas returned to retrieve Naomi's body. And the rest, you know."

Lin wiped the tears oozing from her eyes. A man had killed just to keep his . . . business thriving! Astounded at the story, and at Nick Sr.'s violent behavior, Lin didn't know if she would ever be able to tell Will. Maybe when he was older and had children of his own.

"Is there anything you would like to ask me?" asked Dr. Steffani.

Lin watched Jason as he pulled the tripod apart, placing it back inside the duffel. He looked angry.

"I just wonder how you lived with yourself. You took an innocent woman away from her son, a son who might've turned into a decent human being had his mother been around to raise him. You're nothing but a pathetic excuse for a man. You're not even a man. You're a fucking monster! I hope you rot in hell, you son of a bitch! I hope the devil himself makes you his personal fuck boy! A red-hot rod up your ass is too good for you!" Jason was shouting so loud, a nurse ran into the room.

"We're leaving. He gets excited when he . . . hears a good story," Lin said to the woman.

"Jason, let's go." Lin took his arm and led him out the way they had come in. When they were outside, she flew into him. "What in the world was that for? I can't believe you lost it like that. And the devil's personal fuck boy? Where in the world did that come from?"

Jason wiped perspiration off his forehead with the back of his hand. "I doubt that old guy lost one minute of sleep over what he did. He's no better than *Junior,* if you ask me. Both wanted something, and both got what they wanted, and neither cared how they achieved it. Let's get the hell out of here before I decide to go back inside and squeeze the pus from his face."

Lin couldn't help but laugh. "Jason, you amaze me. Beneath that comic-book skin beats a real live heart."

"Whatever. Let's get out of here."

■ ■ ■ ■

Afraid to go home, because she was sure to be confronted by Nick's spies, Chelsea had spent the past two nights at the St. Regis. She'd watched Fox News Channel day and night, just waiting for a photo of her to be flashed across every living room in America. *So far so good.*

She thought of calling Rosa to see if she'd heard anything on Nick's condition, but she'd call Nick the minute she hung up the phone. Where were all of her so-called friends when she needed them? They were in their luxury apartments, thinking of new ways to ask Chelsea for money for their stupid charities, is where they were. She wished she had kept the money for herself, instead of giving it away just to get her picture in the paper.

She had to find out what, if anything, Nick remembered about that night he was taken to the hospital. It was apparent he hadn't died, or it would have made the headlines. The donor drive was still taking place, because the news reported on it constantly. Each time some stupid kid got swabbed or had blood taken, they reported it, so she was positive that if her dear hubby had died, it would be the story of the hour.

Admitting her mistake would get her nowhere. Simply put, she should have given Nick the entire bottle. One thing she was sure of: there was no way in hell she could spend another night in the hotel.

What would happen if she did go to the penthouse? It wasn't like Herbert or Nora knew what had happened Monday night. Nick didn't advertise his personal affairs to the staff. He had class, more than she did, though she would never admit that to anyone. Nick was born into class. It was a way of life for him. He knew nothing else. She, on the other hand, was born and raised in the Bronx. You had to be tough and street-smart just to get by. Add to that the fact that her mother was a drunkard, and she had no clue about her father. Class, no, but she'd had enough ambition to get her out of there.

Now, because she was Mrs. Nicholas Pemberton, she had some class, and she considered herself to be street-smart. Fuck Nick. He hadn't reported her, or she would have heard it by now. She was going home to her penthouse. Nick be damned. She should've had more patience, let the disease kill him. He wasn't going to live much longer, of that she was sure. For the moment, she would just have to bide her time.

She'd leave behind the cheap outfits she'd bought at the Gap. *Dior and Chanel, here I come,* she thought as she dialed down to the front desk to request a limo. Damned if she'd ride in one of those stinking New York taxis.

An hour later Chelsea was at home, soaking in her Jacuzzi tub. Nora and Herbert were nowhere to be found. She couldn't be happier. All she had to do was convince dear old Nick not to press charges against her, if he even remembered his last night with her. Then she'd simply wait. When he died, she would have his money, the penthouse, all their numerous vacation homes, and she would have the most important possession of all, Pemberton Transport.

And she would auction it off to the highest bidder.

Lin looked at herself in the mirror one last time, thinking this could be her last moment of a normal, peaceful relationship with her son. But she'd vowed to tell him about her past, and she would.

They were meeting at Starbucks on campus. Lin took a taxi over, needing the time alone to gather her thoughts, to try and put into words the error of her ways. It was her hope that when she finished with her story, Will wouldn't look at her with disgust or, even worse, pity. She didn't know if she could bear that from her son.

When the taxi let her off in front of Starbucks twenty minutes later, her hands were shaking as she paid the fare.

Please, dear God, let me find the right words to say to my son, she prayed silently. She spied Will before he saw her. He looked so much like his father, it was downright scary. She allowed herself a few moments to feast her eyes on him just the way he was.

"Hey, Mom! Over here," Will called when he saw her watching him from the door.

She waved. "I'm going to get a latte. Want anything?"

He shook his head.

After giving the barista her order, Lin moved to the side of the line. When her drink was ready, she walked over to Will. He'd gotten a table with a view of the campus. She'd wanted something with more privacy, but it didn't matter at that point. She was there to speak to her son.

"Mom, you look like you're about to ride one of the roller coasters at Six Flags. What's wrong?"

Lin sat down across from her son. She took a sip of her latte. "Nothing is wrong.

Just feeling a little queasy. Nothing a good jolt of caffeine won't cure. I've become addicted to these silly things lately. I don't think we have a Starbucks in Dalton. Do we?"

"Yeah, there's one in Barnes & Noble in the mall, remember?"

"Oh sure. I'll have to send Kelly Ann out for them to satisfy my cravings."

"Mom, I know you didn't fly to New York to talk to me about your newfound love for Starbucks lattes. Seriously, what did you want to talk to me about?"

Will had opened the door for her. All she had to do was step inside. *Here goes,* she thought as she jumped headlong into the matter that would change so many lives.

"Do you remember when you were twelve and I told you about your father?" Lin's voice was low, almost a whisper.

"Sure. You said he died in some kind of accident. How did he die?"

"There was no accident, Will."

He looked curious but not angry. "Oh, then how did he die?"

Here goes. "He didn't."

"What's that supposed to mean? I don't get it," Will said, an anxious look settling over his handsome features. For a minute Lin was back at that apartment in Atlanta.

She blinked to clear her vision of the past.

"Your father didn't die, like I said he did."

Silence.

And more silence.

Lin picked at the cardboard wrapping around her cup. "Will, please say something."

He nodded. "I'm thinking. I'm wondering . . . Never mind. Go on. Finish the story."

"Will, I'm telling you I'm sorry now. I know I shouldn't have lied to you, but the circumstances weren't . . . ideal."

"I'm not getting this, Mom. You're saying my dad is alive, has been alive and well for the past eighteen years, and you're just now telling me about it? Don't you think it's a little too late? I'm a legal adult now. Why now? Why not when I needed a father to escort me to all those Little League games, or all the times I watched my friends playing with their fathers? Why does it matter now!"

Customers were looking at them. "Lower your voice, Will. This isn't something the entire crowd at Starbucks needs to hear."

"Sorry," he said in a lower voice, but the anger was still there. Lin didn't blame him. He had every right in the world to be angry at her.

"Want me to continue?"

He nodded. "Of course I do. You've gotten me interested in the ending, you know, how it turns out. Happily ever after and all that crap."

"Will, I'm still your mother, and you will respect me. I know you're angry, and you have every right to be angry. You just said you were an adult. I think it's time you acted like one." She hated talking down to him, but it couldn't be helped.

"Okay. Say whatever it is you have to say."

She'd expected him to be mad, but sarcastic? No, that wasn't the Will she knew. God forbid, maybe some of the Pemberton traits were finally beginning to show themselves.

"Don't interrupt me. This is hard for me, Will. I know you could care less about my feelings right now, but trust me, this is the most difficult thing I've ever had to do in my life." She laughed smartly, with an edge that she didn't know she possessed. "This is worse than spending night after night on my knees while my father spit on me when I didn't recite the books of the Bible in the proper order. I think I was seven or eight the first time he actually spit on me. After that, it was the strap. He called it the devil's tongue, I remember. Said it was hot and angry like the fires of hell. Those scars on

411

my back, the ones you used to ask me about when you were little? They're from the devil's tongue. After a while your skin thickens with scars. If I was lucky, he'd hit me there. The skin was tough by then, and it didn't even bleed as much as before.

"Did I ever tell you what the kids in school called me? Miss Stinky Pants. I was Miss Stinky Pants all through elementary school. It was true. Want to know why I was called that? Of course you do. My father forced me to pray on my knees night after night for hours, until I peed my pants. And if that wasn't bad enough, he wouldn't allow me to bathe. Hence the nickname. Then came the surprises. Remember, I don't like surprises, either? I'm going to tell you why." Lin knew she was being way too harsh, but if Will didn't have a clear picture of where she was coming from, he would never understand why she had done what she did.

"Mom, you don't have to do this."

"Yes, I do! I asked you not to interrupt. Surprises. Yes. As I got older, my father refused to allow me to shut my bedroom door. It didn't matter that I wasn't hiding anything. Hell, what would I have hidden? Once, when he came home, I had mistakenly closed my door. He took it off the hinges. When I would shower, I had to leave the door open —"

"Mom!"

"I never knew when he was going to come inside the bathroom and yank the shower curtain aside. That's why I don't like surprises, Will. That is what my father called them. Surprises. And you know what he thought? He actually believed he would catch me doing something obscene and vulgar! I never wanted you to know any of these horrid details of my life. I wanted to protect you from men like him. I wasn't going to allow anyone to abuse or threaten my child as I'd been abused and threatened."

Tears shimmered down Will's face. Lin was so very sorry she'd had to tell him some of the atrocities she'd endured. And those were the tame ones.

"One weekend I was allowed to go to Atlanta, to a math competition, and stay with a girl who had been on the math team. That was really the first time in my life I was allowed out of the house on my own with no curfew, no restrictions. All my father said to me that day when I left was that I'd best win, or he and the devil's tongue would be waiting for me when I came home. We won, of course. But I'd lied to my father. I'd told him the competition lasted a week,

413

when in reality it was only three days. We went to a party at someone's apartment. I can't even remember who, not that it matters now. I met your father there. He was the most handsome young man I'd ever seen. I spent the next few days with him. I don't need to tell you the details, but that's when you were conceived. I came home happier than I'd ever been. He promised he'd call and that we would find a way to be together. But he never called, and it wasn't until much later that I even knew how to reach him.

"My father heard me throwing up in the bathroom one morning two months later. He assumed I'd been drinking, but of course I hadn't. I was suffering from morning sickness. He made me memorize the book of Genesis that day. I was so sick, I threw up in the middle of the living room while I was supposed to be praying. He hit me. Then the next thing I knew, I woke up lying in a pool of vomit and urine. A few days later I told my father I was expecting a baby and intended to keep it. He threw me out into the street with nothing but the clothes on my back, and I never went home again."

Lin's insides trembled with her recollection of a past she'd tried to hide, a past she wanted to deny, but in the end it'd caught up with her. Was it possible the truth had the power to set her free?

Will ducked his head, wiggled in his chair. When he finally looked at her, she saw his anger, and she saw his sadness.

"And my father was like your father?"

Lin shook her head. "That's just it. I never knew. Beyond those few days, I never saw your father again. Two months before you were born, I managed to get an address for him and began to send him letters. I sent dozens of letters over the next year or so. They would always come back unopened, marked 'return to sender.' "

"Why tell me this now? Why did you have to . . . do this? I'm okay with not having a father. Heck, you know that. You did a fine job, Mom. Really. There were times when I wished for a dad, but it didn't ruin me. Those things I said a while ago were said in anger."

This was her son, the young man she'd raised to be decent, honest, and compassionate.

"You need to know who your father is. I've struggled with this decision for weeks. Ever since your freshman banquet."

"Why then? Was it because I'd left home? What happened that made you feel it was . . . I don't know, urgent, to tell me this."

"Because your father was a guest speaker at the banquet, Will."

Lin knew he was trying to recall all the guest speakers, trying to put a name to a face that, what? Reminded him of himself?

"It's Mr. Pemberton, isn't it?"

"How do you know?"

"Because you asked me not to donate the bone marrow. You want me to sit back and watch him die, don't you?"

CHAPTER 17

"I can't believe you have the nerve to show your face. I should have you arrested."

"Yeah, but you won't. It'll look bad in the family album." Chelsea sat down next to her husband's hospital bed.

"I've still got a few tricks up my sleeve, Chels. I'm not dead yet. Besides, after giving our 'situation' some thought, I realized having you arrested for *accidentally* giving me too many sleeping pills wouldn't solve anyone's problem. So when the police showed up, I told them I was mistaken, that I must have taken a few myself and forgotten to mention it to you. Doesn't that sound feasible? Like something I would do. Me, the guy who rarely takes an aspirin."

"So what is it you want from me? I know you too well."

"Right now I can't think of anything. But the time will come when I do, and don't you ever forget it."

"I'm sure if I do, you'll remember to remind me. While we're baring our souls to one another, there is something that I've wanted to tell you for such a long time. I just could never find the right time to say it. When I thought I could, then boom, something came up, and it just didn't happen."

"Spit it out, Chelsea. I know your tricks. If you think you're going to use one of the many women we both know that I've slept with to blackmail me, or some such stupid scheme, think again. It won't work."

"I don't care about your stupid flings, Nick. I've had a few of my own. Though as much as I hate to admit it, none of them have been half as good as you are in the sack."

"If you think I take that as a compliment, think again."

"I don't care what you think. Now, where was I? Oh yes. I was about to confess something that I'd tried to in the past but never seemed to find the perfect moment. Well, Nicky dear, as the old saying goes, there's no time like the present." Chelsea paused. She wanted to see the look on the bastard's face when she told him her "little" secret.

"Stop playing games, and say whatever it is you think you must say. I'm tired. Those pills aren't out of my system yet. Amazing, wouldn't you say?"

"Remember why we got married, Nick?"

"How could I forget? You were stupid enough to get pregnant, though savvy enough to make sure you told my father. That was a good one, Chels. I hate to admit it, but going to the old man assured you the kid would carry the Pemberton name. It's a shame he or she never lived. I could use a blood relative right now." Nick laughed at his own wickedness. Chelsea was in for quite a shock when she learned that he had known most of what she was about to tell him for quite some time. In the meanwhile, he was going to kick back and enjoy watching her squirm.

"It wouldn't have made a difference either way."

"Why is that?" Nick prompted, enjoying himself immensely.

"First, the kid wasn't yours. It couldn't have been, since you and I never slept together that first night. I gave you knockout drops and made sure we woke together in the altogether. Secondly, I didn't miscarry. I had an abortion." There! Chelsea almost choked when she saw the look on her husband's face. "It wasn't that I didn't want a kid. I did, but not Ricky Salvadore's. He was a Puerto Rican from my neighborhood. It would've been obvious the kid wasn't yours. Anyway, I really tried to get pregnant, give you an heir to carry on the family name, but after good old Ricky's bastard, it just wasn't meant to happen."

"You really are a coldhearted bitch! But, you know something, Chels? Except for the information about whose kid you were carrying, I knew the rest of it already. When I discovered that you had set me up, I was going to divorce your ass and leave you penniless. But then dear old Dad stepped in to save your hide. So, you see, since I can't divorce you without suffering the consequences, I just decided to let things ride and make the best of a bad situation. Most of the time it was easier to let you have your way, since all it cost me was money."

"Okay, so you knew all about it. And while you could probably make the world believe that you didn't know anything about it should word that you were duped into marriage leak to the media, it would be just one more black mark against the Pemberton name. And I don't think you want to go there. Or do you?"

"Did you set up that kidnapping scheme? It was you who fixed it so I couldn't access my bank accounts! You really set me up, didn't you?"

"As much as I'd like to take credit for those antics, I had nothing to do with them. I'll take a lie detector test if you want. Wonder who did, though? And why? I'm sure it's one of your business associates."

"I would have to pay my business associates to kidnap you. Oh, some of them might want to sleep with you, but that's all. You're too scummy for the public eye. And now that you are aware that I've known most of your little secret all along, I'll make sure to keep you tucked away safely somewhere where Nora and Herbert can keep an eye on you. I know how much you enjoy their company."

"Oh, fuck off, Nick. I'm going home."

"Actually, since you left the house a little while ago," Nick lied to get a rise out her, "the locks have been changed. Did you really believe I would allow you to live under the same roof after you tried to kill me?"

"So what? Now I have to live downstairs in the servants' quarters? Give me a break."

"No, I thought that was too good for you. Since you're really nothing but trailer trash without the trailer, I had Rosa rent one in Newark. All your things are being transported there as we speak. I hope you don't mind. Nora wanted to pack them in suitcases, but I told her to keep your Louis Vuitton for herself and use some of those dark green garbage bags. You know, the ones that line the streets of Manhattan at night." Nick laughed so hard, his sides hurt. The look on Chelsea's face was priceless. The stupid woman actually believed him. "Now go on. Herbert is waiting downstairs to drive you to your new digs."

"Fuck you, Nick."

"No thanks. That's what got me in trouble in the first place."

Evan chose that moment to enter Nick's room.

"Hello, Evan."

"Nick. Mrs. Pemberton, you'll have to leave now."

"What? You can't tell me to leave! This is my husband!" Chelsea screeched.

"Save it, Chelsea. He knows what you did with the pills. Leave now, or I'll have Dr. Reeves call security," said Nick.

One look at her husband's face told Chelsea that Nick meant every word. She turned on her heel and left without another word.

"So, when are you going to let me go home? I'm sick of this place."

"Not just yet. I hate to be the bearer of more bad news, since you've had so much

422

lately, but I had the lab run a complete blood count this morning. Your red blood cells are low. Your white count is back up."

"Damn. Just when I thought I was kicking this mess."

"We'll have to begin the chemo again. I've arranged for you to have a treatment this afternoon."

"So what about the marrow drive? Any lucky winners?" Nick hated it that his voice sounded so fearful.

"We're still working on it. You're not at that stage yet, Nick. The chemo should bring you around."

"Let's hope so. I would hate to die and give Chelsea the last laugh."

Evan shook his head. Nick Pemberton was the most outrageous patient he'd ever had. What was even stranger was that he was even starting to like the guy. "Hang in there, Nick. I'll see you later."

For the first time since he'd opened his practice, Evan asked one of the other doctors to cover for him for the rest of the day and into the next. He hadn't spoken to Lin, and she hadn't returned his calls. He thought they had something, or at the very least the beginning of something, but apparently Lin didn't feel the same way.

He finished a few last-minute details on a

patient's chart, then went downstairs in search of a taxi. The same taxi driver who had recognized him from the paper was waiting at the curb.

"Doc, you're going home early. What gives? All your patients get well and go home?"

"I wish. Just some business to attend to. I need to get to SoHo. Can you take me there now?"

"Sure, just give me the address."

Evan spelled out Lin's address. He felt like an anxious teenager. That was how anxious he was to see the woman who had captured his heart on such short notice. He wondered why she hadn't returned his calls, but more important, he wanted to make sure she was okay. Though he'd known her only a few days, he knew in his heart she was the type of woman who kept her word. Something had happened that night in the emergency room, and he intended to find out exactly what it was.

"Here you are." Evan gave the driver another hefty tip, wondering if he should ask him to wait. Deciding against it, he hurried down the sidewalk to Lin's apartment.

He rang the doorbell, praying she was home and praying she wouldn't slam the door in his face. For all he knew, she could have gone back to Georgia. After all, she had a business to take care of.

Evan pushed the orange neon button again. He heard the dead bolt being unlocked.

"Evan! What are you doing here?"

"I was worried about you and Will. You said you were going to wait. The desk nurse said you ran out like you'd seen a ghost or something."

Lin opened the door all the way and stepped aside so he could come in. "I'm sorry, Evan. There are things going on in my life right now that are more of a priority than sitting around in the middle of the night at a hospital." When she saw the look of hurt that crossed his face, she wished she could take back her callous words. She hadn't meant to hurt him, just to tell the truth. That was going to be her new motto. *Tell the truth, no matter what.* "Please come in so we can talk. I guess I owe you an explanation."

"If you're sure. I don't want to do anything to cause you any more trouble. If you'd rather I leave, I'll understand." The teenager that he'd reverted to made him cross his fingers that she would insist he stay.

"Honestly, I'm glad you came by. I have

some questions that only you can answer."

"Would it be those personal questions that brought you to my office?"

"Yes. I don't know where to start, so I'll start at the beginning. I've told Will what I'm about to tell you, just so you know."

"Okay." Evan sat on the sofa beside her.

Lin began her tale for the second time in one day.

"Will . . . this is the most difficult thing I've ever had to do in my life. This is worse than spending night after night on my knees while my father spit on me when I didn't recite the books of the Bible in the proper order. I think I was seven or eight the first time he actually spit on me. After that, it was the strap. He called it the devil's tongue, I remember. Said it was hot and angry like the fires of hell. Those scars on my back, the ones you used to ask me about when you were little? They're from the devil's tongue. After a while your skin thickens with scars. If I was lucky, he'd hit me there. The skin was tough by then, and it didn't even bleed as much as before.

"Did I ever tell you what the kids in school called me? Miss Stinky Pants. I was Miss Stinky Pants all through elementary school. It was true. Want to know why I was called that? Of course you do. My father forced me to pray on my knees night after night for hours, until I

426

peed my pants. And if that wasn't bad enough, he wouldn't allow me to bathe. Hence the nickname. Then came the surprises. Remember, I don't like surprises, either? I'm going to tell you why."

"Mom, you don't have to do this."

"Yes, I do! I asked you not to interrupt. Surprises. Yes. As I got older, my father refused to allow me to shut my bedroom door. It didn't matter that I wasn't hiding anything. Hell, what would I have hidden? Once, when he came home, I had mistakenly closed my door. He took it off the hinges. When I would shower, I had to leave the door open —"

"Mom!"

"I never knew when he was going to come inside the bathroom and yank the shower curtain aside. That's why I don't like surprises, Will. That is what my father called them. Surprises. And you know what he thought? He actually believed he would catch me doing something obscene and vulgar! I never wanted you to know any of these horrid details of my life. I wanted to protect you from men like him. I wasn't going to allow anyone to abuse or threaten my child as I'd been abused and threatened.

"One weekend I was allowed to go to Atlanta, to a math competition, and stay with a girl who had been on the math team. That was really the first time in my life I was allowed out of the house on my own with no curfew, no restrictions. All my father said to me that day when I left was that I'd best win, or he and the devil's tongue would be waiting for me when I came home. We won, of course. But I'd lied to my father. I'd told him the competition lasted a week, when in reality it was only three days. We went to a party at someone's apartment. I can't even remember who, not that it matters now. I met your father there. He was the most handsome young man I'd ever seen. I spent the next few days with him. I don't need to tell you the details, but that's when you were conceived. I came home happier than I'd ever been. He promised he'd call and that we would find a way to be together. But he never called, and it wasn't until much later that I even knew how to reach him.

"My father heard me throwing up in the bathroom one morning two months later. He assumed I'd been drinking, but of course I hadn't. I was suffering from morning sickness. He made me memorize the book of Genesis that day. I was so sick, I threw up in the middle of the living room while I was supposed to be praying. He hit me. Then the next thing I knew, I woke up lying in a pool of vomit and urine. A few days later I told my father I was expecting a baby and intended to keep it. He threw me out into the street with nothing but the clothes on my back, and I never went home again."

"And my father was like your father?"

"That's just it. I never knew. Beyond those few days, I never saw your father again. Two months before you were born, I managed to get an address for him and began to send him letters. I sent dozens of letters over the next year or so. They would always come back unopened, marked *'return to sender.'*"

"Why tell me this now? Why did you have to . . . do this? I'm okay with not having a father. Heck, you know that. You did a fine job, Mom. Really. There were times when I wished for a dad, but it didn't ruin me. Those things I said a while ago were said in anger."

"You need to know who your father is. I've struggled with this decision for weeks. Ever since your freshman banquet."

"Why then? Was it because I'd left home? What happened that made you feel it was . . . I don't know, urgent, to tell me this."

"Because your father was a guest speaker at the banquet, Will."

"It's Mr. Pemberton, isn't it?"

"How do you know?"

"Because you asked me not to donate the bone marrow. You want me to sit back and watch him die, don't you?"

"My God, this is a nightmare! I can't

imagine what you must be going through." Evan raked his hands through his hair repeatedly. He couldn't begin to put himself in Lin's place. He'd had such a normal childhood, or as normal as one could expect with a terminally ill sibling. His parents had made sure he wasn't forgotten and had taken time to do things with him in spite of Emmy's illness.

"I've never told this to anyone, except my best friend, Sally. If not for her, I don't think I would have been able to manage as well as I did."

"Then I say, 'Way to go, Sally.' "

"There's more, Evan."

"I'm not going anywhere, Lin. No way."

She told him about hiring Jason Vinery, told him everything she and Sally had done. Even the silly kidnapping, if you could call it that. She wasn't sure that she could tell anyone about her trip to Vermont.

"It's not something I'd do, but I haven't had to suffer through what you have. In your shoes I might well have done the same thing," Evan assured her.

Lin smiled, relief etched on her brow. "At least you don't hate me. I'm not so sure about Will. He was so angry and upset this morning, he ran out of Starbucks. He needs some time to get used to the idea that his father is alive. I hope he can find it in his heart to forgive me, I don't know what I'd do if Will stopped speaking to me. He can do that now that he's an adult."

"Something tells me he won't do that, Lin."

"Thanks. I wanted to ask you about Nick when I came to your office Monday. It doesn't matter now that it's out in the open, but I was going to ask you to keep Will's identity a secret if you found out that he was Nick's son. I knew, once I read that article in the paper, that Will would step up to the plate."

"I can't say what I would have done. Nick is my patient. I don't really care for him all that much as a person. No, that's not quite true. I was actually starting to like the guy before you told me this. I can't understand why he didn't call or read your letters. His family has tons of money. He should have helped you financially at the very least."

"That's what brought me here in the first place. It's funny how our lives intertwine. When I rented this outrageously expensive apartment, all I wanted to do was make Nick suffer the way I had to. I knew it wouldn't be on quite the same level, since Nick's a millionaire, but I felt I had to make him pay in some way. I didn't want him to know it was me doing all those things. He never even remembered me, so what was the point? Now all I want to do is go home and sit on my porch and smell the night-blooming jasmine. And I want to get another dog. After Scruffy died, I was so involved with the diner, I didn't have the time to devote to an animal, but now I'm going to make time. Life's too short not to follow your dreams."

Evan nodded to show he understood completely. "Tell me about your restaurant. How did you come up with the name?"

"The man that sold it to me is named Jack. He's working for me while I'm away. Jack and Irma, his wife, are like the grandparents I never had. I went to work for them a few weeks after I discovered I was pregnant. Jack wanted to retire but didn't have any children to take over, so when he said he was closing up shop, I said, 'No, you're not.' He sold me the place for a song, and as they say, the rest is history."

"You're a survivor, Lin."

"That's what Sally calls me. I am in a way, but no more than anyone else who's had to go through similar circumstances. Life deals you lemons, you make lemonade and add a little bit of sugar. A cliché for sure, but it's true."

"You haven't said what happened to your mother. Is she still alive?"

"No, she died a few months after my father threw me out of the house. I learned of her death when I read about it in the obits. She fell down the basement steps. Personally, I would bet my last nickel my father shoved her down those basement steps, but with his Alzheimer's, he wouldn't remember, anyway. And if he did remember, there's no way to prove it. My mother had a pitiful, pathetic life with my father. I wanted to do something for her so bad, but I was just a child, and I couldn't."

"It sounds like you both lived a real nightmare."

Lin nodded, suddenly tired. Telling the truth was hard work. There was one person left, two if you counted Nick's wife, who needed to hear her story. Lin wasn't sure how she would go about telling Nick he had a child, but guessed the letters that she'd carried around all these years might play a big part in the ending to her story.

"It was, but I'm over it now. I've learned a lot about myself the past few weeks. I don't like dishonesty, even though I've lived a lie for more than half my life."

"You have to stop thinking of your life as a lie. You had a child and did whatever it took to protect him. Not telling him about his father isn't the worst thing in the world. When you consider who his father is, it will be a wonder if Will wants anything at all to do with him. If he does, it may be curiosity, nothing more, on Will's part. Don't jump the gun here, Lin."

"I don't know that he will ever truly understand. He was so upset when he ran out on me. Once he's had time to reflect on what I told him, he'll have to decide for himself. I'm through protecting him from a man neither of us knows."

"When will you tell Nick? If it would make it easier for you, I can come with you."

"You'd do that for me?"

"I would."

"But you hardly know me," Lin protested.

"I'd say I know everything I need to know. And I want to get to know you even better. That is, if you'll let me."

There was nothing Lin would have liked more, but she wasn't sure if it was the right time to get involved with Evan. So much of her life was changing day by day. Could she take him along for the ride? She couldn't answer that just yet. Time was what she needed. Time and a clear head.

"I'd like that very much, but I'm not sure if the timing is right. There's so much confusion and friction in my life."

"And don't you need someone to guide you though the rough spots? Some tall, hunky doctor with the hots for the owner of Jack's Diner?" Evan grinned.

Lin's heart almost leaped out of her chest. She didn't know how she knew, but she knew Evan was serious. "You *could* try and convince me," she said lightly, trying to match his bantering tone.

Evan leaned over and took her in his arms. Lin melted into his warmth, into his protective embrace. *I could stay here forever,* she thought. He kissed her with such tenderness that it brought tears to her eyes. This man was slowly easing his way inside her heart, into a place that she'd reserved for that special someone, whom she had almost given up hope of ever finding.

CHAPTER 18

Tuesday, December 18, 2007
New York City

Nick felt himself growing weaker by the day. The latest chemo treatment had knocked him for a loop. Evan, as he now referred to his doctor, said it was normal. Normal, but he refused to allow Nick to leave the hospital until his blood count was up. He'd received two units of red blood cells and one unit of platelets just that morning, but it was still one of his worst days so far.

The donor drive had ended weeks ago, but Nick knew that had been the easy part. Now it was a matter of taking the thousands of samples and trying to match as many factors as possible — the more matches, the better the chance that he wouldn't reject the donor's marrow, if it came down to that. He'd asked Evan to be frank with him. What were the odds that he'd bounce back from this silent killer that had invaded his body?

The good doctor had said he couldn't say, as he wasn't a betting man. Nick knew it was highly likely that he would die. He'd accepted it.

Trevor had drawn up a new will for him. If he died and a matching donor was found after his death, he wanted whoever it was to have the ten million dollars he'd promised. He might be the biggest bastard alive, but with death lurking around the corner and licking at his heels, Nick had softened. He knew it was highly unusual for a cancer victim to make such a request after his death, but Trevor seemed to understand his need to fulfill his promise. It might change the lucky donor's life. Shit, who was he kidding? Ten million bucks. There was no *might* about it.

The nurses were starting to warm up to him. He'd bitched and griped, yet they continued to smile and treat him with respect, even though he knew they pitied him.

He was forty-three years old. It was highly unlikely he'd see forty-four. Nick had many regrets, but his biggest was that he and Chelsea, bitch that she was, had never been able to have a child.

"Mr. Pemberton?" A nurse, one he wasn't familiar with, stepped into his room.

"Yes?"

"This was delivered to another room by mistake. Just wanted to bring it up. I thought it might be something important."

"Thanks," he said.

The box was almost too heavy for him to lift. He hoped it wasn't one of those god-awful fruitcakes Nora baked during the holidays. Just the thought of all those candied cherries made him nauseous.

There was no address; whatever it was hadn't gone through the USPS. He ripped the cardboard apart. Inside was one of those iPod things all the kids had today. There was a typed note with instructions on what to do. He followed them, curious to see if this was someone's idea of a prank. He placed the earbuds in his ears and turned the volume to a comfortable level.

"Dr. Steffani, I'm Jason Vinery. We spoke on the phone."

"Yes, please sit down. I know you've come a long way. I don't have a lot of time left. Skin cancer, of all things. My actions all those years ago have tormented me. Sometimes I think God is punishing me with this wicked disease, because every time I see myself, I think of it as a reminder. I had Louise take down all the mirrors. There is no way to tell this other than the way it happened. If you have any questions, I would very much appreciate if you would ask them when I finish. This isn't something I've been looking forward to."

"Whatever you're comfortable doing, Doctor. I'm ready when you are."

"Look, Steffani, I've given you hundreds and thousands of dollars for that . . . that nuthouse you run. The least you can do is listen to me!"

"I'm happy to listen, Nicholas. Stop screaming and calm down. You sound like one of my patients. Now, tell me, what seems to be the problem?"

"It's Naomi. I think she's losing her mind."

"And what has Mrs. Pemberton done to make you think so?"

"She hides in her room all day. She won't let Nick Jr. out of her sight. I'm afraid if something isn't done, she might hurt my son."

"Nicholas, just because a mother seems to be a bit . . . overprotective of her son doesn't mean she's out to cause him harm. Has she hurt him?"

"No! Er, not that I've seen, anyway. She's become nothing more than a thorn in my side since she lost that damned baby!"

"What did you just say?"

"You heard exactly what I said. She was pregnant. She carried the kid around for nine months, and it was dead."

"Stillborn is what we say."

"Dead is dead, Dr. Steffani. She's not right in the head. Imagine what my business associates would think if they knew my wife never left her room. She hasn't been out of the house once since the kid died."

"I'm curious, Nicholas. Did Naomi see an obstetrician throughout her term?"

"What do you think I am? One of those backwoods idiots you seem to be so fond of? Of course she saw a doctor!"

"And was there any indication of trouble? The child was active throughout the pregnancy?"

"How the hell would I know? She was disgusting to look at. She was so fat! I wasn't about to touch that . . . thing causing her stomach to protrude."

"And you felt that way when she was pregnant with Nick Jr., too?"

"What does the way I felt about my wife looking like the Blob have to do with her mental status? She's not normal. For all the money I've passed your way, I would think you'd jump at the chance to care for her."

"Nicholas, calm down. You're going to suffer a stroke. Relax. Take a deep breath."

"Cut the psychobabble!"

"If you want me to help your wife, there are certain things I need to know. If you'd rather consult another doctor, I can recommend someone."

"What is it you want to know?"

"That went on for weeks before he actually brought her to the center, as I called it back then. We talked daily on the phone. He would threaten my career. I would try to calm him down. Finally, it got to the point where I refused his calls. That was before he brought her to the center. I thought he would strike me when he brought Naomi in that sad day. She was so thin. Her eyes were sunken and hollow. I'm sure she barely weighed a hundred pounds. What struck me the most, though, were the bruises all over her body. There were dozens, some yellowed, some purple, and the others, well, they were fresh. When I asked Nicholas if he beat his wife, he raised his hand to me."

"I'll make sure you never practice medicine again if word of this gets out, do you understand? She's crazy! Hitting her is the only way I get a response out of her! She makes me do this, Dr. Steffani. Do you understand, she makes me do this to her!"

"Leave her. I'll see what I can do. Maybe some time away from the city, here in the country with the pure air, maybe she will come around in time."

"I don't trust you, *Dr.* Steffani! When I leave here today, the next time I return it will be to

441

arrange for Naomi's body to be shipped — do you understand? — *shipped* back to the city? Do you get my drift?"

"Three months later Nicholas returned to retrieve Naomi's body. And the rest, you know."

Nick removed the earbuds from his ears, his hands trembling like dry leaves in a light wind. If this was Jason Vinery's way of getting even after all these months, he would ruin him. He'd hire someone just like him to do the job.

But something told Nick that Jason hadn't sent the iPod to him out of spite or to elicit a response. Nick remembered hearing his father talk to the man. He had never met the doctor and had no reason to believe the accuracy of the conversation he'd just heard. If what he just saw and heard on the iPod was true . . . What? He'd dig his father's body up and kick his ass? He felt totally powerless for the first time in his life. If his father had paid Steffani to kill his mother, what had really happened to the sister he never knew about?

Reaching for the phone, Nick called Trevor.

"What? I . . . Yes, I knew your mother was hospitalized. Yes, I do recall she was pregnant, but the baby died. Bruises? I never saw any, but I never saw your mother that often, either. Yes, your father had a terrible temper. No, I wouldn't be surprised at all to find it all true."

"Thanks, Trevor." Nick hung up the phone.

What else had that mean son of a bitch who was his father done that he wasn't aware of? At that moment Nick was glad that he was at the twilight stage of his life. He didn't know how he could stand to live while that son of a bitch who called himself a father rested peacefully. And in a gold-rimmed coffin.

If he hadn't been so damn sick, he would have dug up the old bastard just so he could piss on his corpse.

"And the shit just keeps on coming," Nick said out loud.

Lin said to her son, "If that's what you really want to do, then we'll make it happen. Being with family during the holidays is the best. Of course I can come back to New York. It's Christmas. We'll go see the Rockettes or a show. I can ask Sally and Lizzie to come."

"That wasn't what I had in mind when I said I think the family should be together at Christmas."

"Then exactly what did you have in mind? We're the only family you have." *Well, damn, I set myself up for that one.*

"I know, but you know what I mean. Don't you think it would be the perfect time? We talked about Thanksgiving, but you were too busy huddled up with Evan in Colorado."

"We weren't huddled up, as you put it. We went snow skiing, and I'm going back right after Christmas, and before you ask, yes, I'm going with Evan."

"That's cool, Mom. I like him. You deserve to be treated like a queen after what you've been through."

"That's sweet of you to say. I'm just so sorry for the way I told you. I needed for you to understand that my life wasn't a bowl of cherries."

"I'm over it. Enough already! I'm almost nineteen. You don't have to protect me from the big bad wolf anymore, okay?" He laughed into the phone, the sound so sweet, Lin's eyes filled with tears. For a few days at the beginning of November, she hadn't been sure Will would ever want to talk to her again, let alone laugh with her. She should have trusted her son.

"Okay. I'll come to New York."

"Alone this time. No Sally."

"All right. I'll call you with my flight info, so you'd better cancel any dates with all those 'hot chicks' you keep telling Jack about."

"You tell Jack I said he talks too much." Will laughed, knowing his mother was smiling.

"Okay, son. I'll see you soon."

"Thanks, Mom. I knew I could count on you."

He could, couldn't he? How wonderful that her son still knew he could count on her for *anything*.

Lin knew Will was hoping for some sort of magic moment, but she knew Nick was dying, and she didn't have the heart to tell Will. He'd have to see for himself, which was why she'd agreed to return to New York. Evan would be there, too. She couldn't forget that.

Dear Evan, who'd stormed into her life, or rather she'd stormed into his office. And she knew without a doubt they were meant for each other. They'd spent the Thanksgiving holiday skiing. It had been the most wonderful, exciting four days of her life. She didn't even give Sally all the glorious details when she'd asked, preferring to hold it all close to her heart. Her time with Evan was too precious to her. She wasn't ready to

445

share their special moments just yet. Maybe she'd never be ready to share them. And if that was the case, that was okay, too.

Before she got caught up in her daydreams, something she seemed to be doing a lot of lately, she called the airport and booked a flight to New York. She was beginning to love the city as much as the oldtimers but could never see herself living there. She'd told that to Evan, explaining that she was a Southern girl at heart. He'd said he was happy with the way things were for the moment. Lin was happier than she'd ever been in her life. She now knew what it meant when a person said he or she felt complete. Evan completed her, complemented her.

The next trip to New York would be like coming full circle. Never imagining her brief relationship with Nick would turn out this way, she was actually looking forward to closing that part of her life and moving forward to the future. Even with no clue as to what the future held for her, other than that she would always be honest. At present that was enough.

Three days later Lin found herself ensconced once again at the Helmsley Park Lane, only this time Evan would be meeting her for dinner as soon as he finished making his evening rounds.

Tomorrow was the big day. She was nervous, but she would handle it, because she had to handle it. There were no other options at this point in time. Will was excited, but she knew he was as nervous as she was. Together, they would get through the meeting, with Evan as their backup.

She took a long, leisurely bath in the giant-sized Jacuzzi. She was getting her hair and nails done before dinner. Lin wanted tonight to be special because she had something so very special to share with Evan.

After soaking for more than an hour, her skin pruned. Lin slipped on a pair of jeans and went to the salon where she'd had her first French manicure when she brought Will to New York. While it was only four months ago, it seemed like a lifetime to her.

The manicurist painted her nails a bright red. They both laughed when they saw what the color was named: "I'm Not Really a Waitress." Lin giggled when they suggested a pedicure with the same bright shade of red.

She asked the stylist to leave her hair long and loose, flowing around her shoulders, the way Evan liked it. She'd gone to Prada, where she'd bought a smashing red dress that hugged her curves in all the right places. She also had a pair of ruby red sling-backs to complete the outfit.

Back in her room she slid into the sexy red dress. She eyed her reflection in the mirror. The dark circles and jutting cheekbones were long gone. She looked just like the old Lin, only better.

"Okay, get your tail downstairs before you really lose it."

Downstairs, she spied Evan in the hotel lobby, and her heart started a wild dance in her chest. *Damn, he's good-looking.* She admired him, loved the way he treated her and Will. But most of all she admired the fact that he respected her. The feeling was new, unique to her, coming from a man. She was sorry her mother hadn't lived to find someone who loved and cherished her the way she deserved to be. But that was the past, and as good old Jack always said, "The past is prologue, kiddo."

"You'd give Julia Roberts a run for her money. You're the prettiest woman I've seen all day. All week. Ever. Come here." Evan wrapped his arms around her, nuzzling her neck.

"You better stop, or we won't make it to dinner. Then I'll have wasted three thousand bucks on this sexy dress, which I want you to become familiar with later. The zippers and clasps, to be precise." *My God, did I just say that out loud?* she thought. Her face flushed to a rosy hue, and she laughed, the sound tinkling across the lobby. Evan grinned from ear to ear.

They both had the prime rib for dinner with wasabi mashed potatoes and a Caesar salad. Evan ordered a bottle of wine, but Lin passed on it, explaining that wine gave her a headache.

They spent the night in each other's arms, and when Evan left to go to the hospital, Lin relished the scent he left behind. She slept for two more hours before getting up to meet the day and whatever it was going to hold for her and her son.

The day she'd been dreading had finally arrived, but she knew that Evan would be available if she needed him.

She dressed in jeans and a bright red sweater to match her bright red fingernails. She didn't want to look too made up for fear both Nick and Will would think she was trying to make an impression.

Her cell phone rang. "Hello?"

"I'm making sure you're up. I know Evan spent the night at the hotel."

"Of course I'm up, and how do you know Evan spent the night?"

"He told me when he called two minutes ago."

"Oh."

"I'll meet you at the hospital in an hour. You sure you're okay with this?" Will asked his mother for the hundredth time.

"I'm fine. I'll see you in an hour."

Lin snapped the phone off, grabbed her purse and the messenger bag that she'd carried with her for so many years. Forty-five minutes later she was waiting in the main lobby of Presbyterian Hospital, after having stopped off for a minute at Evan's empty office. Will burst through the glass doors like his pants were on fire.

"Are you okay?" she asked.

"Yeah, I screwed up and had the taxi drop me off on the wrong block. I ran so I wouldn't be late."

"Take a deep breath and relax, because we don't have an appointment. We have as much time as we need. Remember, this was your idea to come here so early. Before you say anything, I know it's your first day of Christmas break and you want to enjoy every last minute of each day."

"I did say that, didn't I?" Will laughed at her words

"At least twenty times. Catch your breath and comb your hair. I know this day has been a long time coming, Will. I'm still sad that it came to this, but I can't change my life. I don't think I would if I could."

"Me either, Mom. No matter what happens upstairs, I want you to know that you've been the best mom and dad a guy could want. Don't cry. You'll ruin that mascara you wear all the time now."

Lin sniffed and dabbed at her eyes with a tissue. "Let's go meet your father."

Neither spoke on the elevator ride, each lost in memories of what was and what would be. The silver doors swished open. Lin took Will's hand and gave it a squeeze. He squeezed back.

Together they walked down the dim hallway. When they reached room 267, they stopped outside the door.

Will leaned over and whispered, "You don't think this'll shock him into a heart attack or anything, do you?"

"No, not at all. Evan said it wouldn't affect his health. So before you chicken out, I think you should walk in first. Okay?"

Will nodded and slowly pushed the heavy door inward. Lin remained in the open doorway, where she could watch her son meet his father for the first time.

Will looked like a little boy on his first day of school. He glanced in her direction, his eyes pleading for guidance.

She nodded. "Go on," she whispered.

He walked back to the doorway, where she stood. "I want you with me."

He wasn't so big, after all, Lin thought, suddenly glad that he'd asked her to share this moment with him.

Together they walked toward Nick's bed. He appeared to be sleeping.

"Maybe we shouldn't wake him," Will whispered.

"And maybe you should," Nick said. He rolled over in bed, then pushed himself into an upright position. Even though he was critically ill, he was still as handsome as ever. "You all must have the wrong room. Sorry." He laughed, and Lin smiled herself.

"I don't think so."

Nick looked at her, *really* looked at her. Then he looked at Will. "Do I know you? I've seen you before. It's the eyes." He shook his head from side to side. "No, that's impossible."

"What do you mean, that's impossible?" Lin asked, her heart throbbing in her throat.

"Look, you're in the wrong room," Nick replied. "I wish you were in the right room."

Nick stared at her as though he was trying to figure out where he'd seen her. Lin wanted him to figure it out, felt a small

452

perverse delight in watching him.

Lin waited for Will to speak up, but he seemed to be in a state of semishock. "Dr. Reeves gave us your room number. He told us to visit."

"What are you? A brother and sister comedy team?" Nick asked with a hint of a smile.

Whatever had Will in such a strong hold broke loose, because he burst out laughing. "Did you say brother and sister?"

"Yeah, so?" Nick asked, joining Will in his fit of laughter, not sure why, other than that young people's laughter was contagious.

"Sir, this woman is my mother."

"Will, this isn't the way it's supposed to be. You're an adult, remember?" Lin was about ready to start laughing herself.

"I'll tell you what would be nice. Want to hear it?" Nick addressed the two of them.

"Sure," Lin said. "I'm waiting."

"Just tell me what you want," Nick said. "Did Chelsea put you up to this? I swear, I rue the day I married that woman. She's been nothing but an albatross around my neck from day one, but you don't need to hear all that."

"Who is Chelsea?" Lin asked, even though she knew who she was since she'd had the pleasure of pushing her around Manhattan in a wheelchair.

"Unfortunately, or fortunately, as the case may be, she's my wife," Nick said. "You're sure she didn't send you here to lace my morning tea with Ambien again? If she did, rest assured I won't let her off so easy this time. Or you," he added ominously.

Lin winced. They'd made him angry, and that wasn't in the plan. According to Evan, anger wasn't good for his patient. "Look, Nick, I'm sorry. I shouldn't have allowed this silly banter to continue," Lin said.

"You know me!" Nick said, sounding surprised at the use of his name. "I think I've seen you somewhere. Have we met? And you." He turned to Will. "You remind me of someone, too."

Lin and Will glanced at one another.

Lin had hoped Nick would recognize her, but he hadn't, and at this point in time it was okay. She thought she'd be embarrassed with Will observing her, but she wasn't. If anything, Lin thought Nick was a bit embarrassed himself because he couldn't recall how he knew either of them, or if he did at all.

Taking a deep breath, Lin took a step toward the bed, moving closer so that Nick might instantly remember her from that infamous party all those years ago. "My name is Lin Townsend, and this is my son, William Michael. We call him Will."

"Okay," Nick said, his eyes darting back and forth between them.

Not wanting to drag the moment out any longer than she had already, Lin took a deep breath, squared her shoulders, and looked Nick dead in the eyes. "We met at a party in Atlanta almost twenty years ago." Lin paused, then continued. "Will is your son."

There. Done. Out in the open. No more lies. *I can do this,* she told herself. *I* am *doing this.*

"The girl with the silver eyes! I remember you. You were the math whiz," Nick said, awe ringing in his voice. "Did I hear you say this boy is *my son?* You gave birth to my son, and you never told me! For God's sake, why?"

Lin almost fainted. He *did* know her! And he was acting like he didn't know about Will, and if he didn't know about Will, then he had never received her letters. She had to say something, and say it immediately, that very second. "The one and only." That was certainly clever, she thought.

Nick dragged his eyes away from Lin to look at the boy again. "How old are you?"

"Nineteen come January," said Will.

"And what do you want now, after all

these years?" Nick asked. "Not that I'm offering anything."

Lin's eyes narrowed. How like him to
reduce this to money. "Actually, we don't
need or *want* anything *from you.* It's way too
late for that, anyway. You see, I've been carrying these goddamned stupid letters
around in my bag for nineteen years! I had
a wild hair crawl up my ass the other day
and decided I'd hand-deliver them. Here."
Lin tossed the messenger bag at him, hitting him in the chest. She didn't care how
crude or crass she was coming across as.
Nick Pemberton was a royal bastard, just
like his father. How dare he assume she'd
brought Will there to ask for something?

"Mom, the man is sick," Will cried out.
"Watch what you say. Calm down." He was
stunned at his mother's words, his mother,
who never ever said one bad word to or
about anyone.

"I don't have to watch my mouth, Will.
Mr. Pemberton is still a bastard, sick or
not," Lin said, her anger red hot. "He hasn't
changed one iota. Everything in his whole
life has been reduced to a dollar sign. How
dare you even assume we came here to ask
for something? I wouldn't take anything
from you even if you offered me my weight
in gold. What do you think of that, you son

of a bitch!" Lin shrieked.

"You're for real, aren't you? This isn't some hokey, cockamamy scam. Damn, this is truly for real. Come over here, Will. Sit down and let me look at you." Nick ignored Lin's outburst.

Will walked closer to the bed. Lin felt like she was in some stupid grade-B movie, and any minute she would walk out of the theater, wondering what had made her go see the silly thing in the first place. Nope, this was for real. Big-time.

"Seen enough?" she shrieked again. "He looks just like you. His DNA will match yours, as would that of any son and his father."

"I believe you, Lin. Cut me a little slack here. You just invaded my world and threw me a whammy I never expected. My body might be fading away, but my memory is still pretty sharp. I recall our time together. I often wondered what had happened to you. I tried to call you a few times. You were never home. I guess it was your mother who took my calls. She kept asking me to stop calling, so I did. I figured you didn't want to talk to me and were simply using your mother to deliver the message."

Lin almost collapsed in a heap on the floor. She would have if Will hadn't reached across Nick's bed and grabbed her arm.

Somehow Lin found her voice. "Did you read my letters, Nick? Please don't lie to me. I need to know the truth. Did you read those letters?" She nodded toward the pile of letters heaped across the bed.

"I never read your letters, Lin, because I never received any letters."

"Look at them now! Go on. I need to see you do this. Please," she added as an afterthought.

"All right. Sure." Nick took several of the letters and scanned the envelopes, then placed them on the sheet next to him. "Who told you my address? I don't remember giving it to you."

Will was spellbound watching the interchange between his mother and the man she said was his father. He felt like he was at a tennis match.

"Nancy Johnson. You introduced me to her at the party," said Lin.

"I don't recognize her name, but regardless, this isn't my address. That's why I never got them, Lin. Because they're marked 'return to sender.' Look." Nick motioned for her to look closely at the fading print on the yellowed envelope. "Address unknown."

Speechless. Now she truly understood the

meaning of the word.

Lin felt so light-headed, she had to reach for the bar on the side of the bed to remain upright. "I can't believe after carrying these around for more than half my life, that I missed those two little words. 'Address unknown.' "

Images swirled through Lin's head. She could not identify any of them. Her only thought was that Jason had been right, after all, except it hadn't been Nick's father who had kept the letters from him. It had been the United States Postal Service. And herself. Stupid. Stupid. Stupid. And one more STUPID with capital letters.

"You really called?" That was probably the stupidest question she could ask, but it was the only one she could think of.

"I have no reason to lie to you. I think I called seven or eight times. Different times of the day, in the hopes of catching you in."

To think she'd carried around this hate for Nick all these years. He really *hadn't* had a clue that he'd had a son! He *hadn't* tossed her and Will aside like dirty water. He had tried to call.

"So where do we go from here? It's going to take some time for this to sink in. Sally is going to shit when I tell her," said Lin.

"Mom, stop talking like that! Mothers

shouldn't . . . curse."

Suddenly Lin felt like an ornery schoolgirl. "Shit, shit, shit, and piles of shit. Loads of shit, dump trucks full of shit. There! How'd that sound, Will? Don't you ever tell me what to do and what not to do. I am your mother, and if I want to say 'Shit,' I will say 'Shit.' "

Nick laughed so hard, he became short of breath. "Shit," he gasped. "The most famous and used word in the English language. A word that at times seems to sum up just about everything and anything," he continued to gasp.

Lin began to laugh like she'd never laughed before. Will watched them as though they were two escapees from the loony bin. And then he joined in, because it seemed like the thing to do.

"Hey, what's going on in here? Are you trying to upset my patient?" Evan came strolling into the room like a bright wave of sunshine.

"Evan, you'll never believe this. Not in a million, hell, a zillion years. I think I just might have to pinch myself to make sure I'm not dreaming," said Lin.

Evan reached around her and pinched her on the butt.

"Ouch!" Lin cried.

"Okay, Evan, I think you've got some explaining to do. I just discovered this beautiful woman is the very foul-mouthed mother of my handsome son here." Nick placed a thin hand on Will's knee. "And now I see my doctor pinching her ass. What gives?"

Evan and Lin told Nick how they met, their words tumbling over one another.

"Hmm, so now I've got something of an inside source, I'd say. Seriously, I am happy for you two," said Nick.

All traces of humor gone, Lin, Evan, and Will told Lin's story one more time. Lin didn't leave out the ugly details. She felt as though in doing so, she'd purge her soul of her horrid childhood and the hate she'd carried around for so long. Again, she was reminded of that day so many years ago when she'd taken Will to McDonald's. The fear had left her then, but something had remained behind, leaving her full of unhealthy feelings and thoughts for most of her adult life. Now the fear had left her completely, as though some magical fairy had carried it away on a light summer breeze, leaving her whole and intact.

"So, I guess it's time I get to know my son. What about it, Will? Think you can hang around this . . . shitty hospital for a

461

while? Keep the old man company in his hour of need?" said Nick.

"Mom?"

Lin appreciated Will's consideration. "You're an adult now. Whatever you want to do, you can. Just don't do anything I wouldn't do." Lin added as an afterthought, "Forget I said that. I think I'll leave you two alone so you can get to know one another better. And no cussing, Will. Today was just for fun."

"Listen to your mother, son. Only God knows how I've always wanted to say that!" Giant tears streamed down Nick's pale face, landing on the pile of letters and smearing the old red ink into nothingness.

Lin smiled. It was all turning out wonderfully for all of them, and the best part was they were all getting a clean start for Christmas this year. Lin knew of only one thing that could top this.

They were all teary-eyed and smiling, like they'd been together many times. In some ways they were actually acting like a family. A true family.

Well, sort of, Lin thought as she nudged Evan, a sign it was time to go.

"Hey, what's the rush? I like watching this man cry. I have poked and prodded him with needles as big as my arm and haven't seen him cry. And all you do is walk into the room. Women," Evan teased. "Can't live with them, can't live without them."

"The man who said that never spent a day with Chelsea," Nick said.

They all laughed.

"I'll be fine, Mom. Trust me," Will assured Lin, encouraging her to leave him alone so he could get to know his father.

"I know. Take care, Will. Call me." Lin turned to Nick and said, "Good luck. I mean that, Nick. You know what they say, the past is prologue. I'll keep you in my prayers."

Nick nodded, his eyes welling up again. "I'm sorry, Lin. I wish I had known. I might be many things, but I never would have forsaken you. I want you to believe that."

Lin nodded, because in her heart and in her soul she did believe it.

Out in the hallway, Lin asked, "Is there somewhere we can go to be alone? I need to talk to you. It's personal."

"I only discuss personal issues in my office. Follow me," said Evan.

Once the elevator doors were closed, Evan wrapped his arms around Lin. "I think that just went extraordinarily well. What about you?"

"It's almost too good to be true. I can't

463

believe . . . Forget it. I'm moving forward, not backward. I'm hoping Nick has a little time left with Will. It's too sad to think about after all this."

"Hey, the man's not dead yet! I'm his doctor, remember? And I don't take no for an answer." He kissed her hard on the lips and continued when the elevator opened on his floor.

"Way to go, Dr. Reeves," someone shouted from the waiting room. "Now we know what you do between patients!"

"Hey, watch what you say, or I'll have to order an extra set of blood work," Evan called.

Evan joked with his staff for a few minutes before leading Lin down the hall to his office. He closed the door and took her in his arms again. "I can't seem to get enough of you, Lin Townsend. I'm going to have to do something about it, too."

"Really? And what would that be?"

"This," he said as he kissed her neck. "And this" — he kissed her ear — "and this." He kissed her on the mouth, then deepened the kiss. He loosened his arms around her, dropping them to her waist. "You said there was something personal you wanted to tell me. I'm all ears for the next" — he glanced at his watch — "three minutes. Then duty calls."

Suddenly shy and unsure, Lin didn't know if it was the right time or not. She hadn't told anyone. Not even Will. He'd find out soon enough.

"Two minutes and counting. I don't want my patients to think I'm in here fooling around, so you'd better tell me now, or I'll tickle you."

"You wouldn't dare! I hate being tickled, anyway. Listen, stop! What I have to say isn't something silly. It's life changing, and I want your undivided attention when I tell you. If you have a problem with it, I want you to tell me up front. I can take it. I'm a survivor."

"Now you're scaring me," Evan said.

"No, no, I don't want to do that! I just want you to be honest with me. Truly honest."

"Is there any other way?"

"Actually, from this second on, there isn't." Her hands trembled, and she stuffed them in the pockets of her jeans. She looked Evan squarely in the face. "Do you have any plans this summer? August, to be specific."

Evan squinted. "Not that I know of. But you know how my life is, being a doctor. It belongs to my patients first. Scratch what I just said. It didn't come out right. My time is yours first and foremost, above and beyond anything. If you need me, I promise to jump through hoops or whatever it takes to get to you. I mean that, Lin. I mean it more than anything I've ever said. I'll never mistreat you or Will. Never," he said vehemently.

"I can live with that. Now, about August. Why don't you check your calendar just to make sure? I'll wait right here."

"Really, I don't think I have anything going on other than work, and I can rearrange a few things if it's that important to you."

"Just check your calendar. Pretty please," Lin coaxed.

"You're persistent, I'll give you that. And way over your three-minute time limit."

Evan went to his desk, where he opened his day planner to the month of August. Looked at the empty pages and saw that they were blank. Wedged in between the pages was a small white disk about the size of a large pack of Wrigley's chewing gum.

Lin watched Evan as he removed it from the day planner. He looked up at her after he examined the object a few times. "Is this what I think it is, Ms. Lin Townsend? Because if it is, you're about to become Mrs. Evan Reeves. Am I reading this right?"

Lin nodded, smiling at the man she loved

more than life. "Doesn't matter if you're reading it right or not, because in about seven months and two weeks you'll have it figured out."

Evan practically jumped across his desk to get to her. He wrapped his arms around her, then gently pulled her away from him so he could look at her. "This is what you want?"

"I've never wanted anything more in my entire life. This time I'm going to do it right."

"What's that supposed to mean?"

"Wait. Girls first. Was that a marriage proposal I heard a minute ago?"

"It was. I can get down on my knee if it'll make it more official."

"That won't be necessary, Dr. Reeves. I accept your proposal."

"Then let's go shout it to the world! Lin, this is the happiest day of my life."

"Mine, too, Evan. Mine, too."

ABOUT THE AUTHOR

Fern Michaels is the *USA Today* and *New York Times* bestselling author of *Deadly Deals, Vanishing Act, Final Justice, Collateral Damage, Up Close and Personal, Fool Me Once, Sweet Revenge, The Jury, Payback,* and dozens of other novels and novellas. There are over seventy million copies of her books in print.

Fern Michaels has built and funded several large daycare centers in her hometown, and is a passionate animal lover who has outfitted police dogs across the country with special bulletproof vests. She shares her home in South Carolina with her five dogs and a resident ghost named Mary Margaret. Visit her website at www.fernmichaels.com.